MOONDANCE RIDGE
THIN BLUE LINE

I0657488

Also by Melanie P. Smith

MOONDANCE RIDGE

Thin Blue Line Series
Book 2

---

by:
Melanie P. Smith

MPSmith Publishing

www.melaniepsmith.com

Dedication:

To my brother Steve...
For having the patience and endurance
to survive life with five sisters.
For your knowledge, service and strength
and for always standing by your convictions.

Chapter One

Theresa sat huddled in the tiny cupboard, twisted like a pretzel. It was the only way she'd fit into the cabinet under the industrial sized sink. She didn't dare move a muscle. The slightest noise might alert them she was here. The three men standing just outside the thin door were monsters. She'd known that before, but tonight she was learning just how far they would go to get what they wanted. Her husband, Shawn, was paying dearly for his betrayal. She closed her eyes and tried to shut out the sounds, but it was no use. Shawn's agonizing moans echoed throughout the room. It was a sound she knew she would never forget. This moment in time would be burned into her memory for weeks, months and years to come. It was a nightmare she would relive, dissect and ruminate over for the rest of her life. She briefly wondered if that life would last a few short minutes or countless years. *Only time will tell*, she supposed.

Moondance Ridge

She was so angry with Shawn for getting them into this mess. At the same time, she loved him even more for the courage and skill it took to get as far as he had. Yes, that was a paradox that only she could understand. Hating and loving in the same moment. But she wouldn't question her emotions. Not now. There would be plenty of time after this was all over to evaluate her feelings. She knew her husband was going to die. There was no way around it, nothing that could be done to stop the evil machinations of that terrible man. She just hoped Shawn's plan would work and she could somehow survive her predicament.

Theresa's eyes flew open and her body jerked forward, nearly colliding with the closed cupboard door before she forcibly stopped its movement through sheer willpower and fear. The bone crushing sound that reached her tiny hide-away and the agonizing, inhumane sound that resonated from Shawn's limp form, nearly made her come undone. A single tear escaped as she slowly closed her eyes and tried to swallow the lump that was lodged in her throat. Then, the floodgates opened and hot liquid flowed down her dust covered cheeks, slid across her trembling chin and landed on her jeans-clad thigh. She ignored the tears; she ignored the wetness as it cooled and permeated the thick denim; she ignored the way her jeans began to tighten and cling to her skin as the damp circle grew with each passing second; she ignored each and every emotion coursing through her traumatized mind. She had to, her very life depended on her silence. It was taking every inch of self-control she possessed to remain hidden away like a helpless child in that tiny prison under an old, musty sink. She wanted to lash out. She wanted to kill Dominic Zarconi in an extremely violent and painful way. But, revenge and justice would have to wait.

"I think he might be dead boss," Theresa heard the voice loud and clear. She hoped Socks was right. Not because she wanted Shawn to be dead, but because she wanted his suffering to be over.

She couldn't imagine the pain he must be in right now. Theresa knew it wouldn't matter what they did to her husband; he would never tell them a thing. That was true under normal circumstances, but Shawn was protecting her tonight. She might question his methods, but she would never question his love. Theresa was the love of Shawn's life. He had shown her that in so many ways over the years. Tonight, he was showing it with his silence. She just hoped his plan worked. Her husband was confident Zarconi would stay true to form. Once Shawn had been eliminated, Dominic (or Dom as his men called him) would casually move on to his next task as if nothing out of the ordinary had just occurred. And of course, killing a man he considered a traitor wasn't really out of the ordinary for the ruthless mob boss. So, he'd either do the final deed himself or he'd order it done and casually walk away - confident cleanup would be thorough and complete in a matter of minutes. His men had plenty of practice in the art of disposal and would deal with Shawn's lifeless body quickly and efficiently. Both Dominic and Theresa were counting on that – Dom; to ensure freedom from prosecution for his heinous crime – and Theresa; to provide a means of escape.

It would be her only chance. Shawn had given her very specific, very strict instructions on what she had to do once Dominic left the room. She would need to listen for the two goons to follow Dom out, count to twenty then slip unnoticed out the back door. On her way, she was to make a quick stop in the electrical room; disconnect Shawn's phone from the camera system; then, hide it with the rest of the evidence he and Zach had compiled. Once she was out of town, she could find someone she trusted to share it with. If she was able to slip out the back door, avoiding the camera was going to be her biggest challenge; but Theresa was confident she had the plan memorized...especially the blind spots. There was only one camera in Dom's restricted area, located in the alleyway that led

3

to the casino's main parking lot. Once in the lot, the cameras were everywhere; but she could avoid them if she kept to the north entrance. The entrance Dominic used. She'd then make her way to the highway, cross the street, cut through the public park and slip into the parking structure attached to the large shopping mall. Her truck was securely hidden in plain sight awaiting her return.

It was a simple enough plan, but Theresa's heart began to beat a little faster as she considered everything that could go wrong along the way. Dominic's low, menacing voice cut through the fear and brought her back to the current situation. "He's not dead, but he will be."

Dominic crouched in front of the man he had come to despise over the past hour. The kid seemed to hold so much promise. Dominic had brought him in off the street, mentored him and began to trust him with his biggest secrets. With each passing day, Dom started to think of him as the son he'd always wanted. And in return, Shawn Lanza had betrayed him. Thanks to Drago, the traitor had been caught before he stumbled across anything that could damage the operation. Anger flowed through his entire body and the fondness he'd developed for the kid slowly dissipated. Nobody betrayed Dominic Zarconi and lived to tell about it. No exceptions. "This is your last chance, kid," Dom said angrily. "Tell me what you took and where it is. I know you were in my office. Drago saw you leaving. Where did you hide it?" Dom knew it was still somewhere in the building. That too was a relief. Whatever Shawn had been after, it would be recovered...eventually. He had nothing to worry about, but still... he didn't like it.

"Nothing," Shawn choked out. "I told you, I was just dropping off the invoices from Anita." Blood seeped from the side of his mouth as he coughed. His body jerked and began to shake as pain engulfed him. He must have internal injuries. His life was slowly coming to an end. He hated knowing Theresa was seeing this... hearing it. He hated knowing he had failed her. *Please just let her escape unharmed.* He silently prayed. *And give her the strength to walk away.* Something he hadn't been able to do. He'd been so sure he could succeed where his brother Zach had failed, that he'd risked everything...and lost. Now, he was leaving this world with too many unanswered questions. He was leaving his wife in danger without protection. In his obsession to get justice for his brother, he'd risked the only woman he had ever loved. Theresa was going to be vulnerable, but at least Dom didn't know who she really was...who they were. That one secret was the only thing saving her from an equally horrific death. If she stuck to the plan, she might have a chance. *Please leave!* Shawn silently pled.

Dominic stood, disappointed. He was confident whatever Shawn had, it was nothing to worry about. He'd found the kid on the street picking pockets. He had skills, sure...but Dominic never left anything out in the open. Not even in his own office. His files were all tucked away, safe and secure in the ghost partition on his computer. Nobody could access them. Nobody but him. Dom had hired the best hacker in the area to set the system up for him. Sure, there was a chance some up and coming techie out there had the skills necessary to find his records, but certainly not a street rat like Shawn Lanza. Even if somebody was good enough to hack the system, they would never break the encryption code. No, the kid wasn't a threat; but he still had to die. It was the price Dom demanded from anyone that betrayed his trust. He casually slid the Glock from his shoulder holster and pulled the trigger.

Shawn's body barely twitched as the bullet struck him in the left temple. He'd been on the verge of death already without the deadly shot from the .40 caliber semi-automatic that was Zarconi's constant companion.

"Clean it up," Dom ordered as he turned and left the room.

"I'll get the car, you grab that cart over there to move the body. Once we have it loaded, you follow me in the Explorer," Drago instructed.

"Got it," Socks said as he moved to the other side of the room and pushed the bakers cart into position. Once Shawn's lifeless body was secured on top, Socks slowly made his way out the door.

Theresa sat there, silent tears streaming down her face. Her chest tightened and she could barely breathe as her body began to shake uncontrollably. Her husband was gone. Shot dead without a second thought by a mass murderer. Anger surged through her and she finally understood why Shawn had put them at risk. She had tried to empathize with her husband when he quit his job and rented a rundown dive; tried to support his need for justice as he gathered evidence and risked exposure day after day; but she'd failed...until now. Now, she got it and she wondered if her fate would be the same as Shawn's before all of this was over. Could she still walk away? Could she move, start a new life and forget her past? Or would she be sucked into this dangerous world, destined to die a horrific death like her husband and so many others? She couldn't think of that now. Right now, she had to count.

The second she reached twenty, Theresa slowly slid the cabinet door open a crack and peeked outside. When she was confident the kitchen was empty, she crawled forward, pulled her body from her tiny hiding spot and stood. Her left leg gave way and she almost fell to the ground, but she forced her aching muscles to move. It didn't matter that her leg had fallen asleep, nor did it matter that she could barely feel her foot. It certainly didn't matter that her entire body was still shaking uncontrollably and all she wanted to do was fall to the floor and weep. The only thing that mattered was getting that phone and escaping.

The short hallway seemed endless as she fought back her panic and forced her legs to move forward one step at a time. She had to continue. Her survival depended on it. Finally, after what seemed like forever, Theresa was standing before the large electrical room door. She placed a tentative hand on the knob and gently began to turn it. The second the door slid open, Theresa let out the breath she'd been holding and slipped inside. There were no cameras in here, just like the hallway, which seemed odd to her. Why wouldn't you want to know if someone tampered with your equipment? But, she trusted Shawn implicitly and according to her husband... late husband... Dom had been adamant and unwavering. This room could not be tied into the casino's new security measures. The control room, Dom's office and the back entrance, including the long hallway, were to remain surveillance free. She shrugged, not wanting to think about the possible reasons behind that decision. Seriously, he had just murdered a man in cold blood, right out in the open... on camera. What could possibly be worse than that? Theresa shuddered and pushed back her emotions. She had reached the second row of paneling and needed to concentrate. She took an immediate right just as Shawn had instructed then began looking for the phone he had concealed. Half way down the aisle she found it. Theresa carefully disconnected the cell phone, unsnapped the adaptor, and shoved both of them into her large purse. Once the zipper was secure, she rushed to the door confident nobody would know what they had done. Now, she just needed to get to the exit. If she made it to the parking lot, she'd be free.

Once again, Theresa slid open the door just enough to check and see if the coast was clear. When she was certain nobody was lurking in the hallway, she slipped from the room, silently made her way to the loading area and quickly stepped out the back door. For a man who spent a fortune on security, Zarconi's kind of sucked. The outside camera was set at an angle so it would capture anyone approaching from the south but the north entrance was clear. Oh well, his mistake was her salvation. She maneuvered around the concrete platforms holding large, decorative plants near the entrance and practically ran up the alleyway, slid into the crowd and made her way through the casino parking lot.

Once Theresa hit the public park across the street, she let herself relax. Just a few more feet and she could disappear for good. The mall parking lot was packed, another bonus. She was able to blend into the crowd again as she made her way to her vehicle. The moment she climbed behind the wheel of the recently purchased truck, she locked the doors and clambered into the backseat. Crouching on the floor, she carefully pulled back the carpet, slid the hidden panel open and inserted her key into the small safe Shawn had built into the floor just behind the passenger's seat. The metal door unlocked with a soft *click*. Theresa fumbled momentarily with the zipper on her purse, her hands were still shaking as she pulled out the smartphone. She didn't even pause to look inside; just dropped Shawn's device and the cord into the opening; then, secured the lock; slid the panel shut and dropped the carpet back into place.

She doubled checked, making sure the Velcro was secure and the carpet looked natural, then leaned against the back seat in relief. She'd made it and the evidence was now secure. Initially, she had thought Shawn was crazy; but once he finished the secret hiding spot, she changed her mind. He was brilliant. By adding a slider over the top of the box, the locking mechanism and the ring used to open the safe were completely hidden. It provided a smooth surface so when the carpet was dropped back into place there was no outward indication the compartment was even there. If things went bad and Zarconi had one of his men search her truck, she was confident they would never locate her stash.

Theresa slid back behind the wheel and started the truck's engine. Seconds later, she was making her way through the winding maze of the parking garage headed for her tiny apartment. She'd grab her things, Zach's file and the money they'd made from the sale of their house, then head out of town. At least Shawn had the presence of mind to sell their home. She was grateful for that now; she would need the cash to survive. Even if she could locate her uncle after all this time, she would not rely on him for support. She was an adult. She could take care of herself.... maybe. If Dominic caught up to her, if he figured out what had really happened, nobody would be able to protect her from his wrath. She swallowed hard as she pulled onto the highway and headed for home.

Theresa parked her car at the far end of the compound and waited. She sat there for nearly forty minutes before she put her truck into gear and made her way to their building. She pulled into a visitor's spot, locked the truck and rushed inside. As she slid the flimsy door closed behind her, she took a minute to survey the place she and Shawn had temporarily called home. The apartment was exactly how she'd left it, spotless but grungy. Another paradox. One only apartment dwellers could understand. There was a full moon tonight. The mystic orb let off enough light that the small sliver peeking through her curtains illuminated the entire living area. She reached for the light switch then paused. She didn't need it, not with the natural glow of the moon. She understood she was still in danger - Dom's men knew where they lived. Fear swamped her again and her hand began to shake.

Theresa closed her eyes and counted to ten. If someone was watching, if someone had followed her, she didn't have to make things easy. She could do this without the modern convenience of electricity. She slowly made her way to the bedroom and cautiously opened the curtain an inch, just enough to let some light into the room. Suddenly, her body froze. Despair washed over her and reality hit. Shawn was gone forever. Her eyes landed on her favorite photo proudly displayed beside her bed and she crumpled to the floor, exhausted, defeated and so very alone. Maybe she could stay one more night. *Don't be an idiot*, she scolded herself. *It's not safe, you know it's not safe. You promised him you would leave.* She had to get out of here, but she was so tired. Her gaze landed on the queen-sized bed and for a moment she wasn't sure she could go on. Sleeping beside Shawn had always been one of her favorite things. Sometimes, they would fall into bed and quietly cuddle as they drifted off to sleep. Other times, they'd stay up for hours talking, debating and plotting. How was she going to make it without him? *One day at a time, that's how. Now, get your butt off the floor, grab what you need and get out before someone does find you.*

It took effort, but Theresa pushed herself into action. She slid the suitcase out from under the bed, dropped it on top of the cheap comforter, and flipped open the lid. Within seconds, she had the photo from her nightstand; her digital clock that contained a storage card with her best family photos; and the pearls Shawn had given her for their anniversary safely tucked inside. Once the luggage was packed and secured, she brushed back her tears, grabbed the small flashlight she always kept on her nightstand–Shawn had insisted on it after she'd stubbed her toe for the fourth time - and made her way to the darkened closet. Theresa crouched, slid the door closed and flipped on the light. It only took seconds to open the tiny floor safe bolted to the closet floor. She quickly removed Zach's file and her life savings, then slid them into her large purse. She flipped off the light, opened the door and moved back to the bed. Once she had everything she cared for loaded and ready to go, she headed for the door. Tears were streaming down her face again as she paused to remember... one last time... just how good her life had been. With a sigh, she accepted the fact that those days were over for good. Her future was uncertain, she may not even make it out of the city alive. But if she did, nothing would ever be the same again. Theresa carefully made her way through the one-bedroom apartment that had been a ruse for the past several months. She didn't look back as she slid the door closed and walked warily to her truck. *Goodbye Detroit*, she said to herself as she pulled out of the complex and started the long journey to Montana. She was several miles outside of town before she relaxed, confident she wasn't being followed.

Two days later, Theresa was sitting in a tiny mom- and- pop restaurant in Hays City, Montana, when she learned Dominic Zarconi had sent someone to kill her. It was just dumb luck she hadn't switched on those lights herself. Her apartment manager and the man occupying the unit above her, hadn't been as lucky. The local news reported that Cody Paisley, long- time manager of the rundown complex, was dead. The tenant, Steve Dawson, was still fighting for his life. The authorities were investigating, but it appeared a bomb had been set to go off the instant the lights were switched on. Apparently, they were stumped because one Shawn Lanza, who had been living in the one bedroom dive, was also dead; killed in a freak car accident the previous day. Guilt washed over her at the same time panic set in. Did Dom know the truth? Had he somehow discovered her true identity? But how? They were always so careful. Theresa blinked back tears, wondering if her death would be painful or swift. Most likely painful, Dominic liked to make dramatic statements.

Chapter Two

Two years later...

Theresa pulled into the parking lot of the Bar and Grill and shut down her truck. She glanced around nervously. No sign of them...yet. It had been nearly six months since their last visit. Six months of living on pins and needles. Six months of barely surviving the stress. She figured Dom liked it that way. It was another technique he used to get what he wanted. He just pushed his target over the edge, then once they were about to slip into oblivion... he'd pounce.

She slid open the door and stepped from the vehicle. Well, it wasn't going to work. Not with her. She would not be employed by that monster in any capacity. She'd rather die than step foot in

Detroit again. Her life was in Montana now. Somehow, she'd find a way out. She had to, she didn't have a choice.

On her way to the front door, she forced a neutral look onto her face and prepared for her daily performance. She loved the Bar and Grill. She loved working for Rowdy Cooper as much as she had loved working for Max, but it wasn't real. Her real life included poverty, the mob and constant fear. Moments later, she pushed open the front door and stepped into the dimly lit room. Theresa reminded herself one more time that she loved it here. These days it was the only thing she loved. Life inside this building was entertaining and predictable. Outside? Well, outside was more than she could handle most days. She would never tell anyone just how serious her troubles were. Mount Haven was a happy little town where people believed hard work and dedication were rewarded with success and happiness. Little did they know, but Theresa did. She was well aware of just how tragic life could be sometimes.

Theresa had only gone two steps when she spotted the sophisticated man at the bar. He was casually talking to Bailey and Rowdy and wearing an extremely expensive suit. Could he be an old friend? The man was stunning and hopefully just passing through. Her heart beat a little faster and she swallowed the lump that was forming in her throat. She had only experienced this kind of reaction to one man before in her life, and Theresa knew just how toxic that situation had turned out in the end. She would not fall into the trap of loving or depending on a man again. She couldn't allow it... no matter how potent the guy was. She was still paying for the first mistake, she was pretty sure she would never survive a second. Okay, that wasn't fair. Shawn hadn't been a mistake. They had loved each other intensely. He had just made a serious miscalculation. One that proved fatal for him and had altered her life forever. A mistake she was still paying for, one she couldn't seem to escape no matter how hard she tried.

13

Moondance Ridge

Theresa's attention returned to the outsider. Regardless of the danger, she could not take her eyes off the sexy, but cocky specimen sitting so confidently at the bar. His dark brown hair was styled in a classic cropped cut that was a little messy on top but trimmed on the sides in such a way that every hair remained perfectly in place. The man was sporting that GQ tight beard that made Theresa want to run her palms slowly across his face and then kiss him silly.

Now she was being silly. She took a deep breath and approached her boss, doing her best to ignore the eye candy that was now scrutinizing her. Theresa expected to get one of two reactions; blatant interest or disgust. But this guy wasn't openly showing either. Just another thing that drew her in... and made her want to run. This man was danger with a capital "D". "Morning," she hoped she sounded casual as she focused on Rowdy. "Need any help before we open?"

"Hey, Theresa," Bailey said turning to face her co-worker. "Come meet Tony Nazario. Tony, this is Theresa Regan, one of our waitresses."

Theresa chuckled, figures. The guy had a catchy name to go with his custom- tailored suit and cocky grin. But she'd be polite, for Bailey's sake. They weren't exactly friends. Theresa couldn't afford to make friends. But, ever since that night she'd rescued the girl from three drunks, things had changed. Something had shifted and it was easier to get along with her co-worker these days. Theresa welcomed the change. When Bailey started at the bar nearly a year ago, the woman had taken an instant dislike to her. Theresa couldn't blame her. In fact, that dislike had put her at ease. If she could fool Bailey Zander and make her believe the fake town slut disguise, she could fool anyone.

14

She casually glanced over at the cocky intruder then quickly looked away. The man was still studying her; she felt like a bug under a microscope. Yeah, she would definitely need to stay away from this guy. He was way too potent and observant for her liking. That's when she remembered Bailey had just introduced them. She reached out her hand for a polite shake, best to get the niceties out-of-the-way, then she could bolt. When his large hand encircled hers, Theresa felt a jolt all the way to her toes. The instant attraction was such a shock, one she hadn't expected, she yanked her hand away and practically ran to the back room.

Tony frowned. He was still trying to figure out the woman he'd just met. Nothing came to mind. He'd spotted Theresa the second she stepped into the bar; and, at first, he'd pegged her as just another bar bunny. A loose woman who was probably a dimwit and a slut. But when he looked closer, he realized that was a front. She wore tight skirts and low-cut shirts as a shield. *From what?* He had no idea, but her eyes screamed tragedy. For some reason, Tony had always been a sucker for a pretty face in need. Wasn't that how he'd met Bailey all those years ago? She'd been more tragic than most; but this woman...the waitress was a mess. He wondered if anyone else had noticed besides him.

Tony glanced at his dearest friend, then her new boyfriend and decided he was the only one that realized Theresa was acting. Bailey and Rowdy seemed oblivious to the facade. Maybe because they were so caught up in each other they missed something so obvious in their colleague. Tony gave himself an inward shake. He was here to do a job. He was here to get his friend's business back where it belonged. He'd eventually have to decide... stay in Missoula working for Drakker, or move on. He had plenty of time to make his decision. What he didn't need right now was a beautiful woman that screamed disaster. He definitely would be staying away from one Theresa... what was her last name? Oh yeah, Regan.

Moondance Ridge

Theresa Regan. So why was he staring at the back door, anxiously awaiting her return?

* * * *

Theresa stood in the backroom forcing the breath in and out. The last thing she needed right now was a sexy stranger occupying her mind. Socks and Joe were going to surface again and she needed to be ready. Any day now, she'd be blindsided with another demand, another condition to be met if she wanted to remain free. She'd been so naïve to think she could just flee Detroit and live her life the way she pleased. Dominic Zarconi would never allow that. Somehow, he'd learned Shawn's true identity, which meant he had learned Theresa wasn't the girlfriend of a common street thief. She was the daughter of former District Attorney, Jenny Tanner. Former sister-in-law to one Zachary Regan and current widow of Shawn Regan... not Shawn Lanza's bimbo girlfriend.

Dominic had made it his mission to force Theresa into slavery. A life of servitude to the callous, sadistic, murdering monster she hated with every fiber of her being. Well, she wouldn't do it. She might have to flee Mount Haven, but she would never, ever work for Dominic. She would throw herself over a cliff before she'd allow that to happen.

The door to the storage room slid open and Bailey stepped in, "Are you okay?"

"I'm fine," Theresa tried to force embarrassment into her voice as she transformed into the flirty waitress she wanted everyone to see. "He's just so hot! I mean seriously, I'd like to get me some of that." She glanced at Bailey to see her reaction. "But I know I can't. I mean, he's a friend of yours. I make it a rule never to go home with the friend of a friend."

Bailey remained silent as she studied Theresa. Once again, she glimpsed a desperate and terrified woman most likely on the run. Bailey had learned to recognize that look. It's one she had lived with for years. And having been there herself, she knew confronting the problem directly would only make things worse. Maybe someday, Theresa would trust her; but that day was not today. "Tony is an amazing friend, but he has some baggage. Oh, don't get me wrong the man is a sweetheart, but he's also complicated. Look all you want, but be careful. I won't warn you off because I know you can take care of yourself. Just be...I don't know, cautious."

Theresa laughed. "Like I said, no friends. But that doesn't mean I can't look, right? I mean, you snagged the hottest guy to step foot in Montana since Mel Gibson left Stillwater. The rest of us women are stuck settling for second best. But, there's no harm in enjoying the package while he's around."

Bailey decided to leave it at that. She didn't know why Theresa wanted this town to judge her. She didn't know why her colleague wanted the locals to believe she was wild and loose, but clearly that's the image Theresa preferred. Bailey wasn't going to call her on it. She just hoped Tony didn't make Theresa's life more complicated than it already was. She loved her friend dearly, but the man was a tragedy magnet. And when Tony Nazario decided someone needed his help, there was no stopping him. Especially when that somebody was an attractive young woman... a woman like Theresa Regan. "You're right. There's no harm in looking and Tony will be around quite a lot, at least for the next while. So, get your fill. Maybe a little attention is just what he needs to give into my demands and move to Mount Haven permanently." Bailey gave

Theresa a conspiratorial wink. "Anyway, I just came back to grab a bottle of Vodka. Rowdy said he's low and we already have a crowd forming. Tonight is going to be busy, I can feel it."

Theresa grabbed some Grey Goose off the shelf and passed it to Bailey. Inwardly, she was a jumbled mass of nerves. Tony was going to stick around? Fighting the attraction she felt was going to be difficult. *Well, maybe not*, she thought as she absently pulled one bottle of alcohol after another off the shelf. She glanced down and realized she had enough alcohol to restock the entire bar.

Her thoughts returned to the attractive stranger as she slowly made her way back to the main section of the building. Really, there was no indication the attraction was mutual. And the idea that a man like Tony would even think twice about a woman like her was ridiculous. No, she was safe. She just had to avoid the sexy intruder; avoid those pesky tingles she felt at his touch; and above all, make sure the cocky stranger never saw the slightest hint of interest. He'd take advantage in an instant, she was sure of that much. Slutty Theresa would just have to take her performance up a notch tonight. Then, problem solved. She could go back to worrying about her real problem...Dominic Zarconi and when he would strike again. Worse, would she be able to survive the next blow?

* * * *

Tony sat in the corner nursing a second beer. He'd never been a big drinker but Bay had insisted he stick around. No doubt she was trying to prove he belonged here. He wasn't conforming that quickly though. She should know that. Tony Nazario was a drifter by nature. Living in one place for so long these past few years had been a constant struggle. He'd done it out of desperation. He wanted to make sure Bailey could find him when she finally came out of hiding and went looking. His plan had worked, but it had cost him. The past several months had been unbearable. He was determined not to make that kind of sacrifice again. Not even for his best friend.

He studied Bailey for the hundredth time that night. She truly did seem happy and for some reason that made him a little sad. He knew they were only friends, they'd learned that lesson in college. But deep in the recess of his mind, he'd always wondered if they'd been wrong. When Bailey disappeared, he'd been frantic. That panic had quickly turned to desperation and with each passing year, he'd missed the woman with such an intensity it scared him. He'd never felt that kind of connection with anyone else. He didn't understand it, and it terrified him. What if she was the one and he'd lost her to a small-town guy who owned a bar? What if the timing hadn't been right and they were really soulmates after all? What if no other woman ever got under his skin the way Bailey Zander had?

Out of the corner of his eye, he spotted Theresa Regan. Now there was a mystery. The woman was such a contradiction. She pretended to be wild and free, but deep down something was weighing heavy on her mind. She acted like a typical floozy; but every time a guy made his move, she cringed. The girl didn't like to be touched and she never answered a question directly. Despite his decision to steer clear, he was intrigued.

Hours later, Tony watched Theresa exit the bar with a drunk and stupid admirer. He did his best to ignore the uneasy feeling in the pit of his stomach when the guy tried to cop a feel. He told himself the look of terror in Theresa's eyes when her date finally succeeded was none of his business. He clamped down on his annoyance at her backward glance...*At him?*...*w*hen she stepped through the door and let it slam behind her. *Why do I care,* he wondered as he made his way to the bar and settled his tab? He didn't... wouldn't.

It was over an hour later when Tony climbed from his car and slid the key card into his hotel room door. His annoyance had shifted to anger as he pondered the waitress' actions. Why in the world would the woman go home with a man she clearly couldn't stand? Once again, he wondered why he cared so much. But, he did. The hour and twenty- minute drive from Mount Haven to Missoula had only increased his frustration. He was paying far too much attention to the mysterious waitress. A fact that made him even more annoyed as he climbed into bed.

* * * *

Theresa sighed and pulled Spencer's beat up Ford Ranger into his parking stall. She hated going home with drunks but it was necessary. Squatting in a vacant home gave her a place to sleep and protected her from the weather, but now and again she had to manipulate her way into someone's home for a real shower and a place to do her laundry. Since Dom found her nearly two years ago, every spare cent she had was spent securing her freedom. What little she'd been able to save went toward future obligations, kept her free just a little longer each time Dom increased her monthly debt. She knew time was running out, unfortunately she didn't have anything left to give. Theresa sighed, trying to accept the mess her life had become. She forced thoughts of the past and the future out of her mind and focused on the present. She'd be up for another two-to-three hours, but it would be worth it. She'd chosen Spencer because he lived in a condo rather than an apartment. That meant in-house laundry, not a coin-operated common area. She wished she could afford to pay for the service, but her laundry budget was the first thing she eliminated in an effort to meet Dominic's demands. It was only the first step, the first necessity Dom had deprived her of. Fear rippled through her once again. It was past time for him to up the stakes again, change the terms of her supposed debt, and price her out of her freedom. She had no idea how she was going to handle things when that time came. She just knew she would not return to Detroit with his goons. She would not work for Dom...no matter what.

Theresa climbed from the compact truck and walked to the passenger side of the vehicle. She helped Spencer to his feet and up the stairs then deposited him on top of his bed. He'd just have to sleep fully clothed tonight. She silently slid back out the door and locked it behind her. The trek back to the bar...back to her truck, would take at least thirty minutes on foot. Her calves were killing her, but she straightened her shoulders and started on her way. The sooner she got to the truck, the sooner she could make it back here and start her first load. Once her clothing was dried and stacked on the backseat again, she'd slip over to the Wright place and catch a couple hours sleep before it was time to head back to work. She glanced at her watch and cringed, nearly two in the morning. There was a game tomorrow... technically tonight. The bar was going to be packed and crazy. Even more reason for her to hurry. If she didn't get at least a couple hours sleep before returning to work, she'd be sloppy. And sloppy didn't get tips. Theresa picked up her pace. She'd have to be on her toes to deal with the boisterous, drunken frat boys game night always attracted.

Moondance Ridge

* * * *

"Agent Perkins," Skeeter said absently as he silently cursed the interruption.

"Hey, Skeet," a familiar voice said soberly.

Skeet frowned. "Hey, Bryant. What's up?"

"I hate to bother you," Agent Bryant Smith said quietly. "But I have a situation I need to run by you."

"Okay," Skeet settled into his chair. "Go ahead."

"I mean in person," Agent Smith clarified. "I... well, I'm worried the phone might be bugged. I'm in the office of a local restaurant. I don't even trust my cell right now."

"Sounds serious," Skeet observed.

"I'll head to Chicago tomorrow," Bryant advised. "Call you from the airport as soon as we touch down."

"Bryant," Skeeter pressed. "What can you tell me now? I need to know what this is about."

"Dirty agents," he whispered. "I have the names of two but I'm sure there are more."

"Have you taken this up the chain?" Skeet wondered.

"No," Bryant admitted. "I think my boss might be...well, in bed with the mob."

"That's a serious accusation," Skeeter said skeptically. Agents hooking up with the mob? Not likely in this day and age.

"I have proof," Bryant informed him. "You need to see it in person. A few years back a reporter was killed. One of the agents...well, I'm pretty sure he had something to do with it. The journalist was getting too close to the truth and he had to disappear."

"You do understand how this sounds?" Skeet asked.

"I know," Bryant assured him. "And believe me, I didn't want to accept it either. I mean, these guys are my friends. I can't believe they got involved with a man as ruthless as Dominic."

"Dominic Zarconi?" Skeet asked for clarification.

"Yes," Bryant affirmed. "I have to go, someone's coming. I'll tell you everything tomorrow. Please, Skeet... I'm counting on you to keep this to yourself until we meet. As a friend, please do not tell anyone about this conversation."

"Call as soon as you land," Skeet evaded. "I'll pick you up myself."

"Thanks, man." Bryant said before disconnecting the call.

Agent Skeeter Perkins sat staring out the window for several minutes. He should ignore that call and get back to work, but he couldn't. The tone of Bryant's voice, the fear Skeet had sensed, was disturbing. As much as he wanted to blow it off and get back to the job at hand, he couldn't. He needed answers. And there was only one place he could go to get them. Within minutes, he was in his car headed to his friend and mentor's elaborate home. Very few people knew that FBI Director Stanley Burns was in town. Skeet just happened to be on the shortlist.

He pulled up to the sturdy iron gate and waited. It didn't take long for a big burly security guard to appear. Skeet rolled down his window and grinned. "Hey, Dodge. I need to see the old man, is he in?"

"Skeet," Aston Dodge said with a grin. "Yeah, he's up there. Didn't tell me you were coming though. That's not like him."

"That's because he didn't know," Skeet admitted. "Something came up and I need to run it by him."

"Go on up," Dodge decided. "I'll call ahead and warn him to hide the brandy."

"I'm more of a scotch guy myself," Skeeter corrected. "Thanks. By the way, how's the wife and kids?"

A huge smile spread across Dodge's face. "Marnie just got hired to write some fancy jingle for a new car commercial and the kids are doing great. Jeremiah is killing it in football and Elayah is loving dance. Life couldn't be better."

"Wow," Skeet said enthusiastically. "Congratulations on all of it. Knowing Marnie, she's stressed about the new gig but she'll come through. She always does, just like my Angie. We were lucky to find such amazing artists, my friend."

Dodge sobered at the mention of Angela. He was well aware of her past and how the kidnapping had impacted her work. "How is Angie doing?"

Skeeter grinned. "She just had her first big show in San Francisco. It was amazing, but my wife wouldn't settle for anything less."

"That's great, tell her congrats for me," Dodge said as he opened the gate to let Skeeter through. "I won't hold you up any longer. If you drove out in person, it must be important. I'll call ahead and let Stan know you're here."

"It is and I thank you," Skeeter said pulling forward and continuing down the long tree-lined drive. He came to a stop when he reached the elegant mansion. Stanley Burns was the current Director of the FBI, but that's not where he got the money to buy such an expensive home. His wife, Madelaine Burns, was a bioengineer. Laney was considered one of the leading minds in her field and could demand pretty much any figure for one speaking engagement. She currently worked as a guest speaker and advisor at Northwestern Memorial in their training program and loved it. She told him once there was nothing like educating the masses. She truly enjoyed passing her knowledge and experience on to the next generation.

It was her achievements that enabled Stan to purchase their current home and hire armed men for protection. Laney's knowledge and his position put the family at constant risk from evil, greedy dictators, spies and other nefarious individuals. Skeet stepped from the car just as the door flew open.

Laney strolled onto the porch and smiled. "Skeeter Perkins," she called amiably. "Has the earth fallen off its axis?"

Skeet took the stairs two at a time and pulled Laney into a big hug. "Not that I know of."

Stanley Burns stepped in behind his wife. "I know I didn't forget a visit, so what brings you to our humble home at this hour?"

Skeet gave Stan a serious look then pressed a kiss to Laney's temple. They were right of course, it had been ages since he'd visited. He always felt awkward dropping by now that Stan was Director of the FBI. He didn't want to give the impression he was sucking up to get special treatment. Especially when the entire world knew he had already received special treatment after his wife had been abducted.

"I told you to stop the constant analyzing," Stan scowled, motioning the group inside. "You think too much. First, because nobody will ever know how frequently...or infrequently, you stop in to say hello."

"I just..." Skeet began.

"And also, because I don't care if they do. We think of you as an adopted son, Skeet. Don't let them take that away from us. Laney and I miss you and Angela. We want to have BBQ's in the back yard and catch up on Angie's artwork as our schedules permit. Anyone who doesn't like it, can go pound sand."

Skeet grinned. "Sorry, Angie is doing great. Her show sold out and she has half a dozen orders for new projects. I think she's finally healing and the success has been good for both of us."

"I'm so glad to hear it," Laney followed them into the den. "Now, it's obvious you are here on business, so I'll tell Becky to bring in some coffee and I'll get back to my murder mystery. Be sure to say goodbye before you sneak out."

Skeet gave her a wink. "Stan's stories aren't exciting enough? You still find pleasure in those nail biting mystery novels you always favored."

"Stan won't share the good stuff," she teased. "A woman's gotta do what a woman's gotta do." She gave a long, exaggerated sigh as she left the room. "Evasion won't work, sweetie. You better come say goodbye or I promise you will regret it," she called over her shoulder as she disappeared down the hallway.

"She means it," Stan said as he settled into a comfortable lounge chair. "And don't encourage her. It's difficult enough already... keeping the gory details to a minimum. She doesn't need to hear about serial killers and deranged terrorist plots."

"Right enough, sorry about that. Angie used to press me too," he sobered. "That all changed after she learned firsthand just how sadistic the human race can be." Skeet settled into the chair next to Stan.

"And I'm sorry for the reminder," Stan shook his head in remembrance of those awful days. He'd never forget how desperate and helpless he'd felt with each passing hour. "Anyway," he finally said preventing a walk down memory lane for both of them. "What brings you out tonight?

"What can you tell me about Detroit?" Skeet asked.

"Hum, well...it's a shit-hole," Stan began. "Unemployment is up, the structure is crumbling and crime is on the rise. Why?"

"I mean the Bureau there," Skeet clarified.

Stan narrowed his eyes as he studied Skeeter. "What's going on?"

"I got a call today," Skeet admitted. "Well, tonight. Just before I came out. An agent out there was looking for help with something."

"Okay," Stan pressed.

"He said he thinks they have dirt in the Bureau," Skeet provided. "Guys working for Dominic Zarconi. He claims to have proof."

"What kind of proof?" Stan asked immediately.

"I don't know," Skeet admitted. "Bryant was scared, I could hear it in his voice. He said he thinks his phone is bugged, that someone is monitoring him, following him. He's supposed to fly out tomorrow, show me what he's got. I asked him if he reported it, but he said he thinks his boss is on the take."

Stanley stood and began to pace. He hated dirty cops. They gave the rest of the good guys a bad name. Was it possible the mob had infiltrated his ranks? If so, there would be hell to pay. He'd make damn sure of that. Nobody got in bed with the mob, not on his watch.

"Sorry to be the bearer of bad news, but I thought you should be brought up to speed right away," Skeet provided. "I wanted to toss it aside as ridiculous. I mean in this day and age with the technology we have and the capabilities to catch them red-handed, I can't believe an entire group of agents would go dark."

"Money and fear are great motivators," Stan said as he returned to his seat. "We need to keep this between us."

Skeet relaxed, he knew he was going to have to ask for that... for Bryant, but he hadn't wanted to broach the subject so soon.

"I can see you agree," Stan grinned. "Give me a few days to do some digging. See what this Bryant guy brings you. By the way, what's his full name so I know who to protect when the time comes."

"Smith," Skeet said absently. "Agent Bryant Smith."

"Okay," Stanley considered. "We go about this the smart way. We don't trust anyone...and I mean anyone, do you understand me?"

"I agree," Skeeter sighed. "I hate this."

"Me too," Stan agreed. "Any chance your guy's wrong? Any chance he's on the wrong side? You know, coming here to feel you out and see if you know anything?"

Skeet shook his head. "Naw, Bryant's solid. He's a good kid. I've worked with him more than once. He's smart, methodical and solid. There is no way Bryant is dirty. And if he was, he never would have called me. Plus, like I said, he was scared. He snuck into a restaurant and used their phone to make the call. I'm actually worried about him. If he wasn't flying in tomorrow on his own, I would have ordered him to do so."

"Okay," Stan leaned forward and clasped his hands as he tried to work out the problem.

Skeet waited and watched. He'd seen his mentor do this too many times to count. It was how Director Stanley Burns worked a complicated puzzle. His analytical mind and innate ability to solve the most complex situation was what landed him the Director's job in the first place. It was also why the man was respected by so many agents and top officials in Washington. Skeet was pretty sure Stanley Burns had the skills, the resources and the support to accomplish anything if he put his mind to it. They might need that if they were going to take on Dominic Zarconi and his mob.

Moondance Ridge

* * * *

"I called Angie and she's on her way over," Laney announced as she stuck her head into the room.

Stan and Skeeter looked up in confusion.

"I'm starved and so is Angie," Laney added. "We decided to have a lovely dinner together before our men get back to work. We're both looking forward to catching up and if you work too late, the two of you can just crash in the guest room."

"You called my wife?" Skeet asked, feeling slightly guilty. He should have been the one to call Angie. He looked up at the clock and the guilt intensified.

"Don't worry," Laney smiled. "You're not in the doghouse. I told her something happened at work and the discussion with Stan was taking longer than anticipated. She was thrilled I called and said she'd head right over. In fact..."

The two men stood when the doorbell rang. Stan took a step forward then glanced down at his phone when it beeped. He frowned as he read the text.

"I'm sure that's her," Laney rushed to the door and swung it open. Angie Perkins stepped inside and shrugged at her husband.

Skeet moved forward to greet his wife then realized Stan had returned to the den. He frowned at Laney before pulling Angie into a tight hug. "I'm sorry. I lost track of time."

Angie pressed a soft kiss to his lips. "I understand and I'm thrilled. It's been way too long since we've spent an evening with the Burns. And if you two work into the wee hours of the night like usual, Laney promised me a soft bed and an amazing breakfast," Angie grinned. "Please, honey, tell me you plan on working late."

Skeet laughed, then glanced back at the door to the den.

"Go on," Laney encouraged. "Angie and I have tons of girl talk to catch up on."

Skeet stepped into the room just as Stanley was disconnecting a call. "What's wrong?"

Stan motioned for Skeet to sit. "I don't know how to tell you this," he began.

"Tell me what?" Skeet lowered himself into the chair, knowing he was about to get bad news.

"Agent Bryant Smith is dead," Stan said soberly.

"What?" Skeet jumped to his feet. "How?"

"Car crash," Stan said returning to the lounge chair he'd occupied earlier and motioning for Skeet to do the same. "The details are sketchy. My guy tried to get answers from the department handling the crash, but apparently it was quite a mess. Agent Smith hit a concrete barrier, flipped his car and landed sideways in on-coming traffic. He was on the Metro, which made it worse. The other drivers didn't have a chance to stop. I'm told there are two additional fatalities and half a dozen injuries."

"They killed him," Skeet put his head in his hands, horrified by the news. In his mind, Smith's death just verified the accusations.

"We don't know that," Stan insisted, but they both knew he was wrong. They did know. "Right now, the local police are investigating the crash. It's unclear if he was involved in a high speed chase, or if he was just driving beyond his skill level and paid a high price for the mistake."

"Come on, Stan," Skeet shook his head. "We know."

"Yes, we know," Director Burns agreed. "But they don't know we know. And apparently the cops out there are getting conflicting accounts. Some witnesses say a car was chasing him. Others say he was simply driving in a reckless manner and lost control."

"Do you think it's a deliberate attempt to cover up the murder?" Skeet asked. He didn't care what anyone said, Agent Bryant Smith had just been murdered and Skeet knew in his gut who was responsible. Dominic Zarconi had ordered the hit. Now, there were two questions that needed to be answered; who carried out the hit and what did Bryant find that provoked such a desperate response?

"I do," Stan said without hesitation. "And we have to play by the same rules. It's more important than ever that we keep this between us. We both know when the mob is involved, things can get... complicated."

"We do," Skeet's mind was racing. Who did he know that could help them get to the bottom of this?

"What about Andrew Cooper?" Stan suggested, reading his friends mind. "Do you think he'd be willing to help again? Those Cooper brothers did a pretty good job taking down the DeRossi's."

"Coop's the sheriff now. In Montana," Skeet added. "I think Detroit might be a little out of his jurisdiction and Rowdy got out of law enforcement after his injury."

"Okay," Stan stood and moved to the window. "We need someone in-house. Someone I can control. But it also has to be someone we can trust implicitly. If Dominic has infiltrated our ranks, who knows how high that goes. I'd like to believe I can trust my people but to be honest, I don't know most of them well enough to really be sure."

"I feel the same," Skeet said. "Not that I don't trust them to be free and clear of the mob. I don't believe any of the guys in my office are dirty. I just don't trust them to keep their mouths shut. That office is worse than a bunch of old women at knitting club. They love to gossip and for some reason, they think it's okay to share anything and everything if the person they are talking to is another agent. We can't risk it."

"I might have someone," Stan considered. Blake should be done in Italy by now. Could he sneak him back to the states and give him a covert assignment without Blake's supervisor or his colleagues knowing about it? It was worth a shot. "He's a good kid, I knew his father. Died in Iraq and his boy decided to join up with us to fight terrorism in a different way. He's proven to be trustworthy and resourceful. In fact, he reminds me a little of you."

"Then he must be amazing," Skeet teased.

"He is," Stan agreed. "I'll call him before I turn in. He's in Rome at the moment." Stan looked at the clock. "It's just after two in the morning, his time. This can wait a few hours. He should be done with his last assignment by now. I'll call him before I turn in and we'll go from there. The sooner I can introduce the two of you, the better." Stan sighed. "Let's put this aside for tonight. I really am sorry about Smith. He tried to do the right thing and paid dearly for it. We'll take them down, Skeet. That, I can promise. Now, enough about that, let's go spend some time with that lovely wife of yours."

"I thought you said it was me you missed?" Skeet said, following Stan out of the den.

"I said I missed you," Stan corrected. "I never said life revolved around you

* * * *

The bar was packed, more so than usual. To make matters worse, Tony Nazario was perched on his favorite bar stool, observing again. This was the third night in a row he sat there, scrutinizing her slightest move. It was unnerving. The man was getting under Theresa's skin, more than she liked to admit. She turned from the bar, tray in hand, and froze. Theresa nearly dropped the heavy platter, drinks and all. Rowdy would not be happy if she destroyed a dozen orders in one careless swoop and made a mess on his hardwood floor to boot. She caught the tray with her right hand and lowered it back to the counter.

"You okay?" Tony asked from the stool next to her. "You look like you just saw a ghost." He was watching the two men at the corner table. The table Theresa had just glanced at before her tray nearly went bottoms up.

"I'm fine," she barked as she retrieved her serving tray and slowly made her way across the room.

She avoided the two suspicious men, but they were definitely watching her. Something was up and Tony didn't like it.

Theresa did her best to ignore Socks and Drago but inside she was shaking. Why had Dom sent Drago this time? Normally, it was Joe who delivered the bad news. Joe was compassionate and she was beginning to believe he disliked violence nearly as much as she did. Drago loved it. Joe was so much easier to deal with than Dominic's other employees. But, maybe that was the point. Maybe Dom realized sending Crazy Joe out to make contact didn't scare her enough. Well, if that was the case he'd hit the jackpot tonight. Drago terrified her and this time, she didn't have anything to bargain with.

It was an hour before closing when Rowdy stood at the bar across from Tony. "Do you know who they are?" Bailey's 'friend' had been watching the two men since they'd walked through the door. At least scrutinizing the thugs had kept Tony's eyes off Bailey tonight. Rowdy pushed his irritation aside and focused on the strangers. He'd find a way to deal with Tony the 'Fixer' and his obsession with Bailey soon enough. Right now, they had a common enemy to deal with. He couldn't blame the guy for keeping an eye on the duo. Rowdy had been doing the same thing all night. Those two were trouble. He would have thrown them out already if they'd given him a reason. Instead, they just sat quietly and tormented his waitress all night.

"No idea," Tony said absently, not taking his eyes off the pair.

"It's winding down, I was thinking about sending Theresa home early," Rowdy commented. "Any chance you're heading out, too?"

"No," Tony shifted his attention to Rowdy. "But that's a good idea. Send the waitress home, I'll keep those two occupied until she's long gone."

"How?" Rowdy asked, then frowned. Tony didn't answer because he was already halfway across the room.

Theresa stepped up to the bar. "Rowdy," she called over the noise. "Where's my order?"

"I'll take care of it," Rowdy moved to stand closer so they wouldn't have to yell over the jukebox. "It's pretty slow, why don't you head on home. I'll see you tomorrow."

Theresa frowned, she didn't want to leave early. She needed the hours. "I'll stay."

Rowdy glanced at the table then back to Theresa. "I don't know how you know them, or what they want, but it's clear to me they're looking for trouble. I want you long gone before the bar shuts down." He waited several seconds before Theresa gave a quick nod. "Do they know where you live? Will you be safe alone tonight?"

Theresa nearly laughed. Nobody knew where she lived because technically she was homeless. "No, they won't find me." She studied the table again, what in the world was Tony Nazario doing? She should warn him. He didn't know who he was dealing with, but she suddenly wanted to take Rowdy up on his offer. If she got far away from here before Socks and Drago realized she was missing, she'd be free for another night. "Okay, I'll see you tomorrow then." Theresa grabbed her purse from beneath the bar and bolted for the back door.

Once outside, she jumped into her truck and sped out of the parking lot. Her tires flipped gravel as she bounced onto the highway. The entire way back to the Wright farm, she studied her rearview mirror expecting to see headlights closing in. So far, the coast was clear. She pulled down the long drive, passed the house and stopped in front of the huge barn. Within seconds, she had the door open and her truck tucked away, out of sight inside the ancient structure. Once the door was secured, she darted across the yard and slid to a stop on the slick patio. Her insides were shaking as she pushed the glass door open a crack, just enough to squeeze inside, and carefully secured the lock.

The house was eerily quiet. Theresa had finally gotten used to the lack of night-time sounds out here. It was the reason this house was so perfect. But tonight, it made her jumpy. She cautiously moved forward and sat in front of the large picture windows that looked out over lush fields and majestic mountain ranges. She couldn't see them tonight, all she could see was blackness. But blackness was good, it beat headlights, armed men and the inevitable confrontation when Dom's henchmen caught up to her. She remained silent and tense for over an hour before deciding she was safe for another night.

Life was strange sometimes. If Bailey hadn't been kidnapped, Theresa never would have known this place existed. She'd overheard Coop telling his men to drive out and make sure it was vacant. They had all been worried about their friend, desperate to locate her before something bad happened. Correct that, Theresa didn't have friends. Bailey was a colleague... that was all. A colleague that Theresa had come to care for. She'd cried the entire time, wondering what kind of torture Bailey was enduring. It had been a stark reminder of what was in store for her if Dominic ever got his way. A reminder of what had happened to Shawn.

Moondance Ridge

At the time, Theresa had been desperate and homeless... sleeping in her truck with nowhere to go. Six months earlier, Joe and Socks had stopped in to raise her fees. Theresa had known it would happen eventually and she thought she was prepared. She'd been saving money, hoping she could afford the increase, but Dom had nearly doubled her monthly obligation. The extra money had run out quickly. Ultimately, it came down to priorities. She couldn't afford Dom's freedom fee and pay the rent. By the time she learned this place was empty, she'd been living out of her truck for nearly two weeks, sleeping in the park after it closed. Night after night, she'd huddled in the back seat, terrified one of the local cops would discover her secret and arrest her for trespassing. Theresa believed learning the Wright farm sat vacant was fate, and she took advantage of the situation. The same day Bailey was rescued, Theresa became a squatter. She'd been sleeping here ever since.

Depressed now, she slowly stood and moved to the wood burning stove. Within minutes, she had a fire going and was safely tucked into her warm sleeping bag. The accommodations left a lot to be desired, but it was a place to sleep and it kept her out of the weather, so Theresa would not complain.

* * * *

Tony moved casually across the bar room floor and stopped directly in front of the table where the two men were lounging. "Mind if I join you?"

"Actually, I do," a tough looking guy with a scar over his left eye barked.

"Drago," Socks warned. They did not need the locals turning against them. It was hard enough to track down the pesky woman these days. "Excuse my friend," Socks said amiably as he kicked the leg of a chair in invitation. "We've had a long day and he's not much for socializing."

Tony settled into the chair, positioning his body in such a way to block both men from leaving.

"What do you want?" Drago continued to scowl.

"I noticed you watching the waitress," Tony shrugged. "I thought I'd come over and warn you off. She's taken. Off limits. You get my drift?"

Drago straightened and leaned forward. "You threatenin' me, boy?"

Socks shook his head, hoping to stop Drago's next move but his friend wasn't about to back down for anything.

"Naw," Tony said casually, not in the least bit worried. The guy was a typical thug. He'd dealt with far worse in his sleep. As a teen, living on the street, he had to be tough... and smart. Guys like this were a dime a dozen. Tony knew better than most how to handle a bully, some things you never forget. Scarface was trouble alright and Tony was determined to put him in his place. "Just a friendly warning. This time," he added for effect.

Socks could see this was going downhill fast. "Look," he cut in. "We're not looking for trouble. Theresa, well she has business with our boss. He sent us out here to check on her; that's all. We just need to meet with her, have a brief discussion, then we're outta here." Socks studied Tony carefully. Who was this guy anyway? Dom was not going to like this new development. Apparently, Theresa Regan wasn't as vulnerable as she'd been a couple years back or six months for that matter. Maybe the boss didn't need to

Moondance Ridge

know... yet. In the past, it had been easy to intimidate Shawn's old lady. If this guy got in the way, things just might turn ugly. And, Dominic Zarconi didn't like ugly. Well, unless he ordered it that way. "We good?"

"For now," Tony lifted his long neck and took a swig. He wanted these guys to know he was not afraid of them. He needed them to know they would have to go through him to get to the girl. He didn't understand his protective instinct when it came to the mysterious waitress but he couldn't fight it, so he'd just go with it. He hoped in the end, he didn't pay too high a price for his impulsive intervention.

"Where is she?" Drago demanded as he glanced around the room. Theresa had disappeared.

"Who?" Tony asked innocently.

Drago jumped to his feet and grabbed Tony by the front of his expensive shirt. "Where... is... she?"

Tony glanced down at Drago's hand then back to his face. "You ruin that, you buy it."

Socks shoved Drago, forcing him to release his grip. "Come on," he shoved again. "We need to go."

The duo exited the bar and glanced around. Theresa was nowhere to be found. They walked around back and realized her truck was also missing.

"I'm gonna kill him," Drago growled.

Socks was about to respond when his phone chimed. His eyes widened when he recognized the number. "Hello, sir."

"What's the status?" Dom barked.

"Still working on making contact," Socks admitted. "She's moved from the apartment. I think you priced her out of her home. We can't find any indication she's renting somewhere else. Could be she's living out of the truck, which creates a problem. The only place to make contact is that bar. We spotted her tonight but before we could corner her, she disappeared."

"I need you in Vegas," Dominic ordered. "Both of you. Theresa Regan is not going anywhere and Joe needs backup."

"I thought he was just going out to collect from Rodney," Socks wondered out loud.

"Rodney has become a problem," Dom admitted. "I need a word with Drago."

Socks handed the phone over knowing where this conversation was leading. Whatever Rodney had done, it had just bought him a one-way ticket to the grave. And, maybe...just maybe, the delay would help them figure out the Theresa problem. Well, more to the point, the stranger guarding Theresa problem.

Drago ended the call and strolled toward the rental. "We're driving. I'll need a car for this job and we're not done here. Once we've finished up in Vegas, we're coming back to deal with that slut once and for all. And if homeboy in there knows what's good for him, he'll stay out of my way."

Moondance Ridge

* * * *

Rowdy scowled as he wiped down the bar. Tony was ogling Bailey again, but his girlfriend was in denial. Which meant Rowdy was trapped. If he brought the topic up one more time, Bailey was going to blow. The last thing Rowdy needed right now was to be in the doghouse. Somehow, he had to convince Bailey she was better off with a washed-up cop that owned a bar than she was with the slick businessman she had called in to fix all her problems. *Yeah, that was going to work.*

Bailey filled the last salt shaker, turned, spotted the men and sighed. Tony was relaxing in the corner and Rowdy was once again, thinking up ways to torture her friend and hide the body. She'd honestly believed that with a little time, the two of them would become friends. She couldn't have been more wrong. The constant tension was driving her insane. Worse, it was hurting her relationship with Rowdy. She just wished he would trust her. She wished he would get over his ridiculous and unreasonable belief that Tony wanted her for himself. How many times did she have to explain it? Well, she was done. She would not repeat that particular conversation. It was futile and insane. Rowdy would just have to get over himself.

"Hey," Tony smiled as Bailey slid into the booth across from him.

"Pete called," she said referring to her step-father and business partner. She absently grabbed his water and took a sip. "He's worried about Florida."

42

"I expected that," Tony stretched out and relaxed into the booth. He smiled inwardly at the annoyed look on Rowdy Cooper's face. He was winning this round and he planned to gloat a little.

"You did?" Bailey asked in confusion. "Then why did you send him out there alone?"

Tony couldn't answer that question. Initially, he'd planned to accompany Pete on the trip, but the thought of leaving Bailey and Theresa vulnerable had changed his mind. The two thugs hadn't been around for three days now, but that didn't mean they were gone permanently. He shrugged. "Pete needed a chance to try. Since that didn't work, I think you should head out and see what you can do. Flash that warm, friendly grin of yours and assure them things have changed. You know it will work and when was the last time you had a vacation? Take a few extra days and relax on the beach. You've earned it."

Bailey frowned. She was getting the distinct feeling Tony wanted her to leave town for some reason. But why? She ignored the feeling and shook her head. "We both know I can't leave right now. When Pete gets back, we're closing on the cabin. Plus, mom is still upset and refusing to move and I have plenty of work that needs my attention at the office in Missoula. Anyway, that's why we hired you, Tony. You're the Fixer. Fix this."

"You know I hate that name," Tony scowled. Another plan to get Bailey away from her boyfriend for a few days had just failed. Didn't mean he wouldn't keep trying. "Look, I'm not sure Florida is fixable. Think of it from their perspective. Cole went out and made a deal with them but while he was there, he gained valuable inside information about the company. Then he not only exploited it for himself, he shared it with a friend. That would be bad enough.

But to top it all off, every one of their employees endured a lengthy interrogation by the FBI."

"I know," Bailey sighed. "But if we lose them, if we keep losing clients, this company is going to fold. My father's legacy, everything he worked so hard for, will be lost forever."

"Losing Florida doesn't necessarily spell disaster for Drakker," Tony explained. "I mean, that company was in trouble already. It was the reason they brought Cole in to begin with. Everybody knows that, the important companies, the successful ones, they get it. I'm working on something that I think will give us the boost Drakker needs to survive this mess. Trust me, Bailey. I'm not giving up and neither should you."

"I do trust you," Bailey grinned. "You're the Fixer."

Tony scowled and changed the subject. "So, the old man decided to do it then? He's buying the property from you?"

"Yeah," Bailey admitted. "I think he's lost and looking for a way to move forward."

"But is this the way to do that?" Tony countered. "I mean, his son was killed out there. I know, not technically, but that's where Reese issued the final blow. It just seems... I don't know, creepy."

Bailey smiled. "He doesn't see it that way. All he knows is that Cole purchased that place and it's a chance to build a new life. I think he plans to buy a bench or something in memory of his son. Maybe have it engraved. It's actually kind of touching if you think about it."

"And what about you?" Tony asked, still concerned.

"What about me?" Bailey asked, confused.

Tony reached out and brushed his finger lightly across Bailey's cheekbone. The bruising had faded but he would always remember the terror and the anger he had felt when he saw her for the first time after the incident. "Will you be able to return? You and Pete are business partners, in addition to family. At some point, you're going to have to stop by to get paperwork signed or attend a meeting or a barbeque. Can you go back there?"

Bailey knew Tony was right, but she didn't have an answer to that particular question today. She wouldn't lie to her friend, so she didn't answer at all. The two of them sat there in silence for several minutes contemplating. Bailey eventually turned to gaze out the window. Tony's eyes never left her face.

Rowdy watched in agony as Tony and Bailey engaged in an intimate conversation. He didn't want to feel this way, but deep in his gut he knew Tony was trying to force a wedge between them. And, he was succeeding. It took every ounce of willpower he possessed not to throw the guy out when he gently touched Bailey's face. He had no idea what the two of them were discussing. He just knew it was causing Bailey pain.

"She loves you, Rowdy," Maggie said softly as she placed her hand over his on the counter. She hated seeing Rowdy suffering again. She hated the feeling of frustration she felt toward her best friend. She wished she had never met Tony Nazario. Rowdy had suffered so much in his life, he didn't deserve the turmoil that man was causing. He deserved love and happiness and security. For the life of her, she could not understand how Bailey could be so oblivious to the situation.

Moondance Ridge

"Doesn't matter," Rowdy said as he threw the damp cloth into the sink and headed for the office. He didn't realize Maggie had followed until he turned to grab a bottle of water from the fridge and they nearly collided.

"It matters," she disagreed. "But there's nothing you can do about it. Bryan's home alone. Why don't you head over, the two of you can take the horses out? He's been anxiously waiting for you to explore that trail he found the other day. I've got this. You could use a couple hours away from everything. Besides, Coop said he'd be stopping in for lunch so we'll all be safe and secure until you get back." She rested her hands over her stomach, a habit she'd developed since she learned she was pregnant.

Rowdy was about to refuse, citing paperwork, but changed his mind. A little distance, a relaxing ride, and a couple hours with his favorite little man might give him the strength he'd need to get through the day. "I'll have my phone if you need me."

"Good for you," Maggie said, relieved. "And we won't need you. I own this place too, you know? I've got this. Go already," she gave him a playful push for emphasis.

Rowdy only hesitated a second, then he leaned over, gave Maggie a brotherly kiss on the forehead and walked out the door. Maybe a couple hours with his nephew would improve his mood.

Tony frowned. Bailey was upset. He studied her as she watched Rowdy have a brief discussion with Maggie then disappear into the back. She looked so sad right now, just another reason she needed a break from the backwoods cowboy. Unfortunately, she'd made herself perfectly clear, Bailey would not leave Mount Haven until she decided it was okay to go. He inwardly wondered if it would ever be okay. "You know," Tony began.

"Don't start," Bailey cut him off. "You are my best friend, Tony. I expected resistance from my mother. She would never understand my decisions but I thought you would at least try. I thought you would make an effort to get along, for my sake, because it was important to me. I thought having Tony Nazario in my corner would make things better, not worse. But every time I turn around, you and Rowdy are scowling at each other. Either that or you're pushing me to leave when you can see how important it is for me to stay. I can't lose either one of you but with each passing day, I feel like I'm losing you both."

Tony opened his mouth to defend himself, but stopped when Bailey stood to leave. Was he making things harder for her? He knew he'd been doing his best to make things difficult for Rowdy Cooper, but that was his job. Bailey didn't have anyone looking out for her. He had simply stepped in where he was needed. He had always felt this overwhelming need to watch out for Bailey, to protect her. He failed when it came to Cole and Reese, he couldn't fail her again. He had a responsibility to make sure she was happy, to confirm in his own mind that Bailey wasn't making a huge mistake. One she would have to live with for the rest of her life. He also needed to know if Rowdy Cooper was in love with Bailey or if he was only after her money. Because, at this very moment, Tony was not entirely sure he could save Drakker, Inc. And if he couldn't save Bailey's company, all she had was that measly trust fund and her business savvy to start over. There was no way he'd let a washed-up cop step in and steal that away from her. Bailey was one of two people left in the world Tony loved and respected. Everything he did was for her; couldn't she see that? He couldn't ask because his closest friend, a woman he considered family, had disappeared into the back room.

Moondance Ridge

Bailey stepped into the office, expecting to see Rowdy but instead she came face to face with Maggie. "Oh, sorry." She took a step backward then stopped abruptly at Maggie's soft statement.

"You're hurting him," Maggie said without looking up from the computer.

"Stay out of this, Maggie," Bailey requested. But she knew in her heart it was a futile request. Maggie would always take Rowdy's side, whether he was right or wrong. Family loyalty came first for the Coopers. Facts and circumstances came in at a distant second.

"No," Maggie said casually. "Because that man out there is driving a wedge between the two of you and you're letting it happen."

"Where is Rowdy?" Bailey asked, trying to change the subject. She would not debate this with Maggie Cooper.

"He left," Maggie shrugged.

Bailey frowned. Where could Rowdy have gone? He never left the bar in the middle of the day. "When will he be back?"

Maggie studied Bailey for several seconds. Clearly, this conversation was getting them nowhere. "When he gets here, I guess." She picked up another receipt hoping Bailey would get the message. If her friend didn't want to talk about the problem, they wouldn't talk...period.

Bailey turned and stomped from the room even more frustrated than when she'd arrived. That family was going to drive her to drink. She opened the door to the stockroom and began the menial task of taking inventory. She needed to be alone and this was the perfect place to do just that. She glanced out the door toward Tony's table. Her friend had already left. Probably for the best. He said he had an appointment with his realtor. Maybe he would finally find a place to rent here in town. It didn't make any sense to pay for a hotel in Missoula when he spent every night in Mount Haven. Maybe if he was living here, right in town, she could find a way to show both Rowdy and Tony how much they actually had in common.

Chapter Three

Theresa bolted from the sleeping bag and frantically gathered her belongings. After an entire week of very little sleep, she had crashed, hoping to catch a few hours rest before she headed back to work at six. Panic was a horrible wake up call. She paused to glance out the large front window. Still no sign of the car. It had to be afternoon sometime, unusual for Dom's goons but who else could it be? Why would she have an unannounced visitor...to a residence everyone believed was vacant? At least the distinct sound of a vehicle crunching gravel as it left the highway and entered the Wright's driveway had pulled Theresa from a peaceful sleep. Being afraid all the time had probably just saved her life.

Once she was positive everything had been shoved into her bag, she rushed to the front window and gazed up the lane. Apart from the view that was her favorite thing about this house; nobody could sneak up on her. The Wright's had built their home a significant distance from the highway. After a short bend, the driveway followed a long but fairly straight line leading to the house. She could see an approaching vehicle long before they could see her. Her heart beat a little faster as a dark sedan came into view. She didn't recognize the car, but that didn't mean she was safe. Dom's men always picked up a rental near the airport so they were never driving the same car. *Time to run.*

She frantically pushed open the sliding glass door, shoved it closed and darted across the large yard. Today, she was grateful for her paranoia. She always had a getaway plan no matter where she was. The barn was a great hiding place for her vehicle, but most of the time she parked in the woods. It gave her a better escape route if someone came looking... like today.

Theresa slid around the side of the barn and slowly made her way behind the stables. After another quick glance to make sure the coast was clear, she darted across the remaining field and skidded to a stop. For the moment, she was safely hidden behind a large tree. She had to know, was it Socks and Drago? Had they found her once again? She watched in surprise as a middle- aged woman slid the full-length curtains towards the far wall and pushed open the sliding glass door that led to the back patio. Theresa had wanted to do that since the day she'd moved in but was terrified of being seen. Who was this woman? Was she the owner? A new tenant? The woman's presence changed everything. Where was Theresa supposed to go now? This house had been her last hope, the only place left in town where she could find refuge and shelter. Now, that too had been taken away. Well, that just sucked. Defeated and alone, Theresa made her way through the forest, climbed behind the wheel of her truck and quietly drove away.

Moondance Ridge

Her mind was racing and she frantically tried to figure out her next move. She couldn't return to the park, the stress and fear of being caught made it impossible to sleep. There was only one option left. A place she wanted to steer clear of. She had deliberately avoided Moondance Ridge, hoping nobody in Mount Haven would make the connection. Now, she had nowhere else to go. She'd waited too long to come back to this small Montana town and her uncle had passed away mere months before she arrived. Dean Clawson had owned and operated the popular fishing retreat most of his life. Fishermen came from all over the world to drop a worm in the Blackfoot River and relax on the front porch of their rustic cabin as the sun set over the lake. But Uncle Dean's health had changed all of that. Once he'd been diagnosed with cancer, he shut the place down and focused on making it through the day rather than making dreams come true for others. At least that's what Gina Snider, the waitress at a local café had told her.

Theresa always loved that place as a child, but she never returned after her mother had died. As an adult, she'd steered clear to protect the only family she had left. On that fateful day, two years ago, Theresa had pulled into town, tired, afraid, and all alone. She'd been so excited to see Uncle Dean again. Then, the waitress had shattered her last dream...Dean Clawson was dead. She'd driven out anyway, once, just to see if the place was still standing. The following day, she contacted the attorney in charge of her uncle's trust and learned everything had been left to her. Before she had a chance to consider her next move, Dominic's men had found her. The course was clear, avoid Moondance Ridge like the plague. If Dom knew about the property, and its potential, he'd never allow her to keep it.

Theresa didn't care how desperate she got, how miserable her life became, she would not lose Moondance Ridge to Dominic Zarconi... no matter the consequence. He'd taken her family, her life savings and her freedom. He'd murdered her husband in cold blood and was now demanding every penny she could acquire to pay off an imaginary debt she didn't even owe. He would not take her sanctuary as well. She briefly wondered what good a sanctuary was if you could never visit it, but she pushed that thought away. One day, she would visit. One day, she'd claim her property and finally achieve her dream. She'd re-open the resort and run the place herself. It might take time, but fishermen would once again come from all over the country to enjoy the peace and quiet Moondance Ridge offered its guests. Until then, she'd just have to live in a truck.

* * * *

Tony stepped through the front door and surveyed the old building. It actually wasn't in bad shape considering the neglect. He moved across the room and spotted Violet Coulter. He liked the no-nonsense realtor. She'd been upfront and honest with him from the moment they met. He hoped that would continue throughout the buying process.

"Someone has been inside recently," Violet began, pointing to the wood burning stove. "I don't think it's anything to worry about. Probably some high school sweethearts wanting a romantic evening alone."

Tony walked to the stove and opened the heavy metal door. He grabbed the poker leaning against the wall and slowly spread the ashes from one side to the other. Red sparks illuminated the interior. *Not high school kids*, he decided. This was more than one night of romance. Probably a homeless guy looking for shelter. It was spring, but in Montana that still meant cold evenings and chilly mornings. He'd take a closer look before making a decision. His offer would be much lower than he planned if some transient was using the master bedroom as a latrine.

Violet moved in behind Tony. "I'm sorry about that." She motioned to the ashes and the evidence someone had been living here. "George Wright passed away over a year ago. His estate has been in probate. It only cleared last week. George Junior lives in Texas. Well, Junior wants to offload this place as quickly as possible. You could always submit a lower bid than the asking price. We can cite neglect in addition to the squatters to justify the lower offer. It's fair under the circumstances."

"Give me a few minutes alone to look over the place and I'll meet you out back to discuss my price," Tony directed.

"Of course," Violet said, not in the least bit offended. Buyers frequently wanted a minute to themselves but Tony Nazario was unique. She'd recognized that the instant he'd stepped through her door. He was a savvy businessman with a no-nonsense approach. His offer would be solid, fair and non-negotiable. She stepped onto the back porch and settled in with her e-reader, knowing this might take a while. She'd just sit out back, relax and stay out of the man's way.

An hour later, Tony was headed for Violet's office prepared to submit an offer to the owner. He could do the necessary repairs himself. It would give him a project to focus on while he decided what direction he wanted his life to go. If things didn't work out for him here, he was sure he could sell the place and make a profit on his way out.

* * * *

Theresa stepped into the office and frowned. Where was Rowdy? On her way into work she'd remembered the tiny apartment attached to the bar. Maybe, he'd let her stay there in exchange for cleaning the kitchen or something. She checked the storage room then headed to the main area of the building. Voices and laughter echoed throughout the large open space. *Maggie must be here*. As she made her way to the grill side of the business, her nerves set in. She wasn't entirely sure Rowdy's partner and sister-in-law liked her - at all. The woman was always so distant, sometimes bordering on unfriendly. In fact, after all these months, the two of them had barely said more than hello to each other. Could she ask the tiny, pregnant owner for a favor like this, or should she wait to get Rowdy alone?

The instant Theresa entered the room, Jase was up and across the room. "Theresa, you have to come meet my sister."

"Okay," Theresa said hesitantly as Jase took her hand and led her toward the table.

"Marnie's in college now, she just started at the University in Missoula but she needs some extra cash to get by," Jase was glowing. "Maggie agreed to give her a job on the weekends and let her use that small apartment out back so she doesn't have to drive all the way back to town after her shift. I'm counting on you to show her the ropes. Anyway, by staying in the apartment Marnie and I can catch up and spend some quality time together. We've been apart far too long. And, it'll give her the seclusion she needs when she has to study for a big test," Jase announced with enthusiasm. "It's perfect for everyone."

Moondance Ridge

Not everyone. Theresa wanted to be happy for her friend...colleague. She really did, but his sister had just taken away her last hope. Marnie Montgomery and her need 'for a little extra cash' had just ruined Theresa's life. Worse, Jase wanted the two of them to be friends but that was going to be hard under the circumstances. She gave Jase the best fake smile she could muster and mumbled a soft, "that's great," before turning and rushing out of the room.

Maggie frowned. She had tried to like Theresa, but the woman was always so difficult. Today was a special and wonderful day for Jase and his sister, but Theresa couldn't even find the decency to be happy for him. She wondered what could have happened to the woman to make her so self-absorbed and uncaring. Maybe she was just born that way. Maggie would probably never know the answer to that question. Theresa Regan interacted with her coworkers just enough to get by, not a smidgen more. She never socialized and never got too close, well unless she was going home with one of the patrons that is. Plus, the woman never shared anything personal about her life to anyone. In all honesty, Maggie wondered why Rowdy kept her on at the bar. But, that was his business and she had promised not to get involved. She would employ happy, positive people to work the dayshift at the grill and Rowdy could employ whoever he pleased to deal with the drunk, obnoxious evening crowd. She turned to Marnie and rejoined the conversation.

* * * *

Theresa parked her truck in the forest and silently made her way back to the house. It had been a long night but at least the goons hadn't returned. Since she didn't have anywhere to go and hadn't solved the problem of where to sleep tonight, she'd offered to stay late and help clean up. Rowdy welcomed the suggestion and even agreed to pay her overtime. The two of them worked side-by-side in a comfortable silence, each of them lost in their own thoughts, worrying about their individual problems until the place was spotless. Once the work was complete, Theresa had headed for home. She was so tired, she absently drove halfway to the Wright's farm before she realized what she was doing. Instead of turning around, she decided to investigate. She had to know. Was that woman living there now? Had she purchased the old farmhouse? Was Theresa destined to be a pathetic homeless vagabond living out of her truck for the rest of her life? She climbed from her vehicle, pressed the lock and gently closed the door. She'd continue on foot just in case. As she crested the hill, she growled in frustration. That was not the same car she'd spotted earlier. No, that pretentious sports car belonged to one Tony Nazario.

Had the bane of her existence purchased her house? Was Tony responsible for her sudden eviction? Clearly, he was. Theresa practically stomped back to her truck. Well, she had a choice to make. Find a secluded place to hide in the woods, or make the twenty-minute trip to Moondance. She couldn't stay here, Tony-House- Stealer- Nazario would surely see her and call the cops. Theresa grinned, if she were arrested, at least she'd have a hot meal and place to sleep tonight.

Twenty-five minutes later, Theresa pulled up in front of a small deserted cabin and shut down her truck. She just hoped she had enough blankets. Spring in Montana wasn't exactly a tropical paradise. It made her nervous to be here, but she didn't have anywhere else to go. Plus, even if Socks and Drago found her, they would never know the place belonged to her. She'd just tell them she was camping out because she'd been evicted from the apartment. They'd be too busy gloating to dig into her story. When she was finally settled on the backseat, huddled inside her sleeping bag and covered with two additional blankets, Theresa let the tears escape. Would she ever catch a break? Not likely as long as she was fighting the Detroit Mob. No matter how great her success, how inventive her solution, she would always be defeated by Dominic Zarconi. It took another forty-five minutes before she drifted into a fitful sleep.

* * * *

Rowdy pulled into the drive, tired and grumpy. He had a headache from hell and just hoped downing a couple pills would stop the migraine before it developed into a full-blown, incapacitating funfest. Probably not, that was just the way his night was going. He stepped through the door, prepared for Knight's normal ritual. His dog darted across the room and came to a sliding stop as he planted two front paws on Rowdy's chest. He rubbed behind Knight's ears before pushing open the screen door.

His K9 partner bolted outside, happy to mark all his favorite spots. Rowdy let him run for several minutes before calling him back. He tried to push aside the unhappiness threatening to engulf him as he followed his longtime companion into the house. Knight immediately returned to his doggie bed, circled twice then plopped down, resting his chin on his front legs. Rowdy smiled. "Good boy," he whispered as he locked up and headed down the darkened hallway.

Rowdy's heart beat a little faster as he stepped into the master bedroom and spotted Bailey curled up on the bed. Sadness engulfed him as he silently moved to the bathroom, slid open the medicine cabinet and retrieved his prescription. After dropping two pills in his palm, he turned on the faucet and lowered his head to gulp just enough water to down the pills. As he straightened and turned, he spotted Bailey.

"How bad?" she asked, concerned. The last time Rowdy fought off a migraine was the day she'd been abducted.

"Not bad, I caught it early," he moved past her and settled into the chair next to the bed.

"We need to talk," Bailey said as she lowered herself onto the large mattress. "Do you think you're up to it?"

Rowdy's head was killing him but it was nothing compared to the ache in his heart. This was it. Bailey was leaving. He knew it would happen, eventually. He'd overheard Tony, Mount Haven was holding her back. Her business was suffering because she kept putting her life on hold to stay with him. He couldn't let her do that. He knew how it felt to lose everything. Rowdy's gaze fell on the badge resting on top of his dresser. He would never force Bailey to make that choice.

"Never mind," Bailey decided when Rowdy didn't answer. "We'll figure it out later," she pivoted and climbed into bed.

Rowdy didn't know if he was disappointed or relieved. He did know one thing, they couldn't put this off forever. He stripped off his clothes and slid under the covers. The instant he settled in next to Bailey, she turned away from him. Well, if that wasn't a sign, he didn't know what was.

Bailey tried to brush back the tears but they wouldn't stop. She was losing Rowdy and she didn't know how to reach him. She swallowed hard and was surprised when Rowdy wrapped his strong arms around her waist and pulled her against his body. She normally loved this closeness, but tonight it just made her more depressed.

Rowdy realized Bailey was crying. He didn't know what to do to make this easier for her but he had to do something. Maybe he should just tell her it was okay. If she knew he wasn't going to stand in her way, maybe it would be easier for her to move on. "It's alright, baby," he whispered into her ear. "I love you enough to let you go. I always knew this was coming... we both did."

Bailey jumped from the bed and glared at Rowdy. "You are the most stubborn, idiotic, moronic...ugh...man," she threw her hands in the air, frustrated. "You love me enough to let me go? Seriously, Rowdy? After everything we've been through, after the way I've opened up to you? You knew this was coming?" Agitated, she began to pace the room.

"Um..." Rowdy sat up and leaned against the headboard. He spotted the badge again and knew what he had to do. "I know Tony has been trying to get you to leave town. He seems to believe Mount Haven is... detrimental to the company, to your future...and I don't know probably your psyche or something."

Bailey couldn't help it, she laughed. "My psyche?"

Rowdy scowled. "You know what I mean."

Bailey moved to the bed and sat down next to Rowdy. She took his hand in hers and studied it for several seconds. "Rowdy, I love you enough to stay."

That was the problem though, wasn't it? He once again focused on the badge, hoping it would give him the courage to push her in the right direction.

Bailey saw Rowdy's gaze hit the badge and she finally understood. He thought she was giving up something she loved to be with him. She wasn't. She knew she could have it all, knew she would be happier than she had ever been if she stayed here in this small Montana town. The fact that nobody else believed in her vision was really starting to piss her off. "It's not the same," she whispered.

Rowdy immediately turned to face the woman he loved. "Of course, it is."

"It's really not," she insisted. "I can have it all, if you'll let me. I have no idea why Tony is so hell-bent on getting me out of town. I just know he's wrong."

"I thought he was the fixer," Rowdy pressed. "What if he's right?"

"He's not," she shook her head. "Not about this. He thinks because Peter is Cole's father, he's less effective. That's not true. I know Peter. My father brought him into the company because he was so good at the business stuff... all of it, just as good as dad was. Peter is doing exactly what the company needs him to do. And, I am where I need to be. I am absolutely sure of that. I just wish you could trust me."

Rowdy lifted Bailey's hand to his lips and kissed her knuckles. "I do trust you. I would trust you with my life," he grinned. "I already trust you with my dog."

"I'm serious Rowdy," Bailey didn't smile. "I know what I'm doing. Drakker is in trouble. Serious trouble. We lost three big accounts after that debacle with Cole. The only way we're going to get through this is together. Tony's acting like Peter's a liability. He's not. He's the best person to go on this nationwide mission.

Moondance Ridge

Peter is our biggest strength. He's an asset and our clients need to see that first hand. I really don't know why Tony keeps trying to get me out of town." She studied Rowdy. "Do you? There has to be more to this than he's telling me."

"I'm not sure," Rowdy evaded...unsuccessfully.

"Rowdy?"

"I really don't know," he insisted. "It's not like your friend has had an actual conversation with me."

"I know," Bailey sighed.

"But, he seems to be pretty protective of you."

"Don't start with that again," Bailey warned.

"Just hear me out, Bay. There were a couple guys at the bar awhile back, they were focused on Theresa. I think she knew them. Not like friends, she was afraid of them. I sent her home early and your man went over and had a talk with them. He might be trying to protect you from trouble. You'll have to ask him what was said, because I have no idea. Like I said, we don't talk."

Bailey ran her hand through her hair. She'd let the 'your man' jibe go for now. "Do you know why Theresa wants everyone to believe she's the town slut? Is she on the run like I was because that doesn't make sense to me? I wanted to fade into the shadows, she wants as much attention as she can get."

"I don't know," Rowdy admitted. "But, she is hiding, she's just hiding in plain sight. Maybe the same as you, but somehow different as well. Maggie must be really off with this pregnancy thing because she's been fooled by the exterior image. I can clearly see the protective shell Theresa erected to keep people away. Maggie has missed it completely, she doesn't understand what's going on and I think it's making Theresa more withdrawn. Anyway, to answer your question, I do have a theory. Tony wants to protect you and shelter you, he wants you as far away as possible in case those men return." Rowdy paused but decided to continue. "And, it might make you angry; but I think he wants to get you away from me."

"Rowdy," Bailey warned again.

"Just hear me out," he pressed. "Look at things from his point of view, I mean I've been trying to do that for days now. For you."

"You have?" she smiled and climbed onto the bed next to him.

"I have," Rowdy admitted. "And, I guess I sort of understand. You are this amazingly smart, savvy businesswoman that already has millions in the bank. I'm a washed-up cop that owns a bar. He has to be wondering if I'm after your money. He probably thinks getting you away for a month or so will clear your head and help you see things more objectively."

"I know you're not," Bailey said seriously. "After my money that is. But, I also know it's the money that makes you think my leaving is inevitable. I don't need it Rowdy, any of it. If it would fix things with us, I'd give it all away. Peter is serious about wanting to buy the cabin. The one Cole purchased with my trust fund. I told him today we could work out payments. I don't need the cash and he's going to be strapped until he sells his place on the beach. Maybe I should just give it to him, for free."

"I don't want you to give it away," Rowdy sighed. "None of it. I... how do I say this? When I lost the badge, I lost more than a job. I lost my identity. I lost my soul. For the longest time, I had no idea who I was anymore or what I was going to do with the rest of my life. I felt like... well, like I was broken. Like I was only half a man because of my injuries; and also, because I had no identity. I was a cop. I'd always been a cop. Then suddenly, it was gone. Everything I knew, everything I was, suddenly vanished. Now, I own a bar. I'm doing my best to overcome my physical limitations, but it's going to take time. Having Tony here has driven home all the questions I already had about us. Why would you want me when you could have anyone? Tonight, while I was sweeping the floor and throwing out the last of the empty beer bottles, something hit me. If you leave, it won't be because of Tony Nazario. If you leave me, it will be because you need more... and that's okay." He turned so he was facing her before he continued. "It's okay to need more. Before I was shot, none of this would have been enough for me. I needed more. I needed the city, the action. I needed SWAT. I needed to be out there, doing my part to maintain justice. The only reason I'm here is because I can't do that anymore. You can conquer the world. You can be anything you want to be. Don't settle for less, nothing is worth that. Not even me."

Bailey brushed the tears from her eyes, amazed at the man that was sitting beside her. He had just proven, in just a few simple words, why she loved him more than anything else in the world. And, why he was so wrong. He was worth it. "You are not broken, which is why no matter how many times you try to give that badge back to Coop, he is not going to take it. And I told you this once before, whether you have that badge or not, you will always be a cop in here." She pressed her palm to Rowdy's heart. "And because of that, you will always have a place in here." She moved her hand to her own heart. "I'm going to keep telling you this until you believe it, because it is absolutely one hundred percent true. I am in Mount Haven because it's where I want to be. Because of you, because of Maggie, but also because I love it here. I can run my business anywhere. I want to run it from here. Well, in Missoula primarily... but here. That is true whether I'm with you or not, Rowdy. But, I don't want to do it without you. I love you. I need you and I will always be here for you."

"I love you too, baby." Rowdy closed his eyes and tried to ignore the headache that hadn't subsided. In fact, it had now developed into a full-blown migraine and was getting worse by the second.

"We can finish this tomorrow," Bailey frowned. "I can tell those pills aren't working. What can I do to help?"

"You've already done it," Rowdy said as he slid into bed. "Just being with you is enough."

Bailey settled in next to him. They still had some things to work out, but she was fairly certain they had just cleared the largest hurdle; and from here on out, they could handle anything as long as they did it together.

* * * *

Rowdy woke to Bailey tossing and turning in the bed next to him. He immediately realized she was having a nightmare. Skeet had told him that Angie had flashbacks for months after she'd been rescued. He'd expected this; but until tonight, it hadn't occurred. He reached out and brushed the hair from Bailey's face then pressed gentle kisses to her temple, her forehead and then her lips. "Bay honey, it's okay. You need to wake up now."

Bailey's eyes popped open and she gasped for air. She hadn't had a nightmare since before the abduction. She focused on her surroundings and immediately her nerves settled. *Rowdy*. Seeing his eyes focused on her, feeling his touch, made the terror subside. "Hi," she whispered.

"Hi, back," Rowdy grinned. "You okay now?"

"Yeah," Bailey said as she sat up in bed. "I..."

"I know, you were having a nightmare. I expected this and to be honest, I'm surprised it didn't happen sooner." Rowdy shifted so he was sitting next to her.

Bailey shook her head. "It was different this time."

"This time?" Rowdy asked, confused.

"When I initially went on the run, I had the same nightmare night after night. Eventually it came less frequently until finally it only returned when I panicked, when I thought Cole and Reese had caught up to me. This was the same nightmare, but instead of me running, terrified and desperate, it was Theresa." Bailey frowned, what did that mean?

"Do you think the nightmare returned because we were talking about her? Because I told you about those two men? Maybe you projected your fear into her situation and your mind dealt with it through a bad dream," Rowdy suggested.

"Maybe," Bailey considered. "Theresa is scared and she's trying to hide her true self for some reason. Most likely because of the men you saw. After that dream, I'm going to be on edge. It's going to be impossible to stay out of this, I have to watch out for her. We need to protect her, Rowdy. She's in trouble... I know she is. She doesn't have anyone to confide in, or she doesn't think she does. It was a huge step for me to tell you I was running. But once

I did, it made it easier for me to rely on you. Theresa is not alone, but she thinks she is. Will you help me protect her?"

"Of course," Rowdy promised as a smile spread across his face. "Now, I don't have a headache anymore. I guess those pills did work after all. What do you say we make up?"

Bailey laughed as Rowdy tackled her.

* * * *

Tony scowled when Rowdy and Bailey burst through the door and made their way to the bar. Something had changed. Each day, they seemed to grow closer. He still wondered if Bailey was right and he'd been the problem all along. At least seeing them like this, happy and in love, proved there was more to the relationship than greed and opportunity. He was beginning to think they truly loved each other. And if that was the case, he was going to be happy for them.

His thoughts turned to his house. It was coming along nicely. The deserted old place had been occupying most of his time the past couple weeks; but this morning, he'd landed a new client. Bailey would be thrilled. It was the first step in re-establishing Drakker's reputation. And he had to admit, Peter came through for them. Sure, they lost Florida but Tony had known that horse was dead long before Peter made the trip. He also believed, in the long run, they would all be glad they cut those ties and moved on. There was something about the company that just didn't sit right with him. He believed the owner leaked the insider trading info on purpose to cover up an internal problem. One that faded into the shadows when news of Cole and Reese's death, and their suspected activities, hit the national news... and the corporate grapevine. Regardless, Tony was glad to be rid of them. He was also surprised they were the last company to bail. Peter had signed new contracts with each one of their remaining clients. Drakker was safe for now. Not out of the woods completely, but well on its way.

Tony watched as Theresa Regan stepped through the door and slowly made her way to the back room. She looked tired and underneath that smooth exterior, she appeared defeated. Whatever she was dealing with, Tony could see it had gotten worse. He just didn't know how to help her. He smiled when Marnie Montgomery slid into the booth across from him. Here was another girl whose world had been shattered. She was a good kid and just needed a little boost. Tony was confident that eventually the girl would figure things out and get back on track. Venturing out in the open, applying for college and taking a job here at the bar were all indicators she was finally starting to live again. "Hey Marnie," he said amiably.

"Hey," she said softly as she glanced across the room at Jase. She owed so much to her brother. He not only convinced her to get out of her self-imposed prison at their mother's house and test out the college scene, but he'd gotten her a job here at the bar. The people were so kind and Tony was amazing. He'd become such a good friend and mentor. She could talk to him about anything. Even things she didn't dare mention to her overbearing, protective brother. Little by little, she was starting to feel human again. With each passing day, life seemed to get a little easier. Jase did that for her, but Tony... well, Tony was helping her realize that the past didn't define her. She could emerge from the horror a better person. But more than that, it was okay to feel like a woman. Yes, she'd been attacked and raped by monsters but life could go on... if she let it.

"What's up?" he pressed. This was their regular routine. Marnie would join him and he'd push her until she opened up and told him what was on her mind.

Marnie took a deep breath, sipped her water, then began. Once she got started, the dam broke and she found herself telling Tony about the guy in her biology class that was gorgeous and a little intimidating. She admitted her fears and listened while he gave advice and subtly pushed her just a little further away from her comfort zone. It was in that moment she realized Tony had become important to her. He wasn't exactly like a brother. If Jase had been as direct and blunt as Tony was, she would have packed up and gone running back to her mother's house. But for some reason, Tony got away with it. And his not-so-subtle challenges, thrown down like a gauntlet, were pushing her to do things she may never have done without him. He was forcing her to trust again not only to trust herself and her strength, but also to trust others.

It was strange really. Tony wasn't all rainbows and unicorns about it like her mother had been. He frequently warned her that living life meant disappointment, heartache and pain. Those were emotions she would also have to learn to deal with. Lessons she couldn't hide from. She knew that, somewhere inside, she really did know that. But hearing it, out loud, from her new friend, somehow made her feel like she could survive. When she first met Tony, she'd had a little crush. Who wouldn't? The man was hot, sophisticated and smooth. But now, the attraction had been replaced by respect. She loved Tony, but she would never be in love with him. He was too important and Brad was the one that gave her goosebumps. Tony... he gave her confidence.

Theresa stepped up to the bar and began to restock the shelf. She spotted Tony with Marnie and her spirits sank just a little more. She shouldn't care. She didn't want Tony Nazario for herself; but seeing him with Marnie, the girl that stole her apartment, the girl who everyone around here loved and protected, twisted that knife just a little deeper. Sometimes life was so unfair. Marnie had been through something horrific and came out the other side with family and friends anxious and willing to prop her up each time she fell. Theresa didn't fault the girl for that; she was just a little jealous. Her life might be different if she had someone that cared, someone to help her carry the burden when it became impossible to bear. The way it was now.

Theresa had also been dealt a cosmic blow, but unlike Marnie, she was left to deal with her problems alone. Destined to live in fear until one day, she would just disappear forever. She knew that was her destiny. Either Dominic would abduct her and force her back to Detroit against her will, or he'd simply kill her and hide the body. Either way, she'd be gone. Would anyone even notice? Probably not. She avoided relationships, refused to make friends, forced anyone and everyone away that got too close. She'd done it for their sake, to protect them, but knowing that didn't make it any easier. It didn't make life any less lonely.

She sighed and glanced at the table again. Well, Tony could have Marnie. They'd make a great couple. Maybe. He did seem a little too old for her, but who was she to judge. She'd just focus on work and ignore the budding relationship. She had enough to worry about as it was. Mooning over a man that would never want her, didn't even make the list.

* * * *

Tony was fuming. Theresa had ignored him all night and even made Casey take over his table so she didn't have to interact with him. There was something about that woman that drove him insane. And now, she was up to her typical antics. *Well, not tonight*. She was not going home with that deceitful pervert.

Theresa glanced at the clock and sighed in relief. Twenty more minutes. She could survive that long. Her truck was loaded with dirty laundry and Spencer was well on his way to being totally and completely drunk. She'd done this before, it would work again. The second Rowdy announced last call, she was standing in front of Spencer's table. It didn't take long before he invited her back to his place...just like she knew he would. "Sure, just let me check out and grab my stuff."

Tony gritted his teeth and made a decision. It was obvious Theresa thought the prick was falling down drunk, but he wasn't. Tony had watched him all night. Each time he ordered a drink, he'd pass it to his friend. The redheaded buffoon was about ready to pass out, but the other guy...the guy Theresa was helping out to his truck...was as sober as a priest on Sunday. Tony dropped enough money to cover his tab plus a generous tip on the table and followed them out the door. His gut was telling him trouble was looming and he planned to be there to stop it. He was sure the woman wouldn't appreciate his help, but she was going to get it anyway.

Theresa slid behind the wheel of Spencer's truck and pulled onto the highway. For the tenth time in about five seconds she wondered if he really was drunk. He was acting drunk, but something wasn't right. In fact, if history was any indication, he should be asleep by now, head resting against the window for support. But he wasn't. He was staring at her as if he were a hunter and she was his prey. Well, she'd just park the truck and tell him she changed her mind. She could walk back to her truck, she'd planned to do that, anyway. The laundry would have to wait, not ideal, but she'd figure something out later.

Moondance Ridge

Theresa pulled into Spencer's parking spot and turned to address him. She dropped his keys on the seat and shrugged. "Well, I'm beat. Here you go, home safe. I'll see you around." She turned to open the door and was surprised when Spencer forcefully grabbed her wrist and stopped her.

"We had an agreement. You said you'd come home with me. I'm home. We're going to finish this. We both know last time you skated because I was too drunk to stop you. Not tonight, sweetheart. Tonight, I'm nearly sober and I want a piece. The piece that was promised to me weeks ago." Spencer grabbed his keys and pulled her across the seat, yanking her out of the passenger side door.

Tony was out of the car and across the parking lot in seconds. He stepped between Theresa and her attacker in challenge. "Let her go," he demanded.

Spencer growled. "This is none of your business. Walk away while I'm still willing to let you."

Tony gripped the man's wrist and twisted. Spencer immediately released the hold he had on Theresa's arm as he tried to get free of Tony's grip. "Get in my car," Tony demanded. "Now."

Theresa stared at Tony, confused. She'd been sure he would hang out with Marnie all night. Why had he followed her? Could he be working for Dom on the side? It was getting just a bit too convenient that he was always turning up at the oddest times. Was he trying to gain her trust by saving her from danger only to snatch her up and deliver her to the gates of hell?

"Theresa," Tony pressed.

Theresa turned and rushed to Tony's car. At the moment, she didn't really care if he was working for Dom. He just saved her from Spencer. She'd deal with the rest later. As she slid into the passenger seat of Tony's expensive vehicle, she wondered what kind of man he really was. Obviously, he was wealthy and a respected businessman; but right now, he was up in Spencer's face, clearly threatening the overzealous creep in a way that had Spencer fuming. The guy's face was bright red and he looked like he was ready to blow.

Theresa sighed inwardly. This was all her fault. No, it was actually Dominic Zarconi's fault. If he hadn't taken all her money, she'd still be living in her modest apartment where she had access to laundry facilities. Not on the run, living out of her truck, desperate for a free place to wash a load of clothes. The only thing she still owned was that truck... and Moondance Ridge. The two possessions she wasn't willing to sacrifice, not even to save herself from the mob. The truck was her only means of escape. Plus, it contained all the evidence she had against the ruthless murderer. Everything Zach and Shawn had acquired was still carefully tucked away in Shawn's secret compartment. The fishing retreat was her future. Both were essential. "Thank you," she said softly when Tony climbed behind the wheel. Tony didn't answer.

Theresa rode in silence, lost in thought until Tony pulled off the road onto the lane that led to the Wright's farm. "Where are we going? I need my truck."

"I'll take you to get it in the morning," he said without even looking her way.

"Tony," she tried for diplomacy. "I need my truck...tonight." Did he think just because he saved her from Spencer, she'd hop in bed with him out of gratitude? If so, he was going to be mighty disappointed.

Tony pulled into the garage and hit the button to close the door. "What's the difference? You planned to leave it at the bar while you shacked up with that punk. We'll get it in the morning just like you intended." He pushed open the car door and climbed out, not even pausing as he opened the side door that led to the kitchen and stepped inside.

Theresa frowned. Actually, she didn't plan on leaving her truck at the bar. She hadn't planned to shack up either. She just needed the man's washing machine. Tony's would do, but she'd have to find a way to sneak back inside after she made the long hike to the bar and returned with her truck. Worse, how would she explain the mysterious appearance of her large vehicle to the pushy, control freak standing just inside the door?

Tony stepped back into the doorway and waited. The woman was exasperating. After several minutes, she got the hint and slowly climbed from his car.

"Wow," Theresa gasped when she stepped into the kitchen. "It looks different." She caught herself but not soon enough. How could she possibly know what this house had looked like before? "I mean, it looks like you've done a lot of work in here. Mr. Wright was old and could barely get around. If the inside looked anything like the outside, you've been busy since you moved in." She continued to study the kitchen, careful to look everywhere but in Tony's direction.

Tony frowned and studied Theresa. Was this just nervous rambling, or something more? Did she think he was a troll, some deviant that brought her here for more than an escape? Clearly, she did. "The guest room is at the end of the hall. There's a bathroom right next door. Make yourself at home, I'll drive you over to the bar first thing so you can retrieve your truck."

"What makes you think I don't want to go home right now?" she bluffed.

"My place, his place... should be all the same. You obviously didn't have plans to head home twenty minutes ago. Nothing's changed but geography. Goodnight, Theresa. I'll drive you over in the morning." Tony stepped to a small box on the wall, next to the door, and punched in his code to set the alarm.

Theresa panicked. That was new, and there was no way she'd be getting out of this house without alerting the new owner. Would it be so bad to have one night in a real bed, with real heat and real food in the morning? She deliberated with herself, analyzing the situation for several silent seconds before she ultimately decided she'd take advantage of this rare opportunity. It might never present itself again. "Goodnight," she said as she made her way down the hall and into the guest room; closing the door securely behind her.

Tony stood at the bedroom window, gazing into the darkness. Something was off... he couldn't figure out what was going on, but the entire situation perplexed him. Theresa had willingly left with her customer from the bar; but the minute she realized he wasn't drunk, she tried to bolt. What was her end game? Why go home with a guy if you didn't plan to sleep with him? She'd been tricked for sure, but he was beginning to wonder if she'd selected Spencer on purpose. Because she believed he was too drunk to try anything. It fit. How many times had he watched her cringe at the slightest touch? That was not the way a woman responded if she slept around with any willing man. But why? None of this made sense to him. Did her aversion to men have anything to do with the two thugs he'd dealt with over two weeks ago? Tony ran his hand through his hair in frustration. The mystery was getting more intriguing by the day. And, right now, he had more questions than answers. He stripped off his clothes and climbed into bed. He'd figure it out, eventually. Then he'd decide how to help.

* * * *

Tony pulled up beside Theresa's truck and waited for her to climb behind the wheel. He glanced at the back seat and frowned. It looked like the woman was living out of her vehicle. Was she just a slob or was there another explanation? Instantly, her comment last night popped into his head. "It looks different." Was it possible? Could Theresa be the mysterious squatter? No, he knew for a fact Rowdy and Maggie paid their waitresses well. *But still...*

"Thanks again," Theresa called through the window before she backed out of the parking space and made her way across the empty lot.

Tony only hesitated a second. He pulled in behind the truck and waited for her to get a safe distance away, then followed. He needed to know where the woman lived. Well, he needed to know so much more, but that was a good start.

* * * *

"It's done," Drago said into the phone as he dropped onto the uncomfortable hotel room chair.

"Any problems?" Dom asked, expecting the answer to be no.

"Not exactly a problem," Drago said hesitantly. "Just a minor complication."

"Tell me," Dom said in irritation. He hated complications.

"Well," Drago began. "Rodney had a partner. Some street rat who thought he was a big shot. The guy got in the way. You got a two-for."

"And you just decided this on your own?" Drago was starting to get out of hand. Dominic knew he'd have to rein Drago in eventually, but he'd mistakenly believed Joe and Socks would keep him in line throughout this mission.

"Didn't have a choice," Drago said calmly. "You know I would have run it past you if there was time, but the situation was...dynamic. I had to act fast or he would have been in the wind and a much bigger problem."

Dom wasn't buying it, but he wouldn't jump to any conclusions until he spoke with Joe. Socks would cover for his friend...to an extent. Joe didn't approve of Drago's tactics. He'd tell Dom exactly what had happened, good or bad, no deviations. Dom could decide where to go from there. "I don't know what you've been doing, but you've milked this assignment long enough. It should have been a quick in and out, two days tops. You arrived in the city nearly three weeks ago and this is the call I get? Clean it up, then get back to Theresa. I want that woman in Detroit before the end of the week. Tell Joe to head straight home. I have another delicate situation that only he can handle. I'm counting on you and Socks to take care of the girl. No more games, I'm out of patience with that woman." He disconnected the call and settled behind his desk. Soon he would have answers. He was pretty sure Shawn hadn't gathered anything of consequence; but until he tied up this last loose end, he wouldn't know for sure.

Anger surged through him, just as it always did when he thought of Shawn Regan. The guy had nerve that was obvious. Same as his big brother. When Dom received the packet Zachary Regan had been compiling from Darrow, he had panicked. Then, he realized the information was safe. Having an agent in his pocket proved to be beneficial after all. If Zachary Regan had published even half of what he'd gathered in the Chronical, life would be very different for Dominic Zarconi and his entire operation. He'd been lucky. They'd stopped the journalist in time. But what information did Shawn possess? Nothing had been recovered, even though the guy had been inside Dominic's personal office. When Darrow recognized the kid as Zach's brother, Dom had once again become obsessed. He needed to know what Shawn had been after. His men had torn the casino apart three times, but still no sign of what the kid had taken. He knew there was no way anything left the building, just dumb luck again. But, Dominic Zarconi did not rely on luck...ever. He needed to know why Shawn Regan risked exposure. Before the break in, he'd been moving up the chain...quickly. Dominic was definitely missing something, and Theresa Regan was his key to getting the answers he so desperately needed. Dom smiled, he couldn't wait to get started.

* * * *

Theresa slowed, cautiously checking her rearview mirror. The coast was still clear. She let out a huge sigh of relief and made the turn off the main highway onto the gravel and dirt road that led to the campground. The place wasn't ideal but she could wash her laundry in the lake and hang them out to dry in the sun. The spring temperatures still dropped substantially after sunset; but during the day, it was pleasant and warm—especially out here next to the lake. There was a slight breeze today, but Theresa didn't mind. It would help the clothes dry faster. She might have wrinkles, but that couldn't be avoided. She'd just have to deal with it. Tonight was a jeans and t–shirt kind of night, anyway.

As she pulled into the spot she'd been occupying for over two weeks now, she climbed from her truck and gathered her loose clothing into a large pile. If she shoved them in tight, she might be able to do it all in one trip. She studied the lake. It wasn't that far, but it was going to be cold. She glanced around, looking for some kind of rope or twine to string a line between the trees and found just what she needed in the bed of her truck. Now for her clothes. She pulled the tattered basket from her backseat and was again reminded of just how pathetic her life had become. Her plastic clothes basket looked more like a duct taped science project gone wrong than a mechanism for transporting laundry. Theresa sighed. She wouldn't dwell on the negative, she had laundry to do. As an afterthought, she grabbed her iPod and started her favorite playlist as she somberly made her way toward the lake.

Her thoughts immediately shifted back to her childhood. She had always loved it out here. She'd loved her uncle, but she also loved how beautiful and peaceful it was in the country. She'd marveled at how drastically different everything seemed from the city where she lived with her parents. Here, in the wilderness, she was surrounded by the serene lake, the sparkling river and the majestic pines. Birds chirped cheerfully as if they didn't have a care in the world. What would that be like? How would it feel to be happy and content instead of terrified all the time? Until she dealt with Dominic and the threat he posed, she would never know. Fear and desperation overcame her as she focused on her dilemma. What was she going to do the next time Dom's men confronted her?

Moondance Ridge

* * * *

Tony slowed and pulled to the side of the road. Theresa hadn't spotted him, yet. His mind shifted to the last time he'd done this. The last vehicle he'd followed, the last prey he'd hunted. He swallowed hard and tried to push those thoughts from his mind. Back then, he'd failed. A fact that still galled him. But, Travis Beynart was now in prison and the world accepted his punishment as justice. Tony disagreed. The man had murdered the only father figure he'd ever known. Beynart deserved death, not a cell. A long, agonizing, painful death. Anyway, Theresa wasn't his prey. Although, this little detour made him realize one thing. He might be a wealthy and prominent businessman these days... but underneath it all still lurked the wily, cunning predator he'd been when he lived on the streets. Impeccably dressed, savvy entrepreneur, Tony Nazario was still the clever street rat that could overcome and adapt when life threw an obstacle in his way. Something that might come in handy if he was going to figure out the enigma named Theresa Regan.

He once again focused on his current predicament. What in the world was she doing out here in the middle of nowhere? He raised the binoculars and watched as her truck pulled off the main highway onto an old dirt and gravel side road. He waited as long as he dared, then pulled back onto the highway and followed.

As he neared the overgrown path Theresa had taken, he realized it was a private road of some kind. The large pine archway that spanned the length of the drive looked sturdy enough, although it could use a fresh coat of stain. He paused to admire the intricate carving of a trout and the name *Moondance Ridge* engraved in large fancy letters. Somebody had spent a lot of time sculpting it, so why the neglect? He was even more confused now than he'd been minutes before. He took the first turnoff and headed into what looked like an abandoned fishing resort. The main building was situated at the base of a hill overlooking the enormous lake. As he proceeded through the maze of cabins and picnic tables, he spotted Theresa's truck in the distance.

Tony wasn't ready to be discovered. He still had questions and he was fairly certain Theresa Regan would not be forthcoming with answers. Once he parked his car behind a nearby cabin, Tony made his way through the tall pine trees. He wanted a closer look at the area Theresa was occupying. Eventually, the thick forest emptied into a manmade but private alcove. He stopped to glance around, careful to remain hidden in the shadows of the trees. Theresa's truck was parked at an angle and a sleeping bag was dangling over the side of the bed. Upon closer inspection, it became painfully obvious the woman was living out here... in her truck. He was seething as he moved to the large picnic table to wait. Did this have something to do with the two thugs he'd encountered a few weeks back? Tony's gut told him it did and he was going to get to the bottom of this if it killed him.

* * * *

Theresa hung the last shirt on the makeshift clothesline and headed back toward her camp. Hopefully, they'd dry quickly in the wind. She glanced up and spotted the man sitting casually at her picnic table. He was silhouetted, engulfed masterfully in the shade of a nearby tree so she couldn't make out his face. Had Socks and Drago found her? She squinted and tried to get a closer look, tried to determine which one of her foes she'd be dealing with; but it was no use. The shadow provided the perfect cover. Was this an

Moondance Ridge

ambush? Theresa began a frantic search of the area. Was the other one lurking, waiting for just the right moment to pounce?

With that thought, Theresa's knees buckled and she nearly tumbled to the ground. Her breathing became labored and her hands began to shake. She focused on a nearby bush. She had to pull it together. Her life might depend on it. They didn't know she owned this place, they couldn't. She'd pretend she was homeless. Pretend? Heck, she was homeless. She'd tell them she didn't have anywhere else to go. Well, that would be easy enough, it was the truth. Unfortunately, the knowledge did nothing to sooth her panicked mind because Theresa suddenly realized she was out in the middle of nowhere with two sadistic murderers...and she was alone.

Tony stood, frowning at the terror that was written all over Theresa's face. Sure, he was furious with her, but he didn't want her to go into shock. He slowly made his way across the tiny campsite, not stopping until he was standing directly in front of her.

Theresa blinked, then blinked again. Not Dom or his men. Tony. Why was Tony Nazario at Moondance Ridge?

"You live here?" Tony demanded, he couldn't help himself.

"That's none of your business," Theresa growled as she pushed past the irritating man that somehow kept learning all of her secrets. She was still angry at him for his strong-armed tactics the night before. Well, that wasn't entirely true. To be honest, she'd slept better last night than she had in the past six months. Actually, knowing Tony was in a room just down the hall had made her feel safe. Safer than she'd felt since that night two years ago when she'd fled Detroit. Safer than she'd felt since her husband had been murdered. So, as much as she wanted to be angry with him for forcing her hand... she was actually grateful. He didn't need to know that though.

"Theresa!" Tony barked. "Are you listening to me?"

"No," Theresa said honestly as she lowered herself onto the bench of the picnic table. Why was he here? Had he already answered that question and she missed it because she wasn't paying attention?

Tony placed his index finger under Theresa's chin and forced her to look up. When she tried to move her head, to look away, he tightened his grip. "Why are you living out of your truck? Rowdy pays his employees nearly double a normal waitress. Plus, this is Mount Haven, prices are reasonable. I want to know why. Does this have anything to do with those two men?"

Tears began to form in Theresa's eyes and she immediately slammed her lids shut. She might not be able to look away, but Tony would not see how upset she was. He would not see how desperate and vulnerable she was. If he saw, he'd demand answers. Answers she couldn't provide. Telling him anything would put him in danger. She couldn't even protect herself, there was no way she could protect him. His presence here was proof of her failure. If Tony had followed her, if she hadn't seen him coming, how would she ever avoid Dominic's men?

Tony ran his hand through his hair in frustration, knowing he wouldn't get anywhere with Theresa like this. He was beyond livid. The woman was stubborn and independent and frustrating as hell. *Now what*? Well for starters, she was moving in with him. Was this how Conrad felt when he learned Tony was living on the street? Probably. He turned to face Theresa then changed his mind. She was in no condition to be reasonable... he'd just have to take matters

Moondance Ridge

into his own hands and deal with the consequences later. Tony hesitated as he studied her carefully, wondering how she would react. He had no idea, but that didn't matter. He turned and strolled purposefully toward the lake. Once he'd gathered up her clothing, he marched back to her...hobo camp, and dropped the pathetic basket on the table.

"What do you think you're doing?" Theresa demanded.

Tony ignored her. He marched into the thick pine trees, retraced his steps back to his car and took the winding pathway until it emptied out in front of her truck. Tony was doing his best to keep his temper in check but he was getting more and more peeved by the minute. He threw open his door and approached the table. "I'm not leaving you here. You'll stay with me until you decide to come clean, then we'll figure out a solution together. Get what you need, I'm not coming back here tonight."

Theresa glared, dumbfounded at the sexy but pushy businessman. "You think I'm going to what? Move in with you? I don't think so."

Tony grabbed the laundry basket and tossed it onto the backseat of his car. He watched Theresa and smiled inwardly as emotion after emotion flitted across her face. First, there was defiance; then shock, which instantly turned to anger. Tony sighed as he waited, knowing the sexy brunette was not going to give in willingly. He bent slightly, grabbed Theresa behind the knees and threw her over his shoulder. She was still kicking and screaming when he unceremoniously dumped her into his passenger seat and locked the door, thankful for the invention of a child lock for the first time in his life. He was smiling as he rounded the hood, opened the driver's side door and slid behind the wheel. He gave her a triumphant glance, then nearly burst out laughing when she raised

84

her middle finger and shifted away from him in a classic pout. Theresa Regan was definitely going to be a challenge. Tony waited in silence as he pondered the situation. Why exactly did that fact intrigue him?

"You are the most arrogant, annoying, aggravating..."

Tony did laugh now. "You might want to move on, sweetheart. The alphabet has twenty-six letters and you're still stuck on A." He started the engine and pulled his Lexus onto the gravel roadway.

"Ugh," she growled and turned to stare out the window. That's when she realized Tony was serious. He was going to leave all her belongings and her truck at the campsite. "I can't leave. I need...things."

Tony just continued to smile. "Guess you should have been thinking about necessities instead of adjectives, huh?"

Theresa shoved at Tony's shoulder then lowered her head into her arms and growled again. Was he really going to take her all the way back to Mount Haven, back to the Wright Farm without all her belongings? What if someone stole them? It wasn't much, but it was all she had. "I really need my truck, Tony. Please, take me back. I have to work tonight."

Tony glanced at Theresa then reached out and placed his hand over the top of hers. He hoped they could form a truce, but he knew Theresa would go into any negotiation kicking and screaming. "You can finish your laundry at my place and I'll give you a ride into work. We'll get your truck later. I know you're pissed, but relax. I'm only trying to help. I'm going to be here for you Theresa; I'm here to help you whether you want me to or not."

Moondance Ridge

Theresa knew she should pull away. She knew she should throw a fit, insist he turn around and go back to her truck, threaten to call the police... but she didn't want to. His hand holding hers in comfort gave her strength. For the first time in a long time, she didn't feel so alone. She felt a sense of power over her own life that she hadn't felt for so very long. And, maybe she could give in gracefully; enjoy a few nights rest in a bed instead of a hard, cold, uncomfortable backseat; then leave. She'd do her laundry, sleep in his guest room, then figure a way out of this mess. She had to get out...if Dom ever learned Tony was helping her... she swallowed hard. Dominic couldn't learn. If he did, Tony would be dead. But Drago and Socks had disappeared weeks ago, maybe a couple nights wouldn't hurt. Only a couple of nights, then it would be time to move on. If that meant leaving Mount Haven, then so be it. She would not be responsible for the death of Tony Nazario. Bailey would never forgive her. Worse, Theresa would never forgive herself if that man killed one more person she cared about. The couple traveled in silence, each of them lost in their own thoughts, all the way back to Tony's house.

Tony pulled into the garage and closed the door. He casually stepped from the sleek pearl gray luxury sports car and wondered if he needed a truck. He wasn't in the city anymore, he was in Montana. Winter was over...for now. But he'd have to decide soon, no more than a few months. If he decided to stay in Mount Haven, he would definitely need four-wheel drive. He opened the side door leading into his mud room and waited.

Okay, Theresa told herself as she inhaled one deep breath then another. Finally, she pushed open the door and reached into the back for her laundry. It was still soaking wet. She hoped Tony's dryer was a good one. She hoped Tony had a dryer. As she took one step after another toward the cozy home, she felt like she was headed for the gallows. The instant her foot touched the top step,

Tony shifted. He moved further inside as he continued to hold the door, providing ample room for her and the basket.

"The laundry room is that way," he pointed down a hallway. "First door on the left. You can keep the guest room as long as you want," Tony paused. If it were as long as she liked, she'd be gone by morning. "Scratch that. You are in the guest room. What time do you need to be to work?"

Theresa glanced up, confused. She had already started down the long hallway but Tony remained in the doorway. "Um," she tried to remember. "Oh, five. I need to be there at five."

"Okay," Tony gave her a nod. "Well, make yourself at home and I'll be back around four-thirty."

"Back?" Theresa asked hesitantly. "You're leaving?"

"We both know you're uncomfortable and don't want me here. I have work, anyway. I'll be back at four-thirty. Until then, finish your laundry, get situated and there's a big screen in the family room. I don't have a ton of snacks, but you can have anything that's there. We may need to go shopping tomorrow."

"Tony," Theresa began.

"We'll talk about this later, when you're in a better frame of mind. You shouldn't make decisions while you're angry." He continued out the door and moments later was pulling back onto the highway headed for Missoula. It would be a short day at the office, but he could use the solitude the drive would provide and he needed the network to look into Moondance Ridge. There was a reason Theresa had gone there. There was a reason the place was neglected and deserted. He intended to find out why. As a bonus, if he got lucky, he just might find out who had sent the two mysterious goons

Moondance Ridge

to harass his new roommate. That was about the only valuable information he'd garnered from his little chat with the dynamic duo. They were here because their boss had sent them. Priority number one, find out who exactly the boss was. Priority number two, discover what he wanted with Theresa Regan. Step number three, deal with the problem...permanently.

* * * *

Several hours later, Tony sat in a booth at the Spurs Bar and Grill. Theresa was still giving him the silent treatment, and had been since he picked her up for work. He was pretty sure this was just the calm before the storm and they'd have it out eventually. He wished he could talk to Bailey about the situation, but she was clearly busy - popping in here and there, but mostly working in the back office tonight. With everything she had to worry about at Drakker, Tony couldn't understand why she was still managing this place. Her time would be better spent convincing their clients the trouble really was in the past. Convincing new clients they were worth the risk. When Bailey moved behind the bar and reached for a bottle on the top shelf, he watched and grinned out of habit. He could see from the corner of his eye that Rowdy had seen him, but for some reason it no longer irritated the man. Good. Maybe that meant the cowboy really did care for Bailey. Tony hoped so, his friend seemed happy. In fact, he'd never seen Bailey this calm and content before... not even in college. That had to be a good sign, right?

Bailey knew she should be in the back, going through the records, preparing for the audit but she was so bored. The action was out here. She could admit it, she sometimes missed being a waitress. So, she'd saved her work, closed down the program and headed to the bar to help her man. It was a busy night and she knew he'd need the shelves restocked before the night was through. She had just snagged an empty bottle of Jack and was turning to place it on the counter when she spotted Tony in the small mirror. Her eyes widened in shock, then fury as she realized what he was doing.

Rowdy knew the instant Bailey spotted Tony. Once again, the man was trying to make him jealous but it wouldn't work. The slick businessman's antics didn't matter anymore. Bailey loved him. He had finally accepted that. Things were good between them again. They were better than good. For the first time in his life, he thought maybe he could have the kind of partnership Coop had with Maggie. The kind of love his father and mother had shared since the moment they met. He sighed, realizing Bailey was upset. He couldn't stop her anger toward Tony, but he could try to make things easier. He moved to Bailey's side and wrapped his arms around her waist, pulling her gently against him. "Don't be too angry. It doesn't matter," Rowdy whispered softly as he gently rubbed his thumb against the base of her neck.

"Seriously?" Bailey practically screamed. "All this time...I trusted him. I defended him. I thought you were being ridiculous. I can't believe he would do that to me. I can't believe he would do that to you!" She pivoted and marched back to the office. She was going to confront Tony about this, but right now she was just too angry to think straight. The man had nearly ruined the best thing that had ever happened to her. She'd believed in him, trusted him, adamantly defended him...and all along he was doing exactly what Rowdy and Maggie had claimed. She plopped into the chair behind the desk and tried, without success to calm her temper.

Tony frowned when Rowdy slid onto the bench across from him. He glanced at the bar, expecting to see Bailey, but instead Theresa was filling orders. "What happened to Bay?"

Moondance Ridge

"She's pissed," Rowdy said. He had always taken the direct approach and didn't see a reason to deviate tonight.

"Okay," Tony said, confused. Why was Rowdy telling him?

"At you," Rowdy added.

"Me? I haven't even talked to her tonight." Tony shook his head and glanced around the room, thinking maybe this time Rowdy was messing with him.

"She saw you," Rowdy provided. "In the mirror. When she was reaching for the empties. She saw you."

Tony furrowed his brow, still confused at what Rowdy was saying. Then it hit him. Out of habit, he'd pretended to be interested. His mind had been on Theresa, the resort, and the information he'd uncovered at the office. Pretending to have a thing for Bailey had become second nature these days. Not that it was doing any good. Rowdy wasn't biting. Apparently, the man had gotten over whatever jealousy bug bit him the minute Tony arrived in town. "I guess I better go explain." He stood and headed for the back.

"By the way," Rowdy called after him.

Tony stopped and turned, waiting.

"We're cool," Rowdy said casually as he stood and returned to the bar. "I know why you did it and we're cool. Bailey...now that's another story entirely."

Tony hesitated, wondering if he should take a minute to clear things up. But Rowdy was busy with customers and Bailey had a way of simmering on low until she finally boiled over. He needed to catch her before she reached that point or there was no telling what he'd find. If he waited too long, they may not be able to repair the damage. He knocked on the door and waited. No answer. "Bay, it's Tony. I'm coming in."

Bailey was out of the chair and across the room in mere seconds. She flung the door open with so much force it would have banged against the wall if Tony hadn't caught it.

"So, a soft boil but not a raging inferno yet. Glad I caught you in time." Tony entered the room and silently closed the door behind him. He stepped to the guest chair and sat...waiting for Bailey to begin.

Bailey dropped into the desk chair and narrowed her eyes at him. "You were prepared. How?"

"Rowdy," Tony shrugged. "Look..."

"No, you look," Bailey jumped to her feet, too angry to sit. "I called you here to help me...and Drakker, but mostly me. I was so glad I could finally come out of hiding and have my life back. I was excited to have my best friend back. The first person I called was you. I wanted you here. Tony, I needed you here. But, instead of the loving friend I expected, you brought this...angry, manipulative stranger." She dropped back into the chair, barely holding back the tears. "You betrayed me. You nearly ruined my relationship with Rowdy, and Maggie is barely speaking to me. I don't know why you did it, but I'd like you to leave. Stay away from me for a while. I can't stand to look at you...I can't stand to be in the same room as you. I can't stand to feel so...I don't know, my heart just hurts." The tears did come now, Bailey couldn't stop them so she didn't try. "Tony, just go. Please, I need you to go," she stuttered through ragged breaths.

Moondance Ridge

Tony stood, trying to figure out exactly where he'd gone wrong. He'd leave, for Bailey he would leave. If she needed time away from him, he could give her that. He hadn't meant to hurt her. He was trying to protect her. Trying to shield her from getting hurt and somehow, he was the one that messed up. He was the bad guy here and he had no idea how to fix it.

Rowdy watched as Tony stepped back into the bar area then turned to leave. The look on the man's face told Rowdy everything he needed to know. He was across the room and blocking the exterior door before Tony even saw him coming. "Don't leave like this."

"She wants me to go, so I'll go," Tony mumbled as he tried to move around Rowdy.

"Not yet," Rowdy put a hand on Tony's shoulder. "She just needs some time. It will all work out. I promise, go back to your table. Beers on me. Then if you still want to go, I won't stop you."

Tony nodded once, pivoted and returned to his table. He didn't have the energy to argue with Rowdy right now. How had his world gotten so out of control in a single day? Theresa moving in... the ordeal at Moondance Ridge... now Bailey. Sometimes, life just sucked. He didn't regret using force with Theresa. She needed a place to stay. It was the right thing to do. It just meant he wouldn't have any alone time. He wouldn't be able to wallow and right now, he needed to wallow. He slid onto the bench, still thinking about Bailey.

Theresa spotted Tony the instant he stepped from the back room. She had no idea what that was all about, but he was clearly upset and it had something to do with Bailey. *Did the woman have to monopolize every decent guy within a fifty-mile radius?* That wasn't fair and she knew it. The only reason Tony was here was because Bailey had asked him to come. So, what had happened back in the office and why did Tony look like he'd just lost his best friend? She continued to watch as Rowdy stepped forward, spoke to Tony briefly, then motioned to the empty table. Tony silently returned to the spot where he'd been seated all night and looked out the window, staring into the darkness. Theresa took a step forward, she should go over and see if there was anything she could do to help; he'd been there for her after all -more than once. Her heart dropped with a resounding thud and she stopped abruptly when Marnie bounced up, set a beer in front of Tony and slid in to talk.

Theresa scolded herself as the worst kind of fool. Of course, Marnie would be there for Tony. The two of them were clearly developing some kind of relationship. And, what did she care if the man fell for a teeny-bopper? Theresa sighed and forced herself to look away. Marnie might appear young and naïve, but she was twenty-two years old. Legal, beautiful and free of baggage. Well, not free of baggage. Marnie had a past too, but she was at least free of the Detroit mob... which was more than Theresa could say for herself. A mob that could return at any minute and make demands that Theresa couldn't meet. She forced her mind to relax, plastered on her biggest smile and headed for the table of college boys. If she worked it hard enough, she just might leave tonight with a couple hundred in tips. Surely, that would help with the Dom problem. It had to.

Rowdy checked on Bailey who insisted she had work and wasn't leaving the office for several hours. He moved back behind the bar and waited for Marnie to finish her break. The instant she stood and returned to work, Rowdy made his move. He grabbed two bottles of beer and headed for the table. When he sat down Tony studied him, clearly surprised. "We need to talk."

Moondance Ridge

"I didn't mean to hurt her," Tony sighed. "So, I don't need the macho threats on top of everything else tonight."

"Good," Rowdy said as he took a sip of his beer. "I'm glad we cleared that up."

"Now, you're a wise guy," Tony shook his head and grabbed the second beer. "I messed up this time. I mean, I really screwed the pooch on this one. I didn't mean..." he studied Rowdy, not sure how to explain his intentions.

"We're good," Rowdy said again. "I figured it out, eventually. I would have realized what you were doing sooner if I wasn't so out of it myself. Once I stopped worrying about losing her and saw the situation for what it truly was," Rowdy shrugged. "I got it. Like I said, we're good here."

Tony smiled, surprised he could smile after the day he'd had. "I'm glad," he finally said. "I think you're good for her. I've never seen Bay this happy. You hurt her and I'll kill you, but I don't think you will. I think..." he settled back in the booth. "I think you are too far gone to ever hurt that woman. I'm glad. She deserves something good in her life. I tried... back in college. I tried to get that girl to loosen up and have a little fun but something was always weighing on her. Something was simmering under the surface. I never knew what. Oh, I suspected after I ran into Cole and Reese at that debacle in Monterey, but I never knew and she wouldn't tell me. I'm glad you were here. I'm glad you took care of them. I'd never tell her or Peter that, but I'm glad. Cole Hughes and Reese Weathersby were rabid animals. They were sadistic psychopaths who got off on hurting women simply because they could. The two of them needed to die. So, I'm glad you were there for her and I'm sorry you had to be the one to do it."

Rowdy waited, this was the first real conversation he'd had with Tony Nazario and he wanted it to count. He needed it to. For Bailey's sake, he and Tony were going to have to find a way to be friends. If they couldn't be friends, they'd have to at least tolerate each other. So, Rowdy waited and listened.

Tony smiled. Maybe Bailey's anger had been the last straw in a difficult day, maybe it was the beer, maybe it was just the man sitting across from him... but for the first time since arriving in Montana, Tony relaxed. He was rambling, he knew it but he didn't care. There was something about Rowdy Cooper that made Tony believe they could actually be friends. Real friends, not just casual acquaintances for Bailey's sake. Rowdy wasn't the cocky, hotshot cowboy Tony originally believed. As the man quietly sat there, listening, Tony realized he had depth. The former cop had a subtle alertness, keen perception and an underlying calmness about him. Tony watched as a German Shepherd with the same qualities strolled across the room and settled in at Rowdy's feet. "Enough pathetic whining," Tony finally said. "I need a favor. Do you have to stick around until closing?" He hoped he was right about this because, at the moment, Rowdy was the only person in his life he thought he could trust. Well, Rowdy and John but his childhood friend was in New York and unavailable.

"What do you need?" Rowdy studied Tony and waited.

"Road trip," Tony shrugged. "Probably take about an hour or so, if you're free. I need a shuttle and I have something I'd like to run by you."

Rowdy glanced up when Coop stepped through the door. "I think my schedule just freed up. Give me five and I'll let you know." It only took three minutes before Rowdy returned. "If we head out now, I can swing an hour. Bailey's still working so Coop will take both her and Mags home and close up. You need to check out with anyone before we go?"

Rowdy was looking at Marnie, but Tony's gaze fell on Theresa. "Doesn't Jase live on the other side of Maple Drive?"

"Uh," Rowdy frowned. "I believe so, but you'd have to ask him." His frown deepened when Tony disappeared into the kitchen. When the man returned, he glanced around then made a beeline for Theresa, had a brief discussion, and headed back to Rowdy...who was still frowning.

"Okay," Tony motioned for the door. "I'm set, you ready?"

"Sure," Rowdy motioned for Tony to lead the way.

"What about the dog?" Tony asked. "Don't you need to bring him?"

"Coop said he'll take him back to the office with Bailey," Rowdy supplied. "If she's going home alone, I want him with her." Rowdy followed Tony out the side door, even more curious than he had been before. Once they climbed into Rowdy's pickup, he turned and waited. "Where to?"

"If you take a left out of the lot, the road will take you most of the way there. I'll give you plenty of notice before the turn. Once we leave the main highway, it's only a couple miles to the driveway," Tony buckled his seatbelt and settled in.

"There's nothing out there," Rowdy objected. "I guess I should warn you, I have a gun."

Tony laughed. "Seriously?"

"Well," Rowdy shrugged then shifted into gear. As he pulled onto the highway he glanced at the sophisticated businessman. "You said you wanted to talk about something."

"It's not your death so relax. I haven't been tempted to kill anyone in years. I might be persuaded to beat the shit out of you... with the right motivation."

Rowdy laughed. "As if."

Tony grinned then sobered. "This is kind of serious," he began. "I was planning on waiting until we got there but it's a long ride so here goes."

"I have a feeling I'm not going to like this," Rowdy set the cruise control and stretched his leg. He hadn't had an episode for weeks, but the last few nights had been busy and his leg was starting to cramp.

"I know you pay your waitresses well," Tony began.

"Funny, I don't remember an application."

"Yes, I checked. I checked you out, thoroughly, when Bailey told me she was serious. I know about the shooting. I know you used to be a cop but got forced out because of the injuries." He glanced at Rowdy's outstretched leg. "I know there were several animal rights groups that came after you. I know you protected Knight like you would your own child. Let's just say I know about all there is to know. I also know what happened out here. Not just Cole and Reese, but the others. What I didn't find in the papers or on the internet, Bailey provided," Tony admitted.

"You think I didn't check you out as well?" Rowdy countered.

"I have no doubt you did." Tony wasn't sure how he felt about that. He hadn't considered it, but of course Rowdy Cooper, the ex-cop, would do a thorough search the instant he hit town. How much did he find? Maybe someday he'd ask.

"So, why the interest in what I pay my employees?" Rowdy asked, redirecting the conversation.

"We're heading out to an old fishing resort," Tony began. "It used to be owned by Dean Clawson. Dean never married. Some of the locals remember family... city folk that visited a time or two. Yet, in his later years, he never had one visit from his relatives. Well, not as far as I can tell. His friends said he was a kind, hard-working, honest man. They remember a sister, a woman who used to bring her daughter out when the kid was little to spend a week at the resort. Then later, nothing. Not even when he was diagnosed with cancer and ultimately died." Tony had spent the entire afternoon on the phone contacting friends and neighbors. By the time he pulled away from the office, he knew Dean Clawson better than most of his clients.

"My family is new to the area, so I can't say I knew the man," Rowdy said absently, still unsure where this was going.

"The turn is up there to the right, about two hundred yards," Tony pointed to a sign up ahead.

"I see it," Rowdy slowed the vehicle and took a right as directed.

"I ran a search of the place today," Tony continued. "I was curious to see who the current owner is. Dean Clawson died about two and a half years ago. The place is deserted, a little neglected but still worth a fortune."

"You plan to get to the point in this lifetime?" Rowdy pressed. "And explain what any of this has to do with my payroll?"

"It took some digging," Tony continued, undeterred. "Dean Clawson created a trust before he died. The trust is set up to automatically pay all taxes and insurance on the property plus any fees levied by the county for the next ten years."

"Before we go any further I need you to know, I'm tapped out. I put all my extra cash into the bar and recent renovation. If this is some ploy to get me to buy a deserted fishing resort, I'm out," Rowdy admitted. "So, do I continue on or should I turn around and head back to town?"

Tony grinned and shook his head. "Seriously, man? I have enough to buy that place five times over and still leave enough mad money to last a lifetime. This is not a ploy. It's certainly not a business proposal. Do you honestly believe I would make that kind of commitment with a man I had my first real conversation with less than an hour ago? Apparently, Bailey provided far more information about you than she did on me."

"Okay," Rowdy relaxed. "I just...well, this seems to be going nowhere. Would you get to the point already?"

"I'm pretty sure Theresa owns the place," Tony admitted. "But she's homeless. Living out of her truck. From what I've gathered, she picks the drunkest guy in the bar to go home with when she needs something. Laundry services for one."

"What do you mean, she's homeless?" Rowdy asked, confused. Maggie had stopped by Theresa's apartment four, no five months ago to get a receipt signed so she could make the deposit at the bank. When had Theresa moved out? And why? She made good money at the bar. He would know, he signed her paycheck. Then add in the tips and Tony's statement didn't make a bit of sense.

"It shocked me, too," Tony admitted. "Turn there, to the left just after that mile marker."

Rowdy took the turn then focused on Tony. "Why do you think she's homeless?" He didn't want to believe it, but it all made a strange kind of sense. He never could understand why Theresa lived the way she did. Why she acted so flirty when clearly the last thing she wanted was a man in her life. Why she went home with drunk patrons she barely knew.

"Now take a right and head toward that building over there... on the hill. It's hard to see because the power to the building has been shut off and the large nightlight appears to be burned out," Tony instructed.

Rowdy saw it. He'd worked his entire career in the dark. The place stood out like a beacon on a hill. Well, it did to him anyway. The building was fairly large and obviously abandoned but in relatively good shape. "Why are we here?"

"A couple reasons," Tony sighed. "I followed Theresa out here this morning. She went home with a guy who only pretended to be drunk. When they got to his place, Theresa decided to leave. He decided to forcefully prevent her escape."

"What?" Rowdy slammed on the brakes. "Did she call the cops? No, I would have heard about it if she did. That's something Coop would have mentioned."

"No," Tony agreed. "Because I was there. I had a little chat with the faker and then took Theresa to my place. She spent the night in the guest room and insisted on bolting first thing. I dropped her at the bar where she retrieved her truck. That's when I spotted all the laundry in the backseat. I was curious, so I followed her. She came out here, washed a batch of clothes in the lake, and hung it out to dry before I intervened."

"And by intervened you mean?" Rowdy was still in shock. Why would Theresa live out here in the wilderness with no power, no running water and worse, no neighbors to step in and help if some loon attacked her? It was dangerous and irresponsible. But so was going home with drunks from a bar. Something was seriously wrong here.

"I mean I gathered up her laundry, carried her to the car and forced her to stay at my place," Tony said softly. It sounded much worse when he said it out loud...admitting you kidnaped a woman by force to an ex-cop no less, well it probably wasn't the smartest thing he'd ever done.

"I'd appreciate it if you didn't make me an accessory to kidnapping and hostage taking," Rowdy grinned. "We're just not that close."

"She's onboard with it now," Tony insisted. "Anyway, we are here to get the rest of her stuff and shuttle her vehicle to my place."

"Once she has her truck back do you honestly think she'll stay at your place?" Rowdy wasn't sure. In fact, he was pretty sure Theresa Regan would make a mad dash for the front door the instant she thought she had a clean break.

"No," Tony sighed. "I'm not. I'm just hoping she'll listen to reason. If she insists on leaving, I'll have to go camping... in the wilderness...by a lake...that probably has mosquitos. I hate mosquitos."

Moondance Ridge

Rowdy laughed. "That might do the trick." He pulled up in front of the large building and looked around. "So why are we here? I don't see Theresa's truck."

"That's the rest of the story," Tony admitted as he climbed from the vehicle and waited for Rowdy to join him. "Dean Clawson had a trust. He left everything to his sister. But not under her married name, under her maiden name. Which wasn't Clawson. The executor of the trust is Jenny Boland. It took me all damn day, but I finally found her. Jenny Boland married Steven Tanner just after college and became Jenny Tanner. Her maiden name was Boland because she and Dean are half-siblings. They have a mother in common and different father's... thus the different last names. Jenny and Steven had one daughter; Theresa Tanner. In the event of Jenny's death, control and sole ownership of this property is automatically transferred to her only daughter."

"And this daughter, I assume you believe it's Theresa," Rowdy surmised as they walked from the truck to the large wrap-around porch attached to the majestic wooden structure.

"Yes, but that's the strange part," Tony said, leaning against the wooden railing as he focused on the lake. It was too dark to see how beautiful it was here, but he loved how the moon danced over the water illuminating the fish as they jumped just below the surface. Tony wasn't a fisherman, but he was pretty sure it was feeding time.

"Strange how?" Rowdy asked moving in beside him.

"I've seen a lot of trusts in my time. It's pretty normal for large corporations to tie things up tight and ensure the family gets exactly what the owner wants the family to get," Tony provided. "It's a routine part of my job. You can't fix a company's problems if you don't have all the facts."

"Oh, yeah," Rowdy grinned. "I guess the Fixer would have pretty extensive knowledge of trust laws and family wills."

"You do know how much I hate that name, don't you?" Tony scowled.

"Sure, that's why I used it," Rowdy teased.

"I have never... ever, seen a trust that doesn't specifically name the beneficiary. It's unheard of, especially in business. This place is worth a fortune. I have no doubt that with a little cash infusion and a ton of work, it would be back up and running in no time. I did a little research on that as well. The place was booked solid, a year in advance, before the old man had to shut down. Once he was diagnosed, the cancer hit hard. He apparently couldn't keep up."

"And, with no family to help, he finally shut down," Rowdy surmised.

"Exactly," Tony agreed. "But, he had family. Not his sister. Jenny died in a plane crash years ago. He had Theresa, formerly Tanner now Regan."

"Do you think this has something to do with those two men?" Rowdy's mind was in overdrive. There were still too many pieces missing to put the puzzle together, but he was pretty sure Tony was on the right track.

"I think it has everything to do with those men," Tony said soberly. "They're bad news and we both know they're going to come back."

"We do," Rowdy considered. "But if Theresa is no longer renting the apartment those two men have no idea where to go looking. That gives us an advantage."

"How so?"

"Because they have to come to my bar to find her," Rowdy smiled. "And, when they show up, we'll be ready."

"Right," Tony smiled. "So, are we in this together?" He didn't know Rowdy well, but over the past hour, he'd realized they were a lot alike and he was sure he would have no trouble working through this with the ex-lawman. Rowdy had already proven he could handle dangerous when Cole and Reese came to town. He seemed to be pretty good at reasoning things through, too. He probably would have made a damn good detective.

"Count me in," Rowdy nodded. "I'm going to bring Coop up to speed as well. It never hurts to have the backing of the local sheriff."

"I'll trust you on that," Tony decided. "He's your brother, you tell him what you think he needs to know."

"What do you plan to tell Theresa?" Rowdy wondered. "And Bailey?"

"Well, since Bay isn't speaking to me at the moment, I get a pass on that one. Theresa, that's going to be tricky. I'll figure it out when I need to. Until then, I'm not going to rock the boat. I'm going to have a hard-enough time convincing her she needs to camp out in my guest room rather than out here... in the great outdoors. Throwing in our plans to protect her might just shove her over the edge."

Rowdy laughed. "Tell me again why we came up here... to the lodge I mean."

"I just wanted to see it up close. It's a beautiful old building. Could use some work though. Shame it has to stand empty for a while longer. I wonder what Theresa plans to do with it." Tony paused to consider the possibilities. "Anyway, let's head over to the campsite and load everything up. It's late and I don't want Theresa left alone too long. The last thing she needs is too much time in her own head."

Rowdy followed Tony as he returned to the vehicle. They proceeded to the campsite where they maintained a comfortable but friendly silence as they gathered up Theresa's belongings and secured them in the backseat of her truck. Both men had been thinking the same thing... if they'd met under different circumstances, without Bailey in the middle, they probably would have hit it off immediately. Maybe, there was still time to make things right.

Rowdy glanced at Tony and knew he was worried about the blowout. He thought he might be able to help. This guy was Bailey's best friend and neither one of them would be happy until they worked through this. "She'll come around. Just give her a couple days."

Tony looked up and frowned. Was he really that transparent? "She's never been like this before. Sure, we've disagreed, had heated arguments now and again, but she's never said she couldn't stand to be in the same room as me."

Rowdy didn't know the details of the argument but he wasn't surprised. Tony had been the catalyst for weeks of tension between them. "Then, give her what she asked for. She loves you."

"Let's not go there. It's what got me into trouble in the first place," Tony mumbled.

"She's not in love with you, stupid. She loves you," Rowdy corrected. "And, that is not in any way a conflict- not between the two of you, not between us and not between Bailey and me. It's the rest that you have to atone for. Just give her some space. Have you ever heard the expression, 'be careful what you wish for'?"

Tony grinned. "I think right about now Bailey is wishing I'd fall over the nearest cliff."

"Naw," Rowdy said as he casually sat on the picnic table, feet planted firmly on the attached bench. He leaned forward, resting his elbow on his thighs as he considered. "Bay loves you. She doesn't want anything bad to happen to you. And, deep down, she doesn't want you to stay away from her either. Absence makes the heart grow fonder."

"What are you? A walking motivational calendar?" Tony barked as he settled in next to Rowdy.

Rowdy laughed. "No. I've just been spending entirely too much time with my sister-in-law. Forget that. My point is this... Bailey is angry and thinks she wants time away. But, what she really wanted was this," Rowdy moved his hand from side to side indicating the two of them. "She wants us to get along. Once she sees that has happened, she'll need to be a part of it. Knowing Bailey, she'll need to be smack dab in the middle."

Tony stared into the darkness and considered. "You get her, don't you?" he finally decided.

"We get each other," Rowdy corrected. "And we have enough to worry about with Theresa right now. Give Bailey a little time. If I'm going to be stuck with you for life anyway, we can use her distance to our advantage. I'm not opposed to grabbing a beer now and again... in the spirit of trying to understand each other, of course."

Tony laughed. He'd gone about this all wrong. He was beginning to realize Rowdy Cooper was a standup guy. One he should have taken the time to get to know before he crawled under his skin and gave a big shove. "Why aren't you mad?"

Rowdy shrugged. "Because I get you and I would have done the same thing. In a way, I did when Coop started seeing Mags. I was young and stupid so Maggie saw through me almost immediately, but it still caused a few problems in the beginning. I should have seen through your fake interest and well-placed shots directed only at me. I would have if things had been a little different. But, when you got here, I was still dealing with a few personal issues of my own. All I saw was a slick businessman that could give Bailey everything I can't. I'm usually more astute than that. Under normal circumstances, I would have recognized your antics as the test they were, not as a challenge and an obstacle."

"I'm sorry," Tony glanced at Rowdy and hoped the man knew he truly was sorry for the trouble he'd caused.

"Like I said, it's all good," Rowdy grinned. "So, did I pass? The test that is."

"Yeah," Tony stood. "You passed. Now, let's get out of this place. I think the water has some voodoo chemical that makes real men turn into little girls. I haven't shared that much with another person since...well, ever."

Rowdy laughed and stood. "I'll wait until you get the truck going and head out, then I'll follow you. Stop by the bar tomorrow afternoon and we'll have a cold one."

"You sure that's a good idea?"

"Best idea I've had all night," Rowdy said confidently. "I want Bailey to see you and me getting along. I need her to see us working towards an amiable... camaraderie. Time will tell if we can become true friends but she needs to know we aren't enemies. It's all in the plan, just go with it."

Tony climbed into Theresa's truck and rolled down the window. "You really do get her, Rowdy. I'm glad. Bay deserves a man like you. And, for the record, she doesn't care if you're a hotshot businessman. She loves the man you are, not what you can give her."

"Thanks," Rowdy turned to leave then paused. "By the way, I finally figured that out on my own. It's the reason I didn't break your nose a week or so ago. Lucky for you, I'm a quick study."

Tony laughed and rolled up the window. *Yeah buddy, you keep thinking that.* He might be a sophisticated businessman on the outside, but on the inside Tony was still an alley cat cautiously waiting for the next attack. His gut told him one was coming. One he'd be ready for. Only this time, he wouldn't be defending himself, he'd be protecting Theresa Regan.

Chapter Four

Theresa paced the living room for the hundredth time. Where did Tony and Rowdy go, and why was Bailey so angry with her longtime friend? Did all this have to do with her? She discarded that possibility. Tony might not even be with Rowdy. He may have returned to the bar, to Marnie's apartment. He might not come home tonight. On that note, Theresa turned and headed down the hall. *Time for bed.* She'd only taken two steps when she heard it. The distinct rev and pop of her truck engine. The sound was unique to her truck, something Shawn had done to improve gas mileage. She pivoted and headed for the kitchen determined and confused.

Tony stepped through the door and spotted Theresa. "Hey," he said casually as he moved cautiously into the room. "I guess we need to talk."

"You think?" she said sarcastically.

"I can admit I got a little... overzealous earlier."

"So that's what we're going to call it? Overzealous?" Theresa challenged.

"What would you like to call it?" Tony asked.

"Well, the rest of the free world would call it stalking, kidnapping, and imprisonment; but if you want to go with overzealous..."

"I didn't stalk you," Tony objected.

"No?" Theresa raised her eyebrows. "You just happened to be at Spencer's apartment last night when he attacked me."

"No," Tony said moving to lean against the counter. "I followed you because I could see trouble written all over his face. It had nothing to do with you. I would have followed him no matter who he conned. His victim just happened to be you." Okay, so maybe that was a little white lie since he wouldn't have noticed if the guy had gone home with anyone else.

"Right," Theresa dropped onto a kitchen chair. "And this morning? You just got a wild hair to head out into nature and what? Chase a squirrel?"

"No," Tony crossed one ankle over the other. "I got suspicious after I dropped you off and followed to see where you lived. Because I suspected, and I was right, that you were living out of your truck."

"And, kidnapped me, then brought me here without transportation and left me imprisoned in your home," Theresa argued.

"No," Tony said in a tone that sounded like he was speaking to an unreasonable child throwing a tantrum. "I was a little overzealous in my determination to help. And, you were never imprisoned. You could have left at any time. I told you I was headed into Missoula. It's not like I could have stopped you if you wanted to leave. I won't stop you now." He reached into his pocket and pulled out the keys to her truck, straightened and crossed the room. The minute he reached the table, he took Theresa's hand and dropped the keyring into her palm. "I would appreciate a ride back to the bar, though."

Theresa studied Tony that was not the reaction she had expected. Would he really let her walk out the door? She wasn't buying it. "Why?"

"Why what?" he asked.

"Why did you force me here this morning, now you're willing to let me go?" she glanced at the door leading to the garage and realization hit. "You and Rowdy went out to get my truck. What did you tell him? You had no right to tell my boss..."

"Yes," Tony agreed. "Rowdy gave me a lift. We had some things we needed to talk about. I hate to burst your bubble, but it wasn't all about you. I needed to get him away from the bar and having him give me a lift seemed like the best way to do that."

Theresa wondered what exactly that meant. *It wasn't all about her*? "What did you tell him? What explanation did you give for my truck being there?" she wished she could drop it but nobody could know she'd been staying at Moondance Ridge.

Moondance Ridge

"Theresa," Tony sighed. "Bailey and I had... well, let's just say she has some serious issues with some of the things I've been doing since I arrived. I needed a place I could talk to Rowdy about the situation. It was a short ride, we worked some things out. Then I got the truck and came back here. Now, it's late; and I have an early morning. Will you please give me a ride back to the bar so I can retrieve the Lexus? Otherwise, I have a long walk ahead of me. Either way, I need to go."

"And once I drop you off?" Theresa asked. "Then what?"

"Then I'd like to come home and get a few hours' sleep. You're free to follow me home and occupy the guest room. Or, you can head back out to that fisher's camp. I prefer my bed, but I am so tired right now the hard ground and a sleeping bag probably won't bother me. I really do hate mosquitos though. I'm hoping you at least have some good repellant."

"If I stay at Moondance, you think you're staying there too?" the man was out of his mind.

"Of course," he said casually. "If I caught you by surprise, anyone could. I know you don't want to tell me about those two men who stopped in a few weeks back, but they were dangerous. Standing by, watching you return alone to the outskirts of town, where there's no cell service and nobody around to hear if you run into trouble, that's not something I can live with. So, you stay there...I have to stay there. Like I said, I'd prefer the comfort of my soft mattress and a bug free room, but it's your call."

"I don't get you," Theresa admitted. "Why are you helping me? Won't Marnie be upset when she finds out we're living together? And how will Bailey feel about it?"

Tony frowned, confused. *Why would Marnie care? Or Bailey for that matter?* Did Theresa think he was dating Marnie? "Well, since at the moment Bailey is not speaking to me, I doubt she'll care who I live with."

"I'm serious," Theresa urged. "Why?"

"Let's just say I'm paying it forward," Tony shrugged. "Now, am I walking back to the bar or are you willing to give me a ride?"

"I'll take you," Theresa played with her keys for several seconds. "On one condition."

"What?" Tony asked, sure he wouldn't like the condition.

"I'll drive you to get your car and I'll stay here for a few days as a guest. If we can work out a more... equal arrangement, I might agree to stay longer."

"Equal arrangement?" Tony asked.

"Yeah, like you let me paint a room or sand a floor. I work for my keep," Theresa decided.

"That's not necessary," Tony didn't need Theresa's help and he didn't want her to feel like she had to work full time at the bar and then come home and rehab his house.

"It is if you want me to stay here," she insisted. "And when we get back, you tell me what you mean by paying it forward."

"That's easy," Tony shrugged. "I'll give you the short version now. When I was a kid, I was homeless like you. I got into a bit of a bind and a good man stepped in, gave me a place to live and I guess you could say he provided protection. I owe it to Con, I'm simply returning the favor to someone who needs it."

Moondance Ridge

Theresa's mind was running a mile a minute. Tony homeless? She couldn't picture it. He was so... successful businessman inside and out. She'd just assumed he'd been born with money. She didn't like knowing she'd judged this man the way others had judged her. Unless, he was lying to gain her cooperation.

"Are we leaving?" Tony waited.

"So," Theresa pondered. "This Con guy... where is he? Can I talk to him and verify your story?"

"No," Tony leaned back against the counter, obviously they weren't leaving yet. He glanced at his watch and waited. He just hoped he could deliver in the morning. There was a lot riding on him this time.

"Fine, I should have known you were making things up to get your way. Let's go," Theresa huffed as she practically stomped past him and out the door.

Tony slid into the passenger's seat and waited. Once they were on the highway, he decided to answer. "I didn't make anything up. My mother died when I was thirteen and I lived on the street until I was fourteen.... well, nearly fifteen. Conrad stepped in and gave me something I never had... love."

"But, you won't let me talk to him," Theresa didn't know why that was so important to her, but it was. Maybe because of everything she'd been through in Detroit. She no longer had the luxury of trusting solely based on a person's word. That's what had gotten Zach killed. Which was the reason Shawn was murdered. She'd learned her lesson the hard way and she wouldn't deviate. President Reagan said, "Trust but verify." Theresa's motto was simply verify. There was no longer such a thing as trust in her life.

"Conrad is dead," Tony said as he stared aimlessly out the windshield.

"But you said..." Theresa began.

"I said he protected me," Tony glanced at her then back into the darkness. "He did, and it cost him his life. So, I can never repay Con for taking in a troubled kid, for protecting me from one of the most dangerous men in the city, or for loving me like I was important and... worth it, even if I wasn't."

"You don't think you're worth loving?" Theresa scowled... this was a side of Tony Nazario she had never expected.

"Maybe now," Tony shrugged. "But then again, Bailey might disagree. Not then. I was a mess back then. I was lost, confused and extremely angry. Conrad showed me there was another way. He saved me."

Theresa knew Tony wasn't only talking about the outward stuff. Sure, this Conrad had given Tony a place to sleep, but clearly their bond went much deeper. Somehow, she got the feeling Conrad had saved Tony from himself. Maybe they did have something in common after all. And maybe...just maybe, accepting his offer to help was exactly what she needed right now. She pulled through the parking lot and came to a stop next to his fancy car. "Tony, I have no idea what you told Rowdy about that trip out to Moondance Ridge, but I would appreciate it if from now on, you'd keep all of this to yourself. Nobody can know I spent time out there. Nobody, not even Rowdy can know I agreed to move into your home. There's a reason for the secrecy. One I can't share with you right now, but my living arrangements have got to stay a secret. Otherwise, I have to move on. And, this time, I won't just go to Moondance Ridge. I'll have to leave town for good."

Moondance Ridge

"I'll keep your secret because it's not mine to share," Tony agreed as he stepped from the truck. "But I think you are underestimating Rowdy and this town. I know you are underestimating me. Nobody will hurt you again. They'll have to go through me, and that's not an easy task."

"That's what worries me," she mumbled as she shifted into reverse and headed back to Tony's new house. She'd just play things by ear, work through one day at a time and maybe eventually an answer would come to her. Because she may have solved her housing problem, but she had not resolved her mob problem. She was beginning to believe there wasn't a solution-not one she could live with, anyway.

* * * *

Theresa dropped the wet brush into the flimsy plastic tray. She'd forgotten just how much she loved decorating. Shawn hadn't understood her need to remodel every single room in their previous home. In fact, he'd gotten more than a little peeved when she moved all the furniture out of his masculine study to repaint the walls. That had been their worst fight ever. Once she finished her project, he'd come around. In fact, he loved that room even more because of her vision. And, it was all that hard work that had increased the value of the house significantly when they sold it. Equity she had planned to use to fix up the resort. Theresa sighed and pushed those dark thoughts aside. She glanced out the window and hoped Tony would be happy with her work. He'd left early that morning, so early she'd still been sound asleep and hadn't heard him leave. She had a late breakfast and showered then immediately discovered she was bored. Instead of waiting another day, she'd driven to the hardware store and picked out the perfect color to bring the living room to life. Now, she was more than a little nervous. What if he hated it?

She supposed she could always repaint. That thought depressed her. She loved the new look; and when she picked the color, she'd been sure Tony would love it too. It had only been a couple days since he'd physically forced her to occupy his guestroom but somehow it seemed like longer. Maybe because she'd lived here before and was comfortable in the house. She'd occupied that living room for so long it felt like she belonged there. She stood and pushed the feelings of home from her mind. This was not her home, it belonged to Tony. A man she still didn't understand and probably never would.

Once she cleaned the paint from the brushes and the tray, she made sure the can was secure and headed for her room. It was time to get ready for work. Theresa climbed from the shower and pulled on the thick, cotton robe Tony had bought her. She sighed and wondered if she'd ever get used to the man or his generosity. He was an enigma. One she didn't understand. One minute he was negotiating deals with a guy in San Diego; the next having an intimate conversation with Marnie at the bar; and then he was casually dropping the softest, most comfortable robe she'd worn in her life on the couch beside her without a word. No explanation, no expectations, nothing. Was it part of the paying it forward thing? Had that Conrad guy provided the necessities, so Tony thought he had to do the same? She tried to talk to him about it, tried to tell him to stop with the presents, but he'd just told her to drop it and retreated to his room for the night. The worst part, after only forty-eight hours, she knew she was falling for the guy. It had started weeks ago, the instant she met Tony Nazario. The constant contact only made it worse. Now that she'd moved in, all of those feelings had intensified. If she stayed here much longer, she'd do the unthinkable. She'd fall head over heels in love with Tony Nazario.

Moondance Ridge

Suddenly, her heart started racing and she couldn't breathe. Theresa extended her arm and reached for the bed. Then, she slowly lowered her body until she was sitting on the edge of the queen-sized mattress. *Get a grip*, she scolded. A tear slid down her face and she impatiently brushed it away. So many thoughts and emotions were cluttering her mind. Mostly, they were thoughts about her late husband. She'd always believed Shawn would be the only man for her. The only man she'd ever love. The man she would spend her life with, grow old with. Then suddenly, Shawn was gone and she was left all alone. She was left to deal with the mess he had created. She was left desperate, lonely and defenseless. After two long, hard years, she was also completely broke— financially and emotionally. Dominic Zarconi had taken everything and he would keep taking until he destroyed her. If he knew she loved Tony, he would take him away from her, too.

Dom was ruthless and relentless. The more she cared for her new roommate, the more likely the outcome would be death. Somehow, she knew that. And, the knowledge that she might lose Tony; and that he may die a horrible, painful death because of her, nearly shattered her completely. No, she couldn't love Tony. She couldn't continue to live with him, either. It was finally time to leave Mount Haven. Time to repay Tony for his selfless act of kindness... time to pay it forward. She'd get through tonight, then tomorrow she'd spend the day developing an escape plan.

* * * *

Theresa pulled through the parking lot and maneuvered her truck to the rear of the large building. Had that really been Tony and Rowdy on the front porch lounging casually while they drank a beer? *Well, wonder's never cease.* She rounded the corner and

118

spotted the duo. Yep, Tony and Rowdy were sitting there shooting the breeze, just as casual as can be. To see them now, you'd think they were lifelong friends.

"Theresa," Rowdy acknowledged as she ascended the stairs.

"Hey, Rowdy," she glanced at Tony and again wondered what his reaction would be when he saw her handy work. Nerves fluttered in her stomach and she could only nod as he raised his bottle in greeting.

"Bailey's on one today and Maggie's in one of her moods so you might want to watch your step in there," Rowdy warned.

"So," Theresa grinned. "A typical day in the neighborhood?"

Tony laughed, Rowdy shook his head and watched as Theresa disappeared into the building.

Theresa stepped through the doors and immediately heard the muffled disagreement. She paused to determine who was arguing but still wasn't sure. As she stepped into the back to hang her jacket and gather the items needed to restock the bar, she spotted Bailey and Marnie a few feet down the hall. They were clearly having a heated discussion about something. Not wanting to get involved, Theresa darted into the supply room.

"You owe him an apology," Marnie insisted.

"I appreciate the help you have given us around here, but you need to learn to mind your own business," Bailey warned.

"What does that mean?" Marnie pressed. "If I point it out when you're out of line, I'll be fired?"

Moondance Ridge

"No," Bailey sighed. "This conversation is over. Tony is here because I asked him to help me. I hired him, I talked him into moving to Mount Haven. I will decide when and if I talk to him. And, if I do, what I will and will not apologize for. Butt out, Marnie. This is none of your business, anyway I'm not the one that was out of line."

"He's my friend, too," Marnie pushed. "And, I won't sit by and watch while you make him miserable. He doesn't deserve that. You need to apologize."

Theresa glanced up when she heard Marnie stomp down the hall and shove open the door that led to the main area of the bar. She focused on the task at hand but was interrupted by Bailey.

"Need help?" Bailey asked as she stepped into the small storage area.

"Sure," Theresa gave a sideways tilt of her head, motioning to the shelf on the other side of the room. "We need some Irish Cream and Kahlua, I think I have everything else."

Bailey studied Theresa for several seconds. "No lecture from you?"

Theresa smiled. "Nope."

"Why not?" Bailey asked. "I can see the way you look at him. You like him. I can't blame you. Tony's... unique. All I'm going to say is what I already told you. He's got skeletons. Remember that. There's more to him than expensive suits and fast cars."

"I'm not going to lecture you because I have learned, first hand, just how infuriating that man can be. He's used to getting what he wants, no matter the cost," Theresa said softly. "And, because it's none of my business. I have no idea why you're mad at him. Apparently, he's talked to Marnie about it because she seems to have a pretty intense opinion on the matter. Me? Not so much. And, everyone has skeletons," Theresa turned and left the room.

Bailey frowned. What in the world was Tony doing? He wasn't interested in Marnie why was he letting Theresa believe he was? "Ugg," she growled. "Well, if you weren't shunning your best friend, you might actually know what was going on in his life." Her frown deepened. *Did Rowdy know?* Those two seemed to be best buddies these days. Which is what she had wanted all along, but when exactly had it happened? And, why in the world did that fact annoy her so much? Bailey shook her head as she left the storage room and headed for the bar. She had liquor to stock.

* * * *

Marnie slid onto the bench across from Tony and frowned. "You're awfully quiet."

"Hey, kid," Tony gave her a halfhearted smile. "You working tonight?"

"Nope," she shrugged. "It's not that busy so Rowdy didn't need me. I've been studying for a big test but I can't concentrate."

"Brad?" Tony asked, knowing Marnie's new crush was the reason she was feeling so restless.

"Is it that obvious?"

"To me," Tony settled back and waited.

Moondance Ridge

"I thought he really liked me. He acted like he did," Marnie frowned. "We went to coffee between classes and I thought we hit it off, like maybe he'd ask me for a real date sometime."

"But?" Tony asked casually as he glanced around the room. No sign of the two goons, so why did he feel so antsy tonight?

"He skipped class... twice," Marnie moaned. "He showed up yesterday, but he was... I don't know... distant."

Tony refocused on the woman sitting across from him. She was so young and insecure. "Have you ever stopped to consider that maybe it's not about you?"

Marnie frowned.

"He missed class, you told me before he's dedicated to his studies just like you are. So, why did he miss class? Family emergency? Broken toe? Stomach flu?"

"I have no idea," Marnie admitted.

"Well," Tony said slowly. "Maybe that's why he was distant. Maybe he thinks you lost interest in him. Maybe he's going through something and needs you to reach out to him. Talk to him. See what's going on before you decide to bail. Maybe you could skip the trip to Mount Haven next weekend, see if he wants to hang out, get pizza... whatever you college kids do these days."

Marnie smiled, Tony always had the answer and he knew just how to cheer her up. She wished she could do the same for him.

Theresa had just escaped the clutches of a drunk, amorous college hotshot. Would tonight ever end? She pivoted and headed across the adjourning room, anxious to reach the bar and possibly take a few minutes away from the madness. When she rounded the corner, she spotted Tony and Marnie once again engaged in some kind of intimate conversation. She froze in place as Tony leaned forward and spoke to his companion. Marnie's face broke into the biggest smile Theresa had ever seen. Okay, so there was something going on with those two. Her chest ached and she knew her heart was breaking, but did it really matter? She was leaving town... soon. *Not a minute too soon*, she told herself. I'm falling for him, he's falling for the young, vivacious college kid. Well, that's one thing she wouldn't miss; watching Marnie Montgomery get everything Theresa always wanted. She wished she didn't feel this way, she wished she could just be the friend Jase wanted her to be, but she couldn't. Maybe that was a good thing. It would be just one more person she'd have to leave.

"Hey, Theresa," Rowdy said as she stepped around the bar to fill two beer mugs.

"Hey," she answered absently.

"Everything okay?"

"Sure," she took a deep breath and forced a smile in his direction. "Everything's fine."

Rowdy knew she was lying but he couldn't force her to open up to him so he dropped it, positive it had something to do with Tony and Marnie. The woman had to know there was nothing going on there, didn't she?

Theresa glanced at Tony's table again then turned back to Rowdy. "Do you mind if I take a break? I haven't had a chance yet and Casey should be able to handle things for a few minutes. I just need some air, then I'll be back. I'll hurry, I promise."

"Sure," Rowdy agreed. "Go ahead. I got this." He picked up the two beer mugs and started for the far table.

Theresa pushed through the door and headed into the employee area. She glanced at Rowdy's office but realized Bailey was inside so she continued down the long hallway and stepped outside into the cool night air. She walked several feet out, away from the building, then closed her eyes and tried to force her mind to relax. She couldn't deny it any longer. She already had strong feelings for Tony Nazario. He was pushy, cocky for sure, drop-dead gorgeous and the most aggravating man she'd ever met. He was also kind, unpredictable, challenging and... perfect. If only her life were different. If she were free to live the way she wanted to; then, she might stay and fight. But, that wasn't possible. Dom controlled her life now. Dom controlled her every move and she would not put Tony in danger.

She opened her eyes and glanced up to study the stars. She'd done this with Shawn a million times. They'd spread out on the ground, in the tall weeds, the cool grass, they'd even dropped onto the hard surface of a parking lot one night and took turns naming the constellations. Her eyes began to water and she blinked quickly to hold back the tears. She still missed Shawn so much and knew deep in her soul that she always would.

A car came to a screeching stop mere feet from where she was standing. Her heart began to thump in her chest and she couldn't breathe when Drago and Socks jumped out and rushed toward her.

"Don't say a word," Drago warned.

"We don't want to hurt you," Socks added. "The boss, he just wants to talk to you."

"Theresa started to turn, hoping she could take them by surprise and make it to the crowd that was forming in the front parking lot. She pivoted and took two steps forward when Socks tackled her from behind. They both went down, hard. Theresa landed face-first on the ground. Her hands skidded across the asphalt, ripping the skin from her palms. Tiny rocks imbedded in the mangled mess and she cried out in pain just before the entire weight of her enemy came crashing down, knocking the wind out of her. She tried to gasp for air, but couldn't breathe. Seconds passed as she frantically tried to force air into her lungs, a loud wheezing sound echoed throughout the night. She gulped, then gulped again, but with the weight of Sock's body still holding her firmly to the pavement; she was struggling just to catch her breath. Suddenly, he disappeared. His weight was gone completely. She turned, confused, and was terrified at what she saw.

* * * *

Bailey watched Theresa disappear down the hallway. She frowned and stood. Something was wrong. As she entered the bar area, it all became crystal clear. Within seconds, she was standing next to Tony's table. "I don't know what game you're playing now, but stop it. Theresa is dealing with enough, she doesn't need you messing with her emotions."

"What?" Tony asked, confused. "Where is Theresa?" He began to frantically glance around the bar. She was nowhere to be found.

Bailey glared at her friend and sighed. "She's on a break. I think she stepped outside... out back. She looked upset when she walked by my office."

Moondance Ridge

Tony jumped to his feet and ran for the door. He had a bad feeling about this and he'd learned long ago to always trust his instincts. Bailey frowned. Marnie stood and hesitantly followed in his wake.

Tony pushed through the back door and spotted the trio. Theresa was on the ground pinned in place by one of the goons from the bar weeks earlier. The second goon was standing over them, impatiently waiting for his friend to get control of a squirming Theresa. Within seconds, Tony was across the opening and pulling Socks off the helpless woman. He gave him a hard shove in the opposite direction. Socks couldn't get his footing, he stumbled then collided with the large garbage bin. His shoulder took most of the impact but he also struck the metal container with the side of his head. When he tried to stand, he was dizzy and immediately settled back to the ground.

Drago growled. "I told you to stay out of my way."

Tony turned to face Drago head on. He knew what was coming, he'd been in too many street fights to number. The man came at him, fists clenched, head bowed. Tony sidestepped the attack but wasn't able to miss the large man's left elbow to his ribs. He planted his feet and counter punched. The fight was on.

Marnie reached the back door and peered outside. The instant she saw Tony and the two men, she screamed in terror as she crumpled to the floor. Once her hand hit the cold tile, she closed her eyes and tried to breathe, that horrible fight in the apartment years before came back to her; and she sat paralyzed by fear as the sounds echoed around her. This wasn't Cole and Reese. Not her brother. This was Tony, her friend and mentor. Would Tony be forced to go into hiding like her brother had all those years ago?

Could he win the fight against two, clearly experienced fighters? Tears streamed down her face as she struggled for composure.

Bailey was still frowning as she approached Rowdy. "There's something wrong," she said softly. "Let me man the bar. You need to get out back."

Rowdy frowned, but didn't hesitate. He was headed for the back door when Jase pushed past him, nearly running toward the back room. *Now what was that all about?*

As he rounded the corner, Rowdy spotted Marnie on the floor, clearly terrified. Jase was trying to comfort her. The back door was slightly ajar and he could hear fighting just outside the building. He cautiously stepped into the darkness and frowned.

Tony was fighting for his life. His ribs were killing him and he was going to have a black eye for weeks, but at least his opponent was in worse shape than he was. He kicked out and knocked Drago into the brick wall, then struck his opponent in the face, the stomach, the ribs. The man didn't have a chance, not against Tony and his extensive experience on the streets. He wouldn't stop punching until the man stopped moving. Unfortunately, Socks regained his composure and struck from Tony's blind spot. The wily thug joined the fight, armed with a large switchblade. Tony saw Socks coming from the corner of his eye but before he could react, he felt the sting of a blade across his left side. He did his best to ignore the pain, but knew the cut was substantial. Hot wet liquid saturated his t-shirt as he forced his mind to concentrate on the two men closing in on him, menace in their eyes.

Drago smiled as the knife sliced through his attacker's mid-section. The impact gave him the edge he needed to get free. He dodged to the side, prepared to finish off the nosy man who was interfering with his mission. Now it was his turn to inflict a little payback. As he raised his arm, something hit him from behind. His legs gave way and he went sprawling across the pavement. Before he knew what was happening, his arm was practically pulled from the socket and he realized Socks was yelling at him. He stumbled to his feet and let his partner lead him to the car. Within seconds, the two of them were speeding away from a bar Drago was starting to hate.

Theresa saw the moment Socks recovered from the blow Tony had inflicted. She tried to stand, tried to intervene but the instant she took a step forward, pain shot through her ankle and she stumbled to the ground, bracing against the fall with her already mangled hands. She swallowed hard and picked a tiny rock from her palm. Tony needed help. She had to get to his side. Maybe she could crawl but she'd need a weapon. She was frantically searching the area for something... anything to use against the two men when Rowdy strolled out the door and threw Drago towards the parked car. She silently watched as Dominic's men sped away. It took every ounce of will power she had, but she finally stood and limped toward her boss.

"Get him inside," Rowdy ordered as he pulled out a phone and dialed his brother.

Theresa stood over Tony and held out her hand. "Let's get you cleaned up." She was trying to sound composed, but was sure she'd failed. The instant she'd seen Tony attack Dom's thugs, she'd panicked. He would be a target now. Drago wouldn't let this go even if Dominic did, and that was unlikely. Once again, she was going to lose the only person in her life she'd come to care for. Why had she ever believed she could fight the Detroit Mob? Maybe if she surrendered, Dom would let Tony live.

128

Tony stood and took Theresa's arm. She was limping, her ankle would need ice and rest...that's if it wasn't broken. "You okay?" He glanced at her hands then her ripped jeans and his frown deepened.

"Better than you, I think," she frowned and shoved him into one of the visitor chairs inside Rowdy's office.

Bailey stepped through the door and gasped. "Tony!"

"I'm fine," he tried to reassure her but could see she wasn't buying it.

Bailey rushed across the office and crouched in front of her friend. "Who did this?"

Tony shrugged. "Ask Theresa."

Bailey swung around and glared at the woman who was now looking at the floor.

Several seconds ticked by before Rowdy stepped through the door. "Coop's on his way." He dropped into his chair and studied Tony. "Any reason you took on two men like that without help?"

"No time," Tony shrugged. "One of them had Theresa pinned to the ground. She was in danger and I had to act."

Bailey grabbed a bottle of water and a towel then returned to Tony. "I'm going to take off the shirt and see how bad the cut is. Rowdy, I could use some hydrogen peroxide and another towel."

"On it," he said as he stepped from the room just in time to see Jase escorting Marnie to the tiny apartment in the back. The scene behind the bar would be a setback for the girl but Jase could deal with his sister, Rowdy had enough to handle before Coop arrived. He returned to his office just in time to see the damage to Tony's midsection. The knife wound was large, but not too deep. Tony would need stitches, but it wouldn't keep the guy down for long. "Before you do anything, take a couple pictures with your phone. Coop is going to need evidence. I gave him the license plate but those guys are well out of town by now. He's headed over but can't stay long. Maggie's still weak and can't keep anything down. He doesn't want to leave her alone longer than necessary."

"He doesn't need to come," Theresa insisted. "They're gone for now. They'll report in and it will probably be days, maybe weeks before they launch another attack."

"Report in to who?" Bailey asked, not taking her eyes off Tony's wound as she proceeded to clean it.

Tony winced but tried to straighten. He wanted an answer to that question as well.

"Their boss," Theresa evaded.

"That boss got a name?" Sheriff Cooper asked as he stepped into the room.

Theresa swallowed. "Uh, yeah," she sighed. It was time to come clean. "Dominic Zarconi."

Coop and Rowdy frowned at the same moment. Tony glanced around the room wondering if the two lawmen recognized the name.

"Rowdy?" Coop turned to his brother. "Why don't you fill me in on the details, then we'll go from there." He turned to address the trio. "Nobody goes anywhere, I want to talk to each one of you... privately."

The two men walked out of the room and headed for the rear of the building.

"Okay, now tell me what this is all about," Coop sighed when they stepped outside. "It has a familiar ring to it, one I didn't like the first time around."

"Don't remind me," Rowdy frowned. "A few weeks back two guys came into the bar. They didn't cause any kind of disturbance or anything but the minute they stepped through the door I knew they were trouble. They behaved, otherwise I would have thrown them out. But, they made Theresa nervous. She knows them, has a history of some kind for sure. Tony was keeping an eye on them as well. Between the two of us, I'm sure they knew they were on shaky ground. Tony distracted them while I sent Theresa home early. The men left and we haven't seen them since... until tonight."

"Okay," Coop glanced around. "Why didn't you tell me this before?"

"Mags is having a difficult time with the pregnancy, you have enough on your plate and they disappeared. I figured if they surfaced again, I'd bring you in," Rowdy explained. "I was a cop, bro. I know when I need backup and when the problem's been neutralized or at least delayed. This problem was delayed. Plus, they don't know where Theresa is staying. Their only option was the bar. I thought we could protect her and deal with the thugs on my turf. I had no idea we were dealing with mob guys."

"I get it," Coop glanced around the area. He didn't like it, but he got it. "There's blood on the trash bin, more over there on the pavement... and the wall. I'm going to need forensics out here. Can you secure the scene while I make the call?"

Moondance Ridge

"Sure," Rowdy shrugged. "I'm sure Bay needs some time with Tony, anyway. I've got this, do what you need to do. Will you also thank Derek for me? He arrived just in time. There's no way I could have guarded the evidence and checked on Tony at the same time. He jumped in and I know he's off-duty enjoying a rare night off. You should write a letter or give him a bonus or something."

Coop was shaking his head as he walked away. They both knew a cop was never off-duty, but he would take care of his man. It was always nice to be appreciated.

* * * *

Theresa watched as Bailey pampered Tony. She wanted to be the one to help him. This was all her fault after all. But she wouldn't try to come between the two friends. She might if she were staying, but tonight had only reaffirmed what she already knew. She had to leave. No time for a plan, she'd just pack up her belongings and disappear into the wind. She'd have to warn Tony and Rowdy. They would now be on Dom's radar. Could she protect them, bargain her life for theirs? She had to try; but right now, she needed some time alone. As she stepped into the hallway, she realized there was nowhere to escape. The bar was still open, the patrons would stay until they were forced out at closing. Tony and Bailey were in the office and Marnie was occupying the small apartment. Her eyes landed on the storage closet; and she rushed to the door, shoved it open and stepped inside. She didn't even bother with the light, just slid to the floor, wrapped her arms around her knees and cried. Her hands were killing her, but her heart felt like it had broken into a million pieces. She was so alone, desperate and terrified. Worse, she had brought good, decent people into her mess and she didn't know how to fix it. Somehow life was getting worse, not better.

* * * *

"Bailey, stop," Tony insisted. "I'm fine."

"You're not fine," she swallowed hard. "You could have died out there. You could have died and I never would have had the chance to apologize."

"Hey," he pulled her into the chair next to him. "You have nothing to apologize for."

"Marnie said I do," Bailey argued. "She's right."

Tony frowned. "She's wrong. When did you talk to Marnie?"

"I didn't actually talk to her. She was yelling at me earlier today. She said I was being cruel and I owed you an apology," Bailey provided.

"I'm pretty sure if anyone owes the other an apology, it's me," Tony gave her hand a quick squeeze. "And, I am sorry. I don't know what I was thinking. I should have trusted you, should have gone about things... differently. I like him, he's a good man." He smiled and waited for Bailey to look at him.

"I knew you would," Bailey smiled back. "I was so angry with you. I said some things I didn't mean. I told you I couldn't stand to be in the same room as you. I..."

"Yeah," Tony raised an eyebrow. "I was there. Can we maybe skip the recap? It wasn't that pleasant the first time."

"My point isn't a recap. I just wanted to say I'm sorry and I'm glad you and Rowdy are getting to know each other. He's amazing and I knew you would see that if you just took the time to get to know him," Bailey frowned.

"But..." Tony pressed.

Bailey shrugged. "I don't know, I guess I feel... left out. I mean my man and my best friend have been spending an awful lot of time together. Every time I turn around, you're having a casual beer or just shooting the breeze. I wanted to join in and be a part of it, but I couldn't. I was still mad at you and not ready to make up. I hated it."

"Rowdy nailed that one," Tony grinned when Bailey frowned. "He knows you. He gets you. You have my blessing if that matters now. And, I am truly sorry for any trouble I caused. I was out of line and if I could take it back, I would."

"You're forgiven," she rested her head on his shoulder. "Now, what do you mean Rowdy nailed it?"

"I was all gung-ho to track you down and make you forgive me. He had a different approach. One that worked far better. If I had cornered you, we'd still be at odds. You're stubborn and unyielding when you get mad like that. His way? You got what you wanted all along... the two of us getting to know each other, and that made you want to join in. Which meant you had to forgive me, but not until it was your idea. Like I said, Rowdy gets you. He knew you wouldn't be able to resist for long."

"I can't decide if I should be mad or grateful," she admitted.

"Grateful," Tony said immediately. "He only wants what's best for both of us. And you know if you hadn't gotten in the way, I think Rowdy and I would have hit it off immediately. It was my overprotective, brotherly love that clouded things from the start."

"And, as much as I wanted to strangle you when I figured it out, I also love you for it. I'm not sure you realize just how much you mean to me. Overprotective, brotherly instincts and all," Bailey sighed when Tony turned and brushed a light kiss on the top of her head.

"I love you too," he whispered just as Coop and Rowdy stepped back into the room.

"Where's Theresa?" Coop asked immediately.

Tony frowned.

Bailey stood. "I'll find her, you can start with Tony but keep it short. He's injured."

Bailey found Theresa in the storage room. As she pushed open the door and flipped on the light, it was obvious her friend had been crying. "You want to talk about it?"

Theresa brushed away the tears and stood. "Not really."

Bailey grinned. "I can understand that. You know I get it because you know my history. Well, at least part of it. I do understand you, Theresa. I've been there. I recognize the unhappiness, the desperation, and the fear in your eyes. I lived it for years and you know what?"

"What?" Theresa brushed her palms against her jeans then winced.

Bailey moved to her friend's side and took one of her hands. "We need to get these cleaned." She wasn't taking no for an answer. She wrapped her hand around Theresa's wrist and pulled her into the kitchen. Once the water was lukewarm, she motioned to the sink. The message was clear.

Theresa slowly slid her hand under the running water, expecting pain. It was a little uncomfortable, but the temperature was perfect and soothing. "You're good at this. Dare I ask why?"

"I've had my share of trouble," Bailey answered as she looked around for something to use to pick the rocks from beneath Theresa's skin. "And, I learned that no matter how careful I was; no matter how many times I pushed the people who loved me and wanted to help me away; no matter how strong I tried to be... I was lonely, vulnerable and one breathe away from a panic attack. I once lost it completely because I saw a dead cat on the side of the road. It was obviously a stray, but I was so stressed out that dead animal pushed me over the edge and I cried for hours. The only way to stop this is to face it head on. Otherwise, it's going to tear you apart. We can help you if you'll let us."

Theresa began shaking her head.

"I get it," Bailey soothed. "Trust me, I get it. You are so sure that if you let someone in, if you open up, share the burden, you'll be sentencing someone else to a life of misery. That's not true. I promise you that is not true. As strong as I was, as smart, clever, secretive... Reese still found me. I had to face him and you have to face this, too." Bailey glanced up when Tony stepped into the room.

"And like Bailey said, you don't have to face it alone." He was across the room and picking at her hand before Theresa knew what happened. "I tried to explain that to Bailey, but she was too stubborn to listen. Don't make the same mistake she did. We can help. I can help."

"Ouch," Theresa tried to pull her hand away but was unsuccessful. It hurt a little, but what hurt the most was the knowledge that she'd dragged him into her impossible situation. And in the end, he was going to die as a result.

"I know you're tougher than that. Let me clean this, then Coop needs some information," Tony was careful as he gently picked each and every rock from her palm. Then he pushed up her pant leg and studied her ankle. "I don't think it's broken. Can you walk on it okay?"

"It's sore, but fine. Let's get this over with," she stepped away from Tony and limped down the hall

"When we get home, I'll need to finish bandaging that," Tony called after her.

Theresa stopped in her tracks. "Nobody is supposed to know about that. You promised."

"I figure once Coop asks for your address, the cat's going to be out of the bag, anyway. Bailey won't say a word... will you Bay?" Tony glanced pleadingly at his friend.

"My lips are sealed," Bailey assured her. "Let's get this over with." The three of them stepped into the small room and settled into folding chairs Rowdy had arranged inside.

Coop stepped to the door and closed it securely. "Theresa," he settled into his own chair. "I spoke with Tony and got his statement, now I need yours. Let's start with the basics. Your full name, date of birth, address, phone number."

Theresa rattled off her full name, her birthdate and then looked at Tony, swallowed and straightened in her chair. "I'm staying with Tony for now. If he gave you the address and phone number, it will be the same."

Coop glanced up at Theresa, then moved his focus to Tony. "Okay, let's start with the two men. Do you know their names?"

"Drago and Socks," she whispered. "I doubt those are real names. Most likely Dom came up with them, or the other guys did. I'm not sure. I've never known them as anything else."

Coop frowned. Hopefully he could get at least one name off the car rental contract. "Okay and they work for Dominic Zarconi?"

"Yes," Theresa wondered if the sheriff knew who that was.

"And are you from Detroit?"

Okay then, I guess he does. "Yes," Theresa admitted. "I lived there most of my life."

"Okay," Coop scribbled something on a pad then looked Theresa in the eyes. "What is your connection to the Detroit mob?"

"They want me dead," she said flatly. "Or working for them. At this point, I don't know which."

"I see," Coop softened. "Do you know why?"

"Um, yeah," Theresa admitted. "It's a long story but my husband... my ex-husband crossed Dominic. So now, he's after me."

"Did Zarconi do something to your husband?" Coop asked.

Theresa studied her hands. How to answer that question. She thought she could trust Sheriff Cooper. She was pretty sure she could trust Rowdy, but she'd been keeping this secret for so long.

"We'll come back to that," Cooper answered for her. "You say Zarconi is after you. How long have you known... well, let me change that. Why do you think he wants you to work for him?"

"I've known for nearly two years," Theresa said. "He found me a short time after I landed here. Max was great, he gave me a job almost immediately. I found an apartment and settled in. I was stupid, I know that now. I thought once I left Detroit, Dom would leave me alone. But, he didn't. He had Joe and Socks track me down a little over a month after I arrived; they gave me an ultimatum."

"Joe?" Coop asked.

"Another one of Dom's men," she supplied. "He has... well I have no idea how many he has but there are a few that belong to his inner circle. A half a dozen men he trusts to take care of the more... sensitive matters."

"And you were a sensitive matter?" Coop pushed.

"I guess," Theresa nodded.

"So, they tracked you here and told you what?"

"Joe said I owed Dom... for Shawn's betrayal," she supplied. "He said I had to pay up right away, or I had to go back to Detroit with them and work for Dom to pay off the debt."

"Doing what?" Coop asked.

"He didn't say," Theresa whispered.

Moondance Ridge

"But you know," Coop pressed.

"I think I know," Theresa looked up defiantly. "I will not be pimped out like some worthless piece of meat to whatever scumbag friend Dom needs a favor from. I'll die before I work for that monster."

"I won't let it come to that. I can assure you," Coop said forcefully.

"You won't be able to stop it," Theresa closed her eyes to stop the tears. "Nobody can. I can't win. He just keeps upping the payments. I can't afford my freedom anymore. He's priced me out of my home, my dignity and now he's come to up the price again. I'm out of options. Nobody can help me now."

"I'd be offended; but I think under the circumstances, I understand your hesitance to believe anyone can beat the mob," Coop sighed. "Let me just say there are two people in this room right now that have taken down a ruthless mob boss. We're not in the least bit worried about doing it again."

That did get Theresa's attention. She studied the sheriff for several seconds then shifted her gaze to Rowdy. "Who?"

"Leon DeRossi," Rowdy said, his contempt evident as he spoke the name.

"Chicago?" Tony asked.

"Chicago," Coop confirmed. "And, all of his top men. We know what we're doing and we can protect you if you let us. Dominic has been extorting money from you? How much?"

"At first," Theresa bit her bottom lip. How much to tell? "At first, they showed up and said Shawn betrayed Dom. They said Dom needed fifty thousand immediately; or I had to go back with them, work off my debt. Shawn's debt was my debt because we were married. Shawn owed forty he allegedly stole and ten as a penalty."

"How did you come up with fifty thousand so quickly?" Bailey was impressed.

"He added on the penalty to make sure you couldn't pay," Tony surmised.

"That's what he thought," Theresa nodded. "But Shawn had sold our home before we left. Before I left. So, I had the proceeds from that. It cleaned me out but I thought it was worth it. You know, to buy my freedom. To pay Dom, so he would leave me alone for good."

"But it wasn't enough," Tony pressed.

"No," Theresa told him. "It never will be. Dom is still peeved that I came up with that initial outlay. He sent Joe out about a week later to tell me the debt wasn't settled. He said I had to pay for Shawn's brother's transgressions. He said Zach's debt was bigger and his offense was more egregious."

"So, both your husband and his brother were somehow connected to Zarconi's enterprise?" Coop asked, a little confused. Clearly, Theresa didn't want to tell him how her husband had gotten involved in something so sinister. Maybe the brother, this Zach guy, had brought him in.

"Zach was an investigative reporter for the Detroit Chronicle," Theresa provided. "He was investigating Dom. He found some... damaging information that he was going to use to expose Zarconi and his entire organization. Then he turned up dead."

"Oh, Theresa," Bailey was across the room in an instant. She immediately wrapped an arm around her friend's shoulders and pulled her into a one-armed hug. "I'm so sorry." Then she turned to Rowdy, hatred showing in her eyes. "We will stop that monster for good. The Cooper brothers will stop him. Theresa, you will not pay that man one more dime, do you hear me?"

"At this point I don't think it matters," Theresa admitted. "He'll just keep upping the amount until I can't pay. Then he'll have Drago and Socks snatch me up and I'll disappear for good. Nobody will ever know what happened to me."

"Over my dead body," Tony stood and moved to crouch in front of Theresa. "I won't let that happen. Rowdy, Coop, they won't let that happen. If you disappeared, we'd come find you. But, you won't disappear because I'm going to take care of the problem myself, before it goes any further."

"What do you mean?" Theresa panicked. "No, you can't. Dom is already going to come after you. Both you and Rowdy. You interfered, he won't allow that to go unpunished. If you go after him in any way, you will end up dead; just like the others. You have to promise me, Tony. Please let this go."

"No," Tony shook his head. "I won't make that promise."

"You two can discuss that once you leave here," Coop shot a look at Rowdy then Bailey and Tony. "For now, let's finish this up. But, I warn you, Tony... you have just threatened a man in my presence. I would be very careful where you go from here. The last thing I want to do is testify at your murder trial."

Tony grinned. "I got the message sheriff, consider me warned."

"This isn't funny," Theresa practically shouted. "You don't know what that man is capable of."

"I think I do," Coop disagreed. "Like I said, I dealt with DeRossi. They're all the same, under it all. I think you should take Bailey's advice. Do not pay any more installments to that man, not another dime. Give me a couple days. Rowdy and I will come up with a plan. Do not run, Theresa. I know that look and I caution you... do not take off on your own. Think of it this way... Rowdy and Tony are on this guy's radar now. Running won't solve anything. He's going to come after them anyway, he doesn't have a choice. They interfered. It won't matter if you're here, still working at the bar, or on the run. This Dom guy will come after Tony and Rowdy. That makes it our fight now whether we wanted it or not. I hope you'll help us deal with it. We can protect you if you let us. We can keep you safe but we need you here to provide information."

Theresa considered. Coop was right, Tony and Rowdy were in danger and it was all her fault. She should have run days ago...weeks ago when they'd dropped by with a new demand. But, she'd hesitated and now the Cooper brothers and Tony were going to pay for her mistake. "Okay," she agreed. The sheriff was right, if she ran at this point, she'd just be out there on her own, alone, trying to come up with a plan. If she stayed, maybe she could help the people she cared about get out of this mess. It was worth a shot and she'd need to stick around to be part of it.

"Rowdy," Coop turned to his brother. "Maggie's been alone long enough. Stop by my office in the morning and we'll see what we can come up with. I still have my old file on that op in Chicago.

Moondance Ridge

I think it might be a good idea to refresh my memory. If you have anything, do the same. The mob is the mob and refreshing our memories might help somehow."

"I'll be there at eight," Rowdy agreed. The two men stood and Rowdy walked Coop to his car. "We both know they'll return. Next time, it could be worse. Tony got lucky tonight. That man's got grunge fighting in his past. Next time they'll be prepared, probably send more men." Rowdy paused and stared into the darkness. "I have to take this fight to Zarconi, we both know it. Plus, dealing with this in Detroit is safer than bringing who knows how many of those men to Mount Haven."

"Let's not get ahead of ourselves," Coop disagreed. "I'll study my file tonight; and in the morning, I'll work on getting as much information as I can on this Dominic guy. We'll put together a plan from there, you got me?"

Rowdy grinned. "If you're asking me not to hop the redeye tonight, you have my word."

"Good," Coop put a hand on Rowdy's shoulder. "This could get ugly and with Mags down, I'm stretched thin. We might need to find a place to stash that girl out-of-the-way for a while. Tony, too."

"I'll talk to Bailey," Rowdy promised. "But, I don't think Tony will go for it. He's tough and he's been around the block."

"The suit?" Cooper grinned.

"Don't let the image fool you," Rowdy countered. "I've spent time with him. He's solid and I'm afraid he might be fearless. I'm just warning you, any plan that involves Tony Nazario hiding out like a sissy, is not going to fly."

"I'll meet you at eight," Cooper climbed behind the wheel. "We'll figure something out after we've had a good night's sleep."

"What about Skeet? Can he help?"

"Maybe, but I don't want to bring him in just yet. He's still at odds with his supervisor over the last one. I guess my country charm didn't go over all that well," Cooper grinned.

"You never were that charming," Rowdy laughed. "You might want to consider sending Mags and Bry to visit friends," Rowdy added hesitantly. "We both know how the mob guys love to take out their frustrations on family." He watched his brother close the door and leave the parking lot without answering. Rowdy's gut told him the only solution was to take the offense. To do that, he'd need to head to Detroit. Plus, if he took the fight to Dominic, Mags and Bryan would be safe. So would Bailey and his brother. He just had to find someone he trusted to serve as a back. This was one mission he couldn't handle alone.

* * * *

Rowdy stepped back into the room and wrapped an arm around Bailey. He needed to feel her close for one more night. The future held several weeks of loneliness and danger, he was sure of it.

"Tony is going to take Theresa home," Bailey provided. "They would like us to keep Theresa's living arrangements a secret for now. I think that's a good idea. The men that attacked them tonight believe their only hope of finding Theresa is here, at the bar. I'm thinking that limits their options and will help protect Theresa. We just have to make sure she's never alone. Tony is going to work from home for a while. If he needs information or personal contact at the office, I'll handle it for now. That should give you and Coop time to come up with a plan. One that will keep everyone safe. Deal?"

Rowdy grinned and kissed the top of her head. "Sounds like a plan."

"Sounds like a terrible plan," Theresa pouted. "I've heard how your company is struggling. I don't want Tony to neglect his job just so he can babysit me."

"We'll see you guys tomorrow," Tony said pushing Theresa toward the door. He wasn't going to justify her objection with a response. He would protect her. He would get her out of this mess even if that meant putting Drakker on the back-burner for a few weeks. The company was doing fine now and with Peter hell-bent on traveling every waking minute of his life, it would probably be twice its current size by the time this mess was over. Plus, Tony landed another new client this morning, so things were good at Drakker, Inc. He walked Theresa to her truck and waited for her to climb inside. "Wait for me," he said forcefully. "Once I get to my car, pull up beside me then follow me home."

"Oh, for the..." Theresa began.

"For me?" he pressed. "Just do it for me, for one night, just do what I ask for one night?"

"Okay," Theresa saw something in his eyes and couldn't deny him. She'd caused this, the worry, the pain he was in, the danger that was waiting in his future. So, if it made him feel better, she could do what he asked for one night. Well, maybe. Once they reached the house, she was going to look at that cut and see if Tony needed stitches. If so, they'd be headed to the hospital, no matter what the macho man said.

Chapter Five

"What in the world?" Tony was speechless.

"Oh," Theresa froze the minute she stepped through the door. She'd forgotten all about her painting project. However, now that it had dried, it really did look fantastic. "With everything that happened today, I completely forgot."

Tony was staring at the walls in amazement. He'd left the living room and open dining area the way it had been because he just couldn't visualize the perfect design. No matter how many nights he'd sat on the couch and stared at the walls, nothing had come to him. Theresa had nailed it.

"I'm sorry," she took a step back and tripped over the couch that was now sitting in the middle of the floor. Before she could regain her balance, she fell backwards, toppled over the arm rest and landed unceremoniously on the cushion.

Tony laughed and walked toward her. "Sorry for what?" he asked as he gently slid her legs around so she could sit then settled onto the couch beside her. "I love it. You read my mind... before my mind even knew what it wanted. You have talent, serious talent. How in the world did you do all of this in one day?"

Theresa smiled, relieved. "Uh, well... I have practice. You really like it? You're not just saying that?"

"No," Tony said slowly. "I love it. Seriously, I skipped this room because the vision just wasn't coming. I moved down the hall, tackled your room and the master - all the while frustrated because I just couldn't find the right look. You seriously nailed it, woman!"

"I'm so glad you approve," she was grinning now. "I got caught up, then I was worried I overstepped. It did exceed my expectations, though."

"So, I guess you redecorated your own home... the one you had with your husband?"

Theresa's smile evaporated. "Yeah, a long time ago."

"We don't have to talk about it tonight," Tony wrapped an arm around her shoulders. "I think we've both been through enough."

"That reminds me, I need to see that cut," she sat forward and lifted Tony's shirt slightly so she could see the bottom half of his torso.

Moondance Ridge

Tony laughed. "If you wanted to undress me, all you had to do was ask, sweetheart."

Theresa dropped the shirt immediately.

Tony grabbed her hand and refused to let her pull away. "It was a joke. Apparently a bad one, but a joke. I'm fine, nothing a few butterfly strips won't fix. Let's go to bed and we can figure this out in the morning." He stood and frowned when Theresa just sat there. "What's wrong?"

"I um..." she wasn't sure how to explain. "I'm not sure I can sleep. I think, if it won't bother you, maybe I'll just work on putting things back the way they belong. In this room, I mean. Maybe I can work a little."

Tony crouched in front of Theresa and placed his hands on both sides of her face. He should have considered that. She was afraid, terrified really; and he couldn't blame her. He leaned forward and pressed his lips to her forehead. "Why don't you sleep in my room? Come to bed with me. I promise, I'll be a perfect gentleman. I won't even make another joke." She was getting ready to decline, he could see it. "For me? Please? I need to have you close so I know you're okay. If you won't do it for yourself, do it for me. I need my beauty sleep and I have an early morning."

Theresa stared at him, confused. "I thought you were working from home."

"I am," Tony said wrapping his large hand around her wrist. He pulled her to her feet and led her toward the bedroom. "But first, I'm going to attend a meeting at the Sheriff's Office. I need to know what the Coopers are planning."

"Tony," Theresa paused at the foot of the large king-sized bed. "I meant what I said, Dom is dangerous. This isn't a joke. This isn't.... well it's not like dealing with some cutthroat businessman. Dominic Zarconi really will cut your throat, then he'll charge me for cleanup."

Tony slid the shirt over his head then moved to his dresser. He was sure he had a pair of pajama pants in there somewhere. "Your opinion of me is a little insulting but I'll let it slide because you're new in my life. You have no idea how I grew up or what I'm capable of. I guess I thought after the fight tonight; and what I told you before about living on the street, you'd realize I can handle myself. I can also take care of you." Tony stopped rummaging through drawers and turned to look at Theresa. "Let me take care of you... at least for a little while. I have a feeling you've been alone and afraid for far too long."

Theresa opened her mouth to argue, then stopped. Tony was right. He had handled himself against both Socks and Drago no less, two of Dominic's best hitmen. Drago terrified her. He was ruthless and calculating and he was going to return soon to exact his revenge. Drago would need to make Tony pay for that fight tonight, but that was a worry for another day. Right now, she had to figure out what she was going to wear to bed. The answer hit her square in the face. *Note to self, pay attention when in a room with Nazario.* The man was unpredictable and a little dangerous. She pulled the t-shirt away from her face and rolled her eyes as she marched into the master bath to change. The instant she stepped into the room she realized Tony had more talents than he let on. He was in the process of completely remodeling the bathroom and from what she saw, he was as good as any professional. If he ever failed in business, he could make a fortune flipping real-estate.

Moondance Ridge

Tony watched Theresa close the door and smiled. She was definitely nervous about their arrangement. He slid open the bottom drawer and finally found what he'd been searching for. The cotton PJ's were wrinkled beyond redemption but they would do for now. He glanced at the closed bathroom door then slipped out of his jeans and pulled on the thin cotton bottoms. When he climbed into bed, the pants twisted and tangled around his leg. Maybe he should just find a pair of gym shorts. He stared at the ceiling, considering his options. Suddenly, the door swung open and Theresa's silhouette appeared in the opening. He watched as she stood there, clearly memorizing her path before engulfing them both in darkness.

Theresa sighed, flipped off the light and slowly made her way across the room. Once she reached the bed, she gripped the hem of the t-shirt with one hand as she placed the palm of the other on the soft mattress. Pain flowed through her and she hesitated. Maybe she should find some antibiotic cream and a roll of gauze before settling in for the night. She sat motionless on the edge of the bed for several seconds before Tony wrapped a strong arm around her waist and pulled her onto the bed. Theresa screeched, then buried her head in the pillow embarrassed by her outburst.

Tony pushed his weight up onto one elbow as he focused on Theresa's form and smiled. In one fluid motion, he yanked the pillow from her face and pressed a soft kiss to her lips. She was so beautiful, no wonder Dominic wanted complete control over her. The reminder infuriated him; and he vowed then and there, he would never let anything happen to this stubborn woman who had somehow crawled under his skin and wouldn't let go. With or without her blessing, he was going to take care of this mess. A mess her ex-husband should have fixed long ago.

"You're staring," Theresa objected as she snatched her pillow back and sat up. Once she had it situated exactly how she wanted it, she settled beneath the covers, her back towards her bed partner... for one night. *Only for one night*, she silently promised herself.

Tony wrapped his arm around Theresa's waist and pulled her closer. He closed his eyes and enjoyed the feel of her body securely pressed against his. When she tried to pull away, to force space between them, he tightened his grip and leaned forward. "Relax, I've got you. I promise I won't let anything happen to you. Just relax," he pressed a soft kiss to her neck just below her left ear.

"Please stop," Theresa said breathlessly.

"Why?" Tony asked as he kissed his way down her neck and finally reached her lips.

Theresa sat up abruptly, clutching the blanket to her chin like it was a lifeline.

"Hey," Tony sat up. "Talk to me. If I misread you, just say so. I'll back off."

"What happened to being a gentleman?" she whispered.

"I was being gentle," he smiled. "Tell me what's going on in that head of yours."

"If I ask you something, will you be honest with me?" she studied his face for the slightest sign of deceit.

"Of course," Tony reached out and brushed a stray hair away from her face. "I will always be honest with you."

"What about Marnie," she asked.

Tony frowned. "What about her? Sure, she was upset tonight but Jase was there. She's fine."

153

Theresa hadn't known Marnie was upset. That wasn't the question she was asking. "I mean is there something between you two? Are you seeing her?"

"What?" Tony asked, perplexed. "Of course not, she's just a kid." Then he remembered what Bailey had said. She thought he was messing with Theresa, did Theresa think so, too?

"You two seem..."

"Marnie's a good kid, but she's had a rough past," Tony began. "I assumed you knew her situation."

"I know a little," Theresa admitted. "I know about the rape and her brother having to hide out because of it."

"Her mom's been supportive but too protective, I guess," Tony provided. "Marnie barely left her room after the attack. She was still trying to come to grips with the entire incident when Jase went into hiding. She lost her brother, her confidence and her self-respect in a matter of days. Only now, after what happened out here at that cabin, after Cole and Reese died, was she able to start living again. Being able to work at the bar with Jase has helped a lot, but she still has insecurities. That's where I come in. She needed a friend. She was broken and lost. I'm just helping her find the way, nothing more."

"You guys spend so much time together and you seem pretty close. It's different from the friendship you have with Bailey," Theresa argued. "I can see that."

Tony considered, Theresa was right but still wrong. "Bay and I go way back. When I first met her, I was drawn in. Yeah, she was beautiful and initially I was interested. However, it became immediately clear Bailey was also a little broken. Not like Marnie, well at least I don't remember her being that insecure, ever. Not even at her worst. But it was painfully obvious what Bailey needed was a friend, not some random guy hitting on her. So, I filled that void. At first, I thought I was doing her a favor, but eventually I realized she was also filling a void I had in my life. We were equals and that drew us even closer, I think. Bailey and I will always be friends. We will always find a way to forgive each other's shortcomings and come out the other side even stronger. She's the closest thing I have to a sister and I will never do anything to ruin that. Marnie is different because we're not equals, if that makes sense. She's a kid struggling to get back on her feet; and every once in a while, she needs someone to talk to. Someone that isn't going to placate her or shield her. Someone who will challenge her to live her life, ups and downs, disappointments and triumphs, but live. Jase can't do that and neither can her mother. That's where I come in. I'm more of a... mentor and advisor than a friend, I think. Eventually, Marnie won't need me. She'll move on with her life, find love and happiness and I'll just be a fond memory. A guy that helped her get through a rough patch."

Theresa frowned as she considered what Tony was saying. "And me? Am I just another broken soul that needs fixing?"

Tony smiled then pulled Theresa against him. His mouth connected with hers, this time the kiss wasn't gentle. It was intimate and invasive and mind-blowing. When the two of them came up for air, Tony gave her a cocky grin. "Does that answer your question?"

Theresa couldn't breathe. She had never been kissed like that in her life. Not even by Shawn. Her husband had been gentle and loving, not forceful and erotic. She wasn't quite sure what to think of her emotions right now. She lifted her hand to her lips and tasted blood. Her eyes grew wide and she glanced down at Tony's injury. "You're bleeding."

Moondance Ridge

Tony glanced down and wiped the blood from his mid-section. "It's nothing, come back here."

Theresa jumped from the bed. "Where are your medical supplies?"

"This is a home, not a hospital," he smiled. "The kind of TLC I'm looking for doesn't require dissolving thread or a nurse's uniform." A smile spread across his face. "Although, a nurse's uniform might be interesting."

"A simple first aid kit would suffice," she scowled. "We need to clean your wound and at least tape it so it can start to heal."

Tony sighed, stood and left the room. When he returned, he had a large case that looked like a tackle box in his hand. He moved to the bed and sat on Theresa's side of the mattress. "Come on, let's see what we need to do to fix your hands then I'll let you look at my scratch."

Theresa settled in next to him, placing her hands on her thighs, palms up. They were still raw, but she was pretty sure he had removed all the rocks and debris while they were at the bar.

Tony stepped into the bathroom and returned with a large towel. "I'm going to dump hydrogen peroxide on your entire hand, this might hurt a little."

"I'm fine," Theresa said, gritting her teeth against the pain. Seconds later, the bubbling stopped and Tony began to dab at her wounds with a soft piece of gauze covered in antibiotic ointment. The cold cream soothed the throbbing almost immediately. She remained perfectly still as he pulled out a roll of gauze, folded two large squares then placed them on her palms. Finally, he began wrapping her hands with the white bandage. Once he was sure they were secure, he ripped off a strip of tape with his teeth and secured the end.

"You look like a mummy with fingers, but I think it will hold."

"Now it's your turn," Theresa grabbed the kit before he could close it back up. "If you lie on your back, this will be easier."

Tony leaned back and rested his weight on his elbows.

Theresa studied the wound. He really could use stitches. "I think we should go to the emergency room. They can stitch you up, and it won't leave much of a scar."

"A bandage will do," Tony disagreed. "Either you do it, or I will. We just need to make sure I don't bleed during the night."

Theresa studied his face for several seconds and realized the man was just as stubborn as she was. He would not go to the hospital no matter how much she begged. She pulled out a cotton ball and covered it with peroxide.

Tony cringed, then gritted his teeth and endured the pain as Theresa cleaned his wound. He probably should get stitches, but he'd had worse, and they'd healed just fine. All he needed was a little TLC and a few days. Who cared if he had a scar? He had plenty of them already. Once she was finished cleaning the cut, Theresa gently covered it with ointment and secured three butterfly bandages over the area. "See, good as new," Tony declared as he looked at her handy work.

"Not quite, but I think it will hold." She shook her head and began to clean up her mess. "I guess we'll see in the morning."

Moondance Ridge

Tony took the garbage from Theresa and dumped it in the trash. Then, the two of them climbed back into bed. This time, Theresa snuggled up against him on her own; and they both fell into a deep, dreamless sleep. Each of them feeling a level of contentment they hadn't known for a very long time.

* * * *

Theresa felt the warm sun on her face and slowly opened her eyes. Where was she? Oh, yeah... Tony's room. She pushed her body upright and sat against the headboard as she took a minute to slowly peruse her surroundings. She hadn't really gotten a feel for it the night before. In the dim light of the moon, everything had fallen into shadows. Now, she smiled as she took in every facet of Tony Nazario's personal space. It was neutral but masculine at the same time. Decorated in deep browns and creamy off whites. He had added a splash of red here and there to introduce color with the curtains, the throw rugs, the lamps. Tony Nazario had once again impressed her. She glanced at the clock and wondered if he'd left already. Rowdy and Coop planned to meet at eight. She knew Tony would be there bright and early to ensure he was included, but it was only seven. Maybe he was still around here somewhere. She climbed from the bed and made her way into her own room. Once inside, her eyes landed on the cotton robe. She snatched it up and pulled it on as she walked briskly down the long hallway.

Tony was in the kitchen, sipping coffee and reading something on his tablet. She stopped to wonder if it was top of the line or an old favorite. Knowing Tony, probably top of the line. Not that she could tell the difference. It had been years since she had the luxury of owning the market's newest gadgets. "Morning," she mumbled as she headed for the coffee pot.

"Hey," Tony glanced up absently then returned his focus to the tiny screen he'd been studying.

"Bad news?" she asked as she settled into the chair next to him.

"Huh?" he looked up and smiled. "No, not really. Just a minor complication." He pressed a button and the screen went black. "How are you this morning?" He took one of her hands and turned it slowly back and forth as he studied the bandage. "No bleeding I see."

Theresa smiled. "They're fine. I thought I'd remove the gauze when I shower. I think they'll be okay without it. You're the one that could be bleeding. That knife injury went pretty deep."

"Not really," Tony disagreed. "It was longer than I would have preferred but not that deep. I should have stopped it. Guess I'm getting rusty in my old age." He stood and gently kissed Theresa on the lips then turned to leave.

"Are you coming back? Afterwards--I mean," Theresa blurted. She felt like a needy child but couldn't help herself. Tony pivoted so he was facing her again. He was dressed casually today, wearing an old university sweatshirt and jeans. She couldn't help but wonder why nobody had snatched him up and married him already. Tony being single was one of those life mystery's that just didn't make sense.

"Yeah," he gave her his award-winning smile. "I have some paperwork I need to finish later but not much else today. Depending on how long this meeting goes, I should be home for lunch. We don't have much here, you want to head into Missoula with me? I could stop at the office and pick up a few things; then, we could grab a bite before heading back home."

Moondance Ridge

"Sure," Theresa smiled back. *Heading home.* That sounded nice. Oh, she knew it couldn't last; but it was still an amazing feeling to have a home once again. Even if it was temporary.

"Great," Tony said cheerfully. "I'll call you when I leave the station, let you know I'm on my way."

"See ya," Theresa said lamely. She just hoped it wasn't going to be weird now that she'd slept in Tony's bed... and kissed him like there was no tomorrow. She sobered, maybe there wouldn't be - for either one of them. That thought terrified her, she wasn't sure she could get through another loss. Her mind drifted back to their night together. She had slept better than she had in years, knowing she was safe and secure in his arms. What it all meant, she had no idea. She just knew things were going to get worse before they could ever get better.

* * * *

Tony waited in the parking lot until Sheriff Andy Cooper pulled in beside him. He climbed from his car and waited for the lawman to react. It didn't take long.

"What can I do for you, Tony?" Coop asked, knowing precisely why the man was there. He still didn't have a feel for Tony Nazario. He knew Rowdy had run a background on the guy when he showed up in town. He knew Tony and Bailey had a long history and Bailey loved and respected the man. He knew in the business world, they called him The Fixer but Tony didn't like the title. Beyond that, he knew basically nothing. His instincts told him the guy was okay, but there was something simmering just below the surface.

"I'm here for the meeting, but you already knew that," Tony said casually as he followed Coop into the building. "Looks like I'm a bit early."

"What makes you think I'd allow your involvement in a police matter?" Coop asked as he settled into his executive chair.

"Because you'd prefer to know what I'm doing as opposed to hearing it through the grapevine," Tony provided. "I'm already involved, like it or not. This way, you get to decide the parameters."

"I'm surprised you got through the front door," Rowdy said casually as he settled into one of his brother's visitor chairs. "The old man must be getting soft."

Coop scowled then returned his attention to Tony. "For now, you stay. But if I hear you've so much as jaywalked in an effort to go after this Zarconi guy... you'll answer to me."

Tony nodded once, gave Coop a crooked grin and relaxed. Round one was over. It was time to get down to business.

"I stopped by the car rental agency this morning," Coop began. "That was pleasant, let me tell you. I get the feeling these guys rent from the same outfit each time they visit. They were less than cooperative, but I did get a copy of the agreement. The vehicle was reserved through a company called Diamond Cleaners out of Detroit."

"A shell corporation?" Rowdy asked.

"Not entirely," Coop shook his head. "The company's legit, as far as I can tell. But if it's tied to the mob, we both know it's most likely a front. I haven't been able to determine what they're into. Dominic owns a casino. I'm sure he's laundering everything but the kitchen sink through there, it's the easiest way to clean money." Coop focused on Rowdy. "It's going to be difficult to find the specifics."

"Any info on the driver?" Tony asked.

Coop smiled. "That I can answer. He had to provide a driver's license before he could check out the car. The man that sliced a chunk out of you was one Brodie Salvatore, AKA Socks." Coop slid a photo across his desk for Rowdy and Tony to study.

"Yep," Tony sat back. "That's the guy."

"Any luck on the second man?" Rowdy asked. "I get the feeling he's the more dangerous of the two."

Coop frowned. "I was hoping this guy was the ring leader. I figured since he pulled the knife, chances were good he was in charge."

Tony shook his head. "Nope. The other guy, he's the one to steer clear of. I got that loud and clear the first night I met them. Drago is a loose cannon just waiting to go off. Socks tried to reign him in, at least that first time. Last night, well let's just say I might have pushed his buttons. It's probably the only reason he pulled the knife... desperation."

"Okay," Coop retrieved the photo and placed it in a file. "I'll keep that in mind."

"I read through my file on Leon last night," Rowdy provided.

"Yeah," Coop frowned. "Me too."

"And I haven't changed my mind. Our best option is to take the offense. That means I'm going to Detroit," Rowdy pulled out his Reserve badge and placed it on Coop's desk. "It's time I gave that back. This might get sticky and I don't want you pulled into it."

"Keep the badge," Coop shoved it toward his brother. "We both know that if... and that's a big if... you go to Detroit, you just might need the leverage. Where there's a significant mob presence, there are almost always dirty cops; or at least cops who are a little blind when necessary."

Rowdy sat back and eyed the badge. It was a two-edged sword. He knew the rules could not apply if he was going to take down Zarconi for good. He also knew Coop was right, the badge might be the only thing that saved him if things got too bad out there. It wasn't a decision he could make at the moment, so, he left the symbol of honor on the desk.

Coop shook his head. "This discussion isn't over."

"I got that loud and clear," Rowdy grinned. "So, what precautions do we need in place; I mean out here? How do we protect the others from what I'm about to do?"

"What we're about to do," Tony corrected. "If you're going to Detroit, I'm coming with you."

Coop studied the man sitting before him. "What can you add? Why would you be an asset rather than a nuisance if Rowdy agrees to your company?"

"For starters," Tony shifted into negotiation mode. "I have a plane. Best mode of transportation you got. This Zarconi character won't see us coming."

"And?" Coop pressed.

Moondance Ridge

"Money," Tony shrugged. "Plenty of it. Rowdy can't be on the clock, he's a Montana cop at best. His certs in Chicago aren't even valid. He's going to be vulnerable in Detroit. We all know that. Money talks, I might be willing to have a conversation."

"That just muddies the waters," Coop disagreed.

"He's right," Rowdy said soberly. "I can help out here on occasion, volunteer to uphold the law as time allows. I might even be able to swing a few favors in Illinois, but Michigan? No way. My legitimacy ends the moment I cross that state line. I understand your position. You want to do this the legal way; but I've gone over this time and time again, I need the freedom to be flexible. That badge needs to stay right where it is. I cannot bring this down on you. I won't jeopardize your career that way. When the Mayor gets a call, and we all know he's going to get a call, he needs to be able to say in no uncertain terms that I do not work for Mount Haven or this county."

"I disagree," Coop said flatly. "But that's not my decision to make. It's not even yours. I'll let Mayor Herlin know how you feel."

"Don't make this harder than it needs to be," Rowdy said softly. "We can figure that out when I get back." He pointed to the badge. "You know I'll have to walk a fine line, one some PC snowflake might not approve of. One that could get me fired from this profession. I'd hate to bring Jon Herlin into an already dicey situation for nothing."

"That's precisely why I think you need to have it," Coop sighed. "You are going to walk a line. You always have. I was there, in the gutter with you and Skeet when we saved his wife from a sadistic killer. I was there when we took down Leon DeRossi.

Things could have gone a different way. If you had pushed, if things hadn't turned for us, I could be visiting you in prison instead of stopping by the bar to enjoy a beer now and again. I hope you don't take this the wrong way, but I think having that badge in your pocket might help remind you what's important. What you have and what you could lose."

"We both know nothing I did was illegal. The reference to prison is a gross exaggeration," Rowdy said flatly.

"Okay," Coop conceded. "I'll give you that, but we both know it could have been sticky and impossible to defend if anyone learned the truth."

"I get it," Rowdy shrugged. "But I don't need a badge or my big brother standing over my shoulder to know right from wrong. I might bend the rules here and there, but I've never crossed the line and you know I never would."

"What about him?" Coop motioned to Tony. "What do you know about his line crossing philosophy?"

Rowdy laughed. "Oh, I suspect Tony here isn't above crossing a line or two if it gets him the end result he's looking for."

"That doesn't exactly put my mind at ease," Coop scowled.

"I have a line as well," Tony assured him. "One I won't cross. My moral compass might be a little further in the gray than yours, but I do have a compass. The business world is a little less black and white than the one you choose to live in, Sheriff Cooper. But in the end, we all have to look ourselves in the mirror."

"I'm sold," Rowdy stood. "Now, while I'm gone I'm going to put Jase in charge of the bar; and I'm counting on you to protect my woman. Bailey is not going to be happy with this unscheduled trip, but she'll understand. You get to deal with Mags. She doesn't need the added stress of running the place alone, so I'll make sure Jase has the help he needs to pick up the slack. Coop, you need to bring in your men. We both know once I start messing with this guy, he's going to take his frustrations out on my family if he can. Make sure he doesn't get that chance."

"I've got things covered here," Coop stood and walked around the desk. He pulled Rowdy into a brotherly hug. "Be careful... and check in now and again. I need to know what's going on out there. I need to know you haven't gotten yourself killed or thrown in a cell."

"I'll check in," Rowdy promised. "But don't be a mother hen. I've got this. It's not my first rodeo, you know."

"I know," Coop stepped back. "I just wish I could be there with you. We make a good team and I'm not all that comfortable sitting this one out."

"We make an awesome team," Rowdy corrected. "And you're not sitting out. You're guarding the home front. When I make things too hot in Detroit, he's going to send a team out here to go after you. I don't like that idea any more than you like me heading to Michigan without you."

Coop studied Tony for several seconds. "Take care of my brother, he's the only one I have."

"We've got this," Tony assured him. "I might not be a cop, but it's not the first time I've dealt with a man like Dominic Zarconi. We'll leave in the morning. Any information you can provide on our target between now and then would be appreciated."

Coop settled into his chair and watched the two men leave the building together. He just hoped he was doing the right thing. Once they pulled out of the lot, he picked up the phone and dialed the mayor.

"Hey," Tony said when Theresa answered the phone. "I'm afraid I have to cancel lunch. I have a long list of unexpected to do's that I need to get started on. Can we hook up for dinner? At the bar maybe? I hear Jase is serving his signature brisket tonight. My treat?"

"Yeah, I guess," Theresa said hesitantly. Something was up and she was pretty sure she wasn't going to like it. "What time?"

"How about seven?" Tony suggested.

"I'll be there," Theresa sighed as she hung up the phone. Something happened in that meeting and she was going to find out what. If Tony wouldn't tell her, she'd just corner Bailey and demand answers. Her new friend would fill her in, she was sure of it.

* * * *

Skeet glanced at his phone, *finally*. The text was in code, from a burner being used at the moment by Agent Blake Cochran. He kept hearing rumors his new partner was in Greece on a big top-secret case. That couldn't be further from the truth. Once again, Director Stanley Burns had come through for him. Blake was one of the best agents Skeet had ever worked with. If he could just rein in his temper and follow the rules a little better, he'd have no problem moving up the ranks.

Moondance Ridge

"Am I boring you?" Special Agent in Charge, Kyle Donahue asked his subordinate. Skeeter Perkins was even cockier these days than he had been before - something Donahue hadn't thought possible. He would have to go straight to Burns on this one. The Director created the problem, he could deal with it.

"Not at all," Skeet said impatiently. He glanced at his watch. He could give the insufferable prick ten more minutes but not a second more. If he didn't dislike the man so much, he might actually feel sorry for him. Since the completion of their case in Mount Haven, the guy had shown his true colors and then some. Kyle Donahue used to be tolerable. These days, he was on a power trip, determined to put Agent Skeeter Perkins in his rightful place. Well, the guy was in for a disappointment. If he went to Stan one more time, he was going to find himself running a satellite office in backwoods Nebraska.

"I want you to handle this case yourself," Donahue ordered. "You'll need to head out of town in the morning. Plan accordingly, you'll be in Miami until we can wrap this one up. We need to catch this guy before he moves on. Could take weeks... or longer." He studied Skeet, clearly waiting for an objection.

"I assume you cleared this with Director Burns," Skeet said confidently. Of course, he hadn't cleared anything with the head of the FBI. Donahue believed this was a local matter. A power play between him; as the local SAC, and one of his men. It wasn't. Everyone in the Bureau knew Skeet no longer went on extended trips... to anywhere. Not even the Special Agent in Charge would change that. Although, in light of the current situation, that actually might change. Donahue didn't need to know that though. And, this topic was not up for debate.

"You take your orders from me, Perkins," Donahue was turning a bright shade of pink. He didn't like to be challenged in front of others. You would think he'd learn from his previous mistakes. This wasn't the first time he tried to pull this trick in front of a room full of agents. In all likelihood, it wouldn't be the last. "I say you're going to Miami. Pack for Miami."

Skeet glanced at his watch, less than ten but close enough. He stood and left the room without a backwards glance. Donahue could interpret that response any way he wanted. The instant he was in his car, he dialed the number.

"You alone?" Blake asked in greeting.

"Why? You want me to talk dirty?" Skeet grinned.

"How soon can you get to Detroit?" Blake asked, ignoring the jibe.

"If I can get a flight, tonight. What's up?"

"I haven't been able to determine if the boss is dirty," Blake admitted. "He's a desk jockey, doesn't spend much time out in the field. It's going to be hard to know one way or the other. But, I hit on a guy... Agent Troy Darrow. He is most definitely as dirty as they come."

"How do you know?" Skeet asked. He didn't question Blake's assertion, he just wanted the facts before he spoke with Stan.

"I watched him rough up a guy," Blake admitted. "He was looking for information, but I couldn't get close enough to hear on what. He took whatever he got straight to the casino. There's no doubt, trust me."

"I do," Skeet sighed. "I'll report in, update the boss; then, I'll check on flights. I'll text you the time. Meet me at the airport, and we'll figure out a plan."

"Out," Blake said as he ended the call.

Best to do this one in person. Moments later, Skeet pulled into his driveway and slowly made his way up the walk. Angela said she was ready for this, but was he? "Hon? Where are you?"

"In the kitchen," Angela called back. "What's up?" She glanced around in question then frowned when she saw her husband's face. "It's time?"

"I'm afraid so," Skeet moved forward and pulled her into his arms. "You sure about this?"

"Positive," she said as she swallowed the lump in her throat. "Laney's going to stay in town no matter how long this takes. We'll be fine. I promise."

"I don't like it, but I can't come up with another solution," Skeet said soberly. "Believe me, I've tried."

Angela pushed up on her toes and pressed her lips to her husband's. "It's been long enough. We both knew this day would come, eventually. I'm lucky enough to have Laney by my side. Don't fret about this. You can't go into a case distracted. I'll go pack, give me just a minute. Do they know we're coming?"

"Not yet," Skeet admitted. "I needed to talk to you first. Go pack, I'll call Stan

* * * *

The couple pulled up to the gate and waited. Aston stepped forward and watched Skeet roll down the window. "He's waiting for you," the guard informed him. "Evening ma'am."

Angela grinned. "Hey, Aston. How's the family?"

"Right as rain," he took a step back. "The boss seemed pretty anxious when I called up. I won't keep you. Good to see you both. I'll say "hey" to the family."

"Be sure and do that," Angela said cheerily as they pulled through the iron gates and down the elaborate drive. "Why do you think Stan is anxious?"

"Same reason I am," Skeet reached out and took his wife's hand in his. "We'll both be happy when this particular case is over."

"Okay," she knew not to ask questions. Skeet had already told her as much as he could, which wasn't much. "I'll be waiting when you get back. Please, don't worry about me. The security here is better than Fort Knox. Laney and I will have a wonderful visit while you take care of business."

Skeet stepped from the car and moved around the vehicle to get the door for his wife. He loved her more than words could say. This was going to be hard on her, he hadn't gone out of town for an undetermined length of time without her since the abduction. She was nearly over it now; as much as a person could get over what his wife had gone through. He just hated leaving her alone this way. He'd promised her, the instant he found her, he would never leave her alone again.

Moondance Ridge

"Stop it, Skeet," Angela scolded. "I know what you promised and I understand. Things change. Life can't always be controlled. You have to do this. It's time, we both know that. It's the next step. I need to do this, for me and for you. It's the last restriction binding us to the past. Let's make the most of it and never look back."

They had reached the front door. Skeet wrapped his arms around his wife's waist and pulled her close, pressing a gentle kiss to her lips before resting his forehead to hers. "I love you, baby."

The door opened and Director Stanley Burns stood tall and proud. "And I'm sure she loves you, too. Get inside, we need to talk."

Skeet frowned as the two of them stepped into the elaborate foyer.

"Angela," Laney Burns glided into the room. "Let me show you to your room." She paused to kiss Skeet on the cheek then gracefully ascended the stairs. Angela followed.

Stan watched the two women for several seconds then turned and headed for the study. Skeet followed. Once inside, Burns shut the door and moved to one of the lounge chairs.

"Something has happened," Skeet surmised. "Is Blake okay? I talked to him less than an hour ago."

"Blake is fine," Stan sighed. "I have two developments. First, I got another call from Kyle Donahue."

"About that," Skeet began.

"Nonsense," Stan interrupted. "No explanation necessary. He's overstepped this time. Demanding this and that as if I worked for him. He will never understand the pecking order if I don't do something drastic. By the time you get back, he'll be relocated. I'd like you to take his place, as SAC."

"Um..." Skeet frowned. How would that look to his peers?

"Trust me on this," Stan assured him. "I've got it covered and nobody will think you got some kind of special treatment or that Kyle got the boot so you could have his job. I'm going to be holding interviews. As far as anyone knows, you were just one of the many I considered for the position. Rather than follow me to Washington for this impromptu promotional process, you'll head to Detroit as planned. Blake needs your help out there."

"I talked to Blake before we came over," Skeet stood and ran his hands through his hair. "He can't get a bead on Percy Seeger; apparently, the man rarely steps out of the office."

"I was afraid of that," Burns said, frowning. "I'm not sure he's dirty, maybe just complacent."

"We'll figure it out," Skeet promised. "He does have one name, Troy Darrow. Blake is sure he's in Zarconi's pocket. He's done all he can on his own and said he needs my help."

"I agree, it's time for you to head to Detroit," Stan reiterated as he relaxed further into his chair. "Angela will stay here with Laney. It's safer here. And this way, she won't be alone and you won't worry so much."

"I'll worry," Skeet disagreed. "But yeah, if she's here I won't panic."

"If you need to come back, to check on her or whatever, do it. This case is important, but it's not going anywhere. I need your

Moondance Ridge

mind clear if we're going to succeed. This has to be legal, all on the up and up. No shortcuts. I do not want Dominic Zarconi getting off on a technicality."

"I agree," Skeet sighed. "I need to leave tonight. You got an in? On a flight that is, headed for Detroit?"

"Actually," Stan brightened. "I think I might; but first, there's been another development."

"Oh?" Skeet asked, what else could possibly go wrong?

"Yeah," Stan sobered. "DeRossi got a call. We've been monitoring his communication since he entered our humble eight-foot cell. Nothing for years-then all of a sudden, he gets a call from Nico Depiro."

"The one that got away?" Skeet said softly. "I thought he moved to New York."

"He did," Stan affirmed. "The call was cordial, a little too cordial for my liking. They talked about coffee beans."

"Sure," Skeet settled back in his chair. "Because that's what two mob guys discuss the first time they make contact in years."

"No doubt it was code, but so far nobody has cracked it," Stan frowned. "We all believe Nico is a hitman. We knew that when we took down DeRossi's organization we just couldn't prove it. If DeRossi ordered a hit... we have no idea who he's after."

"Why tell me?" Skeet asked. "What does this have to do with Detroit? As far as I'm aware, there aren't any coffee bean entrepreneurs in Michigan."

174

"One of my guys sent me a report," Stan explained. "The ties are flimsy at best, but the theory is plausible. He has connected Nico, through his mother to his Aunt Zaphrina Zaraconi. My guy thinks Nico is now working for Zaphrina."

"And Zaphrina is connected to Dominic how?"

"She's married to him," Stan provided.

"So DeRossi's hitman is the nephew of Dominic by marriage," Skeet sighed. "Can't be coincidental."

"No," Stan agreed. "Be careful. DeRossi's put a hit on you and the Cooper brothers. In the right crowd, you're worth more dead than alive. It could get ugly if anyone recognizes you."

"I'll keep an eye out," Skeet said as he stood. "I'll also have someone watch Nico. I have a contact in New York I can tap. That call might be a coincidence, on the other hand... it could be a connection to whatever is going down in Detroit. Eventually we'll figure it out. Now, you need to arrange my transportation; and I want to talk to Angie before I go."

* * * *

Two hours later, Skeeter Perkins was making his way across the tarmac headed for the private jet of one Tyrone Hollick - esteemed real estate mogul, billionaire playboy extraordinaire and Stanley Burns favorite golfing partner. He ascended the stairs and came face to face with a man in his mid-sixties, distinguished, dressed in a polo and slacks, two drinks in his hand. He had salt and pepper hair, which was thick and perfectly combed, not one hair out of place. *Nature or imitation*? Skeet couldn't begin to guess.

Moondance Ridge

"Welcome aboard, mate," Tyrone said with a smile. "It's nice to finally meet you." He held out one of the glasses in greeting.

"Thanks again for the lift," Skeet said as he sniffed the rim. *Bourbon.* Not as good as scotch, but it'd do.

"Stan said you were in a bind," he turned and headed into the main section of the aircraft. "Unfortunately, something has come up and I'm afraid business calls. You may not see me for most of the flight. But please, make yourself at home. The fridge is stocked and once we're airborne, the cable will work. I planned to watch the game. Guess that's out now. Anyway, glad to have you on board. Maybe next time we can talk about Stanley. I do love an embarrassing antidote about my biggest competitor. It gives a fairly mundane game like golf an intriguing twist. At my age, you have to be more creative when it comes to entertainment. Anyway, Misty will get you anything you want. Excuse me," he added as he answered his ringing phone and disappeared into what Skeet assumed was an office.

A woman appeared and walked Skeet through the flight instructions. She tuned the television to ESPN then shut it down until they were safely in the air, cruising at altitude. Skeet grinned. If he had to travel, this was definitely the way to go.

* * * *

Theresa stepped through the back door and immediately spotted Bailey. She looked stressed and maybe a little upset.

"Hey, Theresa," Bailey said immediately.

"Is everything okay," Theresa asked hesitantly.

176

"Yeah," Bailey tried to sound upbeat. "I just got some bad news from our liquor supplier. Apparently, the truck transporting our delivery rolled and the entire load was destroyed. He needs me to inventory our supply and get back to him with the bottom line. He can only provide a fraction of the order and only those things that are absolutely necessary." She shrugged. "Looks like my evening just got a lot busier. I'll have to visually check our stock, then list what we'll need to get through the weekend... and we have a game this Saturday."

"Sorry," Theresa cringed. "Do you need any help?"

"I think I'm good," Bailey told her. "But I could really use a minute with Tony. I know you're off duty and came here tonight specifically to meet with him, but do you mind?"

"Not at all," Theresa reached out and grabbed the clipboard Bailey was holding. "I'll get started on the inventory while I wait. Let me know when you're finished."

Before Bailey could argue, Theresa was down the hall and stepping into the large storage room. She frowned, worried. Clearly, Theresa didn't know what the men were plotting... yet. What would her reaction be when she learned the plan? When she realized the guys were going to Detroit. Not good, Bailey was sure of that. If only the woman would let her help. Bailey turned and headed for the family eating area. She happened to know Tony was hanging out on the tame side of the building, rather than the bar tonight.

Tony smiled at Bailey and waited. The woman clearly had something on her mind.

"Mind if I join you for a minute?" she asked.

"Not at all, but Theresa should be here any minute."

"Actually, she's in the back. I'll get her after I talk to you. She said it was okay," Bailey added.

"What's up?" Tony asked, hoping Bailey wasn't here to try to stop him, to talk him out of joining Rowdy on this trip to Detroit.

"I've been thinking," she began as she settled across from him. "When I left, when I ran and went into hiding..."

Tony reached out and took Bailey's hand. "That's all in the past now."

"When I disappeared," she continued. "I was only thinking of myself. I panicked. I decided it was the only way to deal with the threat. I was terrified of Cole and Reese and I believed it was necessary to shut out everyone in my life if I wanted to survive. I was wrong and I'm sorry. Until recently, I didn't really consider how that might impact the people who loved me."

Tony sat back, wondering if the situation with Theresa had brought this on.

"What I'm trying to say is... I'm sorry," Bailey repeated. "I was selfish. I know that now. I keep wanting to scream at Theresa or shake some sense into her. Somehow force her to talk to me, to let me in, but I know it wouldn't do any good. Because if anyone had done that to me, I would have rejected it. I feel helpless and frustrated and..."

"Abandoned?" Tony asked.

"No, but I'm sure you did. I wish I could go back, take away all the pain I caused you," she said. "There are so many things I'd do differently, but I can't. All I can do is say I finally understand. I finally figured it out, and I'm not proud of the way I handled things. I hate knowing how frustrated and hurt you must have been when I disappeared without a word. Especially when you tried so hard to get me to trust you. I also feel like I should say this... while you're there, in Detroit, remember that Theresa isn't thinking straight. When you tell her about the trip, she might insist on dealing with the problem herself. In fact, I'd bet on it. I know you won't let her do that but be prepared for anything. No matter what she says or does, I truly believe she is looking for someone to trust. Don't give up on her. She couldn't find a better confidant than you."

Tony stood and pulled Bailey to her feet. "I love you, too." He was choked up and at a loss for words so he just gave her a long, tight embrace.

Rowdy smiled as he stepped into the room and spotted Bailey and Tony. He was glad things were back to normal. He made a stop at the bar, grabbed two beers and headed for the duo.

"I know that look," Bailey said as she stepped away from Tony. "You two talk, I have work." She leaned in and gave Rowdy a quick kiss before heading across the nearly empty room. She knew that wouldn't last long, soon the place would be packed with patrons demanding their favorite concoction. She needed to get the inventory complete, so she'd be free to help Rowdy at the bar.

* * * *

Maggie pushed through the door and immediately spotted Bailey and Theresa. Her steps faltered and her heart felt like it was going to jump through her chest it was beating so fast. Why did the mere sight of Bailey always do this? They used to be such good

179

friends. Now, the woman just made her angry. Maggie sighed, seeing her like that with Theresa only intensified her emotions. She realized the anger was caused by her pain. She'd lost her best friend and it hurt. This was Tony Nazario's fault. If that man had never come to town everything would be fine and Bailey wouldn't be so chummy with the waitress. Well, they deserved each other. The three of them used people and discarded them like a pair of old shoes. They were self-absorbed human beings who only cared about money, prestige and attention. Maggie blinked back tears as she stepped into the office and tried to get lost in the paperwork.

Bailey was so focused on the job ahead, she didn't see Maggie at the desk until she was already inside the office. "Oh, sorry." She took a step back then straightened her spine and held her ground. "I need the inventory sheet, that one on the corner of the desk."

Maggie frowned. "Why? The delivery's not due until tomorrow."

"Because it's not coming, and I need to figure out what we ordered and what we are desperate for." She took a step toward the desk but stopped when Maggie picked up the paper.

"What do you mean they're not coming?" Maggie studied the printout. "We have a game this weekend. We need that delivery."

Bailey sighed. "That's why I need the invoice. The truck rolled. They want to make good, but supply is short for a few days. They need to know the essentials."

"When did you plan to tell me there was a problem?"

"I don't know Maggie, maybe never." Bailey was tired of this. She hated the back and forth that always went on these days when Maggie was in the room. Would the woman ever forgive her? Didn't look like it.

Maggie narrowed her eyes at the manager. "This might be the way you and that hotshot suit run your corporation, but around here..."

"Don't bring Tony into this," Bailey warned.

"Why?" Maggie stood. "He's the crux of the problem. Before he sauntered into town and graced all us little people with his presence, things were working just fine."

"You're not mad at my friend, you're mad at me," Bailey said wearily. "You don't know Tony, so don't take this out on him."

"I know you think he hangs the moon. You were willing to throw what you have with Rowdy away because of him, but where was he when you needed help?" Maggie challenged. "In New York hobnobbing with his elite friends, that's where. He couldn't be bothered to put his life on the line like we did. Us! I'm the one who was driving that car when it was pushed over a ledge. I'm the one who nearly drowned. I'm the one who sat up hour after hour scouring through documents to find you. Me, my husband and Rowdy. Tony wasn't even in the state."

"Tony had no idea where I was," Bailey said softly. "And that's my fault, not his."

* * * *

Theresa grabbed the pen and tried to make a notation but nothing came out. She pressed harder, still nothing. Frustrated, she began scribbling a circle at the top of the page. "Ugg," she tossed the empty pen in the trash and stepped into the hallway. The moment she heard the dispute, she stopped. *Now what?* Bailey and Maggie were arguing in the office, and that's the only place they had spare pens. She was about to turn when she realized they were discussing her.

"That man has torn this place apart and he's taking Rowdy with him," Maggie continued. "And on top of it, you seem to be best friends with the waitress now. What are you, the Three Musketeers? I can't say I'm surprised. Theresa is selfish, just like you and Tony are. You only allow people into your lives if you can get something from them. And Theresa, she's so self-centered, she couldn't even be there for Jase and Marnie. That family has been through so much pain. All he asked her for was a little enthusiasm, a little excitement and support, but she couldn't even give him that. Apparently, the only people Theresa has time for are drunk patrons at the end of a long night. Well, I don't care what she does in her free time but I do care that she's dragging Rowdy into this. He's sacrificed enough. He's risked enough. He doesn't need to fly halfway across the country to fix a problem created by that floosy. You know you're only going along with this because Tony's involved."

Theresa stood in wide-eyed shock. Maggie truly detested her. The woman had always been distant, but that wasn't a casual dislike, it was hate.

Bailey shifted and saw movement in the hallway. She took a step forward and spotted Theresa. The horrified look on her friend's face told her everything she needed to know. She rushed to the doorway hoping she could fix it. "Theresa, she didn't mean that. She doesn't understand."

"I'm leaving," Theresa decided. "Here's the inventory sheet, Bailey. Tony's waiting for me."

Bailey watched as Theresa rushed through the door that led to the main section of the building. The girl had just received another blow, one that was completely unnecessary. Maggie might be her friend, but she was out of line. "Maggie," she began.

"I didn't know she was there," Maggie said, frowning.

"Then I guess you should be careful what you say. That way, you won't destroy what little hope a woman has left after her entire world has been ripped out from under her."

"I have no idea what you're talking about," Maggie said dismissively.

"That woman has been through more than you or I could imagine," Bailey began. "Tony and Rowdy... this trip? It's her only hope. That's why they're going to Detroit. That's why Rowdy is risking his life. That's why we both believe she's worth helping. It has nothing to do with Tony's involvement. I realize you're pregnant and everyone wants to protect you, but this has gotten out of hand. I've gone along, tolerated your mood swings, and made excuses for you - until now. I'm done. You have hurt a woman who's endured more than enough heartache in her lifetime. She doesn't need the pain you just inflicted simply because you feel the need to throw a tantrum.

I don't know what's wrong with you. You haven't been yourself for weeks. I do know this angry, malicious, depressed person you've become isn't the woman I became friends with. I know you're still upset with me. Fine. Be angry if you need to, you can even hate me and never talk to me again. But treating a victim like Theresa with such contempt? That is not the Maggie Cooper I

Moondance Ridge

know. Hating Tony simply because he exists? Well, I never thought I'd see the day when someone as caring and accepting as you behaved that way. It's none of my business, but I truly believe there is something wrong with you. Physically, medically. For the baby's sake, I hope you will seek professional help." Bailey turned and silently left the room.

Maggie waited until she was sure Bailey was gone, then she let the tears flow. Bailey was right, she wasn't acting like herself. She had no idea what was going on with Theresa. She only knew Rowdy was headed to Detroit to deal with a dangerous problem. Maybe it was time to corner her husband and insist he tell her the truth, all of it. Not just the parts he thought she could handle.

Theresa pushed through the door and glanced around, looking for her date. It only took a second to find the two men. Tony and Rowdy were huddled together, obviously in plotting mode. She started for the table and stopped dead in her tracks as realization hit her. She finally understood what Maggie was saying and she was furious. Rowdy glanced up and smiled, which only fueled her anger. That got Tony's attention and he too looked her way. The instant their eyes met, Theresa was marching across the room. She stopped directly in front of their table and glared at the two men. "What in the hell do you two think you're doing?" she demanded.

Rowdy's cocky grin lit up his face as he glanced at Tony then back to Theresa. "I think I'm enjoying a cold one," he drawled as he lifted the bottle and took a slow deliberate sip of his beer. "What do you think I'm doing?"

"Don't get cute with me Rowdy Cooper," Theresa countered. "Maggie already told me you think you're going to Detroit."

Rowdy wondered why Mags had mentioned the trip to his pissed off waitress. They had both agreed to stay out of it and let Tony break the news himself. She must have had a reason although he couldn't imagine what it could be. "We are going to Detroit, Theresa. I have a very specific message for one Dominic Zarconi. One that needs to be delivered in person."

"I won't let you do this," Theresa said, frantic at the prospect of Rowdy and Tony coming face to face with that madman.

"I'm afraid you can't stop me," Rowdy said soberly. "Theresa, look at you. Just the mention of that man's name has you on the edge of panic. It's past time someone put a stop to this. He's a bully, one you need out of your life for good. Tony and I can make that happen, you need to trust us."

Tony hadn't spoken yet, he was watching Theresa intently. Her breathing had become ragged, her hands were shaking and she could barely stand. "Theresa, come and sit down." Tony waited but when Theresa didn't respond, he added, "Please?"

Theresa reluctantly slid onto the bench next to Tony. "You don't understand," she tried to swallow but the fear she felt knowing Dom was about to kill two more people she cared about was too much. "You don't know what that man is capable of."

Tony put an arm around Theresa's shoulder and moved in closer. "It's going to be okay. I promise, we can handle this."

Theresa jumped to her feet and glared at the two men. "No!" She inhaled a deep breath and slowly exhaled, trying to calm the panic that had taken over every inch of her body. "I can't let you do this. I won't. Dom is dangerous. He's ruthless and violent. Nobody can stop him...nobody," she reiterated. "Don't you get it? If you confront him he'll kill you, just like my husband. Shawn thought he could handle this, too. Now he's dead. If you won't back off for me, do it for Bailey. She can't lose the two people that mean the most to her. I know how it feels to watch that monster kill the love of your life. I won't let Bailey suffer like I have." Theresa leaned forward and pressed both palms on the table. "This is my problem. I'll handle it...alone. I want both of you to butt out." Then she turned and practically ran out of the bar.

The two men watched as the heavy wooden door slammed shut. Seconds later, Tony stood. "I'll go," he had only taken two steps when Rowdy called his name. Tony paused then turned to face his new friend, "Yeah?"

"This doesn't change anything. Not for me. I'm leaving for Detroit in the morning. I'll understand if you change your mind but I'm going with or without you. That man sent two of his goons to my town...to my bar for the sole purpose of intimidating and threatening one of mine. The coward is going to learn a valuable lesson. One I intend to teach him in person. Nobody messes with a Cooper. Nobody."

Tony grinned. "I have to disagree with the part about Theresa being yours, but I'm on board with the rest. Nothing has changed. The plane leaves at eight. Nobody messes with what's mine either, man." The menacing look on his face held the promise of what was to come for Dominic Zarconi. A fate the man would never see coming.

Tony stepped through the kitchen door and paused, listening. The second he heard Theresa's muffled cry he was across the room, marching down the hall, headed for the guest room. He stepped into the doorway and paused. The stubborn, independent woman was a sobbing mess. He took a minute to assess the situation. She looked completely shattered, but she was also the most beautiful, challenging, infuriating woman he had ever laid eyes on. In that moment, he realized he'd fallen for her. He was head over hills in love. *Damn.* Instead of celebrating the epiphany, he was torn and confused. He didn't know how to handle her right now. He didn't know how to deal with his own feelings. She'd just declared, in no uncertain terms, that her deceased husband was the love of her life. How could he compete with that? And had she really witnessed his death? Surely the trauma would make that bond run even deeper. He didn't stand a chance. Wasn't that the story of his life? Always falling for the wrong woman? Always walking away broken and defeated? When would he learn? Every broken soul he came across had a story...a history. One that didn't include him. He wasn't some kind of hero junkie so why did the damaged ones always draw him in like a magnet? He ran his hand through his hair in frustration. When he looked up, he realized Theresa was staring at him.

"What do you want?" she asked as she tossed a pair of jeans into a suitcase.

"Where are you going?" Tony avoided the question. He didn't have an answer for that one right now.

"I told you this is my problem," she said casually as she yanked on a drawer and started pulling out socks. "If anyone is going to Detroit, it's me."

Tony was across the room and blocking her path in an instant. Theresa turned to pack another t-shirt and collided with his chest. His strong arms wrapped around her waist to prevent her from falling. "No," he said shaking his head. "I won't let you. Those two men were here to abduct you. You'd be giving him exactly what he wants."

Moondance Ridge

Theresa pushed Tony away and took a step back. She was furious with him. She would not take orders from anyone...not even Tony. She straightened her spine and glared at him in defiance.

Tony realized his mistake the second the words left his mouth. This was not the way to deal with Theresa Regan. She was headstrong and independent. She would not tolerate being told what to do. His temper was speaking for him again. That would never work. He needed to take a step back and come at this from another direction. "I'm sorry, I didn't mean that." Tony aimed for soothing and hoped he hit his mark. "What I'm trying to say is that Rowdy and I are better suited for this. We've both handled men like Dominic before. Tea, you have to trust someone."

Theresa's eyes widened at the casual nickname. She hadn't been called that in years. Emotion flooded her mind and she slowly lowered herself to the edge of the bed, shocked at the intense feeling of loss that overcame her.

"You have to let us handle this. Please, just stay here in Mount Haven where Coop can protect you." Tony glanced at Theresa and frowned. *Now what?* He'd said something wrong again. She was sitting on the edge of the bed in a daze...but why? Then it hit him. He moved to her side and slowly sat next to her. "That belongs to him, too? I'm sorry Theresa. I wasn't thinking. I should have known Shawn would have a nickname for you. I won't use it again."

"Not Shawn, Zach." She looked up and tried to blink the tears from her eyes. "He was my hero. Zach was so full of life. He was seven years older than me, which made him perfect. I grew up idolizing Zach. He was the cool kid...the one that had all the answers. Then one day, he was gone. Shawn actually hated that nickname and refused to use it. He said it wasn't classy enough for me, but when Zach said it...it was exactly right. He made me feel special. It was something only the two of us shared, like our own little secret I guess. It's okay if you use it, Tony. I don't mind, you just took me by surprise that's all. In fact, I think I like it. I think Zach would like it, too."

Tony took Theresa's hand in his. "I'm sorry. You've lost so much." He reached up and brushed a tear from beneath her left eye. "If I could take it all away, shelter you from more sorrow, you know that I would."

Theresa rested her head against Tony's chest and sighed. She'd hurt him today. She hadn't meant to. But the minute the words were out of her mouth, she knew she'd caused him pain. She'd been so angry, and she was really just trying to make a point to Rowdy. Trying to make him understand he couldn't risk his life for her. Bailey needed him and Tony. After everything she'd gone through with her family and Reese, she needed to be surrounded by loyal friends and the man she loved. If anything happened to Tony or Rowdy, Theresa would never forgive herself. She couldn't live with it. So, she'd flown off the handle and hurt the only man that had made her feel again...the one person that helped her understand it was okay to live. "I'm sorry," she whispered.

Tony wrapped his arms around Theresa and pressed a soft kiss to her temple. "Sorry for what, sweetheart? You have nothing to be sorry for."

Theresa pushed away, stood and began to pace. "I hurt you and I think I need to explain."

Tony knew exactly what she was referring to, but he didn't need an explanation. He got it...a little too well, actually. He shook his head in an attempt to stop her.

Moondance Ridge

Theresa turned and stood before the large bedroom window. She wasn't ready for this, but it was time. She had to trust someone and she did trust Tony. She only hoped she could get through this without breaking down. Being wrapped in Tony's arms as she wept for her husband wouldn't be fair to any of them.

"Look, Theresa," Tony began. "I understand. I knew from the beginning there was someone else. It's okay. You still love your husband. I can't fault you for that. I had hoped that somehow you might be ready to give us a shot, but now I know. It's too soon for you. That doesn't mean things have to change. You and me...we can still be friends. You can still trust me. You can depend on me. You can confide in me. I'm here for you...in whatever way you need me." The words tasted bitter as they left his tongue but he meant every one of them. If he couldn't have a relationship with Teresa, if they couldn't be intimate... he would just be her friend. Her confidant. The man she could lean on until she got back on her feet.

Theresa sighed deeply. This constant need to live in the past was ruining her future. She moved back to stand in front of Tony and held out her hand. "We need to talk. Not in here, let's move into the living room. I have a lot to tell you."

Tony stood wearily and wondered what tiny sliver of information she was going to share. He'd take whatever she was willing to give. The more knowledge he and Rowdy had when they confronted Dominic, the better. But, he wouldn't get his hopes up. He'd done that before. No, Theresa wouldn't give him much and he worried that this was some kind of tactic on her part to distract him from the real issue. He was still going to Michigan; and with any luck, he'd convince her to stay in Mount Haven where it was safe.

The couple walked hand in hand down the hallway and settled onto the large comfortable couch. They sat in silence for several minutes...both lost in their own thoughts.

Theresa was the first to speak. "When I said that Shawn was the love of my life I meant it, but..."

"Theresa, it's okay." Tony said again.

"But..." she said more forcefully, "that was a previous life." She moved in closer and nestled her body against Tony's. "Our mothers were best friends. I knew Zach and Shawn all my life. We would have remained close, even if Shawn and I hadn't fallen in love. My relationship with Zach proved that. Mom always said Zach was the Yin to my Yang... even as a baby we had a special bond. Anyway, my mom and Wendy met in college and hit it off immediately. After graduation, mom went on to law school and Wendy moved to New York. That didn't impact the friendship though. I think it only made them closer. Each year, our families got together for an extended family vacation. We grew up together. Shawn and Zach were my best friends.

Oh, I had girlfriends as a kid, but nobody compared to the Regan brothers. They were both so cool and charismatic...I missed them all year long and couldn't wait for our summer vacation to begin. I was fifteen when our parents were killed. Zach and Shawn were there for me in a big way. I felt so alone until those two showed up on my doorstep. Zach promised that everything was going to be okay...and it was for a while. When Zach was killed, Shawn and I felt like we only had each other. We isolated ourselves from everyone else. When Shawn was killed..." Theresa paused. How could she explain the hole that was left in her life? The intense feeling of despair and desperation she felt from that loss. Could anyone really understand it?

191

Moondance Ridge

Tony leaned down and pressed his lips to the top of Theresa's head. "It's okay. I understand, really I do."

"But that's the thing, Tony. I don't think you do." She shifted so she could look him in the eyes. "I loved him...more than words can express. I think somewhere deep in my heart I always will. But because I loved him, you think I can't love again. You think the love I had for him will always prevent me from moving on, from loving someone else, from giving myself to someone else completely, from building a relationship with another man. I think that love will help me form a stronger bond. I can love again, Tony. And, I don't want us to just be friends. We're already more than that...so much more. I don't want to take a step back...not with you. But if that's something you need, I'll do it. I'll give you space because I care, and I know how difficult this must be for you."

Her thoughts were interrupted when Tony pulled her onto his lap and pressed his lips to hers.

Tony didn't know if she meant what she was saying, but he wasn't about to give her the chance to change her mind. He had never felt this way about any other woman in his life. He planned to spend every minute she would let him showing her just how much she meant to him. And maybe with time, she would come to love him, too. What they had was fragile. It certainly wasn't a guarantee, but it was real... a hope of something lasting and permanent if they could only eliminate the pending threat. Tony pulled back a little uncomfortable at the realization of just how much he loved her. How much he wanted this chance. How easy it would be for her to destroy him completely. He should run...but all he felt at the moment was love and contentment. He could run later, tonight he needed to know everything. He needed to know what had happened to her parents. What had happened to Zach and the details of what had happened to Shawn. "Can you tell me about it?" He watched her, waiting for the tiniest indication she was going to deflect.

Theresa swallowed. "I think I have to." She looked at him with terrified eyes. She trusted Tony. She trusted Rowdy. It was time to tell them everything. It was time to ask for help. "But do you think Rowdy would mind joining us? I really only want to tell the story once and if you two are going to Detroit, you need to know everything."

"So, you've come to grips with that fact?" Tony asked.

"No," Theresa said honestly. "I don't think it's a good idea. In fact, the thought of you stepping foot in that city scares me to death but I also know nothing I say is going to stop you. I still might go with you, but we can make that decision together. We'll talk about it after I tell you the rest. After I tell you my story."

Tony pulled his phone from his pocket and dialed Rowdy. He explained Theresa's request then said goodbye and ended the call. "Bailey is coming, too. I hope that's okay. I couldn't say no. She has a right to know what Rowdy is walking into."

"And you," Theresa added. She stood and walked to the kitchen returning with a can of soda. "Do you want anything?"

"No," Tony shook his head. "Come over here for a minute."

Theresa returned to the couch and sat down next to Tony. She set the cold can on top of the coffee table then gave him her undivided attention.

"Does my relationship with Bailey bother you?" he finally asked.

Moondance Ridge

"No," Theresa said honestly. "At first it did. I think I was jealous. I mean she has this amazing man in her life already. Seriously, Rowdy is hot and sweet and kind. Then you come to town, and she had you too. For a while there, I thought you were a jealous ex-boyfriend here to win back her love. It almost made it worse when I found out you were like a brother to her. It felt like Bailey had it all, you know? Bailey had everything and I had nothing."

"And now?" Tony asked, truly curious.

"Now I understand. You have the kind of relationship with Bailey that I had with Zach. I could never fault her or you for having that kind of bond. I loved and adored Zach the instant I met him. Even as a baby I was drawn to him. It's difficult to explain, but I think that's the kind of connection you have with Bailey. It's the reason I'm so worried about you facing down a man like Dominic Zarconi. If Bailey loses you over this...she'll never be the same. She'll probably hate me and she should...this whole mess is my fault."

"None of this is your fault," Tony insisted just as the doorbell rang. He stood then paused. "And we both know Bailey isn't the only one that would be devastated if anything happened to me. I won't be the reason you suffer again. I won't be the cause of more heartache for you. I'm not going to let anything happen to me or Rowdy. Please just try to trust me on that." He crossed the room and opened the door.

Rowdy and Bailey stepped inside and headed straight for the living room.

Bailey sat down next to Theresa, pulled her into a one-armed hug, then took Theresa's hand in support. "You're not alone,"

Bailey said softly. "We're here to help you. Let us help. I know how hard that is. I know what it's like to feel like the weight of the world is on your shoulders and there is nobody out there you can trust. I'm sorry for the things Maggie said. I hope you won't let her get to you. She's not herself right now. She didn't mean any of it. Now is not the time to break off all ties with everyone, or to reject help. I did that," she turned to smile at Tony. "I even pushed Tony away, and I couldn't regret that more. He is the one person I knew I could trust, but my fear stopped me from accepting his help. Learn from my mistakes. Let these two help you. They are probably the only two people in the world that can."

"Thank you, Bailey. That means a lot to me," Theresa said sincerely. "But after you hear what we're up against, you might change your mind. I promise that's okay. I'll understand if you don't want either one of them involved when you know the truth." Theresa swallowed hard. She didn't want to think about the life she'd be leading if they changed their minds...if they decided it was too much and they all wanted out.

"Nobody is going to change their mind," Rowdy assured her as he took a seat across from the couch. "I need you to tell us everything. Do not leave anything out. Tony and I will need all the information we can get if we're going to take this man down." He smiled when Theresa started to protest. "I know you don't think that's possible, but we might have a few surprises up our sleeves. Don't count us out just yet."

Theresa took a deep breath then focused on Tony. He was her rock now. Zach had always held that position in her life, but Tony had somehow gotten under her skin and filled that void almost immediately. It was strange really, he was nothing like either of the Regan brothers, but he filled a void their absence had left so

Moondance Ridge

completely. "I know this is going to be a long story, but I think I need to start at the beginning."

"Take your time. We're in no rush," Bailey assured her.

"My parents were Jenny and Steve Tanner," Theresa began. "They met mom's final year of law school. Dad was working at the university at the time. He was just finishing up an internship and was looking forward to becoming a college professor the following year. The two of them got married right after mom graduated. Dad had already been offered a position at Wayne State University, and mom gave him her full support. She didn't care where she practiced law, she just knew she wanted to be a prosecutor. They moved to Detroit a few days after their honeymoon. Mom studied hard, took the bar and was immediately hired part time at the local D.A.'s office.

Wendy, Shawn and Zach's mother, was already living in New York by then. She was my mother's best friend since their first year in college. Her fashion design career had finally taken off and she was a rising star in New York. By this time, she had married Kendrick Regan, a stock trader on Wall Street. The two of them were doing fairly well for themselves. Both couples were busy with their own schedules but always found time to spend the summers together. As the years went on, the four of them grew even closer. Wendy and Kendrick gave birth to Zach and then Shawn. Mom continued to pursue her career as a lawyer. I was born a couple years after Shawn. My mother had gained a reputation for being tough on crime. She was popular with nearly everyone, except the criminals of course. So, she quickly moved up the ranks and became the youngest lead prosecutor Detroit has ever had. Our families were close, and I grew up with Zach and Shawn. They were like distant brothers that I only saw in the summer.

Everything changed when I was fifteen. I had joined a business club in high school and decided to attend a competition in marketing. My parents were so proud of me when I won first place in the region. Unfortunately, that meant the state competition would be held during the first week of our scheduled vacation with the Regan's. Zach and Shawn offered to stay with me while I competed, and then Zach was going to drive the three of us out to the cabin. It was a summer oasis the Regan's had purchased years before. Our parents agreed to the arrangement and decided to fly out as originally planned. Zach was twenty-two at the time. I didn't understand why my parents were so surprised when he offered to be our chauffer."

Bailey laughed. "He must have cared for you a great deal. I can't imagine a guy in his early twenties offering to take a road trip with his seventeen-year-old brother and a fifteen-year-old family friend."

"I know, right?" Theresa said. "I get it now, you'd think spending time with us would be a major downer for a hot young guy... especially since he was single. But, Zach was always amazing like that. And, it was a dream come true for me. I was fifteen, trying to pretend I was something special and the two coolest guys I knew were taking me on a road trip."

"Okay, we get the picture already. Teenage fantasy in technicolor...move on already." Rowdy grinned and gave Bailey a friendly wink.

"Anyway," Theresa continued, scowling at Rowdy's interruption. "The Regan's flew into town and arrived early in the afternoon. Our families had a wonderful dinner together and caught a movie before returning to our house to play board games late into the evening. Our parents planned to fly out the following morning,

197

Moondance Ridge

but Kendrick received a phone call notifying him their pilot had been hospitalized for food poisoning. Wendy was beside herself, he wasn't just another employee, the pilot had worked for them a long time; and they trusted him completely. Kendrick decided to call in a favor and was able to find a replacement pilot that could fly on short notice. Mom was worried about the sudden change, but the Regan's told her things like that happened all the time. I guess in their world, it did. Not in ours.

The plane crashed not long after takeoff killing everyone on board. That day we lost everything, we just didn't know it. When the final report came in, the crash was attributed to a mechanical failure. They said the plane was not maintained properly and negligence caused the engine to stall resulting in loss of control. The plane crashed into a building killing six additional people. The family of the pilot sued, the loved ones of the people inside the building sued and Shawn, Zach and I were left with nothing. Well, almost nothing. Shawn and Zach lost everything, their mother's business, their home, the cabin and every penny their parents had to their names. After the verdict, they moved to Detroit to live with me. Since the plane belonged to the Regan's and my parents were considered victims, I still had my house."

"Did you have to go into foster care?" Tony asked.

"No," Theresa smiled. "I would have, but Zach saved me...saved us. I knew he was going to petition the court to give him guardianship over Shawn. He was seventeen anyway, so the system wasn't the place for him. I was only fifteen though. I had no idea Zach petitioned for me as well. He was granted temporary custody. My house went into a trust that was managed by Zach. My parents had enough life insurance between them to cover funeral expenses and pay off the remaining mortgage. It was a major life changer for the Regan boys and in a way for me, too. Not financially, but things were so very different without my parents."

"So, that's how you all became a family," Bailey said in understanding.

"Yes, I guess so," Theresa agreed. "By that time, we already felt like family...just a summer family I guess. Now it was permanent. Full time and we had to get used to each other's constant presence. Zach quit college and got a job with the Detroit Chronicle. Life went on that way for nearly a year. Shawn graduated high school and Zach surprised him by announcing there was a trust. Their parents had set aside money in the boy's names for college. Because Zach was an adult and the money was his, not his parent's, the courts couldn't take it. He surprised us once again after I graduated when he announced there was enough for me, too. Shawn and I attended Wayne State on a reduced tuition program for the children of professors. Shawn didn't really qualify, but the Dean chose to bend the rules. Everyone liked dad and Zach had been there for me in my time of need." Theresa paused to glance around the room, suddenly realizing she'd left out a very important part of the story. "I need to take a step back. I forgot something important."

"Okay," Tony said in support. "What did you forget?"

"Mom was the District Attorney when she died. She had a reputation for being tough on crime and rarely lost a case. She had been gathering evidence on Dominic Zarconi and his organization for years. The guy was slick and nobody was ever willing to talk. Witnesses either disappeared or changed their stories before trial. She was frustrated but determined. A few weeks before they left on vacation, mom came across some very damaging evidence. There were two business owners, guys that were standing in the way of Zarconi's casino. One day, they suddenly disappeared. Mom said she could prove Dom was responsible. She was ecstatic and so confident she could win this time. I was just a stupid teenager, so I never paid attention to specifics; but I knew it was something big, and I was happy for her. She was finally going to take down a very bad man."

"Then they crashed," Rowdy said, not buying that as a coincidence.

"Then they crashed," Theresa confirmed. "Once I started college, Zach became obsessed. Life went on, but it changed. We didn't see much of Zach. He took assignments out of town a lot. Any free time he did have, was spent digging things up on Zarconi. A year later, Shawn graduated at the top of his class and got a job with Meditech. We decided to buy our own house, and Zach moved back into my parent's home to save money. We worried about him, but didn't realize just how much trouble he was actually in. One night, Zach called and asked us to come over for dinner. That's when he showed us all the evidence he had gathered against Dom. There was a lot. Stuff on the crash, evidence on specific crimes and a list of people who worked in the system and also worked for Dom.

There were so many crimes Dom was connected to but Zach couldn't get the Chronicle to run most of his articles. When they did give in, they were immediately harassed and threatened by Zarconi. Eventually, they refused to run anything that even hinted at his involvement in anything hinky. We believed we had enough evidence to finally make him pay, but we couldn't go to the police. Zach found at least three dirty cops in the Detroit PD, and we were pretty sure the new prosecutor was in Dom's pocket as well. We guessed there could be more, maybe one in every precinct. We didn't know what to do with the information Zach had. The three of us talked well into the night and finally decided to go to the FBI.

Zach insisted on handling it himself and promised to find a contact the following day."

"What happened?" Bailey asked, afraid she already knew.

"We were both busy, Shawn trying to prove himself at work and me with college but when we didn't hear from Zach, we knew something was wrong. We tried multiple times, for three days to contact him with no response. We knew something horrible had happened to Zach, it was the only explanation for his disappearance. We wanted to believe he was okay, just hiding out, looking for a contact or something ...but we knew. Zach never avoided our calls. He always called us back no matter what he was working on.

Shawn and I finally decided to start looking for him ourselves. We entered the old house and found it completely ransacked. Someone had been searching for information. We rushed to the basement...mom had installed a small safe behind a wall. She needed a place to secure her files when she brought home an important case. It was well hidden and very difficult to get to which is probably the only thing that saved it. All of Zach's hard work was still there, hidden away for safekeeping. It also contained a burner phone. When Shawn switched it on, there was one text from Zach. *Agent dirty. Fatal mistake. I love you guys and I'm sorry.*" Theresa paused as hot tears ran down her face. She missed Zach so much...nearly as much as she missed Shawn.

"So, we're not only up against dirty cops in the local PD," Rowdy surmised. "We're also dealing with feds on the take." He turned to Tony. "This could get a little sticky. You still in?"

"Absolutely," Tony said soberly. He'd dealt with criminals before but dirty cops? That was something new. He just hoped Rowdy knew how to handle it because he had no idea.

"I hate dirty cops!" Rowdy seethed. "They give us all a bad name."

Bailey took Rowdy's hand then focused on Theresa. "What happened to your parents' house? I mean, you said those men were here for money. Money Zach owed. Couldn't you sell the house to pay off the debt this Dominic guy says you owe?"

"Dom took it," she said soberly. "I secretly signed it over to Zach. He didn't even know, neither did Shawn at first. I wanted Zach to have something to show for all his sacrifices. He gave up so much to take care of me...of Shawn. He quit college and would never make Editor at the Chronicle because he didn't have a degree. He was going to pay for his love... for his selfless dedication to the two of us forever. I didn't want him to feel like he was a renter or a freeloader. I wanted the house to be Zach's and only Zach's. It was stupid and it backfired, anyway. Zach never even knew what I'd done."

"It wasn't stupid, it was sweet," Bailey disagreed.

"Dom wasn't satisfied with just killing Zach," Theresa continued. "He needed us to know he could take anything he wanted. He sued Zach's estate for defamation of character. He was so angry at him for those articles, the ones that were published. Plus, Zach took copies of his entire investigation to the FBI guy. I assume the entire packet was turned over to Dom. Zach was a thorn in his side. Zarconi finally found someone that he couldn't control; so, he killed Zach and took his house along with everything else he owned."

"If he knew you guys were Zach's family how did Shawn get involved? How did he get close enough to garner Zarconi's attention?" Tony asked.

"He knew Zach had a family, well a brother, he didn't know about me. Dom didn't bother to look into us, what we looked like, where we lived, what we did. We were insignificant I guess. He didn't care enough about us to look into who we were. All he knew was that Zach was Wendy and Kendrick's son and he had a brother. Steve, one of Zach's friends, took on the case. He was a pretty good attorney, but we all knew fighting Dominic Zarconi was futile. Steve went through the motions mostly to be a nuisance, but also to create distance between us and the mob. Apparently, it worked. Dom moved on, believing his threats and intimidation would keep Shawn in line. Zarconi is careful but arrogant."

"That doesn't sound right," Bailey objected. "Zach worked for the paper Why didn't Zarconi sue the Chronicle? How did he win a court case against a reporter for personal assets?"

"Threats...or subtle suggestions, I guess," Theresa answered. "Steve found out later that each of the jurors received little notes. One lady got a message taped to her back door telling her... *Your children want you to make the right decision.* That was it. She knew what she had to do to protect her kids. Every juror received something--just a note or a passing comment from a stranger...on the surface not even a threat. Eventually, the trial was over; and we lost the house to Zach's killer. We were both devastated. Dom had won, again.

I begged Shawn to let it go. That man had already killed our parents; and now, he'd murdered Zach. Shawn promised me he wouldn't pursue it, and he didn't...not at first. We tried to go on with our lives. Things were different; but we moved forward...sort of, for nearly two years. But, the loss, the grief, the entire situation ate at us constantly. We still had each other, but somehow as long as Zarconi was out there...it wasn't enough. Shawn stopped sleeping, I stopped eating...the stress and grief consumed us. I dropped out of school and barely left the house. Shawn worked all the time and rarely came home. We were both a mess and didn't know how to fix it.

I told myself it was over, that I could live with things the way they were as long as we stayed out of Zarconi's way. I knew I was fooling myself, but I couldn't face the truth. Shawn is the one that finally took action. He came home one day and told me he was going to quit his job at Meditech and work freelance with a couple college friends. It would give him more freedom to investigate Dom and still allow us to pay the bills. That was the beginning of the end. We sat at the kitchen table and discussed our options. If Shawn was going to pursue this, I decided to get a job as a waitress. We'd need the money to pay the bills. Shawn didn't like that part of the plan, but I wouldn't budge.

The next day Shawn gave his notice. He left a job he loved to become a freelance computer programmer. That's when we really started to drift apart. Shawn was never home. He was focused on Zarconi. I remember thinking he'd turned into Zach. I was terrified, sure I was going to lose him too. I sat by the phone constantly waiting for his call. A call that rarely came. A few weeks later, Shawn cautiously snuck in the back door and told me he was in. He'd been working the street, trying to gain access to Dominic's enterprise by being a thief. His hard work had paid off. Dom noticed him and immediately brought him into the fold. Shawn explained that he'd rented a rundown apartment on the other side of town, and we were going to have to be apart for a while. He claimed it had to be this way to protect me from Dominic. I went a little nuts and insisted we could deal with anything as long as we did it together. Shawn reluctantly gave in, and I became his live-in girlfriend."

"Were you two crazy!" Rowdy asked. "We're talking about a mob boss, a violent criminal that had killed both your parents and your brother. How exactly did a computer programmer and a college dropout think they were going to take down a man who paid off the cops and killed witnesses to stay out of jail?"

"We didn't know," Theresa admitted. "But, it wasn't right. We couldn't just go on like nothing had happened. Dominic Zarconi was ruining my marriage. We had to do something."

"Did it work?" Tony asked quietly? "Did Shawn find anything that could help?"

"Yes, and it got him killed," Theresa said in defeat. "Shawn was an ace at his job. Not the thief stuff. He was an amazing computer whiz. He somehow got into Dominic's computer and found a hidden hard drive. Shawn called it a ghost drive. He copied everything, but it didn't do us any good. It was encrypted. Those last few months of our marriage were amazing. We had a common goal, we were back together and we were finally fighting back. It felt like somehow, in spite of the odds, we were actually going to win this time."

"So, what happened?" Rowdy asked. Clearly the plan hadn't worked...Shawn was dead.

"Shawn said he needed the passcode for Dom's computer. He said the encryption was complicated and the only way to break the code was to install a keylogger on Dominic's hard drive and that had to be done in person," Theresa answered.

"Please tell me you didn't risk that on your own," Rowdy practically begged.

"We did," Theresa admitted. "We had a plan, and it would have worked if that FBI guy hadn't delayed us."

"What FBI guy?" Tony asked.

"I think he might be the one Zach was meeting that night," Theresa said. "I don't have proof of that, but he was asking some very strange questions and he was extremely pushy. He kept looking at Shawn, then away, then back to Shawn. It's hard to explain, but he was acting guilty and trying to cover it up by being a jerk. Neither one of us had ever seen him before. We only knew he was FBI because he flashed his badge when he cornered Shawn in the casino. I was able to hide in plain sight by sitting at a nearby slot machine and messing around like I was actually gambling. I don't think he even saw me.

Anyway, we had a hard time getting past the guy and once we did, Shawn didn't have much time to take care of whatever he had to do. I hid in a closet while Shawn snuck into the office just in case he got caught. He was able to install the software but Drago saw him leaving. Shawn said he was just dropping off paperwork, but we knew Drago didn't believe him. Shawn begged me to sneak out before anyone knew I was there. He wanted me to leave him; and he'd catch up, but I wouldn't go. I was afraid of being separated. We nearly made it but Socks came in to do the afternoon run early and cut off our escape. Shawn rushed me into the kitchen and stuffed me in a cabinet under the sink. We both knew Shawn wasn't going to survive that night. I barely had time to say goodbye before the three of them walked in and cornered my husband," Theresa stopped. She couldn't bring herself to describe the rest...to remember the torture...to relive the sounds and smells of that awful night.

"They killed Shawn? Right there in the kitchen?" Tony asked.

"Yes," Theresa nodded. "Once it was over, I was able to escape while Drago and Socks removed the body and staged Shawn's death. Dominic probably went to his office and had a drink to celebrate his latest kill."

"You were in the room the whole time? You're a witness to the murder?" Rowdy asked soberly.

"I was in the room but none of them know that," Theresa answered. "Since I was in a cupboard, I'm not sure how much of a witness I am." Should she tell them about the cellphone video? Not yet.

"What about the files? The ones you found in the wall at your old house?" Rowdy asked.

"They're safe," Theresa answered vaguely. She knew she could trust Rowdy and Tony and even Bailey for that matter, but it was so hard.

Bailey took Theresa's hand again. "You can trust us, Theresa. I know how hard that is. I know how scary it feels. After all this time...after hiding all the evidence, keeping it safe...Rowdy is asking you to just turn it over and trust him to do the right thing."

"It is hard, but not because I don't trust you. I know I can. I know you're not working for Dom or anything, it's just..." she trailed off not sure how to explain it.

"It's just that you feel like you need an escape route," Bailey provided. "You feel like you should hold something back, hedge your bet so to speak...just in case."

"Exactly," Theresa said, realizing Bailey understood because she had been through the same thing.

"As much as I understand that Theresa, I need to know what you have," Rowdy said. "Those files might help me take Zarconi down for good. But, before we get into the evidence, did Shawn get the keylogger installed?"

"Yes," Theresa said perplexed. "Why?"

"I'm just wondering where that information went. Do you have that, too?" Rowdy asked.

"No," Theresa admitted. "After Shawn died, I just fled. I got out of Detroit as soon as I could and came here, to Mount Haven."

"Do you know where the information was saved? Shawn didn't know he was going to die that night, so he had to send the files somewhere," Tony pressed.

"He said he was sending it to his cloud account," Theresa said reluctantly. "That's also where Shawn stored his backup copy of all the evidence against Dom." Well, everything except that video. Plus, she had the paper copies.

"Do you know how to access it or was it a paid service that's now gone?" Rowdy asked. If they could get to the files...well, if Skeet could get to the evidence they might have a chance at stopping this guy.

"I do," Theresa said locking eyes with Rowdy. He wanted her to trust him but he didn't realize just how vulnerable that would make her. Up until tonight, nobody even knew she had any evidence against Dom. If the truth came out... she'd be dead.

Rowdy sighed. "Theresa, what do I have to do to convince you I am on your side? How can I prove my loyalty? Because if you don't trust me, we're not going to make it through this. One or all of us is going to get hurt."

"That's not what I'm worried about, Rowdy. I trust you," Theresa also sighed. "Look, I am still alive because Dom has no idea I have anything on him. They tortured Shawn, pushed him...beat him...and still, he protected me. Because he loved me. They have no idea I was even there. They don't know I have any evidence. Now you and Tony are determined to head to Detroit to confront the monster that ruined my life. What if he tortures you? Right now, he doesn't know anything. He only wants me because he can't have me. He was so sure I'd have to rely on him...work for him...to pay off Shawn's so-called debt. When I produced a check for the full amount, he was livid. But, he couldn't alter our deal because he showed up in Mount Haven with potential clients. He was stuck, to alter our deal, to go back on his word, would undermine his position with his new customers."

"I think I'm missing something here," Bailey interrupted. "You said Dom tracked you to Mount Haven. But, you also said he didn't know who you were. How did he figure it out? And, why is he still after you? I thought he settled Zach's debt with the house."

"After they killed Shawn, I escaped just like Shawn told me to. I avoided the cameras, hid in a crowd and made it back to our truck. We parked it at the mall so nobody noticed me leaving. I stopped and grabbed the essentials from the apartment and skipped town. I thought I was free. I was sure Dom didn't even know who I was. I was wrong. He figured it out somehow. In answer to your question, I don't know how. Maybe it was the FBI guy. But once he knew who I was, he tracked me down. I wasn't as smart as you, Bailey. I didn't change my name or even try to hide. I moved to

Moondance Ridge

Mount Haven and started my life over. Max gave me a job and everything seemed to be going great. Then, a month later, Dom showed up and demanded restitution.

I was told that Shawn had stolen forty thousand dollars in cash from Dom and was headed out of the city when he crashed into a house. The car caught on fire and Shawn was killed instantly. The money was lost in the fire and I had to pay the debt. He tacked on another ten thousand as a penalty. I knew it was a lie, but I couldn't challenge him without revealing I was there. Then, he threw me a bone...if I didn't have the money, I could go work for him. The idea of being pimped out to all Dom's scummy friends made me want to vomit, but I held it together and told him I would think about it. He said he'd come back the following morning. That gave me time to head to the bank and close out my account. It cost me every penny I had, but I thought it would ensure my freedom. It didn't."

"Can you answer one more thing for me?" Tony asked.

"Okay," Theresa turned to look at him. He'd been awfully quiet this entire time.

"With Shawn, Zach and your parents gone... why are you still paying an imaginary debt he claims you owe for Zach? Are you just afraid he'll kidnap you and take you back?"

"That's part of it," Theresa swallowed the lump in her throat. "The other part has to do with a girl. There was a woman, Callie. Zach fell for her, hard. Unfortunately, the feeling wasn't mutual. She was still in love with some guy she met in college. Zach and Callie became close friends while he was investigating a story in New York. She's some big fashion designer and Zach helped her get connections... because of his mom. Anyway, she broke his heart but they stayed in touch. I guess they became pretty close friends.

She came to visit a few times and he still traveled to New York on occasion. Somehow, Dom found out about her. If I don't pay Zach's debt, he's going to go after her. From what I saw, she's pampered and naïve. She'd never survive Dom. Zach would want me to protect her, so I do."

"If she's a hotshot fashion designer, she probably has the funds to pay Zach's debt," Tony growled. "You were living out of a damn truck."

"Yeah," Bailey frowned. "I've been meaning to talk to you about that. However, I don't think tonight is the best time to hash that one out."

"You don't get it," Theresa said. "She is a successful fashion designer, but that only means the debt would be greater, the payments higher. Dom isn't owed a debt, it's fictitious. He can demand anything he wants and your only choice is to go along, get kidnapped or die. I went along. I'm sorry if you don't understand. All I can say is Zach would have done the same for me. I had to protect Callie. Zach is dead, which makes it even more important. I won't let him down, I owe him so much. The least I can do is protect the woman he loved."

"A woman that didn't love him back," Tony said softly.

"Yes," Theresa turned and glared at him. "A woman that didn't love him back."

Tony stood and walked outside, Rowdy watched for several seconds before he stood and followed.

"Are they mad?" Theresa asked.

Moondance Ridge

"If I had to guess, I'd say Tony is frustrated. Rowdy," she paused. "He's a little frustrated, too. He needs those documents and anything else you can provide. To be honest, none of us are sure you're going to be forthcoming with the evidence."

"I told you," Theresa began.

"I know, and I understand." Bailey stood and walked to the large living room window. She could see the two men huddled together in deep discussion. "But you know as well as I do, they're going to need it. I also think you know Tony would never rat you out... even if he were being tortured. Rowdy wouldn't either but I don't expect you to understand that. It's taken me a long time to figure that man out, and I'm in love with him. I can't expect you to get it overnight."

"I don't know anything about that keylogger thingy," Theresa insisted. "I can get into the file, I know the username and password. That's not a problem. Maybe Rowdy will understand the code stuff, maybe he won't. Shawn was careful, so are his friends. The cloud isn't a typical storage system. It was developed by Shawn and some hacker friends he knew in college. There's no fee associated with the system, nobody can access it but them. I just feel like I need to protect Shawn's friends. They don't deserve the FBI crashing down on them because they did Shawn and me a favor."

"You can trust Rowdy," Bailey said again. "Tell him what you just told me. He'll understand and he'll know how to protect Shawn's friends."

Theresa considered that for several minutes and decided Bailey was right. Rowdy wouldn't care about a couple hackers that had nothing to do with the case. "Okay," she whispered. "When he comes back in, I'll tell him."

Chapter Six

"So," Rowdy stepped up beside Tony. "There are holes but I think she told us most of it."

"Yeah," Tony agreed. He was positive Theresa was still hiding something, but he wasn't going to press her. He knew it wouldn't do any good. "The woman is willing to protect everyone on the planet but herself."

"You say that like it's a bad thing," Rowdy bumped Tony's shoulder with his own.

"Not bad," Tony sighed. "But, it complicates things. We both know, based on what she just told us, there is no way she'll stay in Mount Haven and let us head to Detroit to fix her problem."

Moondance Ridge

"True," Rowdy sighed. "It complicates things, but we can handle it."

Tony glanced at the ex-lawman. "I guess I better tell you, I have no idea how to deal with dirty cops. Dirt bag mob scum? No problem. But feds and locals in one fell swoop, I'm out of my league on that one."

"Well," Rowdy shifted and casually leaned his back against the wooden railing. "Lucky for you, I've had a little experience in that area."

"You've taken down one of your own?" Tony asked for clarification.

"No," Rowdy scowled. "The minute they went dirty, they lost that classification. They lost the distinction. The guys Coop and I took down had long before stopped being one of ours. I know everyone thinks there's this blue family that shields bad cops and hides the truth to protect anything and everything no matter how egregious. That couldn't be further from the truth. Good cops hate bad cops more than the public ever will. They tarnish the badge, they damage our rep and they betrayed their oath. In my eyes, there's nothing worse. So, in answer to your question... yeah, it's going to be more complicated; but a bad cop is nothing more than another bad guy that belongs behind bars. I have no problem helping him find the way."

"Makes sense," Tony decided. "So, if Theresa is willing to turn over the evidence what do you plan to do with it?"

"If I can talk her into cooperating, we might have to leave a little late tomorrow," Rowdy decided. "Can we reschedule for ten or eleven?"

214

"Sure," Tony shrugged. "Private flights have more leeway. We can just play it by ear. Why?"

"I'd like to take whatever she has to Coop," Rowdy admitted. "He can start digging, he has resources we won't have. It makes more sense than you or me searching the net for crumbs. Coop can access federal files and local databases. He'll have to be careful but he'll be able to take each name, run them and provide up-to-date information on whatever the reporter collected–names, places, tax info, you get the idea. The fed worries me. He's going to be harder to single out. Chances are pretty slim his name is in the file; an investigative reporter wouldn't have trusted him if it was."

"I might be able to get somewhere with the Chronicle, maybe scrounge out Zach's files he had there," Tony considered. "I'm pretty sure I can get my hands on any stories they were too afraid to publish, at least the ones Zach submitted. From there, we'll just have to play it by ear."

"Are you *Dear Abby*? Maggie is going to be ecstatic. She might even start to like you if you can answer all her deep, dark secret questions about life."

Tony ignored him and pulled out his phone. "Give me a minute to reschedule the plane, then I'll be in. That should give you time to push without my interference. Just don't hit her too hard. I'm starting to like you. It'd be a shame if I had to kill you already."

Rowdy laughed. "Thanks, man. I'll be sure to keep that in mind."

Moments later, Tony stepped back into the house.

"We need a laptop," Rowdy said immediately. "Theresa is going to access the storage so we can see exactly what we have."

Moondance Ridge

Tony disappeared down the hall and returned with a sleek new computer. He set it on the table and settled in next to Theresa. "You okay?"

"Not really," she said, relaxing as he took her hand in his. "But, I think I'm doing the right thing, so that helps."

"You are," Tony gave her hand a little squeeze. Once the machine booted up, he clicked open the internet and pushed the device toward Theresa.

Theresa glanced around, took a deep breath and punched in the web link. Within seconds, a login screen appeared. She typed in Shawn's information and then pushed the computer back toward Tony as file after file filled the screen.

"Holy cow," Bailey was standing behind Tony, glancing over his shoulder. "That's a lot of information. Is all of it about Zarconi?"

"Yeah," Theresa admitted. "Shawn had a different account he used for personal stuff. This was everything we had going in plus all the keylogger data that's come in over the past two years. That's why there's so much. He set it up to log results daily, creating its own folder at the beginning of the day. Each folder has a date, see? The first one is today." She pointed at a folder on the screen.

"Okay," Tony glanced at Rowdy and sighed. "So, now the million-dollar question. What are you willing to do with this stuff?"

"What do you mean?" Theresa asked, confused.

"I mean, are you willing to let us use it?" Tony clicked on the folder labeled with the current date and glanced up. "If so, we're going to need a professional. Someone that can decipher this and tell us exactly what's in there. I'm pretty good with computers but this is way over my head."

"Me too," Bailey sighed. "I was hoping I could help but not with this. It's all code and gibberish to me."

"Who do you want to share it with?" Theresa studied Tony, sure she wouldn't like his suggestion.

"I was thinking Coop for starters," Tony admitted. "I'm not sure he's going to know what to do with all of this, though."

"He won't," Rowdy sat in the chair across from Theresa. "Coops worse than me when it comes to computer mumbo-jumbo. We could talk to a friend in the FBI, someone I know we can trust. Someone I would bet my life is not involved with Dominic Zarconi."

"I can't," she glanced at Bailey momentarily. "This cloud is not a typical cloud. It was set up by Shawn and a couple buddies he went to school with. Bottom line? They're hackers and they don't always fly on the right side of the law. I can't... I just can't turn this over to the FBI. I will not be responsible if the feds find something they don't like and round these guys up. Think of another way."

"Theresa," Rowdy said clearly annoyed. "Skeet will not go after the messenger."

"I can't risk it," she shook her head. "These guys kept all this going, even after Shawn died. They have protected his information, his secrets, his... life work. Some of which is also considered illegal. If they start snooping around in there, in the storage... I might end up behind bars, too."

"How much data are we talking?" Bailey asked.

"Several gigs," Tony said, scrolling through the folders.

"What about that external hard drive we just gave you?" she asked absently. "I thought Kit said she bought extra memory... two terabytes if I recall correctly. Will all the files fit on that drive?"

"Probably," Tony said cautiously as he scrolled down the list. "Yeah, I think so."

"Then get it," Bailey shoved at his back. "Copy the data, give it to Coop. He can extract the basics...whatever he can and send the rest to Skeet. Agent Perkins will have experts who can break the code."

"Is that okay with you?" Tony asked Theresa before standing.

"I guess," she was still nervous about FBI involvement.

"But?" Rowdy asked.

"But Zach tried this already. Zach went to the FBI and he's dead. How can you be so sure this Agent Perkins can be trusted? After everything I've been through... I just don't like taking the risk."

"Skeet's as clean as they come," Rowdy sat back and considered. "We go way back. He helped us take down the DeRossi's in Chicago. He helped me save Bailey and... a few years back, Coop and I helped him save his wife. The only person I trust more is my brother and Skeet is a very close second. If you can't trust Skeet, trust me."

Theresa turned away, her gaze landed on the window and she stared absently into the darkness as she considered. There wouldn't be a trace back to the server or Shawn's friends. There technically wouldn't be a trace back to her and if they turned it over to Coop, who then turned it over to the feds, well... that might work in her favor and keep her safe if the guy was dirty. "I don't want anyone causing trouble for Shawn's friends. They're good guys and don't deserve to be harassed over this."

Rowdy smiled. He wasn't sure how 'good' a hacker was, but he'd protect them. For now. Their involvement was minimal and irrelevant to the case. "Tony, you got that hard drive here?"

"Yeah," he stood and once again disappeared into the back room. He returned with a small device not much larger than a cell phone and plugged it into the computer. "Theresa? You do this, copy over the files but leave them in the cloud for now. We might need to access them and once they're transferred to the Federal Boys, we'll never see those files again."

"That's true," Rowdy conceded. "Leave them in the cloud. That way we can access it from anywhere that has internet."

"Okay," Theresa began to copy the files. She paused before clicking on the folder that contained the info from Zach. "You're sure about this?"

Tony wrapped an arm around her shoulders. "Do it, babe. We have to trust someone, sometime. If Rowdy trusts this Skeet guy, I think we should trust him, too. He helped Bailey, I'm guessing he can't be all bad."

"I trust him, too," Bailey added.

"Okay," Theresa said after giving the copy command on the last file. "There's a lot of information in there, it will take a while."

Moondance Ridge

"I delayed our departure," Tony advised the group. "We're set for ten, but can push that back again if necessary. I suggest we all try to get a little sleep and pick back up in the morning. The files will be transferred by then, and we can stop by the station and drop the evidence off to Coop."

"I know you want me to stay here, but I think I should go with you," Theresa said, looking at Tony. "There are a couple reasons for it. One, I know Dom, his men, his tactics. I can help. But also, because leaving me here, leaves everyone in this town vulnerable. I'm sure you've already put Coop on notice and he's briefing his men; but it's a small town and the regular guys aren't prepared for an invasion. If Dom knows I'm still out here, there will be an invasion. He won't care who ends up dead. There will be a lot of casualties and most of them will be innocent citizens who never saw it coming. If I go to Detroit, I'm at risk... a little, but nobody else has to get hurt."

"The people of Detroit might disagree," Rowdy said flatly. He agreed with her, but he didn't like it.

"They're already used to it. They stay out of his way. They're prepared for his violence. It's not the same." She studied Tony, anxious to know how he felt about it.

Tony knew this was coming and wasn't at all surprised. He didn't like it. He planned to mess with the mob boss while he was there and didn't want the added risk to her safety. But, he also knew there was no talking her out of it; and on the bright side, Bailey, Maggie and the rest would be relatively safe in their absence. He nodded briefly then stood.

Rowdy also stood and moved to stand beside Bailey. "I'll come by first thing, we'll visit Coop together then plan out the rest of our day."

"Sounds good," Tony walked the couple to the door and focused on Bailey. "If I don't see you tomorrow, kid... stay safe. We're dealing with an unpredictable man here, don't let your guard down just because we're in Detroit. He could still send someone out here to get back at us."

"I've decided I don't want to know your plan. I'm sure it would only terrify me. Just be careful, both of you. And, we'll do the same out here, I promise." Bailey hugged her friend goodnight, then stepped through the door. Rowdy silently followed.

* * * *

Joe stepped into the dimly lit office and paused. "Sorry, Anita said you wanted to see me. I can wait outside."

"No," Dom motioned his man inside. "This is my nephew, Nico. He's visiting from New York. He decided to accompany two of his men, Dreven Killian and Talon Woods out personally."

Joe turned to the man Dom indicated was family. "Salve," he bowed his head slightly to demonstrate his submission.

Dom nodded in approval. Joe had always been one of his best soldiers, unlike Drago. *Speak of the devil himself.*

Socks and Drago stepped into the room together. Socks immediately froze and took a step backward. Drago continued to glide nonchalantly across the room. "You rang?" he asked before dropping into a chair across from the antique desk.

Dom scowled. "You noticed I have company?"

"Of course," Drago shrugged. "Hey."

Dominic's patience was wearing thin. Drago's attitude and incompetence had sealed his own fate. "Come on in here, Socks."

Socks slowly made his way across the room, briefly glanced at Joe, then cautiously lowered himself into the chair next to Drago. He was terrified and worried, more than he'd admit, about this meeting.

"Socks," Dom said in a low, menacing tone.

"Yes, sir?" Socks gulped.

"I've heard Drago's account of what occurred in Vegas... and I've heard from Joe. I haven't yet heard from you. Is there anything you would like to add?"

"No, sir." Socks squirmed and shifted.

"I see," Dom sighed. He had a decision to make. His focus moved from Socks to Drago and back to Socks. "Then let's discuss Theresa Regan."

"I'm sorry about that boss," Socks said immediately. "We clearly blew it out there. We didn't know about the guy."

"What guy?" Dominic frowned.

"Some poser that got in the way," Drago barked. "If the owner hadn't stepped in, that punk would be history and the Theresa problem would be rectified."

Dominic studied the disruptive fool. "It appears this poser, as you put it, defeated you. If your face is any indication, you were outshined and outclassed by a stranger." He turned to Socks. "What do you know about the man?"

"Not much," Socks admitted. "We first encountered him before we went to Vegas, just briefly. He didn't even drop his name. We were at the bar, looking for the girl and he got in the way. We didn't find her that night and then you sent us out of town. Once we returned, we nearly had Theresa. I grabbed her and was trying to get her to the car when the same guy stepped outside and attacked. He didn't say anything, I don't even know how he knows her. It's possible he's just a bouncer at the club."

"That's a new development," Dominic considered. He didn't like it. Was someone guarding Theresa or was it just bad timing? The answer would make all the difference in the world. But, that was a problem for another day. "Joe," Dominic called. "Look into this. I want to know if that club has hired muscle or if the man was somehow connected to our girl."

"On it," Joe answered, before he turned and disappeared out the door grateful for the escape. He had a pretty good idea what was coming.

"The guys a no-good nuisance," Drago growled. "Say the word and I'll take him out for good."

Dominic raised an eyebrow. "So, I'm in charge again? That's good to know."

Drago frowned. "I told you about that, the op was dynamic. I had no choice."

"You tracked the man down, which I understand took days, restrained him with zip ties and used him as a punching bag. Then, you drove him ninety miles south and drowned him in the Colorado River. You call that dynamic?"

"He was a problem, I tell you." Drago insisted. "He threatened to expose you. He ran, I chased. Like that hot pursuit thing the cops use. Sure, it took a couple days but I did it for you. You said take care of the problem, I resolved the problem. The guy was a street rat, he got exterminated."

Dominic slid the Glock off his thigh and pointed it at Drago. "The man was David Sherman's grandson. Dave called me today and we worked out a solution. One we can both live with." He pulled the trigger, the sound of the gun firing echoed throughout the room as the bullet struck Drago through the forehead. Dominic set the pistol on the desk in front of him.

Socks was terrified. He knew Drago had lost it. He knew eventually his lies would catch up to him, but the man was a friend. Was that friendship going to be the thing that ended his life? He hoped not; but at the moment, it looked like a pretty good possibility. He briefly wondered what Joe had told the boss. Did he know how many times the two of them tried to call for direction. Drago was a man on a mission. Socks and Joe had gone along, mostly because Drago was the one with the car. Joe tried to intervene, tried to stop Drago, but he'd been pistol whipped for his effort. Socks knew he should have helped Crazy Joe, but he was too afraid of Drago to betray him.

Dom stood and slid the .40 back into its holster. "Clean this mess up. Nico and I have a dinner date with my lovely bride. He hasn't seen his Aunt Zaphy for nearly a year. I'm sure Dreven and Talon are more than happy to assist. Get acquainted, they're going to be your new best friends."

"He always like that?" One of the newcomers asked once Dominic left the room.

"Yeah," Socks took a long, deep breath. "Yeah, Dominic Zarconi expects loyalty and perfection. I'd watch my back because I guarantee Dom will be watching your every move and if he so much as thinks you're not reliable and trustworthy..." he glanced at Drago. "Well, I think you get the idea."

"I'm guessing we were present for that on purpose, as a warning right off the bat?" Talon asked.

"I'd say so," Socks agreed. "Now, we should be able to roll the chair straight out the back door. Once we get there, you two stay with the body and I'll pull the car around."

"I thought the place was covered with cameras," Dreven asked.

"Dom likes his privacy. Doesn't want anyone knowing who comes and goes if you know what I mean. He's big on plausible deniability and insisted the area remain surveillance free."

"Makes sense," Talon shrugged. "Let's get this done, I'm starved."

Moondance Ridge

"Okay, what do we know?" Skeet asked the moment he slid into the passenger's seat.

"I was able to follow Agent Darrow out to a warehouse. I'm still unsure what they're dealing, but I think it's something big. Security is tight and around the clock. There were several players coming and going. I got shots of them, thought maybe Stan could run them through the system and see if he gets a hit."

"I can do that," Skeet said absently. "Once I get settled, bring me the card and I'll download them. If the shots are good enough, we might hit them with face recognition."

"I got a suite," Blake advised. "When I checked in, thought when you got here that would make things easier. I've already cleared the room. So far, I don't think anyone knows we're here. That could change. Burns mentioned some connection to a case you had out of Chicago. Some bigwig serving a life sentence that's related to our players out here."

"DeRossi's hitman is Zarconi's nephew," Skeet considered. What could these guys be running? It could be anything, drugs, girls, guns. You name it, DeRossi had his fingers in it. "Hear anything about coffee?"

"What?" Blake shot a glance at his new partner then refocused on the road. "This is Detroit, not exactly the climate for coffee beans. Why?"

"Because Nico contacted DeRossi and they had a long conversation about coffee, and how good the market is doing at the moment. There is no chance they were truly talking crops and water rations."

"Agreed," Blake said, pulling into a long driveway. He made a sharp right into an underground parking garage then pulled into a spot near the elevator.

"Prime spot," Skeet observed. "He saving it for you?" Skeet pointed to a man who was obviously homeless but sporting a new pair of shoes. The man had been lounging in the middle of the parking stall until he saw their car approaching.

"Might be," Blake said with a grin as he passed the man a couple bucks.

The two agents entered the hotel and headed for the elevators. Once Skeet was settled in, he uploaded the photos Blake took the previous day and began running them through the feds database. He hoped the facial recognition program would get a match on at least one of the men.

Nearly forty minutes later, Skeet had the Intel on two of the suspects. He had recognized one of them immediately, a low-level runner that used to work for Leon DeRossi. According to the file, the other was also a low-level employee, but not one Skeet had encountered before.

"I guess I should tell you, these are DeRossi thugs, and the man put a bounty on me the minute he hit a cell. I could be a hindrance if we want to keep our activities a secret," Skeet admitted.

Blake smiled. "I could be a hindrance if we don't."

"Somehow," Skeet frowned. "I think I'm better off not knowing what you mean by that."

"Any luck on the others?" Blake asked, ignoring Skeet's concern.

"No," Skeet sighed. "And there should be. I'm gonna send them to Stan and see if he can do a more thorough search. Hopefully, he'll come up with something."

"In the meantime, you want to head over to the warehouse and take a look for yourself?"

"Sure," Skeet glanced up. "Just give me a minute to send these through. It's going to be dark so visibility will be sketchy. Grab the night vision. I'd like to see what goes on out there when the sun goes down."

* * * *

Tony stood by the large front window and gazed into the darkness. He'd sent Theresa to bed already, hoping she'd be able to relax before their trip. Something he was unable to do at the moment. He ran a frustrated hand through his hair, thinking about Detroit. The task ahead wouldn't be easy... harder with Theresa by their side. For the hundredth time, he wondered if this was the best way to handle things. Unfortunately, he couldn't come up with a better plan. The extortion and harassment had to stop. Instead of questioning their strategy, he decided to work on covering all their bases. One thing he knew for sure, men like Zarconi had achieved status the easy way... with violence and intimidation. He pulled out his phone and called an old friend.

"Hello?" came the groggy greeting.

"John, it's Tony."

"Do you have any idea what time it is, man?" John grumbled.

"Yes," Tony said calmly. "But I'm in a bind and I need a favor."

"This must be some favor if you couldn't wait for a decent hour to do the asking," John returned.

"There's a woman, lives in New York. She's a fashion designer, her name is Callie. I don't have her last name but she knew a reporter by the name of Zachary Regan a few years back. I need you to keep an eye on her for me. I'm about to send a message to some dangerous people, and I don't want her to get caught in the crosshairs," Tony told him.

"Can't you get the name from this Zachary guy?"

"No," Tony answered. "The guy I'm going after killed him."

"Man are you sure about this?" John objected. "I mean you're talking about a killer. Why don't you just hire me, I'm trained for this shit? Better yet just turn this over to the police."

"I'm working with an ex-cop. I'm fine, I just need to make sure the same thing doesn't happen to this Callie woman that happened to Con."

"Not that again," John moaned. "How many times have I gotta tell you, it was not your fault? Is that what this is about? Some misguided mission to atone for Conrad's death?"

"No," Tony sighed. "I never said I needed to atone, that's your hair brain theory. But he did die because of me; we both know that. I crossed the wrong man. He couldn't get to me, so he took his frustrations out on the person closest to me. If I hadn't crossed Voyt, Travis Beynart wouldn't have gone after Con."

"True," John conceded. "But that's on him, not you. There's more to this story, something you're not telling me; and we both know it. I think it's related to your past. You're still kicking yourself because Beynart got away. He's sitting in a cell rather than a grave. I get it, you wanted to make sure he paid for what he did to Conrad, you feel deprived so you meddle in lost causes. But, you're a successful businessman now, stop playing with fire. This mission sounds like a dangerous game, one you might not win. Please just back off, accept that justice was served. Beynart will never leave that cell, it has to be enough."

"We've been over this too many times," Tony frowned. "It's futile to rehash it tonight, let's just agree to disagree."

"I can do that if you level with me," John said. "Tell me this case has nothing to do with the past. I don't think you can because this phone call has Conrad Werner written all over it."

"Con is dead because I was a stupid teenager, and I got involved with the wrong crowd. He had no idea what he was taking on when he decided to protect me, Con saved me John. I picked the man's pocket and he took me in, fostered me and treated me with respect. Then, he made the ultimate sacrifice for his generosity. I should have known Voyt would never back off, he was used to getting his way. Until Con, nobody defied him. Voyt was too powerful in that area, he controlled the drug trade as well as the local gangs. I underestimated his power. He underestimated Con. That final showdown was inevitable and since he couldn't get back at me, he killed the one person he knew I cared about. It's not something I can just forget. I'm just glad he didn't know anything about you. Otherwise…"

"Otherwise," John interrupted. "He would have come up against the two of us and he would not have survived that encounter. Stop acting like it's the same. Conrad Werner was an amazing man, but he was soft. He was an intellectual who won his battles with his mind and the law. Con was book smart, court smart and he understood the system. He knew when someone could be saved and when they couldn't. That's why he saved you. But he didn't truly understand the code. He didn't understand how the street worked, and that's what got him killed. A sadistic criminal was looking for revenge and willing to make an example out of the innocent. Voyt is responsible for Con's death and, in the end, he got what he deserved."

"On that we do agree," Tony said softly. "And that's why you're wrong. Voyt did pay for his role in Conrad's death. I'm not living in the past. I'm dealing with the present, which is why I had to take this on. I know firsthand just how dangerous men like this can be. Nate Voyt was powerful and unstable but nothing like the man I'm dealing with here. This guy is much worse. Be careful, just check on the girl for me. Don't make contact. Don't draw attention to yourself or reveal the reason you are there. I do not want you getting involved in this."

"What aren't you telling me?" John pressed.

"I'm going to be dealing with the mob," Tony admitted. "Their ruthless, murdering tactics would make Voyt look like a school boy. Promise me you'll watch yourself. Keep your distance and don't get involved."

"Shit, man," John exclaimed. "Don't do this. Walk away."

"Can't," Tony settled into a chair. "But you can. If you don't want the risk, just say the word. The woman is probably okay. She has no connection to me and only a tentative connection with Theresa."

"Awe," John said in understanding. "This is about another troubled chic."

Tony couldn't deny it so he didn't answer. "In or out? It's your call."

"I'm in. Ain't I always in? Just be careful. Have you at least hooked up with someone that can watch your back? This ex-cop, is he good? I mean there's a reason he's an ex. You didn't recruit some old ancient has-been that reminisces about the good ol' days, did you?"

"Naw," Tony laughed. "He's Bailey's new man. He's solid. Do me a favor and check in. I don't like bringing you in at all but there's nobody else I can trust with this."

"I'll call you tomorrow," John promised. "Now, let me get some beauty sleep. We can't all be baby faced sissy's."

"Whatever," Tony grinned. "I'll talk to you tomorrow. I should be in the air by ten or so. Give me an hour to reach altitude if you learn anything before then."

"Can you tell me where? Obviously, there's not a big mob presence in Montana."

"Detroit," Tony provided. "Get some sleep. I'll be in touch." Tony slowly ended the call and frowned, hoping he'd done the right thing.

"Who was that?" Theresa asked from the hallway.

"Oh, hey," Tony turned. "I thought you were sleeping."

"Can't," she sighed. "I'm worried. This feels like before. First with Zach, then with Shawn. I'm afraid it will all end the same. I'm terrified that one or all of us will end up suffering a painful, tortuous death."

Tony moved forward and pulled Theresa into his arms. "Did they torture him?"

"Yeah," she swallowed. "It was horrible. Those sounds, knowing how much pain he was in. Dom was looking for answers. He wanted to know why Shawn was inside. He endured, suffered in silence as best he could. He was trying to protect me, from Dominic, but also from hearing him suffer."

"I'm sorry," he kissed the top of her head. "This time it will be different."

"Why?" Theresa asked, truly wondering how he could be so sure.

"Because, Rowdy and I are not inexperienced," Tony took her hand and led her to his bedroom. "We've both dealt with evil, sadistic men in our past. We understand him, better than Zach, better than Shawn. I suspect your mother understood him as a prosecutor which is why she worked so hard to bring him down. But, the plane crash wasn't something she could control. That's why it will be different. We are prepared and we know what we have to do. We won't hesitate to do what we need to do. That is one thing this Dom guy won't be ready for. He won't be expecting the destruction I plan to bring down on his enterprise."

Theresa shuddered as she climbed in next to Tony and silently realized she had no idea what this man was capable of. She wondered if Rowdy knew what he'd signed up for. "Who did you tell we were coming?"

Tony jerked around and stared at Theresa. "That sounds like you think I'm working with the enemy."

"I don't think so," Theresa said hesitantly. "I'm just wondering who you called and told about our trip."

"I called a friend who is a security specialist in New York," Tony said wearily. What did he have to do to make the woman trust him? "He's going to figure out who Callie is and check on her from afar. I told him not to make contact and not to draw attention to himself. It struck me that if you are paying her debt, anything Rowdy and I do might just bring heat down on her. I wanted all my bases covered."

"Oh," Theresa said, surprised. "How did you know her full name?"

"I didn't," Tony told her. "I just told him to find a Callie in the fashion industry who knew Zach."

"You could have asked, I know her last name," Theresa said softly.

"I thought you were asleep or I would have," he settled into bed and pulled her close.

"Tony?" Theresa continued. "Please don't bring anyone else into this. I really appreciate you looking out for Callie. I hadn't even thought of that, so thank you. But, the more people that get involved, the higher the body count might be."

"Don't worry about John," Tony told her. "He's a professional. He does this for a living. He'll know how to handle the situation. He'll ensure Callie is safe without anyone knowing he was even there."

"I can't help but think you are so confident because you have never met Dominic Zarconi. I'm not sure you are taking this as seriously as you should."

"Trust me," Tony said again. "I understand, Rowdy understands, Coop understands and so does John. We're just better prepared than you and the rest of your family. I wish you would let yourself have a little faith. Now, go to sleep. We have a long day ahead of us."

"Goodnight," she whispered.

Tony kissed the top of Theresa's head. "Goodnight, sweetheart."

* * * *

Rowdy shoved his last t-shirt into his bag and zipped it shut. He slowly made his way to the living room, knowing that's where he'd find Bailey. She was sitting on the comfortable couch, sipping a cup of coffee. "Hey," he leaned in and brushed a gentle kiss across her lips.

"Coffee's ready," she said as she held out her cup.

He moved to the kitchen filled a mug and returned to the living room, settling in next to her. Bailey immediately shifted and relaxed against him. They sat there for several seconds in silence before Rowdy broached the subject. "While I'm gone, I need you to keep Knight by your side at all times. Do not go anywhere without him."

Bailey straightened. "Even the bar? I'm not sure I can control him if someone gets out of line."

"There's a leash in the truck. I've fastened a hook on the wall, just snap his leash onto the hook. He won't be able to reach anyone unless they step behind the bar. In that case, I want him to bite them."

"Rowdy," Bailey began then stopped when she saw the look on his face.

"I need you to listen to me and promise you will always have Knight with you," Rowdy said again. "Just because you are here, it doesn't mean you're safe. What I'm doing is dangerous. I'm putting you in danger and I'm sorry for that. Think of Cole and Reese then times that by about ten. If they can't get to me, they will come after my family. Coop is taking precautions, and he'll spend more time at the bar but he also has a job to do. That means you have to watch out for yourself, too. Knight will protect you," the dog must have heard his name because he sauntered over and leapt onto the couch, resting his head in Rowdy's lap. "Good boy," he said immediately as he began rubbing behind the dog's ears.

"I promise," Bailey said softly. "I'll stay alert and always have Knight by my side."

"I hate leaving you like this," Rowdy frowned. "But taking you along would be even more dangerous. This is better and between Knight and Coop, you should be safe. Just in case, I have also left a loaded pistol in the nightstand."

Bailey swallowed hard, Rowdy was starting to scare her.

"I'm sorry," Rowdy pulled her close. "I'm so sorry it has to be this way. If I thought anyone else could do it, I wouldn't get involved."

"No," Bailey straightened. "We both agreed on this. You have to help Theresa. You have to get her out of this situation for good. I know you and Tony are the only ones that can take care of this. I trust you, and I'll be fine. I promise, if there's trouble of any kind, I'll call Coop."

"Jase will be helping as well. He's aware of the situation and will be on the lookout for anyone acting suspicious." He paused, then frowned when the doorbell rang. "Stay there."

Rowdy slid his Smith & Wesson, semi-auto from the shoulder holster he was wearing and approached the door. They weren't expecting company, especially not this early in the morning. He cautiously positioned his body to the side of the door and glanced out the window. His body instantly relaxed although now he was more curious than cautious. He reached for the doorknob at the same time as he slid the pistol back into the holster and yanked open the door.

"Good morning," Mayor Jon Herlin said in greeting. "I'm sorry to bother you so early, but Coop said you were leaving this morning; and I wanted to make sure I caught you before you took off."

"Come in," Rowdy said, still perplexed. "Would you like some coffee?"

"That would be wonderful," Herlin said as he shot a nervous glance at Knight, who was now standing, alert next to the couch, watching the newcomers every move.

Moondance Ridge

Bailey recognized the fear in the Mayor's expression. She stood and moved to the door. "Knight, come."

Mayor Herlin took several steps into the kitchen, making sure he put plenty of distance between himself and the dog.

Knight moved to Bailey's side but never took his eyes off the mayor.

"I'm going to take Knight for a walk," she told Rowdy as she pulled open the door. "Take your time, we'll be awhile."

Rowdy smiled and handed Herlin a mug. "Sugar's on the table, do you take cream?"

"Oh, no." Herlin finally relaxed when he heard the click of the door latching. "Thanks, just one sugar for me." He moved to the table, dropped in a heaping scoop of sugar and glanced around, clearly unsure where Rowdy would like to have their conversation.

"Let's move this into the living room. The chairs are a lot more comfortable," Rowdy stepped past the mayor and returned to the couch.

"I'm sure you're wondering why I'm here," Herlin began

"To be honest, yes," Rowdy shifted and set his mug on the table.

"Coop told me you are heading to Detroit this morning. I also know you turned in your badge," Jon said soberly. "I'm here to return it," he pulled the metal police badge from his pocket and set it on the table in front of him. "I know all the reasons you think you can't keep it; but I'm here to ask... well, insist really, that you change your mind."

"I'm at a disadvantage here, Mayor. I'm not sure what Coop told you about my pending trip," Rowdy glanced at the badge then back to the man sitting across from him.

"Enough," Herlin said, relaxing into his chair. "Coop told me enough to prepare me for any conflict but not enough to implicate me if anything goes awry."

"Then you should understand why me having that badge is a bad idea," Rowdy surmised.

"What I know is that you having that badge might help, in some small way, while you're dealing with this… threat." Jon took another sip of his coffee.

"I'm sorry," Rowdy sighed, frustrated. "I'm having trouble knowing what to say here because I don't know exactly how much you actually know about this mission."

"I know you are headed to Detroit to confront the mob; and you could also be dealing with corrupt cops, including the FBI. I know that the minute you cause problems for this Zarconi guy, the first thing he'll do is have his FBI friends call me and lodge a complaint. I'm sure he'll have some argument about jurisdiction, or some other nonsense. I also know, I plan to tell him to go pound sand."

Rowdy laughed. "Okay, but like you just said, I will be out of my jurisdiction. I won't have any police powers, no authority whatsoever."

"If nothing else," Herlin continued. "Having that badge will legitimize any weapons you have on you. That alone makes it a good idea. We both know you might have to use one of those weapons before you return."

Moondance Ridge

"Okay," Rowdy pondered. "I'll give you that. But, I'm going to be walking a fine line. Dealing with the mob is not like arresting your average street thug. These guys play dirty, they have no boundaries, if I play by the rules…I lose."

"I understand that as well," Herlin took another sip of his coffee then gently set the mug back on the table. He leaned forward and looked Rowdy directly in the eyes. "I'm willing to risk it. I trust you to do only what's necessary and nothing more. No matter what happens out there, I'll have your back. That is something you can count on."

"Why?" Rowdy asked. "I mean you barely know me. If you're expecting the same reaction you would get from Coop, you might need to rethink your position. We're brothers, but I'm my own man, and I tend to see things a little less black and white than Andy does."

"I'm well aware of that," Herlin admitted. "I think it's time I fill you in on a little secret."

"Okay," Rowdy narrowed his eyes, wondering where this was going.

"I'm not sure how much you know about my recruitment of your brother," Jon began.

"I know you wanted him as Sheriff, enough that you flew out three times and upped the salary until he agreed to take a look."

"True," Jon nodded. "But, it's a little more complicated than that. His predecessor was… let's say lackluster. I'm actually putting a positive spin on the situation, but I think you get the idea."

"Sure," Rowdy agreed.

"Well, when I won the election, I was determined to make some changes," Herlin began. "Our previous Sheriff had won his last election as well, but only because he wasn't opposed. Not because the community loved him, but because they feared him. He won his third term at the same time I won my first. Yes, I was determined to get Coop out here, and I did my best to lure him with money. But, we both know that wasn't enough. He was ripe for a change, but only if that change included you. I was on board with that. I confess, I always hoped I'd be getting a packaged deal. I wanted both brothers and I still believe in my original vision."

"Wait, what?"

"Yes," Herlin nodded. "I wanted you as well."

"But you didn't know me, you hadn't even met me." Rowdy was confused and not sure he liked learning about this new twist.

"No, I hadn't actually met you," Jon smiled. "But I did know you, in a secondhand sort of way."

"I'm not following," Rowdy admitted.

"I wanted a replacement for the current sheriff. That wasn't going to be easy. I had to time everything just right. I worked with the council to develop a plan. In the beginning stages we didn't have a candidate in mind, just a plan of action to make things right again. I won't bore you with the details, but suffice it to say our plan worked. Coop's our man for the next three years. I have no doubt, with his popularity, he'll win another term easily. I didn't even approach Andy until we had everything finalized. As luck would have it, everything fell into place a couple months after your tragic incident. At the time, Andy was too shocked and despondent to make a commitment."

Moondance Ridge

"Why did you single out Coop in the first place?" Rowdy asked.

"That's the secret I need to share," Jon stood and moved to the window. "My sister, Susan, lives in Chicago. I was actually in town when the shooting took place. Susan's husband and Chief Steven Griggs' wife are siblings." He glanced at Rowdy and saw the surprise he had expected. "I've known Steve for years, long before he became the Chief of Police for Chicago PD. Whenever I'm in town, we always spend at least one evening with the Griggs. Such was the case two days after that fateful event. The whole situation was sickening, and Steve was having a hard time wrapping his head around it. None of it should have happened, starting with the burglaries, to the lack of backup, to the ancient dinosaur cowering in the car instead of coming to your aid. He felt responsible. The worst of it was the end result. We both knew you'd never recover before the deadline. It was obvious that you'd have to take long-term disability. Steve was so worried about you, about how you'd deal with that final blow. He felt responsible for that, too. He was the one that transferred Davis to a patrol car as a means of forcing him out."

"Davis couldn't have saved me," Rowdy objected.

"I guess that's a debate for another day," Herlin said soberly. "It was then, during our discussion when the solution hit me. If I could get Coop, who was also struggling to deal with recent events, to accept a position with my department, I might ultimately get you as well." Herlin paused to smile. "And now that my evil plan has worked, I'm not going away quietly. I want you working for my department in whatever capacity I can get you. I have to admit, I didn't see the new career as a bar owner coming; but if that means I can only have you part-time, I'll settle for part-time. I will not settle for nothing. You are a valuable addition to my department. I want you enough to overlook an excursion to Detroit."

"Mayor Herlin," Rowdy began.

"Jon," Herlin corrected.

Rowdy closed his eyes and took a long, frustrated breath. "Look, Jon."

Herlin smiled in approval, Rowdy scowled.

"I'm not going on some relaxing vacation. I am heading to Detroit to cause problems, as many problems as I possibly can, for the Detroit mob. You do understand that, right?"

"I not only understand, I wholeheartedly approve," Herlin answered.

"Then you also understand why you should distance yourself from this. You need to be able to say, no matter who comes calling, that I am no longer associated with your organization. We can renegotiate that when I return," Rowdy pointed to the badge, hoping it would appease the mayor.

"I disagree," Herlin sat forward. "Rowdy, you think you're going to cause problems for us; but you're not. We're a small Montana town. What we do, how we view your activities will be an internal matter. It's different here than say... Chicago. Our citizens are strong, patriotic, hardworking people. They won't care that you stepped one foot in the gray to take down the mob. In fact, I'm pretty sure they'll commend you for it."

"Once again," Rowdy pushed. "If you think I'll handle things like Coop..."

Moondance Ridge

"I think you'll handle things like Rowdy Cooper," Jon interrupted. "I know you nearly as well as I know your brother... through Griggs, of course, but also because of Donald. Your grandfather was proud of both of you, differences and all. Steven was impressed with both Cooper brothers. He believed the two of you would rise through the ranks just like your father did. I'm not sure you realize just how much Steven Griggs admired your father. Pappy Cooper was his hero for many years. A sort of role model if you will. They were partners during a very difficult time in Steve's life. Griggs felt like he knew you and Andy, nearly as well as he knew his own kids. He couldn't show favoritism, of course. In fact, I think he kept his distance because he knew his bias would be obvious. I knew all about the Cooper brothers years before I ever met either one of you. Partially from Steve, but also from your grandfather. I'm well aware you are not your brother. I also know, with all your differences, you are just as honorable as he is. I'm not worried about anything you might do in Detroit. I am worried about the situation, and I'm determined to do my part to ensure your safety and success. Take the badge, Rowdy. You might not need it; and if that's the case, leave it in your pocket. Nobody will even know it's there. But if you do need it, if something comes up and that badge will help you survive, use it. I've got your back and the council has mine."

Rowdy stared at the simple piece of medal that symbolized so much to him for several minutes. He was more than a little surprised by what Herlin had just told him. He had to know one more thing before he agreed. "What if I can never pass a physical? You said you want me on part-time but Coop didn't have me go through any testing before he brought me on. I won't cut corners and make my brother look bad. If this gets ugly, the media might descend on your little town and start digging. They're going to learn of the shooting in Chicago. The fact I couldn't pass the test will mean I'm not fit to do the job. How will you handle that scrutiny?"

"Coop said you passed the written exam, is that true?" Herlin asked. "It's my understanding the two of you took that test together."

"Yeah," Rowdy nodded. "I took the test."

"Well," Herlin smiled. "That's all our department requires of our officers. There's not a physical exam. Never has been. It's a loophole, I guess you could say. Most of our people come to us fresh from graduation. Typically, they just completed the Police Officer Standards and Training Academy and are looking to get certified. We, as county officials, didn't see the need to put them through one more physical just for the sake of administering a test. If you passed the POST exam, you are just as qualified as any other officer in our department. If the media asks, that's the answer they will receive. I'll also add a little something about how honored we are to have you on the team."

"Did Coop know that?" Rowdy asked. "Did he know you don't require a physical test prior to employment?"

"I can't answer that, but I doubt it," Herlin admitted. "He never asked. I suspect he was worried about the answer. He does know that now, I spoke to him last night. I also told him I planned to visit you this morning. I explained the policy to him and suggested the county would be better off with you on the team than we would be without you. I know you're busy running your business, but I also know you have a little free time as well. You can make your own schedule and hammer out the details with Coop when you get back. Once a week, once a month, I don't care. I think the arrangement will be beneficial to us all. Now, I've taken up enough of your time. I know you have a plane to catch and I'm sure you want some time to say goodbye to that lovely lady of yours." Herlin stood and picked up his empty mug.

Rowdy moved forward and took the cup. "I've got it," he followed the mayor to the front door, setting the mugs on the table as he walked past. "Thanks for coming by," he finally said.

"Thanks for humoring me," Herlin smiled as he stepped onto the front porch. "Hello, Andy." He gave Coop a friendly nod before desending the stairs. He had only taken a few steps before he turned and focused on Rowdy. "I'm sorry I didn't come clean weeks ago. I think by keeping the details to myself, the reason I pursued you so vigorously, you might have suffered unnecessarily. If so, I truly regret the delay." Then he turned, climbed into his car and drove away.

"What was that about?" Bailey asked immediately.

Rowdy glanced at Coop. "Did you know he hoped I would eventually work for you?"

"Not until last night," Coop admitted. "I didn't know any of it until last night. The whole time he was pursuing me, trying to convince me to move out here and take over, he never once told me about his connection to Griggs or our grandfather. I had no idea how much he knew about our careers. I always wondered why he was so set on hiring me, but I never did figure it out. I was just grateful for it when we saw this place and decided to move. I was too grateful for the job to question the reasons."

"Well," Rowdy pulled the badge from his pocket. "I guess you win. I'm still not sure it's the best thing... for any of us. But, you win."

"We all win," Coop pulled Rowdy into a brotherly hug. "Promise you'll be careful."

"I'll be careful," Rowdy sobered. "Promise you won't let anything happen to Bailey while I'm gone. I have a bad feeling about this. One I can't shake."

"I have the same feeling," Coop admitted. "I don't like this, and I'm still not sure splitting up is the right tactic."

"Give me another plan, and I'll stay," Rowdy said immediately. "One that ensures the same outcome. Because I've got nothing. Believe me, I've tried."

"Me too," Coop settled into a chair. "Me too, and for the life of me I can't come up with a better plan. Now, you said you needed to see me. Can we do it here, or do we need to head into the office?"

"Actually," Rowdy moved to lean against the sturdy wooden rail. "We need to head over to Tony's. Theresa has something she wants to give you. I have to warn you though, it's going to be over your head. We have to call in Skeet, there's no other option. I know his supervisor is peeved about the redneck country boy act; but at this point, I think he's the only one that can help. And, you also need to know, there's a dirty agent in the mix. A guy that is complacent if not the actual perpetrator in a murder. Theresa's brother-in-law, Zach Regan. We need Skeet, and we need him to do it on the down low for now."

Coop sighed. "I guess we better get started then." He stood and turned to face Bailey. "Keep Knight close, he's the best protection you've got right now. I'm going to stop at the house and ask Maggie to spend the day here, with Bryan. I'd like her to hang out at your place until it's time to head to the bar. If I can't be here, I want all of you protected by that mutt."

"I agree," Bailey also stood. "I already made a promise to Rowdy. Where I am, Knight goes. It's a good idea to have Maggie and Bryan close as well. We'll be fine, I promise. Go do cop things. I'll see you at the bar later tonight."

The two men disappeared and Bailey went inside to await her neighbor. Maybe this forced time together would help the two friends reconcile their differences.

Chapter Seven

It was nearly ten hours later when the small group landed on the tarmac in Detroit. Tony had arranged for a car, and it was waiting when they arrived. A large, slightly-scary looking man approached; spoke briefly to Tony; then climbed into a second car; and disappeared down the drive.

"Let's get to the hotel," Tony grabbed his bag then Theresa's and moved to the rear of the sleek black car. Rowdy followed, deposited his own bags in the trunk, and slid into the back seat.

Tony had booked one of the Penthouse Suites in the MGM Grand. Theresa had never seen anything like it in her life. "Don't you think it's a little extravagant?"

"Not at all," Tony said casually. "There's a spa downstairs. Feel free to make yourself at home. I was thinking maybe you'd want to book a session for tonight."

"And the two of you?" Theresa asked more than a little suspicious now. "What do you two plan to do all night?"

"Uh..." Tony squirmed. "Well, we were thinking we could check out Dom's casino."

"And you don't want me with you?" Theresa realized.

"I don't want Dominic Zarconi to know you are in town just yet," Tony corrected.

"We need to do a little snooping," Rowdy added. "If you're with us, the security cameras will pick you up the instant you step through the door. If someone recognizes you, our anonymity goes out the door."

"I understand," Theresa dropped into one of the comfortable looking chairs. "I'm not going to be a problem but you two need to be careful. If Drago or Socks sees you, they'll act immediately. Before you know what's happening, you'll be ushered into the back room. Dom doesn't have cameras back there. If you find yourself inside his private office, chances are pretty good you won't live to tell about it."

"We'll be careful," Tony moved to the chair and settled onto the armrest. He took Theresa's hand in his and rubbed his thumb over her palm. "We have to start somewhere. The casino seemed as good a place as any. You'll be safe here, I've asked for extra security and tipped the concierge to keep our presence a secret. You can move around freely, at least for tonight. There's a spa, a large pool with a Jacuzzi and a sauna downstairs. You're even safe in the hotel casino, just don't leave the building okay? They also have a state of the art fitness area. Make yourself at home. If you order room service, just put it on the room, they apparently have a wide variety of movies available as well."

"Don't they cost extra?" Theresa asked, uncomfortable with the luxury accommodations.

"Tea, I can afford this," Tony pulled her to her feet and wrapped his arms around her. "Let me pamper you a little. This trip is going to be difficult enough. Let me make it easier." He took a step back. "By the way, do you like baseball?"

"I love it," Theresa smiled. "When I was little, my dad took me to a Tiger's game as often as we could afford it. I still remember it to this day. The excitement of the crowd, the warm spring afternoon, the smell of popcorn and hotdogs in the air. It's something I'll never forget as long as I live."

"And you?" Tony glanced at Rowdy.

Rowdy shrugged. "Who doesn't like baseball? That would be un-American."

"Good," Tony grinned. "Because I reserved the suite next Sunday. The Detroit Tigers are playing the White Sox, should be an amazing game."

"How did you manage that?" Theresa asked.

"Money talks, sweetheart," Tony shrugged. "I figured by then we'd need a break and a little fun. It gives us something to look forward to. So, what do you say? A little spa treatment while Rowdy and I go gamble the night away?"

Moondance Ridge

"Actually," Theresa considered. "I think I'd like to relax tonight. Maybe watch a movie and try out the monstrous tub in there."

Tony pressed a kiss to Theresa's forehead. "If that's what you'd like." He studied her face for several seconds. "Are you okay? I mean I know coming back here has to be difficult. Are you sure you'll be okay alone?"

"I'll be fine," she nodded. "Go on, do what you need to do. You didn't come here to babysit me or entertain me. We came here to work, to figure out how to take Dominic and his organization down. Go plot our revenge."

Tony nodded and turned to Rowdy. "There are two rooms, take your pick and dump your stuff; then, let's go."

"Most of the activity happens around back, but there are cameras," Theresa added. "You have to enter from the North. Dom keeps that unsecure. He doesn't want a record of who comes and goes from his private space. The parking garage, up on top, will give you the best vantage point. But, be careful, security sweeps the top floor. It's part of their regular routine. Dom knows it's vulnerable and he's cautious."

"We'll be careful," Tony promised as Rowdy disappeared down the hallway. "I was hoping you would be okay sharing a room but if not, I can make up the couch. It's your call."

"I'd like to share," Theresa said immediately. She knew tonight was going to be tough. She was already a jumbled mess of nerves. Being close to Tony would make her feel safe. She hated feeling weak and vulnerable but was realistic enough to know that was exactly how she would feel until she left Detroit.

"Good," Tony picked up their luggage and headed for the back room. Moments later, he returned. He had changed into comfortable clothes and was now sporting another college sweatshirt and jeans. He focused on Rowdy. "You ready to go lose a few hundred?"

"What makes you think I'll lose?" Rowdy grinned.

"Because we both know if we start winning, it will draw attention. We need to fade into the background; and the best way to do that, is to lose." Tony turned and gave Theresa a gentle kiss.

Theresa wasn't sure what got into her, but a gentle kiss wasn't enough. She pressed her body against Tony's and deepened the contact. They only broke apart because Rowdy cleared his throat and then let out a fake cough.

"Be careful," Theresa pleaded.

"We will, I promise," Tony gave her another quick peck before leaving the room.

The instant the door shut Theresa sank to the couch, exhausted and worried. Being here, in Detroit, was more difficult than she'd ever imagined it would be. She'd been struggling to deal with her emotions since the skyline came into view from the tiny airplane window. Leaving the plane, walking across the tarmac, had felt like a trip to the gallows. She still wasn't confident they would survive this mission. Then, add in all the memories of Shawn, Zach and her parents; and it was nearly impossible to keep it together. In an attempt to distract her mind, she flipped on the television and began to absently surf. A smile spread across her face when she landed on an old classic, one of Zach's favorites. Maybe that was a sign of some sort. She could almost hear his cheerful voice telling her to relax and live a little. *Just go with it, Tea*, he used to say. Maybe this time, she'd try to listen.

* * * *

Tony pulled the vehicle to the top floor of the parking garage and parked at the far end of the structure. He shut down the engine and pushed the seat as far back as it would go. He was surprised when Rowdy held out an expensive pair of binoculars.

"You're going to have a better view of the back door," Rowdy said casually as he rummaged around in his bag.

"Where did a cowboy like you get an expensive pair of night vision like this?"

"SWAT days," Rowdy shrugged and pulled out a second pair of binoculars. They weren't night vision, but they were top of the line. "The department couldn't afford to spring for the good stuff; so, Coop and I did a couple side jobs and bought our own. I had no idea just how frequently I'd need them once I left law enforcement."

"You haven't exactly left," Tony pointed out. "However, the situation with Bailey and now Theresa are... unusual to put it mildly."

"I suppose," Rowdy settled further into his seat and made a few adjustments with the electronic buttons before glancing around the parking garage. "If you've never used night vision, the one thing you need to know...avoid the light. If the back door starts to open, look away. There could be a motion light that's activated by the door. A fraction of a second will fry your retinas. Trust me, it's painful and something you will never forget."

"Sounds like a voice of experience," Tony glanced at his new partner in crime.

"It is," Rowdy grinned. "Coop and I were messing around one night and came face-to-face with the Watch Commanders headlights. Not only was the pain burned into my memory for all eternity; but he scared us so badly, I nearly jumped out of my own skin. We were just lucky Godfrey found us instead of Griggs. Although, I'm beginning to think Griggs' bark was mostly for show."

"Sounds like you still miss it," Tony observed.

"Yeah," Rowdy admitted. "Not as much as I used to, but yeah. I think I always will."

"Bailey wants you to spend more time working as a reserve with Coop," Tony said reluctantly.

"She told you that?"

"She did," Tony admitted. "She'd never pressure you, that's just how she is. But, she said you're happier when you can at least keep your toe in the water, so to speak. She also said you're good at it. I see what she means. There's something different about you. I noticed it the minute you stepped onto the plane. You're in cop mode. That means you're focused, constantly planning five steps ahead; but you're happy. More content than usual, I guess. It's hard to explain, but I understand what she means now that I've seen it firsthand."

Rowdy wasn't sure what to think of Tony's assessment. He was right, of course. But, he didn't realize it was that obvious. He also didn't have a chance to respond because he spotted a light coming up the ramp. "Incoming," he said as he shoved his body onto the floor.

Tony twisted and maneuvered so his body was sandwiched between the front seat and the steering wheel. Then, he reached around and pressed the button to straighten the chair into its natural position. He had just finished when the bright beam of a flashlight swept over the interior of the vehicle. Tony held his breath as he waited to see if the guard would pass by or stop to investigate further. Seconds later, the light disappeared around the corner. He shifted, pushing his body upwards when Rowdy grabbed his arm.

"Wait," he whispered forcefully.

"He's gone," Tony objected. "And this steering wheel jammed into my spine isn't exactly pleasant."

"Wait," Rowdy insisted. Just then, a second flashlight appeared only feet away from the back window. It too scanned over the interior of the car, then moved on, ultimately disappearing around the corner.

"How'd you know?" Tony asked immediately.

Rowdy pushed his body back into the seat and straightened his leg, clearly in pain. "I think they have a playbook or something. They never go anywhere alone, never. And, DeRossi's men used that tactic more than once on me and Coop. We nearly blew it the first time. After that, we knew it was coming. They think they're smart, clever professionals, but as you can see they're easy to evade."

Tony once again pushed the seat as far back as it would go so he could straighten out his back and stretch his muscles. "How bad is the leg?"

"Not bad," Rowdy scowled. "Give me a minute, and I'll be fine."

Tony reached for the binoculars, then leaned forward just as the back door flew open and three men stepped out. Rowdy was right, two bright lights flashed on illuminating the entire area.

Rowdy shoved the regular binoculars at Tony as he reached in his pocket and retrieved two pain pills. He didn't have the luxury of time to recover, he needed to be ready for action. He dry swallowed the pills as the three men moved into an alleyway.

"Now what?" Tony asked turning to study Rowdy. "You up for a little drive?"

"You think you can follow without being seen?"

Tony started the car and pulled through the garage, making his way to the far end of the parking lot. Once the men pulled onto the highway, he'd be ready. He used the binoculars to see inside each approaching car from a distance. Finally, a black SUV headed their way. "That's them," he told Rowdy as he passed over the binoculars and waited for the men to drive by.

"Don't..." Rowdy began then stopped. Tony obviously knew what he was doing and didn't need Rowdy's distraction.

Tony smiled as he pulled onto the roadway leaving several cars between him and his prey. He knew how to tail someone without being spotted. He held back, changed lanes and did his best to look like your average driver headed down the highway. As far as he could tell, the SUV had no idea it was being tailed.

"I'd say you've done this before," Rowdy finally said.

Moondance Ridge

"Maybe once or twice," Tony grinned.

"Care to explain? Or am I better off not knowing?"

Tony sighed. "My mother was a druggie. She sold herself just enough to get her next fix. Not a pro, she didn't have a pimp or anything. Probably because she didn't want to share her profits at the end of the night. She had her favorite corner and a few regulars. I guess that was enough for her. Anyway, we moved around a lot until I was about five. Then, we set up in a dive and stayed permanently. Maybe because enrolling me in school, kept me out of her hair. It certainly wasn't motherly love or concern for my education."

Rowdy split his attention between the vehicle they were following and Tony. Bailey had told him her friend had a rough start, but he hadn't realized just how hard until this moment.

"I was basically on my own," Tony continued. "She didn't care if I was coming or going. In fact, she was usually happiest when I was going. Anyway, once I started school, something awakened inside. I loved to learn, and I was curious about everything. I perfected the art of tailing without anyone realizing I was there at an early age, six… seven maybe. I was good at it. I followed my mother a couple times when she left the house at night; but once I saw what she was doing, I didn't want any part of that. The skill saved my life more than once. If you can track someone without being detected, you also get pretty good at knowing when you have a tail yourself. The skill has served me well over the years."

"So, what happened to your mother?" Rowdy asked. "Bailey said you don't have any family. Is she still around?"

"No," Tony took the off ramp and slowed to let another car slide in front of him. "She overdosed when I was thirteen."

"And that's when you went to live with Conrad?"

"Bailey told you about that?"

"A little," Rowdy admitted. "She said he was murdered, and the man responsible is serving a life sentence."

"The man who pulled the trigger is serving life," Tony corrected. "The man responsible is another story."

Rowdy frowned. "What does that mean?"

"Beynart worked for Nate Voyt," Tony pulled off the side of the road and shut down the headlights. The SUV was slowing, and he didn't want to be discovered just yet. "Voyt was responsible for Con's death. He was using me as a runner."

"Drugs?" Rowdy asked.

"Mostly," Tony admitted. "Although, there were other items as well. I was good. He liked using kids, especially young kids because the cops didn't harass them as much. Before Voyt showed up, the neighborhood was like a war-zone. The Crips and Bloods were battling it out almost daily. The cops were trying to get control, but they always seemed to snag the wrong guy. I wasn't involved in that shit, didn't have any interest in gang life. I spent my free time at the library but, I had to eat and food was a distant second to my mother's next fix. Once she died, I was on my own."

"So, you picked pockets," Rowdy surmised.

"I guess Bailey told you about that, too?"

Moondance Ridge

"She told me how you met Conrad, that he took you in when you needed someone. And, she told me he was murdered," Rowdy hesitated.

"And she told you I blame myself?" Tony added.

"She did," Rowdy nodded. "There can't be much up there. Let's wait a few more minutes before we check it out. In fact," he glanced backwards. "Let me get out and guide you. I think we should leave the car here." Rowdy slowly opened the passenger door careful to press the release button on the side before the light flashed on. He crouched on the ground, fumbled around under the dash for several seconds, then yanked on two wires. When he stood, the door light had been disconnected.

"Guess you've done that before," Tony observed.

Rowdy smiled. "Cop trick." He disappeared behind the vehicle and didn't return for several minutes. "There's nowhere to hide the vehicle here. Oh, and I disconnected your backup lights. Let's move back down that way and park in the lot of that large building. We shouldn't look too out of place among the other vehicles."

Tony pulled back onto the highway and made his way to the lot in the dark. He maneuvered the vehicle around so it was parked facing the nondescript building where the vehicle they were following had disappeared.

"Not ideal, but I think it will do," Rowdy decided.

"Now what?" Tony asked. "You want to head in on foot and see what's down there?"

"Eventually," Rowdy said studying the terrain. "Let's wait another five, though. Tell me what happened to Voyt."

"Disappeared," Tony said hesitantly. How much should he tell?

"Dead then?" Rowdy pressed.

"Disappeared," Tony corrected. "The lead detective told me the guy probably fled the country to avoid prosecution."

"Did he?"

"Are you implying something?" Tony asked, aggravated.

"I can protect you from a lot of things, will stand by for nearly anything," Rowdy paused to consider. "But, I won't cover up a homicide. Not then, not now."

"I didn't kill him," Tony said softly. He didn't have to confess his sins to Rowdy Cooper. He hadn't actually killed Voyt, but some would argue he had a hand in it. Both he and his best friend, John. If anyone knew John drained the brake fluid from the expensive vehicle before Nate Voyt loaded up his luggage and fled for a private landing strip intent on leaving town, they might even say he did the killing. Tony saw things a little differently. Neither he nor John knew the man was planning to flee. They assumed he'd take his regular route to the old warehouse which would be a terrifying journey without brakes, but not lethal. Instead, Voyt had sped away from his elaborate home and turned left instead of right. His intended escape route took him up a steep incline before winding its way around the coast. Voyt finally lost control and veered over the edge, plummeting nearly three hundred feet to his death in the icy waters of the Pacific. The tide was high that day and chances were pretty good his vehicle and his body would never be found. Tony was grateful for the way things ended. It meant he didn't have to answer any difficult questions and John's name could be left out of the situation completely.

"But he's dead?" Rowdy pressed.

"He's dead," Tony admitted. "But I didn't do it. There won't be a homicide charge... over what happened then, or now."

"That's all I need to know," Rowdy pushed open the door, indicating it was time to leave.

Tony wasn't sure he could disconnect his interior light switch as proficiently as Rowdy had, so he climbed over the console and slid out the passenger door. Once he secured the vehicle, he turned to look at the man beside him. "Rowdy," he began. "I told Coop this before, but I'll say it again. I have a line I won't cross, it might not be your line, it most certainly wouldn't be Sheriff Cooper's line, but I have a line. I haven't always walked cleanly on the right side of the law, but I can look myself in the mirror each morning without reservation. Nothing that happens while we're here will change that. But, you also need to know, I might cross a line you're not comfortable with. I hope you can live with the knowledge that it was me, not you, and let it go."

"I'm not sure what that means, but trust me, you cross my line... I will intervene. I'm willing to do what needs done, and my methods just might surprise you. But, I will not sell my soul to bring down the devil."

"Understood," Tony gave Rowdy's shoulder a pat. "I have a feeling your line and my line just might be the same one. Now, let's go see what's happening on the other side."

The two men quietly made their way across the road and slid through a stand of trees taking a position behind the thick foliage.

Rowdy settled onto the ground and pulled out his night vision.

Tony settled in next to him. "You look like you've done this before."

Rowdy grinned. "A time or two."

"What do you think? What are they selling?" Tony asked.

Rowdy studied the building then handed the binoculars to Tony. "Says boat accessories."

Tony glanced around the area then handed the lenses back to his new friend. "Brilliant deduction, Einstein. You could have been a detective."

"Naw," Rowdy disagreed as he once again surveyed the area. "I prefer action. You know, man hunting, car chases, throwing the bad guys in a cell, the fun stuff. Studying paperwork, filing reports, analysis, making phone calls… that was more Coop's thing."

"And now we've come full circle. You love this," Tony observed.

Rowdy glanced sideways and sighed. "Yeah," he admitted. "But that doesn't mean I can have it. Those days are gone for me now."

"Why?" Tony asked.

"Seriously?" Rowdy said sarcastically.

Moondance Ridge

"Seriously," Tony said soberly. "You know you can still do it part-time and you should. You don't have to give this up for good. I'd guess that's the reason Coop and Bailey want it to continue. I agree with them, for what it's worth. It's a part of you."

Rowdy didn't have an answer so he let it go. The two men sat silently waiting for any sign of activity outside the building.

* * * *

Joe knocked on the door and waited.

"Come in," Dom said absently.

"Oh," Joe paused, glancing at the two men sitting near the desk. "This can wait."

"Nonsense," Dom looked up. "Come in Joe, what have you found?"

"Not much," Joe said hesitantly. "I'm sorry, but I can't access their system. What I do know is the man who attacked Socks and Drago was not hired legally at the bar. Darrow gave me access to that E-Verify program businesses have to use now. The last employee the Spurs Bar and Grill ran through the system was a part-time waitress named Marnie."

"Doesn't mean he's not getting paid under the table," Dom said, thinking about the many employees he hired the same way. "The only way to know is to send someone out to look into this personally." He glanced at the two men sitting before him. "I guess I do have a new mission for you two."

Joe glanced at the two men and frowned. He hoped Theresa would be safe but with these two heading to Montana, he couldn't be sure.

"Is there anything we need to know?" Talon asked.

"If you have a chance to grab the girl, Theresa Regan, do it. I want her back here where she belongs," Dom decided. "And if the mystery guy gets in the way again, take him out."

"We're on it," Dreven said, standing. The two men silently left the room.

"Good job, Joe. That will be all," Dominic said in dismissal.

Joe left the room, worried about Theresa, a woman he had come to admire, a woman that had come so close to escaping.

* * * *

"We've been here over an hour and not a soul has left that building," Tony complained.

"Welcome to my world," Rowdy shrugged. "Surveillance work takes patience."

"What do you think the propane tank is for?" Tony asked. "They live in the middle of the city. That building isn't fueled by propane."

"Could be used for the lifts," Rowdy provided. "Forklifts."

"Well," Tony said, considering. "What if we eliminate the fuel and see what happens?"

"What do you mean?" Rowdy frowned.

Tony stood. "I'm going to drain the tank. If they ran a line inside, they'll send someone out to investigate. If not, it should be about time to refuel."

"I'm not sure that's..." Rowdy stopped. Objecting was worthless, Tony was already halfway across the yard headed for the large propane container. Rowdy watched as Nazario did a little crouching run across the opening and hid behind the large tank. Within seconds, he was working on the valve at the far end.

Rowdy glanced up, spotted the camera and considered. If he got rid of it, they would know they had company. If he didn't, his photo and Tony's would be captured on film. Zarconi would know who was after him, and he'd have proof for his dirty cops. Rowdy had to get rid of it. There was no other choice. He glanced around the area looking for a solution. Seconds later, he found what he needed. Rowdy clasped the large rock in the palm of his hand and used it to smash out the lens. Then he shoved the smaller end into the camera until it was securely embedded inside the lens compartment. That should take care of the problem, temporarily. Tony wanted action, Rowdy had a feeling he might get his wish a little sooner than planned.

Moments later, Tony slid in beside his partner. "Now, it's time to wait and watch."

"That was dangerous," Rowdy scolded. "It is dangerous. That open valve is a hazard and uh... we need to move."

"What? Where?" Tony glanced at his partner then snapped up the binoculars when a man stepped out the back door. He approached the propane tank and leaned up against it, pulling a cigarette from a pack in his shirt pocket. He immediately began to fumble in his jeans pockets, most likely for a lighter.

"Again," Rowdy said softly. "Reckless and dangerous."

"Don't do it," Tony whispered. "Walk away. What kind of moron lights up next to a propane tank?"

A second man stepped from the building and approached the first. They had a brief conversation; then the two of them stepped forward, pulled their weapons and pointed them in the direction of the trees.

"Move," Rowdy ordered as he gave Tony a shove. "Now! That way, there's an embankment we can use for cover."

Tony and Rowdy scrambled over dead logs and made their way to the secluded dirt mound several yards to their right. They had just dropped below the surface when the two workers fired. Bullets struck the trees and ricocheted off the rough surface of the ground in the exact spot Tony and Rowdy just vacated... suddenly, the world around them exploded.

Rowdy uncovered his ears and forced his body into a sitting position. He'd been half prepared for the blast. Tony on the other hand looked a little dazed. The massive shockwave from an exploding propane tank would do that to a guy.

"How'd they know we were there?" Tony finally asked.

"Camera," Rowdy said casually as he stood, careful to remain hidden behind a large tree. "I haven't seen any others so I'm guessing they were set up sporadically as an alert system. Probably one on the other side of the building, maybe one or two on the building itself. Just enough to alert the men if someone was lurking in the shadows. Kind of like we are."

Tony stood. "Now what?"

"Now," Rowdy brushed off his jeans. "You stay here while I take a look inside. But, be careful, with that racket police and fire are already on their way."

"Nice try, but no." Tony shook his head as he glanced around the area. His gaze naturally landed on the wreckage from the propane tank. There was no sign of the two men. Guilt swamped him, and he ran a frustrated hand through his hair. It was his fault two men were just blown to pieces.

"Hey," Rowdy put a hand on Tony's shoulder. "Don't feel bad about that. I mean, those two were trying to kill us. If that tank didn't take them out, I would have shot them myself." Rowdy shrugged. "This way it's cleaner. Dom and the authorities will think it was an accident, a malfunction on the tank of some kind. Plus, now it's your fault, not mine."

Tony studied Rowdy for several seconds. "You're serious?"

"I'm always serious about death," Rowdy took a step forward. "Stay put, I'll be back in ten. If it takes longer, head back to the room without me."

"I'm coming with you," Tony moved to follow. "Forget it," he shook his head. "We don't have time to argue about this. I'm your partner, it's about time you started to treat me like one."

"Tony," Rowdy began moving toward the building hoping he could change the man's mind before they got inside. "What I'm doing… this is burglary. The cops are enroute. If I get caught, it means time in a cell."

"Good thing I have excellent lawyers," Tony strolled casually beside him. "However, it would be better for all of us if we just don't get caught."

"Yeah, that's the goal." Before leaving the seclusion of the trees, Rowdy paused to survey the area. Several men had exited the building, but they were all focused on the explosion and the remains of the two men who had been killed. He had to admit, Tony accidentally created the perfect diversion. Rowdy sighed inwardly. He knew Tony didn't understand his viewpoint. Their friendship was too new. Coop or Skeet would get it but the suave businessman was new to all this. Maybe Rowdy was jaded from the job, but to his way of thinking, he was just being realistic and sensible.

Death was death and always something to take seriously. He wasn't thrilled about the loss of life, but he wasn't going to worry about it either. Dom's thugs were trying to kill them. If the explosion hadn't neutralized the threat, Rowdy would have. And, shooting them was complicated. This way was cleaner, and it gave them more time. He glanced around, searching for any sign of trouble before darting toward a side door. He was a little surprised when the knob turned freely, and he quickly slid inside. Tony stepped in behind him.

The two men slowly made their way through the warehouse. The first area they came to was a large, open bay that was clearly used for packing and shipping. Nothing of interest stood out, so they made their way across the open expanse, pausing when they came to a long hallway. Rowdy studied the dimly-lit path before moving several feet forward and darting cautiously into the first room they encountered. It was packed full with large crates. The two men moved around the room, looking for a box that wasn't sealed shut. Rowdy crouched to study the wooden shipping container. The outside was stamped with large black letters on every side… COFFEE. *Not likely*, Rowdy ran his hand over the top crate looking for a weakness. It was tightly secured and impossible to open with his bare hands. His gaze landed on Tony and he shrugged.

"I'm going to check out the room across the hall," Tony decided, shining the beam of his flashlight on the closest pile of crates. "How about a little wager? Five to one that's not coffee."

"Since you're the multi-billionaire and I'm just a lowly bar-owning ex-cop, I'll pass on the bad bet. Be careful. Let me know what you find, more coffee crates or something else. And, watch out for guards. Most of them are dealing with the chaos, but one or two may hold back to guard the merchandise."

"On it," Tony gave a backward waive as he disappeared out the door.

Rowdy retrieved his own flashlight and slowly made his way around the room. He had to find something to pry open the lid. Moments later, he found what he needed. There was a pry bar hidden behind the first row of crates. Rowdy snagged it and went to work on the lid, careful not to make a sound as he slid the wooden top off the box. It was immediately obvious the thing didn't hold coffee. He cautiously brushed flakes of sawdust to the side and spotted the sleek black barrel of a rifle. *Jackpot!* He carefully cleared away the remaining saw dust making sure the entire gun was uncovered then pulled out his phone. The image wasn't perfect, but you could clearly tell the weapon was a new Colt M4 assault rifle. He moved to the second stack of crates and pried open the top. This one contained AK47's. Clearly Dominic Zarconi was into gun running. He was about to replace the lid when he heard voices headed his way. Rowdy frantically slid both lids back onto the crates. He glanced around then crouched and carefully crawled backward, searching for an opening or shallow pocket that would keep him hidden. Once he was in place, he held his breath hoping the duo would continue down the hallway.

* * * *

Dominic Zarconi stepped from his vehicle and surveyed the area. This situation could be problematic. He didn't have anyone inside the fire department on his payroll. It hadn't been necessary. If they insisted on heading inside...well, they were certain to find the weapons. He studied each officer and relaxed. Frank and Corey, two of Detroit's finest, were among the responders. They could clear the building, he'd insist on it. He approached Sgt. Delbert and made his request. Once the supervisor agreed, he stood back and waited. Hopefully, the firemen would be able to determine if this was an accident or foul play. It better be an accident. If they suspected foul play, heads would roll. Nobody messed with Dominic Zarconi and lived. Then again, if it was negligence, the man who put him at risk would need to be punished. He'd have to think about that. Punishment would need to be swift.

* * * *

"I don't like being put in this position, Frank."

"Just do what you're told. Dom's paying you enough to follow directions without complaint."

"What? You get paid?"

"You don't?"

"No, and now that he's singled me out like that, I'm going to be scrutinized by the entire unit. Why do you get paid?"

"Uh, well... I'm sure you will, eventually. Dom likes to make sure he can trust his employees before he works out a salary."

"Like I have a choice. The man threatened my six-year-old son. The SOB had photos of Ken playing at his favorite park. How does he think that shows loyalty? Anyone would do his bidding to save his kid."

"Keep talking like that and you might end up in a body bag instead of on the payroll. Dealing with Dom takes patience. You'll be rewarded soon, and Ken will be fine. As far as the unit goes, shrug it off. They'll look at you funny for a few weeks, but then it will drop. You had no control. He may have selected you, but Sarge gave us this assignment. Don't act guilty, and you won't look guilty."

The two men stepped into the first room and looked around.

Rowdy froze and forced his breathing to slow as he listened to the conversation taking place in the hallway just outside the door. As he inhaled and exhaled, he was careful not to make a sound. His fingers itched to take a photo of the two cops, but he knew the flash would activate and he'd be discovered for sure. Instead, he studied their faces, determined to remember every feature. If Coop finally reached Skeet, maybe he'd be able to get employment photos from the local PD. His breath caught in his throat; and he froze, not daring to move a muscle. The two cops stepped just inside the open doorway and shone a bright flashlight around the room, the beam landed on each pile of crates. Rowdy watched and waited, hoping he replaced the lids completely. If it was the slightest inch off, they might realize someone had been inside the building. That would make escape even more difficult. From Rowdy's angle, he could tell the last crate he'd opened wasn't flush with the base. He tightened his grip on his weapon and prayed he wouldn't have to use it. The two men continued to survey the room for several seconds before pivoting and heading across the hall. Rowdy relaxed, slid his gun into his holster and moved back to the crates for more photos. He just hoped Tony didn't get caught. If he did, those excellent lawyers were going to make their money tonight.

Tony heard voices and moved silently into the large closet and waited. The men would leave eventually. He just hoped they didn't do a thorough search of the room first. With any luck, Rowdy got the crate open and figured out what these guys were into. Maybe the information would help them bring Zarconi and his organization down. But first, they needed to get out of here. He patiently waited, careful not to make the slightest noise as two cops swept the room with their flashlights then immediately moved on. He stayed completely still, waiting patiently as the sounds made by men's footsteps on the squeaky floor slowly grew quieter and quieter until they eventually disappeared. Tony silently moved to the doorway and peeked around the corner, checking for round two. Once he was sure the coast was clear, he crossed the hallway and stepped back inside the room with the crates. "You still in here?" he whispered.

Rowdy climbed out from behind the box he had just secured and headed for the door. "I have everything we need for now. Let's find a way out of here."

"Actually," Tony pushed past his friend and darted across the empty hallway, disappearing into the room he'd just vacated. He glanced back to make sure Rowdy followed, then made a right turn and disappeared.

Rowdy frowned but continued to follow. He turned the corner and glanced around. "What are we doing? The cops are gone for now, but they could return any minute."

"We're leaving," Tony grinned.

Rowdy focused on a tiny window in the far corner and frowned. "Neither one of us will fit through that window."

"True," Tony agreed as he moved to the back of the room and yanked on the wall. It immediately slid sideways and disappeared. It was like a pocket door you would find in a bathroom but harder to see.

"How in the world did you find that?" Rowdy asked.

"I grew up in California," Tony shrugged. "Voyt had one just like it. He wanted a way to reach his boat in case of an emergency."

"You think this leads to the dock?" Rowdy asked as he stepped into a concrete tunnel.

"I'm sure of it," Tony slid the door closed and switched on his flashlight. "The question is where. If we're lucky, it will empty out further down the river. With everyone focused on the explosion, we might just escape unnoticed."

Rowdy pulled out his phone and began to take video of their journey. If they were able to reach Skeet in this lifetime, the footage might help him convince his boss to get involved. He paused as his feet became engulfed in water. "Are we going for a swim? Because an underwater excursion is deadly on night vision. It's also going to render our weapons unusable."

"I doubt it," Tony said over his shoulder. "Voyt's tunnel was built so the water level didn't rise too high. I think the highest point was about knee level. The equipment should be fine."

* * * *

Skeet stood and moved backward, Blake followed. "Let's head to the hotel. I'm not sure anyone is even inside that building tonight. For some reason, the flood of activity has stopped completely."

"I agree," Blake turned and headed for the stairs. "Either they finished early, or they have another warehouse."

"I haven't been able to trace this to Zarconi, but we both know it's his. The challenge is tracing the holding company back to the mob boss. He's had years of experience and is going to be proficient in hiding his assets." Skeet was frustrated. He missed his wife and wanted this case to be finished. Darrow hadn't shown today, which was unusual. Something was up tonight, and Skeet wanted to know what. He slid behind the wheel of his rental and waited for Blake to close the passenger's door. Within minutes, they were secured inside the hotel. Skeet dropped onto the uncomfortable chair and pulled out his phone. He needed to hear Angie's voice.

"Hello?" Angela said softly.

"Hi, honey," Skeet said in greeting. "Sorry it's so late, I just got back to the room and wanted to check in."

Moondance Ridge

Angela began her normal routine of telling Skeet about her day.

"Skeet," Blake pounded on the door that separated their rooms. "Open up."

"Sounds like you need to go," Angie said hesitantly. She missed her husband and couldn't wait for him to return.

"Maybe," Skeet stood and walked to the divider door, swinging it open impatiently.

"You need to see this," Blake pointed to the tiny television.

"I guess I do," Skeet told his wife. "I'll call you tomorrow. I love you, baby."

"I love you, too," Angela whispered. "Be careful."

"Goodnight," Skeet said just before he ended the call. He turned to his partner. "What has you so agitated?"

Blake hit a button and sound echoed throughout the room. "That's Zarconi," he pointed to the upper corner of the television.

Skeet settled on the edge of the bed and studied the scene before him. "Where is that?"

"Some warehouse on the bank of the Detroit River near Atwater Street. Looks like they shut down the Detroit Riverwalk as a precaution. They said a propane tank exploded. I spotted Darrow in the crowd, explains why he was missing tonight. Might explain why they were all missing."

"So," Skeet considered. "That must be a second storage area. Whatever they're selling, it's either large or business really is booming. That's the only reason they'd need two large warehouses. Explains DeRossi's conversation with Nico about the coffee. He said production was up and demand was high."

"If they're shipping coffee, I'm the reincarnation of Elvis here for a reunion concert," Blake grumbled. "And I don't sing."

"Coffee is just a cover," Skeet said absently. He was studying the television set, trying to identify as many people as he could. "I'll call Stan and have him pull the footage. He should be able to get it from the local network."

"See if there's a staff member he trusts to identify the participants. We need a copy as well, but if someone on his end can get the names and backgrounds, that would help. Neither one of us has contacts here in the city. Plus, I'm not ready to be noticed yet, especially with a price on your head. We're better off in the shadows for now."

Skeet agreed as he carefully scanned the crowd for any of the old players. So far, so good. If he didn't recognize them, they shouldn't recognize him. Things just got interesting and that explosion had finally given them another lead.

* * * *

Theresa paced the room, worried. Tony and Rowdy said they were going to the casino. Why had they ended up at the warehouse? Did Dom suspect something? Had Drago and Socks spotted them? Were they dead? She grabbed the remote and increased the volume when the on-scene reporter filled the screen.

"An anonymous source within the police department just informed us two bodies were discovered inside the blast. We are still trying to confirm this report. So far, official channels have refused to confirm any fatalities," the reporter said calmly.

Theresa fell onto the couch and covered her face with her hands. *Two bodies.* She jumped to her feet when the door swung open. Theresa was off the couch and across the room in a matter of seconds. She practically tackled Tony as she began to sob.

"Hey," Tony said as he wrapped his arms around Theresa. "What's wrong?"

Rowdy spotted the television and sighed. "You thought we were dead?"

Theresa nodded, unable to compose herself.

"What? Why?" Tony studied Theresa.

Theresa swallowed hard and tried to brush the tears from her face. "They said there were two bodies."

Tony glanced at the television. "Dom's men, not us. Come here, sit down." He escorted her to the couch and sat down next to her.

Rowdy's phone rang. He glanced at the screen. "This is Coop, I have to take it."

"Go ahead," Tony nodded. "You might want to change while you're at it. I got this."

"Hey, Coop," Rowdy answered as he disappeared down the hallway. "What's up?" He stepped into his room and immediately kicked off his soaking wet sneakers.

"I still haven't been able to contact Skeet," Coop began. "I'm starting to get worried."

"Why?" Rowdy asked as he slipped off his jeans and pulled on a pair of grey sweats.

"When I didn't get a response from him at the office, I called the main number. The receptionist said he's in Washington on assignment. When I pressed, I was told it was top secret."

"So, call Angie," Rowdy suggested as he settled on the edge of the bed. "She always knows how to get a hold of her husband."

"I would but she's missing, too."

"What do you mean she's missing?" Rowdy pressed.

"I've left half a dozen messages at their house. Angie hasn't answered no matter what time I try, and she's not returning my calls either," Coop said in frustration.

"That's not like her," Rowdy frowned. "Did Angela have another show?"

"Not that I know of," Coop sighed. "I'll keep trying. Give me another day. If I still can't reach them, I'll call Burns."

"Sounds like a plan," Rowdy ran a hand through his hair. "Listen, I'm going to text you some photos. This is bigger than I originally believed."

"What does that mean?" Coop asked.

"Guns," Rowdy advised. "Illegal gun running. M4's, AK's. The warehouse is a perfect front--says they sell boat accessories. Crates are marked as coffee. I'm assuming that's the cover but…

Moondance Ridge

well, the Detroit river connects with Lake St. Clair, which is only half US. The other half is Canada. They have easy access in two countries."

"How did they get M4's?" Coop asked.

"The hijacking I'm sure," Rowdy mumbled.

"What hijacking?" Coop frowned.

"Do you even read your own alerts?" Rowdy shook his head. "Two months ago, that semi was hijacked leaving the manufacturing plant in Connecticut."

"How do you know that?"

"Because it was one of the law enforcement bulletin's that came out… you know, the ones you insist your men read and memorize?"

"Oh," Coop settled into his favorite lounge chair.

"You want to tell me what's going on?" Rowdy asked. "You haven't been yourself for a while. Does this have to do with Maggie or is something else going on?"

"Maggie," Coop said, clearly frustrated. "She's not herself. I think it's the pregnancy, but she insists she's fine. I've done everything I can think of to get her to make an appointment with her doctor, but she says her next visit isn't for two weeks. She thinks she's fine, she's not. I'm worried about her. I'm worried about my kid. And apparently, it's now affecting my work."

"That's understandable," Rowdy tried not to sound worried. "I didn't want to say anything, but Bailey also noticed the change. She thinks it could be a thyroid problem or a hormonal imbalance

280

that's caused by the pregnancy. You need to get Mags to the doctor."

"Thanks," Coop sighed. "I was worried it was just me. I was afraid I was misreading the situation or overreacting. I'll do it. Now, back to the case. I tried to access those files, but it appears they are all password protected. Do you think Theresa might know the password?"

"I don't know," Rowdy stood. "Let me see." He headed back toward the open lounge area and spotted Theresa and Tony at the table. As he approached, he realized they were on Tony's computer. He paused and watched Theresa type in a few characters and hit enter. An error popped up on the screen. "I'd say no," Rowdy said into the phone. "Looks like she's trying to access them now, but she's not having any more luck than you did."

Theresa glanced up. "Is that still Coop?"

"Yeah," Rowdy said absently. "And he still can't reach our favorite fed."

"Look," Coop said into the phone. "I'll keep trying Skeet and let you know. I'm going to talk to Maggie, see if I can get her to head to the doctor tomorrow. I'll call you after I find Perkins."

Chapter Eight

Theresa glanced up when Rowdy settled in beside her. "I can't get in. The only file I can access is the one with all the stuff Zach gave us plus the keylogger data, but that stuff doesn't make sense."

"Do you think Shawn's friends could crack the passcode? I mean, isn't that what hackers do?" Tony asked.

"I can't ask them to do that," Theresa argued. "If they get involved, it's going to put them on the FBI's radar. After all they've done for me, for us... I can't involve them in this. I won't be the reason they're suddenly investigated and shut down by the feds."

"But what if they got something out of it?" Tony asked.

"Like what?"

"Leverage," Tony glanced at Rowdy. "You're not going to like what I'm about to say. Consider yourself warned," Tony said to Rowdy.

"Go on," Rowdy nodded.

"Well," Tony took Theresa's hand. "These guys worked with Shawn, they learned together, hacked together and set up a system together. If anyone can crack that code, they can. In return, the FBI won't even want to prosecute them."

"Why?" Theresa asked.

"Because they would never prosecute someone that assisted them in an investigation. It's bad for business. Nobody would ever assist the feds again if they learned the last guys got arrested for helping," Tony continued.

Rowdy shook his head. "Seriously, this is ridiculous."

"Is he wrong?" Theresa asked.

"No," Rowdy said. "He's right. But it's irrelevant. Skeet would never prosecute them anyway. But, if his scenario makes you feel better, he's right. It's bad business to arrest an informant. If word got out, nobody would inform."

"So," Tony said to Theresa. "Will you call them? We need their help. At least until Rowdy finds his agent."

"What do you mean finds his agent? Is he missing?" Theresa asked, worried.

"No," Rowdy answered. "Coop just hasn't been able to reach him yet. His office says he's on assignment, but Skeet never leaves town for long. Coop should make contact within the next couple days. It would help if Shawn's friends tried to decode the files for us. Getting that information is going to take time. If they can figure out Shawn's password, we still need someone to sift through the keylogger stuff and find the code for the encrypted files as well. Everything in there is useless if we can't figure out the code."

"Okay," she hesitantly agreed. "I'll call them; but, for now I want them to remain anonymous. Only I know who they are. I'm the only one that will make contact. If they decide to help, they can also decide who knows their identity."

"Can you live with that?" Tony asked Rowdy.

"Sure," he shrugged. "I don't care who these guys are… well, first I have a question. You said they're hackers. Do you know if they've infiltrated any government systems? Are they wanted?"

"No," Theresa said confidently. "They're good guys. And they're surprisingly patriotic for a couple hackers. I'm not comfortable telling you what they've done. But, it has nothing to do with the government."

"Okay then," Rowdy shrugged and stood. "You call the hackers. I'm going to call Bailey."

"Um," Theresa said quickly. "Before you go, I think we need to go over a couple things. I was hoping that you'd have all the information before we arrived in Detroit. I thought you would have looked at the documents on that disk. But, clearly none of us can access Shawn's files; so, let me tell you the basics."

"Okay," Rowdy agreed as he returned to his seat.

Theresa pulled up a map of Detroit from the internet. She took a screenshot and carefully circled the casino. "As you know, that's Dom's casino. He spends a lot of time there, but he also has other places...warehouses. Shawn and I never figured out what he was dealing, but it's obviously something illegal. He was careful who he trusted with access, and Shawn was never allowed."

"Guns," Rowdy told them both. "I got a couple crates open, and they were packed with guns."

Theresa sat back. This was worse than even she had imagined. "I was sure it was drugs."

"Could be that too," Tony took her hand. "Most of the time, these guys don't stick to one vice, they have several."

"He has three warehouses," Theresa said softly. "So, it's possible."

"Three?" Rowdy asked.

"We think so," Theresa nodded. "Or, I guess we thought so. The one on the river where you were tonight. There's also one here." She pointed to a spot on the map a few blocks from the casino."

"And the third?" Tony asked.

"We never found it, but Dom referred to a warehouse in the park. We took that to mean the industrial park, but I'm not sure about that either. We looked, Shawn and I did, but we never could find it. I have no idea what he's doing out there, but it must be serious. Very few people know where it is, even within his inner circle. Fewer can actually go there. Shawn wasn't allowed at the one on the river either. But, many of Dom's top people went out there a lot... sometimes daily."

"And, the one by the casino?" Rowdy asked.

"Shawn did go there, once." Theresa considered. "He said it was basically for the casino--mostly old slot machines, blackjack and roulette tables, things like that. He wasn't allowed upstairs though. Shawn said it looked like an office area, at least the part he could see; but he never got close enough to find out for sure. He also wondered if the casino stuff was a front. Like, maybe they used the warehouse for something else, but positioned casino items in the open in case someone cased the place. That particular building always had a lot of activity."

"Maybe we should check it out," Tony said to Rowdy. "That could be our first stop tomorrow. We know what's out by the river. Let's see what's in the casino warehouse."

"Sounds like a plan. We'll head out after breakfast," Rowdy stood. "Now, I'll see you two in the morning. I'm going to call my woman." Rowdy turned and disappeared down the elaborate hallway.

"You make your call to the hackers, I have one of my own to make." Tony stood and took several steps away.

"John?" Theresa asked.

"Yeah," Tony paused. "I need to check in, make sure he's okay."

"Callie's last name is North. Just in case he hasn't found her yet."

"Thanks," Tony said. "This will just take a minute."

Theresa watched as Tony stepped across the room and stopped in front of the large window. He pulled out his phone and dialed the number before settling into a nearby chair. Theresa pulled out her own phone and opened her contacts. She hadn't called Shawn's friends in years. Hopefully, they'd still be open to helping. She studied her list for several seconds before deciding on Carson. He'd be more open to her request than Marcos.

"Hey," Carson Gibbs answered. "Theresa? Is that you?"

"It is," she confirmed. "How have you been Carson?"

"Good," he said hesitantly. "What's going on? I mean I'm glad for the call; but after Shawn died, you just disappeared. Marcos and I weren't even sure you were still alive."

"I know," Theresa sighed. "And I'm sorry. I just thought… well, it was dangerous. I didn't want you involved."

"And now?" Carson asked.

"And now," Theresa said. "Now, I think I need your help."

"Help how?"

"The stuff Shawn saved on the server," Theresa began. "He password protected it and the files are encrypted. I need help accessing them."

"Why?" Carson asked.

"I'm going to be as honest with you as I can," Theresa told him. "Shawn didn't die in an auto accident. He was killed… tortured and murdered because of the stuff on that server. That's why I kept you out of this. It's risky, but as long as you don't get personally involved, as long as you stay away, I think you'll be safe. I'm trying to protect you as much as I can."

"Theresa," Carson said, worried. "What are you doing? What are you into?"

"This has to do with Zach," Theresa admitted. "Shawn was trying to get something solid on his murder. That's what got him killed, but the evidence is in those files. He saved everything to that cloud system you guys set up. Somehow the system continued to save even after his death. He got killed setting up what he called a keylogger."

"Why now?" Carson asked intrigued but trying to sound neutral. Shawn told him, just a few months before he died, that he believed Dominic Zarconi had killed his brother. Surely any attempt to cross the mob boss would be lethal for all of them.

"Because I'm desperate," Theresa admitted. "The same man is after me. He tried to have me abducted. I'm working with some friends to try to stop him, but we need those files."

"Who are you working with?" Carson asked. "Are you sure you can trust them?"

"A close friend and an ex-cop. They know what they're doing," Theresa added, hoping she was right. "Rowdy, the cop... his brother's the sheriff in the town where I've been living. They don't have any connection to Detroit. Plus, they have a friend with the FBI. I think we can finally end this, but only if you can help. You and Marc."

"I don't know," Carson frowned. "I mean, you know what the three of us did. You have to know Marc and I didn't just stop.

288

Did you consider what could happen if we join up with the FBI. If they get a look at our system, they might figure it all out. I don't think Marc will go for it. I'm not sure I can."

"I have it on good authority that you'll be safe," she told him. She proceeded to explain the angle and the leverage they would have according to Tony and Rowdy.

Tony moved from the window and hit send as he settled into the comfortable chair.

"Callie North is fine," John said in greeting. "I located her this afternoon. She's oblivious."

"Meaning?" Tony asked.

"Meaning," John said. "She's dedicated to her work and frantically preparing for an upcoming fashion show."

"But…" Tony asked.

"But Nico Depiro has his sights set on her," John announced soberly. "I seem to recall the last favor I did for you involved the so-called retired mobster."

"Not good," Tony sighed. "And, don't blame me for that fiasco. I brought Cindy to you for help. It's not my fault you went bat shit on Depiro's goon."

"He was forcing that family to launder his money through their tiny store by kidnapping their son and holding him hostage," John said softly. "I did what I had to do."

"So, what now?" Tony asked. "You available to stick for a while?"

"Yeah," John said. "I'm on it. The woman's as innocent as they come. She's rebuffing, but that could be just as dangerous. I've got this, it's going to be a little more complicated, but I've got this. You finish up there and don't worry about Ms. North. With any luck, we can tie Nico into this Detroit mess and get two birds."

"I agree," Tony said softly. "Keep me posted. It never sat well that Depiro got off scot-free on that one. And thanks, I appreciate your help."

"You okay?" John asked. "I saw the news and the explosion. Was that you?"

"Sort of," Tony sighed. "I thought emptying the tank would force them outside. Give us a shot at identifying the players, you know?"

"But something went wrong," John surmised.

"The guy, well he was about to light up... a cigarette. He was standing right next to the tank. Seriously who does that? There was nothing we could do. We just had to sit there, waiting, hoping he'd move away when another guy stepped out. The two of them had a brief conversation then they both fired a shot toward our original location. We moved out-of-the-way the instant we spotted the guns, but it was close."

"You said you were with an ex-cop," John said. "Did he fire any shots?"

"No," Tony assured him.

"Good," John said, relieved. "Then the thugs sparked the flame that blew up the tank, and killed the men," John surmised.

"Yeah," Tony frowned.

"That's good," John said again.

"How is that good?"

"Because now you're in the clear. In fact, you could call it a suicide," John grinned.

"That's what you said about Voyt," Tony grumbled.

"And that's the problem, right?" John asked. "You never came to grips with that death, not really. Just because you wanted him dead, it wasn't our fault, Tony. Voyt decided to head up the canyon. He decided to deviate and run. He lost control and crashed. As far as tonight, if those men hadn't been blown to bits, that cop of yours would have been forced to killed them himself. It's better this way. The police are investigating an accidental explosion, not looking for the man who shot two of Zarconi's men."

"Rowdy agrees with you," Tony admitted.

"Because I'm right," John pushed.

"Maybe," Tony said. "I don't know. It doesn't matter. Just take care of the designer."

"I'm gonna go, but Tony I'm right about this. Rowdy's right. Those men fired at you. They were trying to kill you. It's karma. Don't feel guilty about this one. It has nothing to do with you... or Voyt." John hung up, more worried than ever. His friend was playing a dangerous game, and he wasn't sure his head was on straight.

"You okay?" Theresa asked sitting beside Tony.

Moondance Ridge

He took her hand and studied it for several seconds. "Let's go to bed."

"Carson said he'll help," Theresa said softly. "He can't speak for his friend, but Carson will help."

"I don't need their names," Tony stood and held out his hand.

"I trust you," Theresa linked fingers with the complicated man. "Marcos is more cautious, less trusting. He's going to worry about the feds involvement."

"This thing," Tony said hesitantly. "Whatever those guys did. Was Shawn involved?"

"Yeah," Theresa nodded. "They could never have done it without Shawn. It wasn't his idea, but he was right in the middle of it. Where those two were concerned, he always was. He was brilliant when it came to computers. Shawn could have hacked the government, but that's something he would never do. They were just messing around, with people who…"

"It doesn't matter," Tony said as they stepped into the bedroom.

"I trust you," Theresa said again. "I want you to know that. I also trust Rowdy. I'll tell him about the guys in the morning. I still need to be the one to contact them. I'm not ready to discuss their last names. Although, they all went to school together; so, I guess it would be pretty easy for the FBI to track them down if they wanted to."

The two of them climbed into bed. Tony wrapped his arms around Theresa and held her close. He hoped his presence made her feel safe. Being here, in Detroit, had to be difficult for her. Their first 24 hours in her hometown wasn't exactly relaxing or reassuring.

* * * *

Tony stepped into the main area of the suite, headed for the kitchen and coffee. He froze mid-step when the front door slid open and a figure stepped inside. He relaxed when he realized it was Rowdy. He was about to continue into the kitchen when the man's outfit suddenly registered. "Where have you been? I thought we agreed neither one of us would go out alone."

"It was a necessity," Rowdy shrugged as he set two burnt casings and what looked like bullet fragments on the wooden table.

"You went back to the warehouse," Tony realized.

"I woke up, couldn't sleep," Rowdy admitted. "I came in here, thought about the incident and realized at some point the police would search the area, or Dominic would. Once they found the bullets, they'd also know the men were firing at someone. I thought I'd go check it out. See if the investigation had led that far."

"I'm guessing no," Tony said as he prepared a pot of coffee.

Rowdy shook his head. "It was sloppy and unprofessional. A rookie could do better. I have to wonder why. Does Dominic Zarconi pay the department to look the other way or does the department simply not care? Are they so used to incidents at his warehouses they show up, do a cursory look and bolt? Even with the two bodies, they didn't search the area for the casings. It's like they simply don't care."

"That helps us, right?" Tony asked.

"Yes and no," Rowdy moved to the counter and poured a cup of the freshly brewed liquid. "It helps in regard to what happened last night. I recovered the casings, and I snagged the bullets. Now, even if Zarconi goes out and looks around himself, he won't know we were there. Not even with the camera damage. I removed the rock, now it just looks like the blast took it out. The cops have the men's guns. If anyone looks, they might notice they're each missing a bullet. I doubt they'll look, mainly because one of them was on a break about to light up. If I had to guess, I'd say that's what they'll list as cause of death."

"But?" Tony pressed.

"But," Rowdy sighed. "That probably means any other investigation that surrounds Zarconi is also slipshod and incomplete. We can't rely on police reports to be accurate or thorough."

"Will that be a problem?" Tony settled in next to Rowdy.

"I hope not," Rowdy shrugged. "But, I haven't seen any of the evidence. We need those files. We're starting from scratch here; and, it's going to be impossible to bring him down legally if we don't find something in the previous work gathered by the Regan brothers."

"Carson said he'd help," Theresa said as she stepped into the room. She glanced at the bullets and then up to Rowdy. "Are you turning that over to your friend or just keeping it so Dom didn't find it?"

Rowdy stood, gathered the evidence and disappeared down the hallway. Minutes later, he returned. "I'm keeping it as evidence. Now, I have a chain of custody; and it won't be tainted when I hand it over to Skeet."

"Well," Theresa settled in across from Rowdy. "I spoke to Carson. He's in. He said he will talk to Marc, but don't count on both of them. Marcos is more, I don't know, untrusting and skeptical. He had a rough childhood, and he'll need to protect himself and Carson for that matter. He's not going to believe the FBI will give him a fair shake just on my word alone."

"Once Coop talks to Skeet, I'll have a better idea of how to proceed with them," Rowdy provided. "Right now, it's a guessing game. I don't want to speculate on how they'll handle that aspect. It doesn't mean they will pursue them or file charges on their previous bad deeds. It means they might offer them immunity, they might offer a contract, they might do something totally different. Skeet is going to have to work that out. If this Carson guy will help, we'll just have to hope he can find something running solo."

"I'll talk to him later," Theresa promised. "You said you were going to the casino warehouse this morning. What do you want me to do?"

"Is there any of the files you can access," Rowdy asked? "I know the keylogger stuff wasn't protected, but is there anything else?"

"Probably the file from Zach," she shrugged. "I don't know why Shawn put passwords on his new files and then didn't tell me what it was." Theresa wondered if he'd saved the information in the phone. The one back in Mount Haven, in the safe in her truck. Well, she couldn't do anything about that now.

"Instead of messing with the password," Rowdy continued. "Maybe you can work on anything that is available. See if you can make sense of the keylogger stuff. See if that file from Zach is open. If so, scroll through and find names, addresses, anything we can provide to Coop so he can start running backgrounds on the players--that means everyone, prosecutors, business owners and businesses, even those that seem insignificant."

"Okay," Theresa glanced around for the laptop. She spotted it in on the coffee table. "Do you guys know when you'll be back? Should I plan to order lunch from room service or wait?"

"We'll play it by ear," Rowdy decided. "Tony will call if he can. If not and we haven't returned by one, go ahead and order something."

"Okay," she stood and walked to the living area, retrieved the computer and returned to the table. "Might as well get started."

The conversation shifted to the casino warehouse-- what Theresa knew about it, how secure it was, what could be stored in the upper level, everything she knew was discussed. Finally, Tony stood. "Let's go," he motioned to Rowdy and the two men stepped solemnly out the door.

Theresa watched them leave; then, she pulled out her phone and dialed Carson.

* * * *

Skeet adjusted his binoculars and watched as Blake took two steps forward. He studied the man occupying the neighboring roof and frowned. Something was off, the tiny hairs on the back of his neck tingled in warning. Skeet turned and blinked when the magnified view landed on the barrel of a rifle. He slowly followed the black cylinder upwards and shook his head in disbelief as the lens landed on the marksman's face. He pivoted, hoping he could stop Blake's impatient reaction; but he was too late. His partner already had his weapon out, and it was pointed directly at the decoy standing out in the open. *Not a good idea*, Skeet thought. "Blake," he called out as loudly as he dared. "Lower your weapon. Slowly."

"What?" Blake turned his head in shock to study his partner. "Why? He spotted us already and we both know he's armed. Why aren't you covering me?"

Skeet made a motion over Blake's head, then once again raised his binoculars. Seconds later, he took a step into the open and lowered the field glasses. He turned, faced the armed man, and silently waited. Seconds later he relaxed and smiled. *Signal received.*

Blake slowly turned and spotted the man, or more accurately, the distinct barrel of a high- powered rifle. So, there were two of them. How had he missed the second gunman? Blake scowled, and slid his pistol into his holster. He raised his arms slightly, positioning his hands away from his body, palms up until the man lowered the weapon. Blake immediately turned to glare at Skeet and wondered why he had stepped from the shadows. "I thought you were supposed to have my back."

"I did," Skeet shrugged. "That's why I told you to lower the gun." He stepped forward and put a hand on Blake's shoulder. "Let's go."

"Where?" Blake asked, confused.

"Trust me," Skeet said as he turned and made his way to the stairwell. Once they reached the car, Skeet slid behind the wheel and pulled onto the highway. Within minutes, they were back at the hotel.

"What are we doing?" Blake demanded.

"We're meeting a friend," Skeet answered casually as he approached his room. "You want to wait in here with me, or should I call you when they arrive?"

"Who?" Blake asked as he followed Skeet into his room.

"A good friend," Skeet said settling in to wait. It didn't take long. Within minutes, there was a knock on his door.

"You plan to get that, or should I?" Blake asked.

Skeet grinned. "Go ahead. This ought to be fun."

"What do you mean by that?" Blake asked as he crossed the room and paused to peer through the peephole. His scowl deepened when he opened the door and came face-to-face with the same man who had just pointed a gun at his head.

"Mind if I join you?" Rowdy asked casually before stepping past the stranger and moving toward Skeet.

Skeet stood and pulled Rowdy into a brief hug. "I think we have a lot to discuss."

Tony stepped into the room and leaned against the wall. The man speaking to Rowdy was obviously the fed, but who was this other guy? The one with the itchy trigger finger?

"That's Tony," Rowdy pointed to his friend. "He's not too happy about your partner pointing a gun at his head. In fact, we both think it was rather unfriendly and inhospitable."

Skeet grinned. "If I remember correctly, you also pointed a rifle at my guys head. I'd say we're even. Anyway, he should be thanking me--moving out in the open like that was dangerous. Do you have any idea who owns that warehouse? If one of his men had spotted you… well let's just say you guys got lucky."

"Actually," Tony said stepping further into the room and dropping onto the couch. "Luck had nothing to do with it."

"Who is this guy?" Skeet asked Rowdy.

"Tony Nazario," Rowdy answered flatly. "And he's right, there was no luck involved. He was flushing you out. We spotted you in the shadows. Tony thought you'd come out in the open if he did. I guess he was right. I lost that bet, good thing we didn't wager anything substantial."

"You saw us?" Skeet considered. He was losing his touch. He'd been out of the field for too long. Today only proved what he had secretly feared. What was he doing out here, trying to take down a dangerous mob cartel with a rookie? Had he completely lost his mind?

"If it makes you feel better," Rowdy added. "I saw him, not you. I spotted movement in the shadows. Turned out it was your trigger-happy friend. Who is he anyway? He might need a few more weeks at Quantico."

Skeet relaxed a little. At least he wasn't the one that gave their location away. Blake was young and impatient. It made sense someone as seasoned as Rowdy Cooper would spot his partner as he fidgeted on the rooftop. "Actually, that does make me feel a little better."

Moondance Ridge

"Good," Rowdy punched him on the arm and settled into a chair. "Now, why don't you tell me why the FBI is here... staking out Dominic Zarconi's warehouse?"

"Then you do know who you're dealing with?" Skeet asked, surprised. "Maybe you want to fill me in on why a part-time cop from Montana is packing a rifle and spying in Detroit."

"Sure," Rowdy stretched out his legs and crossed one ankle over the other. "After you. But first, you might want to call Coop."

Skeet frowned. "Why?"

"Because we've been trying to get in touch for days. Coop is about to call Burns to demand answers and maybe demand a search party if he's not satisfied. He got so desperate he's been leaving messages at the house, but Angie hasn't called back either. We were starting to worry about you, old man," Rowdy frowned.

"Burns won't give him anything; but if he keeps calling the office, it might turn into a problem. Give me a minute," Skeet pulled out his phone and dialed his friend.

"It's about time," Coop barked. "Where have you been?"

"Detroit, just hooked up with Rowdy," Skeet admitted. "The kid is as cocky as ever in case you were wondering. We still have a lot to hash out; but I thought I'd drop you a line before you cause trouble at the office."

"You're in Detroit?" Coop asked. "Why? Is Angie with you? There's more going on out there than you know. It's not safe for your wife. Maggie would be happy for the company if you want to send her out here."

"Ange isn't here," Skeet admitted. "She's with a friend. That's why she's not calling you back. She didn't get the message, either. Sorry we made you worry, and I appreciate the offer, but it's not necessary. Now, I need to pin down your brother and figure out why he's here. Unless, of course, you want to fill me in? For old times' sake?"

"Naw," Coop laughed. "I'll let Rowdy take care of that. But, you can do me a favor, watch the kid's back. I feel better already, knowing you're there with him."

"Okay," Skeet said after he disconnected the call. "So, I think we might be after the same man. The question is why?"

"Does anyone know you're here?" Rowdy evaded. "Any chance the room's bugged?"

"No," Blake inserted himself into the conversation as he settled into an uncomfortable hotel chair.

"Still," Tony looked at Rowdy. "I'd feel better if we did this at our place. Plus, I think it would help if we were all involved. You know this guy?" He pointed to Blake.

"Nope," Rowdy stood. "But, I know Skeet and that guy wouldn't be here if he couldn't be trusted. I agree by the way, let's move this to our place. I know it's safe and we can talk freely."

"What do you know that you're not telling me?" Skeet asked as he stood.

"Too much to get into here," Rowdy shot his friend a glance. "I promise, I'll tell you everything once we relocate."

Moondance Ridge

As the two men stepped outside, Skeet grabbed Rowdy's arm and pulled him to a stop. "You sure you can trust this Tony guy? And who else is at your hotel?"

"Tony's solid, you don't need to worry about him," Rowdy assured him. "Theresa came with us, she's one of my waitresses. You met her, briefly, when you were in town. Now, I have the same question. The guy with you, are you sure he's clean? I have reason to believe you have dirty agents in this town."

"And you didn't call me?" Skeet asked, annoyed.

"Uh… what part of trying to reach you for days was I not clear about?" Rowdy frowned. "That's why you're here? You're looking for dirt. Maybe you should be a little more diligent about checking messages. I hear it's a great way to know if someone's trying to track you down," Rowdy smiled then sobered. "Let's go, we have a lot to discuss. Be prepared for a long day."

Once they reached the parking lot, Skeet and Blake slid into their rental. Tony and Rowdy climbed into their vehicle. The group pulled onto the highway, Skeet following closely behind as they made their way to the swanky hotel.

"That place is a dive," Rowdy frowned. "Any chance we can swing another room? It would help if we could get one on the same floor."

"You mean any chance I'm willing to foot the bill for another suite?" Tony corrected.

"If you front it, I'll pay you back when we get home," Rowdy bargained. "If we can help it, I'd rather not leave a trail back to the bar. But, we need Skeet close by. He can help with this; and I'm pretty sure he's here working the dirty agent angle. That's why his office didn't know where he was and Angela is staying with friends. He's working covert, I'm sure of it. Which ups the stakes and the last place anyone would look for an undercover fed, is at our hotel."

"That's true," Tony agreed. "I'll see what I can do when we get back. The concierge should be able to handle it. I don't want a couple agents barging in on Theresa. She might freak. Are you sure the other guy is a fed and he's clean?"

"Maybe," Rowdy shrugged as they pulled into their parking spot and climbed from the car. "I didn't ask where he worked. Could be Skeet went outside the Bureau. He'd need someone he was sure he could trust. That's all that matters to me. I agreed to partner with you, didn't I? Skeet may have done the same... brought someone in he knew wasn't, and couldn't be compromised. We'll get answers, I promise. Skeet won't hold anything back."

"I hope you're right," Tony paused. "What do you plan to tell him about last night? About the explosion."

"The truth," Rowdy shrugged. "I stand by what I said last night, it was better for all of us those men died in an explosion. Otherwise, I would have had to kill them, and that would leave questions and complications."

"But will the fed see it that way?"

"Yep," Rowdy said confidently as he unlocked the door and stepped inside.

Moondance Ridge

* * * *

Tony stepped into the room and immediately settled in beside Theresa on the couch. She was watching some series on TV. He grabbed the remote and casually flipped off the power. "We are going to have company. Coop couldn't track the agent because he's here. It looks like he knows Detroit has problems in the Bureau, and he's here to investigate. He has a friend, Rowdy doesn't know him so we're going to have a few questions. Just relax and let us take care of this. Trust us, Tea. We will protect you."

"I trust you," Theresa assured him just as the knock sounded at the door.

"Showtime," Rowdy said as he swung open the door and took a step back.

Skeet and Blake stepped into the room together. Skeet paused to take in the accommodations and shook his head in disbelief. "A bit different from our usual digs. Was this to show off? That's not like you," he focused on Rowdy. "Strike that, it's exactly like you. Okay, you win."

"I'm not showing off," Rowdy said soberly. "I didn't trust your room. Nobody knows we're here. Since I'm not sure how long you've been in town or what kind of grand entrance you made, I wanted to be safe."

Just then there was a second knock on the door. Tony casually moved to open it, spoke to the hotel employee for several seconds then quietly shut the door and moved across the room. Once again, he settled in next to Theresa before tossing a tiny envelope with two keys to Rowdy. "It's across the hall."

"Thanks," Rowdy said, passing the key cards to Skeet.

"What's that?"

"We thought it'd be easier and less conspicuous if you relocated," Rowdy grinned.

"To here?" Blake looked around. "Not on the government's dime."

"No," Tony said flatly.

"You're paying?" Skeet asked.

"Yeah," Tony shrugged. "Call it a donation. In fact, maybe I can write it off, get a tax break or something for taking care of the feds. It's worth it."

"Before I say anything, I need to know who this guy is," Skeet studied Tony.

"Ever heard of Kayer Financial? Micero Industries? Polyescent Pharmaceuticals?" Tony asked.

"You're the Fixer," Blake surmised.

Rowdy burst out laughing.

Tony scowled. "No, I'm Tony Nazario, a successful businessman that is good at his job."

"Okay," Skeet settled into one of the lounge chairs. "We get it, you don't like the nickname. You're also Bailey's best friend. I remember now. I couldn't place it at first …where I heard of you. It just clicked, you're in Victoria's file."

"That too," Tony agreed.

"I thought you were a business legend," Skeet said flatly. "I had no idea you fixed criminal problems as well."

"I don't," Tony shrugged. "Not normally, but for Theresa I decided to make an exception." He reached over and grasped her hand in his.

"I see. Theresa," Skeet said turning to face the only woman in the room. "I don't know if you remember me. We met in Mount Haven."

"I do," she took a deep breath. "You should know, these guys are out here because of me. They're helping me with a problem. A big problem."

"I'm sorry about that," Skeet said sincerely. "I wouldn't wish Zarconi on anyone."

"Why did you automatically assume he was after me?"

"Because of him," Skeet pointed to Rowdy with his thumb. "It's the only thing that would bring him into this. So, who wants to fill me in? There's a story here, I can feel it."

"Not yet," Tony glanced at Blake. "We don't know him."

"Right," Skeet motioned for Blake to join them. "This is Blake Cochran. He's FBI but his father knew Stan. I've been working with him for weeks now, we can trust him."

Tony narrowed his eyes. "Any relation to Tyler Cochran?"

"That depends," Blake said evasively.

Tony turned to face Rowdy. "I'm out. If he can't answer a simple question, I don't trust him."

Skeet frowned. "Answer the question."

"My father's name was Tyler," Blake admitted. "Did you know him?"

"No," Tony said tapping a few buttons on his phone.

"Who are you calling?" Skeet asked.

"A friend," Tony held up a finger. "Hey, John."

"What now?" John grumbled. "I'm still dealing with the first favor, and you already checked in this morning."

"Not a favor," Tony said. "Information."

"What kind?"

"Did Tyler Cochran have a kid?"

John sobered. "Yeah. Blake, would be in his mid-to-late twenties by now, why?"

"I'm standing here with a man who claims to be Blake Cochran," Tony provided. "I thought I'd check him out, see if he was lying."

"Well, I couldn't begin to tell you that," John said. "We never actually met, but if Ty's kid is on the case, I feel better already."

"I haven't come to that conclusion yet," Tony said, studying the stranger.

"You couldn't seriously be talking to John Buckley?" Blake asked.

"You know him?" Tony asked.

"Not personally," Blake admitted. "But dad did. John was his best guy. Dad would have trusted him with his life; did trust him with his life. Tell him thank you for me."

"That's the kid," John confirmed. "Let me talk to him for a minute."

Tony held out the phone to Blake. "John wants to say hi."

"Hello," Blake said hesitantly. He knew more than he should about John Buckley. The man was an unsung hero, one of the best Special Forces soldiers to ever live. His dad had admired and respected the former operator. Blake would, too.

"Hey, kid," John said into the phone. "Tony says you're Ty's son."

"I am," Blake agreed.

"Well, I hope you're telling the truth. Because if I find out you lied, if I learn you are involved in this, on the wrong side…well, I'll come after you myself. Do you understand me?" John said softly.

"I do," Blake tried to sound casual. "But, that won't be necessary. I'm told Tony's after the bad guys. That squares things with me, and I guess that means we're on the same team."

"I hope so," John relaxed. "I thought you were Army."

"I was," John admitted. "But after dad died, I thought I'd do more good in the Bureau."

"Look, Tony's my best friend," John confided. "He's tough, acts like he has it all figured out; but he's too kind hearted to do what I do. What your dad did. And, if you're any kind of cop, what you do. Watch his back for me, will ya? He's important."

"It would be my honor," Blake said soberly. "And thank you. I know I'm not supposed to know what you did, so I don't. But, thank you."

"Don't mention it," John replied. "And by that, I mean seriously don't mention it."

"You have my word," Blake handed the phone back to Tony.

"Well?"

"He's the real deal but if he gets you dead, he'll answer to me," John told him.

"No, he won't," Tony disagreed. "You know what I'm doing here. You will not hold anyone responsible for my actions but me. No matter what goes down while I'm here."

"Call me tomorrow," John said before hanging up.

Tony turned to Blake. "Sorry about that. Forget what he said. I'm responsible for myself."

Rowdy laughed. "Now the rookie's protecting you? That's a relief."

"Shut up," Tony turned to Skeet. "I trust your man."

"I'm not sure what that was all about but okay," Skeet turned to Rowdy. "Now, you want to tell me why you're here?"

"Not yet," Rowdy studied Blake then Tony. "Who is John?"

"A friend," Tony admitted. "I called him in. Asked him to check on Callie. He's keeping his distance. Don't worry."

"Who is Callie?" Skeet asked.

"That's a long story," Theresa answered. "For now, what's important is that she's connected and if Dom gets upset with me, he might send someone after her."

"There is a complication," Tony admitted. "John says Nico Depiro has shown an interest in your girl. Nico's been able to keep his nose relatively clean, but he's still connected with the mob-- could be completely separate, but equally dangerous. So far, she's rejecting him. But, that could be just as perilous. John's going to hang out in New York for a while, until he gets another case. Then, he'll have to bolt."

"Nico Depiro?" Theresa considered. "I don't know him. I've never heard of him. Who is he?"

Skeet glanced at Rowdy. "A hitman. He used to work for Leon DeRossi. He's also related to Dominic Zarconi, by marriage."

"Now that I didn't know," Tony admitted.

"I think we all have a lot to discuss here. Are we good with Blake now?"

"Was your father and this John guy military?" Rowdy asked.

"Yeah," Blake nodded. "Dad was killed on a mission. I decided to take another approach to the whole war on terror thing. Mom wasn't happy, but I think deep down she was glad I didn't go the covert military route."

"Special Forces?" Rowdy asked Tony.

Tony nodded.

"Okay, we're good." Rowdy turned to Skeet. "So, why are you here? You didn't bat an eye when I told you about the agent. Is that your mission? Ferret out the bad seed?"

"Basically," Skeet nodded. "But, before we go any further, I think you should know you and I have a price on our heads."

A slow smile spread across Rowdy's face. "Really? How much?"

Theresa frowned. "That's not funny. Did Zarconi put out a hit on you?"

"No," Skeet also frowned. "Leon DeRossi did, the second he stepped foot in a concrete cell."

"And, Dom is connected with this DeRossi guy?" Tony asked. "Because that might make things a little more difficult."

"Dominic Zarconi's wife, Zaphrina, has a sister, Selma. Selma's son is Nico Depiro." Skeet said. "Nico was one of DeRossi's hitmen, but we couldn't connect the dots. He skated, the one that got away I guess you could say."

"Seems to be a pattern," Tony mumbled. "Doesn't sit well, does it?"

Moondance Ridge

"We finally found something we can all agree on," Rowdy frowned.

Theresa stood and moved to the window. "From the moment I knew I was coming here, I've been terrified. As we broke through the cloud cover and began our decent, I looked over the city," she held out her hand. "This city. It was difficult to breath, my heart began to race and my stomach was tied in knots," she glanced at Tony. "For some reason, the instant you two left the room, thoughts of my parents flooded my mind. Memories I hadn't let myself entertain for years surfaced. Instead of feeling sad and alone, I felt comforted. I know that's strange. Now, I'm just terrified again. The more I hear, the worse it gets."

Tony stood and moved to stand next to Theresa. He pulled her into his arms and pressed his lips to hers.

Theresa was surprised by the kiss. It was different from the others. This one wasn't a quick peck or the erotic contact that always set her body on fire. It was soft and sweet... loving. Once it was over, Tony pulled her into a gentle hug.

Tony knew it was the wrong time for this, but he also knew Theresa needed the contact. He leaned forward and gently kissed her temple. "You're safe, baby. I promise, you will be safe here."

Theresa took a step back, nodded then moved back to the couch. She paused when Tony followed and took her hand. She might be safe, but were they? "Tony and Rowdy already know this, but let me tell you my story." She proceeded to lay out the situation for Skeet and Blake, careful to leave out the part about Shawn's friends.

"So," Skeet considered. "What happened to the evidence? Where did the keylogger stuff go?"

Tony gave Theresa's hand a gentle squeeze. "The evidence is safe; but before we say who has it, we need to cut a deal."

"What kind of deal?" Blake asked.

"I have some friends working on it," Theresa said softly. "Some friends of Shawn's. He password protected everything. Once they crack the password, the files are also encrypted. At least the stuff Shawn got from Dom's computer is. That's why Shawn needed the keylogger. He was looking for the encryption code. Even if they figure out his password, the encryption was top notch. Shawn couldn't decipher it without the code. His friends won't be able to either."

"And these friends." Skeet asked "They're hackers, right?"

"They are," Theresa said. "And that's where the deal comes in."

"Are they wanted?" Skeet asked.

"I don't think they are wanted by the FBI," Theresa said without hesitation. "But, they have messed around, been places they shouldn't be. If you start looking into their system, you might recognize something. Shawn told me every hacker has a signature, you might recognize theirs."

"As in a government hack we never solved?" Skeet asked.

"No," Theresa disagreed. "They never got into any of your systems. That's all I'm comfortable saying."

"Okay," Skeet decided. "You have your deal."

"What? Just like that?" Theresa asked.

Moondance Ridge

"I don't care about a couple hackers," Skeet said. "When I call Stan, I'll have him set them up as private contractors. But, if I do that, I'm going to need their cooperation throughout this investigation. We're keeping this localized. That means I can't send the data over to my people. We can use them, have them work on the password then ferret out the encryption code."

"And in return?" Tony asked.

"In return, they have my word nothing they have done or even what they do to help us now, will cause them problems," Skeet said. "As long as it hasn't jeopardized national security, they're clear."

"I'll call and see what they say," Theresa said. She stood and retreated into the back bedroom to make the call.

"So," Rowdy said after Theresa disappeared. "We're on our own. I think it's your turn to explain what brought you here."

Skeet explained the phone call, the death and the conversation between Nico and DeRossi.

Several minutes went by before Theresa stepped back into the room and settled in next to Tony. "The guys are nervous, but they're willing to continue as planned. I guess they've been working all night. They'll think about the contractor thing; and once they get something, he'll call and we can go from there."

"I can live with that," Skeet considered.

"Coffee, huh?" Rowdy pulled out his phone, still pondering all the new information.

"Yeah," Skeet said. "Why?"

Rowdy clicked on a photo and handed Skeet his phone.

"Where did you get these?" Skeet asked immediately.

"Zarconi's warehouse," Rowdy said flatly.

"The explosion," Blake murmured.

"That was you?" Skeet asked Rowdy.

Rowdy shrugged. "What do you think?"

"And the two dead guys?" Skeet asked. "Cause of death?"

"I haven't seen the official report, but I'd say being blown to bits is a pretty good possibility," Rowdy said casually.

Skeet shook his head. "Be serious."

"I am," Rowdy settled further into his chair. He proceeded to explain the events from the previous evening.

Skeet smiled and nodded. "Good."

Rowdy glanced at Tony, his look clearly said *I told you so*.

Tony shrugged. Maybe he'd been wrong. Maybe he was judging Rowdy and all of them by the standard he'd set years ago. As a teen living on the street, he dodged the police. He certainly didn't look to them for cooperation or assistance. Sitting here in a room full of cops, it didn't seem like anyone had a problem with the way things went down last night. Maybe they wouldn't have come after him for Voyt, either. It was certainly something to think about.

"I think I'm missing something," Skeet said dividing his attention between the two friends.

"Naw," Rowdy disagreed. "Tony just learned a valuable lesson. Now, you said you got a call from an agent. One that brought you out here in the first place. Was he able to give you anything concrete? I know you said he died before you arrived, but can you hook up with his partner, did he stash the evidence somewhere we can retrieve it?"

"Rowdy," Skeet sighed. "The call came in from Bryant Smith and he didn't trust anyone but me. All I know is what he told me on that call. They staged some kind of crash to get rid of him before he could take things further. If I had to guess, they probably snatched up the evidence before the cops arrived."

"Man," Rowdy ran his hand through his hair. "Bryant was just a kid, but he was good. There is no way he crashed on his own, not if he had dirt on the mob."

"I agree," Skeet settled across from him. "He just said he thought there were at least two of them and maybe his supervisor. He was going to give me the proof in person the next morning. He was scared and now he's dead, that tells me whatever he had must have been solid. Something about a journalist getting killed a few years back."

"What?" Theresa said, shocked.

Skeet glanced around. "Okay, once again, I think I'm missing something."

"Theresa's brother-in-law, Zach Regan," Rowdy provided. "He was meeting a fed, said he made a mistake and ended up dead."

"But, he was dead," Blake frowned. "How did he tell anyone anything?"

"Text," Theresa whispered. She moved to the laptop and quickly pulled up the file. Once she was in the folder that contained all Zach's material, she clicked on the image. Shawn had forwarded the message to the cloud for safe keeping, just in case they ever needed it.

Skeet moved forward and studied the screen over Theresa's shoulder. "Do you still have the phone? The one that made the call?"

"I do," Theresa acknowledged. "In Mount Haven. But, it was a burner so I don't think it will be much good."

"It could be," Skeet considered. "Is there anyone you trust to retrieve the phone and mail it to your hacker friends? They might be able to trace the location from the GPS inside the phone. We might be able to discover where Zach was killed."

"I already know," Theresa admitted. "Not the exact spot because Zach was cautious. He set up the meeting himself. We talked about it though, the three of us. We decided on the park," Theresa stood and retrieved the laptop then pulled up a map of Detroit. "We decided right here would be the best location. Zach agreed, he wouldn't meet with anyone that didn't let him pick the spot."

"That's a public area," Skeet observed. "There should have been witnesses. How did the murderer get away with the crime?"

Theresa pulled up another file, the police report on Zach's death. "We identified four police officers who are working for Dom. Frank Dressel was the first officer on scene and then Detective Rosario was assigned the investigation. Dressel handled everything that night, Rosario on the back end. They ruled it an attempted mugging gone bad by an unknown assailant and closed the case."

Skeet glanced around. "I need a place to work. Somewhere I can make diagrams, tack pictures, develop a timeline."

Tony stood. "Let me see what I can do."

Chapter Nine

Tony stepped into the hallway and dialed John.

"Now what?"

"Bad timing?" Tony asked. "You sound like you're in a tunnel."

"Roof, actually. And no," John shifted. "Just watching our workaholic fashion designer. What's up?"

"Can you still access hotel records?" Tony asked, getting to the point. "I need to see if MGM Grand has an executive suite, one with an office space, conference area, something like that."

Moondance Ridge

John pulled out a tablet and began typing. "What room did you say you were in?"

"Penthouse," Tony provided the room numbers for him and Skeet.

"Okay," John tapped a couple additional keys. "You have now rented the executive suite directly below your room. Next floor down. Check in will be after three today. It's under my company name using the credit card attached to that account you set up. The one I refuse to use. I assume you still have a card. Anything else?"

"No," Tony sighed. "That will cover it. You do remember I set that account up for you, not me."

"And I'm sure you remember I don't want your money. But, I will admit, it came in handy today. I put in the notes that my assistant will be checking in, give Blake my business card and the credit card, and let him do it. Now, looks like our girl is on the move. Gotta go."

"Thanks," Tony said before hanging up. He moved to stand in front of the large picture window that looked out over the city and dialed another number.

"Cryo-Comm," came the cheerful female voice. "Felicity speaking, how can I help you?"

"Hey doll," Tony grinned. "It's Tony Nazario."

"Oh, wow," Felicity said. "It's been a while. How've you been?"

"Busy," Tony answered. "Is the boss available?"

"I think he just finished up a meeting," Felicity said instantly. "Let me see if he can take the call."

A few seconds later, the friendly voice came over the phone. "Tony Nazario."

"Martin Ashbury," Tony said. "How's business?"

"Couldn't be better," Martin assured him. "And, I owe that all to you. Not to be rude, but I have a meeting in five. Should I assume you're calling for a reason? In all the time we spent together, you were never the nostalgic type; so, I'm guessing this isn't a social call."

"No," Tony agreed. "I'm actually calling to ask for a favor."

"Anything," Martin didn't hesitate. "Within reason."

"I need some information from one of your subsidiaries, The Detroit Chronicle," Tony advised.

"Name it, I'll call Dale and tell him to put it together," Martin offered.

"There was a reporter working there a few years back by the name of Zachery Regan," Tony began. "I'm told he died in some freak mugging gone wrong or something. Anyway, he was apparently a fairly good journalist and I keep hearing a couple of his articles may be relevant to a job I'm working. Any chance you can get me everything he wrote?"

"Sure," Martin agreed. "No problem, but why do you need me? I mean most of that should be on the internet these days."

"Because several of his articles were never published. I'm not sure why, but my sources are telling me this Zach guy wrote a number of pieces the paper refused to run. I'm also told the information I need is in one or more of those articles. Problem is, I have no idea which ones." Tony hoped this call didn't set off any red flags but Martin would come through for him, Tony was sure of it.

"Could be they couldn't verify the info or had a problem with the sources," Martin suggested. "As long as you use it for business and don't try to make it public, that shouldn't be a problem."

"You know me," Tony answered. "Nothing I do is for public consumption."

"Which is why I'll take care of this for you," Martin assured him. "Give me an hour, if the guy was good, he probably has a decent amount of work to pull. I'll get Dale on it immediately. Just stop by the front desk and they should have a file for you before lunch." Martin paused. "I'm going to tell Dale I want the documents for myself and I'm sending a runner to pick them up. I think it will be cleaner that way and he won't panic about the unpublished work getting out."

"Great," Tony smiled. "I knew I could count on you." He hung up, stepped back into the room and realized Rowdy still had the car keys. As he glanced around, he saw everyone but the man he needed to talk to. His gaze landed on Blake and he moved to stand in front of the agent. "Hey."

"What's up?" Blake immediately pushed himself from the couch.

Tony retrieved his wallet and pulled out a credit card and a business card. "I need you to check in for John. The room is listed under his security company, Isofix Securities." He held out the two cards. "The room is directly below us, one floor down. There are stairs just outside the door and around the corner to the left. Wait until after three to check in. Tell them you're John's assistant. Get half a dozen keys."

"And you?"

"I need to take a road trip," Tony glanced around the room, again. "Where's Rowdy? I need my car keys."

"He said he needed to call Coop," Skeet looked up from the computer he was working on with Theresa. "I think he's in his room. By the way, thanks for the added space. I'll see what I can do as far as reimbursement."

Tony shrugged, dismissing the offer before he disappeared down the hallway and knocked on Rowdy's door.

"Gotta go," Rowdy said to Coop. "Be careful out there and I'll call you tonight to check on those backgrounds."

"You too," Coop sighed. "It shouldn't take long to pull the report so go ahead and go now. I'll tell them to leave it at the front desk."

Rowdy pulled open the door and spotted Tony, he frowned at the look on the man's face. "What?"

"Nothing," Tony shrugged. "I arranged for Skeet's extra room, now I need my keys."

"Sorry," Rowdy stepped past him and headed for the kitchen. "I have an errand to run. You can have the car when I get back."

"What kind of errand?" Tony followed.

Moondance Ridge

"Coop's getting me a copy of the full investigation into Zach's death. He said it should be ready by the time I reach the station," Rowdy stopped to grab his room key off the table and headed for the door.

"Wait," Tony glanced at Theresa then back to Rowdy. "I'm coming with you. We can take care of my errand once we finish yours."

"What errand?" Theresa asked.

"I need to stop at the Chronicle and grab everything Zach wrote for the paper," Tony admitted.

"But they won't give it to you," Theresa objected. "Shawn tried to get Zach's work already. He thought there might be something in there, in the ones Dale rejected and wouldn't publish, but the editor refused to turn them over."

Tony grinned. "Shawn didn't have my connections."

"What does that mean?" Skeet stood.

"It means I know the owner," Tony glanced at Rowdy. "I helped save his company. Not the Chronicle, Martin Ashbury."

Skeet nodded and returned to his seat. "Cryo-Comm, makes sense."

"That's it?" Theresa glanced at Skeet then back to Tony. "Who is Martin Ashbury?"

"I'll explain it," Skeet assured him. "Go ahead, you shouldn't have any trouble. If Tony knows Ashbury, Dale Norris won't cross him. If he does, he'll lose his job."

"Glad we came to the same conclusion," Tony said as he pulled open the door and disappeared.

"Rowdy?" Theresa looked at him in apprehension.

Rowdy shrugged. "I'll be there, it should be fine."

"Sit back down and I'll explain," Skeet nodded to Rowdy who disappeared out the door. Once they were gone, Skeet turned to study Blake. "I need you to run an errand as well."

"Tony said to check in at three," Blake reminded him. "Into the room we're gonna use as an office."

"It shouldn't take long," Skeet motioned for Blake to join them. "Laney Burns had a student a year or so ago. She works at Wayne State now. Laney has arranged for us to use some of their equipment. I need you to head over to the University, to the Bio department, and meet up with Roxie Savett. She'll have some laptops, a router and some other equipment we can use to bypass the hotel WiFi. If Zarconi realizes we're here, the equipment will safeguard our investigation. He won't be able to hack into the hotel system to learn what we know."

"What are you going to do?" Blake asked.

"I need to wait for Burns to call me back, he's working on something."

Just then Theresa's phone chimed. "I'm going to take this in the other room. It's the guys, my um... tech advisors. I'll let you know what they say," Theresa stood and left the room.

"What are you not telling me?" Blake asked when he heard the sound of a door shutting in the distance.

"I think Theresa's friends... the hackers, well... I'm pretty sure they're Robin Hood," Skeet admitted.

"Seriously?" Blake asked, impressed. "No wonder she was hesitant to get them involved."

"Stan is working on a deal," Skeet whispered.

"Like immunity or something?" Blake asked.

"Yeah," Skeet nodded. "They'll be clear of anything they have done from the day they turned eighteen until they sign the deal, but he had to work it through DOJ."

"In return for what?" Blake asked, knowing there would be a catch.

"In return, they agree to consult for us. Stan," Skeet paused to look down the hallway again. "Well, Stan is convinced they could be an asset to the Bureau. Especially if they're anonymous."

"Meaning?"

"Meaning," Skeet settled onto the couch. "They work directly for him. We could use them as needed as well, but he wants to keep their identity a secret. He authorized me to read you in, but nobody else. Do you understand?"

"Does he think there are others?" Blake wondered. "Other dirty agents that need to be weeded out?"

"At this point, we have no idea," Skeet admitted. "We brought down DeRossi in Chicago only to have Zarconi connected in Detroit. The one thing we do know is that Depiro is operating out of New York. For now, we need to keep this contained and just among us. If the hackers agree, they just might be the secret weapon we need to bring the entire organization down once and for all."

"Okay," Blake agreed. "I'm gonna head into town and grab the equipment. I should be back just in time to check in so we can start setting up the war room. Oh, I'll stop at the other hotel and check out on my way back."

"Don't," Skeet decided. "I think we should continue to rent the rooms out there, as a ruse. If anyone goes looking, we need them to find us."

Blake grinned, "Good plan." He'd stop at a cheap retail store and stock up on travel toothpaste and razors. Might as well make the place looked lived in, right?

* * * *

"Carson, is that you?" Theresa was surprised to hear from Shawn's friend already.

"Hey, Theresa," Carson said soberly.

"Did you crack it already?"

"Partially," Carson admitted. "We actually broke through hours ago. Theresa, why didn't you come to us? Why didn't you let us help?"

Theresa frowned. "What are you talking about?" She thought Carson had sounded strange when she talked to him earlier, but he wasn't making any sense.

"We saw the video," Carson admitted. "Marc and I could have helped you. Why didn't you call us? If nothing else, we could have created a new identity. We could have kept you safe. Hidden away where he never would have found you."

"Wait," Theresa's heart began to beat faster. "What do you mean you saw the video?"

"We saw Shawn die," Carson said. "You should have let us help you take that SOB down."

"How?" Theresa whispered. "That's not possible. I didn't upload it. It's still on the phone. How did you see it?"

"Oh, honey," Carson laughed. "We're talking about Shawn Regan. That man was fanatical about backups. Where did you think he was saving the data? He's got at least two weeks' worth of video in that file.

"He saved it," Theresa realized. "He saved it to the cloud?"

"Yeah," Carson said softly. "He saved it."

"I'm so sorry you had to see that," Theresa said softly. "You shouldn't have seen that. Wait you said videos, you lost me."

"We figured out his password," Carson admitted. "The encrypted stuff is going to take longer but Shawn has at least two, maybe three weeks' worth of video saved to the cloud. Marcos and I thought we'd start with the latest one. The last one he saved. We had no idea. I'm so sorry you had to be there for that."

"You saw me?" Theresa realized.

"Yeah," Carson sighed. "We saw Shawn stuff you under that sink; then, we watched as you climbed out and disappeared. I'm guessing you're the one that disconnected the feed."

"Shawn told me to retrieve his phone," Theresa whispered. "He never told me it had been there for weeks. I thought he put it there that day. I thought..."

"It's okay," Carson said immediately, sensing she was upset. "We won't say anything to anyone."

"That's not it," Theresa could barely breathe. "I'm on the video, Dom's video. I have no idea how long he keeps the feed. Obviously, he didn't know before. But, what if that's the reason he sent his men out to kidnap me? What if he knows I was there and he needs me eliminated?"

"I need to know how to contact your fed," Carson said, ignoring her. "I want in. I don't care what happens. I don't care if we have trouble over this. I want in, we want in."

"Skeet is here," Theresa advised. "He said he'll give you a contract and the past doesn't matter." Theresa walked back into the kitchen and stood next to Skeet. Before she handed him the phone, she had to know. "Did Marc see?"

"Yes," Carson said softly. "He's... well, he's having a hard time but he'll be okay. You know how he is. It hit him harder, but he's bouncing back already."

"I'm sorry," Theresa whispered as a tear ran down her face. "If I had known, if... well, I would have spared you from seeing that."

"I know," Carson assured her. "And Marcos will be okay. I promise. Can I talk to the fed? I need to make sure he can protect you. I have a few questions that need to be answered."

"Okay," Theresa held out the phone to Skeet. "Um, my computer guy would like to talk to you, Skeet."

"Agent Skeeter Perkins," Skeet said when he took the phone.

"Do you know who we are?" Carson asked

"Officially? No," Skeet answered. "Theresa said she had to control contact. I'm fine with that."

"Not any more. We want in," Carson swallowed. "I know that comes with risks and we hope you won't come after us for what we've done... I did before. But, we want in. The way that man killed Shawn..." Carson stopped to swallow again. "He needs to pay. If we can help, we want in."

"I understand," Skeet took a deep breath and considered. "So, where are we at on the rest?"

"We figured out Shawn's password; so, we've been able to access some of the files. The ones I assume he collected before that day, the day he died. Those have been copied into another file without the password on the folder. We labeled it Shawn with a video folder inside. The others, the ones from Zarconi's computer, those are all encrypted. We're working on it, but it's going to take time. The good news is the keylogger program Shawn installed was ours. It was one the three of us developed together; so, I have the tools to analyze the data. We never finished the program; it had a few bugs but if there's a code in there, I'll find it. Unfortunately, that just starts the long, arduous task of decrypting one file after another. There are thousands of them. Like I said, it's going to take time."

"Okay," Skeet stood and left the room. He needed privacy for what he was about to ask.

"There's one more thing," Carson added. "Shawn recorded hours of video by dubbing the security system. If that madman watched it, he knows she was there. Zarconi knows Theresa was in the room when Shawn died. It might be why he tried to kidnap her. It all depends on how long he retains the footage. Shawn recorded around three weeks of stuff, it's all in the cloud. It would take months to go through it all. He has at least ten different feeds, ten different rooms and angles. Like I said, hours of video. There could be something that will help you, but it's going to take time."

"I understand," Skeet said as he stepped into Rowdy's bedroom and closed the door. "I'll watch the one about Shawn, I assume it's the latest file in the folder?"

"Yeah," Carson shuddered. "It's awful, but it should be enough once you arrest him. It should keep him locked up for good. Please, I know you have to watch it but don't let Theresa see it again. It's brutal and she doesn't need the reminder."

"I understand. Did Theresa talk to you about my offer?" Skeet asked. "About working for the FBI as a private contractor?"

"Yeah," Carson affirmed. "We're in. Send over the paperwork and we'll sign it. We want to help bring that man down. It doesn't matter what the personal cost is to us. We want in."

"You have my word," Skeet said relieved. "There won't be a personal cost. I'll protect you, my boss will protect you. Do you still want me to go through Theresa? After I watch the video, I'll need to get back in touch."

"Naw," Carson said. "Just call me direct," he rattled off a number. "Now I need to give you admin access to the new folders," Carson decided. "The ones we saved from Shawn's system and a clean version without encryption after we crack the code. You said your name is Perkins? How about Perkins666?"

"That's a bit harsh. If you think I'm the devil, that might make our arrangement a little more difficult," Skeet grinned. "How about Perkins007?"

Now Carson laughed. "You don't seem very James Bond like, but that will do. The password is changeme--all lower case, no spaces. As soon as you're in, you can update it to something you'll remember."

"That won't impact your access or Theresa's?" Skeet asked.

"No," Carson shook his head. "I'm making you one of the admins. We'll still have access through our own login credentials and so will she."

"Okay," Skeet considered. "Once I have the paperwork, I'll get in touch."

"Sounds like a plan," Carson said. "Your all setup in the system, login and like I said you're an admin on that folder; so, you can add anything, delete, download, copy whatever. Let me know when you have the paperwork. In the meantime, I'm going to continue to work on the keylogger stuff. With any luck, we'll crack the encryption code soon."

"Sounds like a plan," Skeet echoed. "Before we continue, I do have to ask you one thing." Skeet was pretty sure he knew who these guys were, but he had to ask.

"Shoot," Carson said, logging back into the system under his own name this time.

"Those things you did before?" he asked hesitantly. "Did any of them jeopardize our country's safety? Or, did you ever share classified information? I can't save you from those two scenarios; but, otherwise, we should be good here."

"Then, we're good," Carson said confidently.

"I'll be in touch," Skeet said as he disconnected. It didn't escape his notice that the man hadn't identified himself or his partner throughout the entire conversation. Hopefully, the hacker would recognize the number when Skeet called.

"You have to watch it," Theresa swallowed the lump in her throat as Skeet stepped back into the room.

"I do," Skeet stopped in front of the large window. "But, you don't. The techie said there's at least two, maybe three weeks of video. That's something I'm going to have to go through myself. There could be a clue in there, one only a cop would catch." He ran a frustrated hand through his hair and turned. "We need more people, but that's not possible."

"We could give access to Coop," Theresa suggested. "Rowdy planned to have him help once we got into the files. He can watch the footage and see what he finds. Maybe he could go through them, try to identify specific faces and then run them through your system. He's already going through Zach's files. And I can help, maybe put names to some of the faces. Shawn and I always thought Zach found something we were missing. Something that made him a target. He had to know something that worried Zarconi."

"That's a good idea," Skeet agreed. "Let's see what we have and then I'll call Coop. It's about time he made himself useful. I'm going to wait to watch that video – the one of Shawn's death. Tony and Rowdy need to see it, too. That way, you only have to leave the room once. Later. For now, let's look at the other video and see if you recognize anyone."

"Okay," Theresa sat next to Skeet, grateful for the delay.

* * * *

Marcos stepped into the large loft and made a beeline for the old refrigerator. The dusty smell of their workspace helped him relax. As much as he'd needed an escape, he was glad to be back. He slid open the door, set the two-liter bottle of ginger ale on the nearly empty shelf, and took several steps toward his desk before he realized Carson was watching him. He dropped unceremoniously into the large, comfortable executive chair and sighed.

"Better?" Carson asked softly. He was worried about his friend. Once he located the folder with the video inside, he'd regretted it. Shawn's death video was the last recording, so they'd decided it was the best starting point. Neither man knew what was coming nor had they been prepared for the brutality they'd seen inflicted on their business partner and friend. Marcos had rushed to the bathroom and slammed the door, but that didn't stop Carson from hearing his friend's agony. Marcos had remained in the tiny room for nearly an hour. After he'd lost his breakfast, the man continued to dry heave, over and over again, until he finally stepped back into the dimly-lit work area. Seconds later, he mumbled something about needing air as he darted out of the spacious loft.

Marcos was tall, about six four and beanpole thin. He was the consummate geek with thick, black rimmed glasses that he had a habit of adjusting with his thumb. His dirty blonde hair was thick, wavy, and a little too long. The man was always in need of a cut which meant he was frequently shoving the long strands out of his face as he worked. His nose was bent, remnants of a break when he was ten. Carson remembered that day like it was yesterday. It was the day they became inseparable. The schoolyard bully wanted Marc's lunch money, Marcos was determined to prevent the theft at all cost. He was on the ground, blood gushing from his broken nose, money grasped tightly in his left fist as Earl Wickes kicked the defiant nerd over and over again. Finally, Carson had enough and stepped in to help. Earl walked away with a black eye that day and Carson and Marcos walked away with a bond that would never be broken.

They'd met Shawn in college and extended their little group immediately. The three of them had so much in common. Each was innovative, a little crazy and determined to push the limits and explore possibilities others shied from. They made the perfect team. Shawn's sudden withdrawal, then subsequent death had shattered the duo nearly beyond repair. Now, he and Marcos had a common goal. Another event that would meld their friendship into an even stronger, cohesive bond. One that would no doubt alter their future. It remained to be seen if the change would be for the better or for the worse.

"I'm fine," Marcos finally said. "What did the fed say? Did we do the right thing?"

"If there's a price to pay," Carson studied his oldest friend. "I'll pay it."

"Not this time," Marcos disagreed. "We'll pay it together. I've increased the firewall and created an alarm. If anyone tries to hack in, we'll know."

"Marcos," Carson began.

"Don't start," Marc shook his head and settled further into his chair, turning away as he studied multiple screens filled with code. "We decided to help. We'll help. And whatever the consequence, we deal with it together. Shawn was my friend, too."

"I know," Carson sighed. "He's preparing the paperwork. Wants us to sign it so he can bring us on as consultants. Official like. That way we can help and be protected from trouble."

"What about the rest?" Marcos said. "If they start snooping around our system, they're going to figure it out. Any first-year techie would recognize our signature, we didn't even try to hide it."

"I'm willing to risk it," Carson said soberly. "I have to do this, Marc. I have to be a part of it. Shawn and Theresa tried to shield us from this. They protected us, but that cost me. It cost us and it deprived me of the opportunity to nail that monster. I can leave you out of it though. You don't need to participate. Or, if you want, you can participate in the shadows. They don't need your info. I can fill out the paperwork and never tell them you assisted."

"No," Marcos began tapping his pen on his thigh. "No, I want in. It's a risk, but we do this together. We risk it together. And, we make sure Dominic Zarconi never sees the outside of a cell. He dies in prison. If the evidence doesn't lead him there, we have that last job we can pin on him. The keylogger is still on his computer. It would be easy to hack in." Marcos shrugged. "Instead of taking from the rich this time, we could give a little and leave an obvious trace." A smile spread across his face as he thought of the possibilities.

"It's a last resort," Carson agreed. "I don't think we're going to need it, though. I mean, that video alone is going to put him away for years. I was thinking…"

"What?" Marcos asked.

"Well," Carson continued. "There has to be something damning in those files. Why else would he be so careful? That encryption code, it looks like the work of Danny Jones."

"But Danny left town a long time ago."

"Almost four years," Carson nodded. "About the time that system was set up."

"You think Zarconi forced him to set up the program then Danny what?" Marcos asked, considering. "Relocated hoping to get out of his reach?"

"Protects his family, to a point," Carson added. "I mean Dan was good, nearly as good as us. I'm not surprised Zarconi enlisted him. Danny J never did care about the moral high ground; but once he was finished, he had to know there could be a price. We saw what he did to Shawn, killing Danny if something went wrong isn't out of the realm."

"You could be right, but does it matter?" Marcos asked.

"Maybe not," Carson considered. "We'll know more once we crack the encryption code. But, if we operate under the assumption it was Danny J's, that alone gives us an edge. We know his style, we cracked his system before."

"True," Marcos drawled. "This one is more complex, apparently Danny learned from his mistakes; but you're right, it matches his style. Nobody is more familiar with Danny's tricks than we are. Let's get started."

They were an unlikely pair. Marcos the poster boy for a computer geek. Carson was an anomaly. He didn't have any distinguishing traits to speak of. His hair was a light brown. He was six feet tall, average build, average looks, average style with a brilliant mind. He was the kind of guy that would never stand out in a crowd but once you got to know him, he was charismatic and memorable. People tended to underestimate Carson Gibbs. Not Marcos, they'd grown up together, learned together, and developed a love of computers together. Once Shawn joined the group, they were unstoppable. Shawn Regan had been a natural. Somehow programming, coding, and development had all just flowed out of him as if his very thought process was the same as the programs they were building. Carson and Marcos together were nearly as good. The three of them made the ultimate team.

They were great friends outside the computer stuff as well. Carson's charm coupled with Shawn's craziness that challenged them and Marcos' inner nerd that kept them in check was the ideal combination. The trio could have conquered the world. All of them were fiercely loyal, intelligent and a little extreme. Dominic Zarconi had ended it, he was responsible for two years of uncertainty and pain. Now, the two friends were determined and unwavering. They would ruin Zarconi's life and make sure he paid dearly for his crimes – especially killing their friend.

* * * *

Rowdy approached the vehicle and immediately spotted Tony. He was leaning against their sleek black RLX casually waiting for his driver. Rowdy grinned. He wouldn't be driving.

Tony frowned when Rowdy approached the passenger side and stopped directly in front of him. "What?"

"You drive," Rowdy said as he dropped the keys into Tony's palm and pulled on the door handle. He was settled in his seat by the time Tony climbed behind the wheel.

"Why?" Tony asked, perplexed. "Not that I'm complaining, but why?"

"Let's go," Rowdy motioned for Tony to start the engine. "I'll tell you on the way."

Once the engine roared to life, Tony put the car in reverse then headed out of the parking garage. They had merged into traffic on their way to the police precinct before Rowdy spoke.

"I'm not sure what we're going to encounter at the station," Rowdy admitted. "Coop called ahead to request the file. He told them he needed it after the abduction attempt on Theresa. Apparently, that appeased the desk sergeant because Coop sent a text confirming success."

"But?"

"Not a but," Rowdy disagreed. "It's just all the rest. We know a couple of the cops are dirty. We were lucky, last night we saw them; but they didn't see us. I'm just not sure how it's going to

339

Moondance Ridge

go down in there. I was hoping you'd wait in the car... with the engine running... just in case we need to make a quick getaway."

Tony considered, sounded reasonable. "I'll park as close to the building as legally possible."

"Good idea," Rowdy's mind was all over the place. He was trying to think up any possible scenario where things could go off the rails.

"Did you bring the badge?" Tony finally asked.

"Yeah, why?"

"It might come in handy in there," Tony shrugged as he took a left turn. "Just be careful and if you smell trouble, forget it. We can manage without the file." Tony hesitated but decided to ask the question that was on his mind. "Is that why you planned to do this alone? You're trying to keep me out of trouble?"

"Maybe," Rowdy grinned. "Don't read too much into that, though. Doesn't mean we're tight or anything."

"Of course not," Tony grinned. He pulled into a slot directly next to the last handicapped spot and turned to face Rowdy. "Don't take any chances. In and out if you sense trouble... bolt."

"See you in five," Rowdy climbed from the car and made his way to the entrance.

* * * *

"Can I help you," a middle-aged woman asked politely.

"I'm here to pick up a file," Rowdy told her. "For Sheriff Andy Cooper. I was told it would be ready."

"Oh, yes," the woman retrieved a sealed envelope and slid it across the counter. "I just need you to sign for it." She passed him a clipboard with a pen attached to a chain.

Rowdy casually flipped it around and scribbled something illegible to the paper. He picked up the envelope and turned to leave.

"Excuse me," the lady called out. "Can I see some ID?" She was studying the signature with a frown.

Rowdy turned, forced his most friendly smile and flashed his badge at the woman. He just hoped it would do the trick.

The lady visibly relaxed. "Thanks. That's good. Have a nice day."

Rowdy once again turned and made his way back to the front door. He was just pushing through when he spotted the man from the night before. The one with the kid, the mostly unwilling culprit. He wished he had a reason to stay and watch, but the last thing he wanted was to draw attention to himself. Instead, he continued out the door and walked back to the car. The instant he closed the door, Tony pulled away.

"Any trouble?"

"Nope," Rowdy paused to look up then went back to prying the flap open on the envelope. "I did see one of the guys from last night, but he didn't react. We're in the clear."

Tony relaxed. "You're sure he didn't recognize you?"

"Positive," Rowdy scowled as he pulled the file free and began to skim the contents. After only a few seconds, he shoved the paperwork back into the envelope.

"What's wrong?" Tony slowed to take another turn.

"The report's shit," Rowdy tossed it onto the back seat. "They didn't investigate that man's murder any more than they investigated the explosion at the warehouse. We risked exposure for nothing. Sorry about that. I was hoping..."

"Don't apologize," Tony interrupted as he pulled into a parking stall. "We're here. What do you say I go in alone on this one? Same plan, but you take the wheel."

"Are you expecting trouble?"

"No," Tony assured him. "Not really. Martin said he'd have what I need waiting at the front desk. I'm sure this Dale guy, the editor, won't disappoint. I just have a bad feeling I can't shake. Could be from the PD, could be the paper," Tony shrugged. "I just think we should be prepared."

"I agree," Rowdy opened the door and climbed out. Tony exited as well. "Hey," Rowdy called.

"Yeah," Tony answered.

"Take your own advice. Any trouble, leave it and we'll do it another way."

Tony smiled. "And you said we aren't tight."

"Go get your paperwork already," Rowdy smiled as he climbed behind the wheel.

* * * *

Dale Norris watched as the good-looking man stepped up to the desk. He knew exactly who it was when Darla reached for the envelope. He glanced at his watch and relaxed. Dom's men should be in position. The instant he'd concluded Martin Ashbury's call, he'd contacted the criminal mastermind that terrified and intrigued him. Dominic Zarconi hadn't been happy about the request, but ultimately decided it was best to fulfill it. They both agreed Dale Norris as Editor-in-Chief for the local paper was essential to them both and needed to continue. Dom told him to pull everything, and his men would take care of things on the back-end. They just needed twenty minutes to get into position. It had been thirty. Dale was in the clear. He continued to watch as the runner Ashbury had sent over grasped the large file, winked at Darla and headed for the door. He casually wondered if the man would survive the inevitable encounter, or if Dom's men would eliminate him the same way they had so many others over the years. *Oh, well. Not my problem.* If he couldn't write about it, he couldn't bring himself to care.

Tony's senses were on high alert, something wasn't right. He picked up his pace and had barely pulled the door shut when Rowdy punched the gas. Had he spotted something he didn't like or were his nerves telegraphing trouble as well?

"Buckle up," Rowdy warned as he swerved around traffic.

Tony barely heard the click as the belt snapped into place when the car swerved around a large van. Rowdy slammed on the brakes, then nearly skidded out of control as he took a left turn.

Tony grabbed the handle above the door and scowled as his entire body was shoved forward. The only thing stopping the momentum was the seatbelt that was now locked into place. "Are you nuts? What the hell, Rowdy?" He glanced in the side mirror just in time to see they were being chased. "Oh."

"Yeah," Rowdy punched the gas again then tapped the brakes and took a hard right. "See if you recognize them."

"Can't see them," Tony turned back around and held on for dear life. "But, I'm kind of glad you're driving. Well, I will be if we live to tell about it."

Rowdy laughed. "This is nothing. I've done it a million times. Just stay buckled up buttercup, and you'll be fine."

After three more turns, the road straightened out and Rowdy floored it. The engine whined and complained but continued to gain speed. Apparently not enough, Tony glanced back in time to see the souped-up Prius was gaining on them. "Now what?"

"Watch and learn," Rowdy grinned just as the vehicle pulled in beside them, then swerved abruptly, colliding with the passenger side of the car. The high-pitched sound of metal scraping metal sent chills down Tony's spine. Rowdy slammed on the brakes, the Prius swerved again, missed, lost control, and rolled. Finally landing in the scooped-out ravine used for a median.

Tony let out a sigh of relief when he spotted two men climbing from the wreckage. "Don't know them but they have to work for Dominic. It's the only thing that makes sense." He tried to steady his hand as he snapped a photo.

"Hold on," Rowdy took the first road that led to the right, punched the gas then tossed Tony his phone. "There's a police scanner app, find Detroit."

"What?" Tony examined the screen for something that looked like a scanner. He had just located the app and tapped the screen to open the program when their tires squealed then caught and the vehicle lurched forward. "What are you doing now?"

Rowdy glanced in the rearview mirror, smiled, took a hard right, another right and then a left. He accelerated again and glanced at Tony. "The scanner?"

Tony swiveled in his seat and frowned. They were being chased by a cop! "Why doesn't he have his lights or siren going?"

"Because he doesn't want anyone to know he's chasing us," Rowdy said a little too nonchalant for Tony's liking.

"You look like you're having fun," Tony observed.

"I am," Rowdy's grin got even bigger. "The scanner?"

Tony shook his head as he began looking for Detroit. Once he located what he needed, he turned up the volume and waited. Nothing. A traffic accident... hopefully they didn't cause that. An auto theft, a shoplifting, a reckless driver...was that them? "He's not reporting in," Tony realized.

Rowdy took another corner and smiled when the cop behind him took the turn a little too fast, overshot his lane and was blocked by another vehicle. The car spun, avoiding a collision then caught and slowly weaved forward, dodging the congestion he had just caused. It was the break the duo needed. Rowdy took a left, then a hard right into a hotel parking garage unseen by his pursuer. He careened around the corner and continued the wrong way taking the first left then another corner that wound around and followed the narrow trail in the opposite direction. It eventually emptied onto a back road. A quick right and Rowdy was winding through an industrial warehouse area. Eventually, the private drive emptied out onto a frontage road. They followed the roadway until it intersected with the next on-ramp. Rowdy entered the highway and sped up again. He was traveling with traffic, just a little faster than most of the vehicles. Every once in a while, he'd change lanes and make his way around a slower car or truck. Nothing unusual, nothing too overt.

"Now are we clear?" Tony asked, looking around for another threat.

"Now we're clear," Rowdy's smile was bigger than Tony had ever seen it.

"You look like a ten-year-old that just experienced his first rollercoaster," Tony observed.

"That my friend was more fun than I've had in years," Rowdy glanced at Tony.

"You and me," Tony shook his head. "We clearly have different ideas about fun."

Rowdy burst out laughing.

"But seriously," Tony pried. "Now what?"

"Now, we play it safe and head out of town," Rowdy told him. "Once I'm sure we're not being followed, we can return to the hotel."

"Should we call Skeet?"

"Yeah," Rowdy decided. "Dial the number then put me on speaker. I'll explain everything."

Once they hung up, Tony studied Rowdy truly curious. "Now that we're traveling at a normal speed, can you explain why he didn't turn on his emergency equipment? It would have made it easier for him to chase us. At least cleared the way some if nothing else."

"The instant he activates his lights or siren, it flips on the dash cam," Rowdy explained. "He didn't want a record of what he was doing. It's the same reason he wasn't calling the pursuit into dispatch. And, it's the reason I knew it had to be one of Dom's guys. Normally, if a cop chases a suspect, he calls in every move, every turn, every road. It gives the other officers time to get into place to spike the tires or block him in. That guy didn't want company."

"So, if he caught us?"

"We'd be dead," Rowdy shrugged.

"I will never get used to the casual way you refer to death," Tony shook his head then gazed out the window. "We're lucky you were driving. I'm good, under normal circumstances; but I never could have outrun a cop."

"Not many can," Rowdy assured him. "But yeah, I'm glad we were prepared for trouble."

It was nearly an hour later when Tony directed Rowdy into a large business that looked a lot like a wrecking yard. "Just pull up to the third overhead door," Tony advised. Once the car came to a stop, Tony stepped out and waited. A large man covered in tattoos stepped through a side door, wiping his hand with a grease-stained cloth.

"What did you do to my baby?" the man practically whined.

"Sorry, Wolf," Tony said sincerely. "It couldn't be avoided. You know I'm good for it, but I'm going to need a new ride."

Wolf looked at Tony like he was insane. "You wreck my ride then have the nerve to ask for a new one?"

"It's important," Tony pressed. "I need something fast but inconspicuous."

"Don't ask much do ya," Wolf grumbled. "Always was a pain in my keister."

Tony handed Wolf a card, the large man wrote something on the surface then handed it back. "I'll take care of it tomorrow," Tony assured him. "Now, a new ride and strip that one down. It needs to disappear... like yesterday."

Wolf narrowed his eyes at Tony. "What did you do?"

"Wolf," Tony warned. "Break it down and crush it, tonight. This can't wait."

Wolf sighed then turned. "Boys," he bellowed. The overhead door slowly slid open and three men stood on the other side. "Break it down and move it out. Morpheus, I need you to haul it down to the graveyard and deal with it tonight. This can't wait, it has to disappear for good. If anyone asks, it was never here."

"Got it boss," a wily black man gave Wolf a solute.

Wolf turned back to Tony. "Now, you are going to explain why I just destroyed my new ride if you want me to sacrifice a second machine to your cause."

"Does Dominic Zarconi know about your operation? Are you on his radar at all, for any reason?" Rowdy asked, realizing they may have just put this man in danger.

Wolf studied Rowdy for the first time. "You brought a cop with you? I told you before my pad is sacred."

"He's not a cop," Tony disagreed. "Not anymore. What about Zarconi?"

"No," Wolf barked. "I stay clear of the man, as far as I know he has no idea I even exist. He has his own operation. Guys he uses. You know, friends he can trust not to mess with the good thing he has going."

"Rowdy's not going to mess with you," Tony insisted receiving the message loud and clear. Wolf was not happy. "If the cops show, lie. We were never here. That car was never here. You hear me?"

"I guess I should feel lucky you shared that much," Wolf started for the corner of the building. "You mess up Nessie and I swear, I don't care who you are or how much of that fancy money you throw at me, we're done."

"If she means that much to you," Rowdy began.

Tony glanced sideways and gave Rowdy one shake of his head. "Nessie will be fine. I appreciate your help Wolf, I always do. And, you know why you have to stay in the dark. Just don't talk to the cops, don't talk to anyone, you have no idea what they're talking about and you never owned an RLX."

"I get it," Wolf dropped a set of keys in Tony's palm. "There she is. I'm serious, take care of her. She's one of my favorites. She's fast but not too obvious and shouldn't draw attention."

"BMW," Rowdy nodded. "It's perfect."

Wolf turned and walked away.

"Nice friends you have, Tony. Real personable and friendly. As much fun as this was," Rowdy held his hand out for the keys and waited while Tony hesitated then dropped them onto his palm. "I think I'll pass on the return trip. Wolfie in there, he needs an attitude adjustment."

Tony laughed. "I dare you to call him that to his face."

Rowdy put the car in drive and pulled away. The challenge didn't deserve a response.

* * * *

Blake rounded the corner then came to an abrupt stop. Someone was exiting Skeet's old hotel room. He immediately backed up and waited. Once he heard the distinct sound of the door closing, he peeked around the corner and watched the stranger turn and disappear in the opposite direction. Blake darted forward and sprinted down the long hallway. Their rooms were situated smack dab in the middle of the building. You could approach the elevator from either direction and it was about sixes as far as distance was concerned. He pushed himself to pick up the pace, knowing he didn't have much time. Blake slid into position just as the man rounded the corner and approached the elevator. He snapped a picture with his cellphone, silently retreated, then made his way back to the room. He planted various travel items in each room, then headed to the new hotel. They had a lot of equipment to assemble and he needed to talk to Skeet about this new development. *Who had discovered them and how?*

Twenty minutes later, Blake had everything loaded onto a luggage cart and was following a bellhop into the newly acquired office. The instant the hotel escort disappeared, Blake yanked open the door, slid into the hallway and quietly pushed open the door that led to the stairwell. He took the steps two at a time and had his keycard ready when he reached the penthouse door. The instant he rushed inside, both Skeet and Theresa looked up.

Skeet stood and approached his partner. "What happened?"

He pulled out his phone and showed the photo to Skeet. "He was at the hotel, in your old room when I arrived."

Theresa stood and moved in next to Skeet. "Crazy Joe."

"What?" Skeet asked.

"That's Crazy Joe, he works for Dominic."

"You're sure?"

"Positive," Theresa looked up. "I've dealt with him more than anyone else on the crew. He was usually the one that Dom sent out to collect his fee. While I was in Mount Haven, that is. Joe was easy to deal with, not like Socks or Drago. What do you think he was doing at your hotel?"

"That's the million-dollar question, isn't it?" Blake asked. "I got lucky. If I'd arrived five minutes sooner, I would have walked in on him. Five minutes later, and I never would have realized he was there."

"Did you go in?" Skeet asked.

"Yeah," Blake moved to sit in one of the chairs. "It's bugged."

Theresa's eyes widened in shock.

"Figures," Skeet also settled onto a chair.

"I bought a few travel items and placed them around both rooms so they look lived in."

"That's it?" Theresa asked. "That's your reaction? We've been bugged. Oh, well. Should we order beer with our pizza?"

The two men laughed, Theresa scowled.

"We expected this," Skeet told her. "Although, I'm curious how they knew where to find us. We've been careful."

Just then the door beeped and swung open. All three of them looked up to see Tony and Rowdy enter the room.

"Still pumped I see," Skeet grinned.

Rowdy shrugged. "It's been awhile. I have to say, today made all that money Tony's throwing away on this excursion worth it."

"What's he talking about?" Theresa asked Tony as he settled onto the couch beside her.

"Don't mind him," Tony said as he pulled her against him and wrapped an arm around her shoulders. "He's like a kid in a candy store because we were followed when we left the paper. Rowdy lost the tail, but apparently he enjoyed it far more than I did."

"How did Dom find out?" Theresa asked. "We've been careful. You said you've been careful, but he bugged Skeets old room and followed you guys to the paper."

"When did your room get bugged?" Rowdy turned to Skeet.

"Apparently this afternoon," Skeet motioned to Blake. "The guy snuck in and almost made a clean break without us knowing."

Blake pulled out his phone again and showed Rowdy and Tony the shot.

Tony turned to Rowdy. "That's the guy from earlier."

"Yeah," Rowdy considered.

"It's Joe," Theresa provided. "The crew calls him Crazy Joe, but I don't know why. They make up stupid names for each other, but Joe's not nearly as crazy as the rest. In fact, he's pretty levelheaded compared to Socks and Drago."

"What do you mean from earlier?" Skeet asked Rowdy.

"I thought he might have followed you from the warehouse," Rowdy began.

"Like we did," Tony added. "He was driving in a pattern and looked like he might be onto you."

"You didn't think to mention that earlier?" Blake asked, annoyed.

"We pulled back, wanting to make sure he didn't connect you with us," Rowdy continued. "We watched you turn into the hotel so we circled the block to get a better look. When we pulled into the lot, he was climbing back into his car," Rowdy continued. "I watched him leave. He disappeared down the highway without a sideways glance. I decided it had to be a coincidence, just a strange quirk. It happens."

"Maybe he did follow us... all the way to our rooms. Once he knew how to find us, he reported in, maybe went directly to Zarconi at the casino who sent him back to bug the room," Skeet offered.

"But if you didn't follow us directly, how did you know which room?" Blake asked. "I assumed you followed us all the way up."

"I asked at the desk," Rowdy said absently. "Which is why you never use your own name when you're trying to be covert."

"Unless you want to be discovered," Skeet countered.

"Yeah," Rowdy grinned. "There is that, apparently it worked."

"Do they do that a lot?" Blake asked Tony. "Because it's kind of annoying."

"No idea," Tony shrugged. "I'm new to the covert spy stuff."

"So," Theresa glanced around the room. "What do we do now?"

"Now," Skeet stood. "We head downstairs and set up the office."

* * * *

Dominic stood, hunched over his desk as he tried to make sense of what had happened. How had his men failed so miserably? He picked up the phone and began pounding the receiver on the antique mahogany. When that didn't relieve his anger, he turned and threw the entire machine against the wall.

Three men stood just inside the doorway waiting for their punishment. Each wondering if they would be leaving this room alive.

"I still don't understand how he got away," Dom turned to face Horatio and Geovanni. "You two, maybe. Clearly the guy was a pro. But you?"

"Like you just said," Frank Dressel responded. "The guy was a pro. If I had to guess, he's been on a speedway. If not a pro, maybe a relief driver or someone who washed out of the big league; but he has skills. You just had that issue in Vegas, are you sure things are cool with Sherman?"

Dom settled into his desk chair and considered. "He was that good?"

Dressel shrugged. "He outdrove me, I think that speaks for itself."

"Good point," Dom acknowledged. Dressel was the best driver Dom had ever met. It was the reason he'd brought him into the fold. His profession was just a bonus at the time. Having a driver that was also a cop solved any messy problems that came up while he was taking care of business. "You're excused."

Moondance Ridge

Dom heard the shock in the men's voices as they discussed what had happened just outside the door. He knew the men feared him, wasn't that the point? All three of them had stepped into his office wondering if today was the day they would meet his favorite Glock. It wasn't. The thought hadn't even crossed his mind. Not for this. It wasn't their fault some pro driver outmaneuvered them. But, Dressel was right, that spoke volumes. Had Sherman reneged on their deal? Drago was dead, Dom had provided proof. And still...

Dom stood and began to pace the room. There were too many connections to dismiss. He'd sent Joe to Vegas initially to deal with Rodney and his failure to pay his debt on time. The man had become cocky all of a sudden, and Dom wanted to know why. Joe got to the bottom of things immediately, it was the reason he sent Joe rather than Drago or Socks in the first place. Rodney mistakenly believed he had leverage. How the nuisance had uncovered one of Dom's biggest secrets was still a mystery. One he had dismissed as irrelevant. Maybe he'd been wrong. Maybe eliminating Rodney and retrieving the documents on the journalist's unexpected death hadn't eliminated the problem.

What if David Sherman had the same Intel? What if his grandson had learned everything? If anyone knew Darrow was on his payroll... that the fed was the one that murdered the reporter... things could get messy. If Sherman had the same documentation they'd recovered from Rodney, killing Drago might not be enough to silence his competitor. But, how did Martin Ashbury factor in? And, why did the man want Regan's news articles? Was it possible Dave knew the Cryo-Comm billionaire? Had Zachery Regan written a clue into one of his stories? Something that confirmed information Sherman already had. Did David Sherman possess damning evidence against Dom and his organization at this very moment? Dom was sure of one thing, there was no such thing as coincidence. So, the connections couldn't be dismissed, but he also needed more information before he decided on a course of action. If he took out Sherman, the man's organization would wage instant war and that was something Dominic would never provoke without a reason. He would, however, do anything necessary to protect his own life and his rapidly growing enterprise.

* * * *

Bailey glanced at the two men again and wondered what their next move would be. She'd spotted them the instant they walked through the door and both of them radiated trouble. Her hand absently rested on Knights head and she gently rubbed behind his ears, to comfort him or her? She wasn't sure. She relaxed a little when Jase stepped behind the bar and moved in next to her. Together they dealt with the growing line of customers, each of them keeping an eye on the two strangers.

"I'll be back in a minute," Jase whispered then disappeared into the back.

The moment the door closed, Jase pulled out his phone.

"What's wrong?" Coop demanded.

"I'm not sure if anything is wrong but a couple strangers are sitting at the bar and they... I don't know. They just ooze danger. They've been staring at Bailey since they sat down. I'm afraid they're planning something, I just haven't figured out what yet."

"Keep an eye on them," Coop ordered. "I'm on my way."

Jase stepped back into the open area just in time to see one of the men grab Bailey's wrist. He moved in next to her for support. "I wouldn't do that if I were you."

"Oh, yeah?" the second guy replied. "Who's gonna stop us? You?"

The two men burst out laughing. Apparently, they didn't notice Knight's response. He was alert, the hair on the back of his neck was standing straight up and he was watching every move the two men made. A low growl rumbled in the back of his throat, but most of the patrons couldn't hear it.

Jase was about to move forward, to free Bailey from her captor when his colleague suddenly yanked her hand backwards. The unexpected force did the trick, the aggressor was taken by surprise and couldn't maintain his grip. The laughter immediately stopped. Dreven Killian leaned forward, a menacing look on his face. "I asked you where the girl is."

"And, I told you I have no idea what you're talking about," Bailey glared back.

"The waitress," Talon pushed back his jacket to reveal a holster that clearly held a handgun.

"Most of our waitresses are female," Bailey said with a shrug. "You'll have to give me more than that."

"You know exactly who I'm talking about," Dreven growled. "Where is Theresa Regan?"

"Oh," Bailey smiled. "Why didn't you just say so? We could have avoided this little... testosterone display. Theresa has the night off."

358

"I'm going to need her address," Talon insisted.

"I'm afraid that's confidential," Bailey stepped closer to Knight. "We believe in protecting our employee's privacy."

"Listen lady," Talon stood. "You have no idea who you're dealing with. Give me the damn address."

Bailey stood frozen, unsure of what to do next. She knew the man had a gun. How could she miss it? He was clearly telegraphing a threat, revealing the weapon only to her and Jase. If Knight got involved, would he be shot? Before she could come up with a plan, the men set things in motion and the bar suddenly became a bloody mess.

Dreven reached across the bar and grabbed Bailey's forearm again, pulling her hard against the side of the counter. With his other hand, he slapped her across the face. Bailey's vision blurred, but she saw the distinct form of her favorite K9 coming to her defense. Knight leapt forward, planting his two front paws on the top of the counter. His teeth sank into Dreven's upper arm with precision. Instead of releasing his hold, he yanked Bailey forward again. Wrong move. Knight tightened his grip, sinking his teeth further into the flesh before he started to shake his head back and forth. Dreven screamed out in pain as blood seeped through his shirt and dripped onto the counter. Knight didn't let go. He continued to yank and pull as his head turned left to right. Blood was now flying across the room, splattering the walls and the patrons. Several women screamed, the crowd fled, exiting through the door into the parking lot.

Talon Woods watched in shocked horror for several seconds before he reacted. He moved behind the counter and approached Bailey from behind, lifting the flap of his jacket out-of-the-way so he could retrieve his gun. Knight saw the second threat and lunged. He struck Talon squarely in the chest. Both of them toppled to the ground, Knight on top, Talon's gun hand securely between his teeth. Again, the man did the worst thing possible, he tried to fight.

Jase was worried about the gun. He studied Knight and decided he had to try. While the man and dog wrestled on the floor, Jase took a step forward and crouched. He froze, terrified when Knight let out a deep, menacing growl that reverberated throughout the entire room. "Good boy," Jase said softly, hoping the dog would recognize him. Moments later, he saw his chance and he took it. The man twisted, turned and kicked out. Jase grabbed the gun at the same time Knight latched onto the man's thigh and yanked. Talon slid across the floor, banging his head against the wooden cabinet when the dog once again used the force of his body to turn his head to the side. The intruder reached out and grabbed hold of the foot rest that ran the length of the bar, then held on for dear life. The instant the man stopped fighting, Knight released his hold. He stood, leaning forward, hair standing straight up as he focused on his prey. Again, that low, menacing growl vibrated in the back of the dog's throat.

Dreven tucked his arm against his side, hoping it would stop the bleeding. He pushed his body into a standing position, steadying his weight on the nearest bar stool as he reached for his side.

"I wouldn't do that if I were you," Coop said, pointing his own gun at the man's head. "Hands flat on the counter. Move."

Dreven froze, glanced to the side and immediately gave up. Fighting a woman and the cook had seemed like a simple task just minutes ago. How had things gone so wrong? Cujo, that's how. He hadn't even noticed the vicious monster before it latched onto his arm and ground his limb into hamburger. Dreven placed both hands on the counter and waited. He screamed out in pain when the hardened Sheriff cuffed him. "Watch it," he stumbled forward, caught his foot on the bar stool and did a face plant into the ancient wood floor. His nose slammed against the hard surface and Dreven saw stars mixed with a large set of black boots.

Matthew leaned down and tied a strip of cloth around the dog bite. "Looks like he may have nicked a vein," he said as he stood over the prisoner.

Coop rounded the corner of the bar looking for the second man and spotted Knight. "Good boy," he soothed. "Bailey, see if you can get control of Knight. He's on that leash so he can't go far. Talk to him, soothe him and see if you can pull him toward you."

"Knight," Bailey whispered. "Good boy. You're my hero, aren't you? Rowdy knew you'd protect me. I had my doubts about this setup; but you proved once again, dad's always right." She waited and watched as Knight turned his head and gazed into her eyes.

Coop moved forward, grabbed Talon by the shirt and yanked. The man began to slide across the floor, out of the dog's reach. Knight reacted immediately. He pivoted, took a step forward then stopped when he heard Bailey's voice. He stood there for several seconds, his attention divided between Bailey, and his target.

Bailey crouched and called to Knight. "Here boy," she held out her hand and offered a strip of doggy bacon. Rowdy would kill her if he knew, but he wasn't here so she'd do things her way. She had to get control of Knight so Coop could arrest her attacker. "That's a good boy. Come here. Come get a treat, you were such a good boy tonight."

"You've got to be kidding me," Talon objected. "That rabid mutt needs to be put down. Just wait. I'm going to sue the pants off you lady. My lawyer is going to chew you up and spit you out. You'll rue the day you let that monster near me and my partner."

Coop cuffed the rambling lunatic and searched him for additional weapons. "Search him, Matt. They were both armed. Let's make sure they're secure before the medics take a look." He crouched until he was directly in front of Talon's face. "If I remember correctly, that dog just chewed you up and spit you out. You might want to think about that before you come back here causing trouble. Because, I guarantee you'll rue the day you met me if we have a repeat. This is my town." He stood and pressed a button on his walkie. "Ben, send in your men."

Two medics stepped through the doors, each moving to a man to render first aid. Coop motioned for Matt to join him away from the group. "I need to make a call, you got this?"

"Yes sir," Matt grinned. "I think I might want to talk to you about a K9 partner once things settle down. That dog is the bomb."

Coop grinned as he stepped into the cool night air. He sighed as he moved to the patio and settled into a chair. This was a call he hated to make, but it was necessary.

"Coop," Skeet said flatly. "This is a surprise."

"We had a situation," Coop gave him the short version of what went down.

"Wow," Skeet walked away from the board he was tacking photos to and moved to stand in front of the large window that overlooked the city of Detroit. "Rowdy's not going to be happy about this. But Bailey's okay?"

"Yeah," Coop confirmed. "The guy clocked her pretty good, she'll have a bruise, but she's fine."

"I always knew that dog was a gem," his thoughts turned to the situation at hand. "We need a delay. Can you take them to the station, maybe have someone interrogate them for a few hours?"

"Sure," Coop said hesitantly. "About what?"

"I'm just looking for a delay," Skeet admitted. "Ask them about, I don't know. Ask them about DeRossi."

"Exactly how would I make the connection to DeRossi?" Coop asked. He was at a loss right now and just wanted to get back inside and check on Bailey and his favorite K9.

"I don't know, think of something," Skeet countered, just as frustrated as his friend. He looked up and sighed when Rowdy stepped into the room. "Here's your brother. Put your heads together and come up with something. I need to make another call." He turned to Rowdy. "It's Coop. Bailey's fine, but they had some trouble. I need your phone. He'll fill you in on the details." They swapped phones and Skeet moved into the other room.

"What do you mean an incident?" Rowdy asked.

Coop ran through it again, this time in detail. "I had doubts about that leash thing you rigged behind the bar, but it saved Bailey tonight."

"So, they were just looking for Theresa?" Rowdy asked. "They don't know we're here yet?"

"Not according to Jase and Bailey," Coop assured him. "They wanted Theresa. We know they're Zarconi's men because of that alone. Which means he still has no idea you are camped out in his backyard."

"We need to keep it that way," Rowdy dropped into a chair. "What did Skeet say?"

"Basically, the same," Coop admitted. "He wants me to put someone on them, interrogate them, keep them busy for a few hours. Problem is, I have no idea what I should interrogate them about. We can't mention Zarconi or Detroit."

"Just start with the basics," Rowdy provided. "You're off your game, bro. Take a deep breath, you're not thinking straight. Start by finding out who they are. Run them, see where they came from. See if there's any way to pin them to other crimes. There has to be burglaries or assaults in the area. See what Missoula has. They always have unsolved burglaries, robberies, whatever. Question them about those. You don't have to get specific, be a detective Sheriff Cooper."

"You're right," Coop said softly. "I am off my game. There was so much blood. When I stepped through that door and saw the mess, I panicked. If anything happened to Bailey, I'd never forgive myself. I was so terrified some of it was hers."

Rowdy's gut clenched and the constant worry he felt for Bailey and her safety while he was so far away intensified. "I trust you," he finally said. "And I trust Knight. As long as she keeps that dog by her side, she'll be fine."

"Well," Coop stood. "I guess he proved that in spades tonight. I'll let you talk to your girl now. I'm sure it will make both of you feel better about this whole thing. I have two suspects to interrogate."

"Thanks," Rowdy said sincerely. "Thanks for watching out for Bailey. I have to finish this, but..."

"We're family," Coop said. "Here's your girl but first, be extra careful out there. We knew what we were dealing with; but, tonight is a reminder. Take care of each other, these guys were ruthless."

"Same with you, be alert and watch your back," Rowdy said. "It's not only Bailey I'm worried about. You can only keep those guys secluded for two days tops. Once they contact Zarconi, things out there might heat up. I need to know if they do. We're making progress but if the troops descend on Mount Haven, we're coming home."

"I'll keep you posted," Coop handed the phone to Bailey. "The boss wants to talk to you."

* * * *

"Thanks for the night out," Theresa said as she and Tony stepped onto the floor below their room and made their way toward the office. "I needed that."

"It was my pleasure," Tony lifted her hand and gave her knuckles a soft kiss. "We will get through this, I promise." He stopped to slide the keycard through the slot and pushed open the door.

"Wow," Theresa said as she stepped inside. "Skeet has made a lot of progress."

Moondance Ridge

Tony glanced around and frowned. Rowdy was on the phone and clearly not happy. Something had happened, he was sure of it. He surveyed the area and wondered where Skeet had disappeared to. Just then, the man in question made his way down the short hallway and moved abruptly toward Rowdy.

"Is that still Coop?" Skeet asked.

"No, Bailey."

"Is Coop still around?" Skeet pressed. "I need one more minute with him, then you can have it back. By the way, tell Bailey I'm impressed. She's as tough as I always thought she was."

"Hey baby," Rowdy began.

"I know, I heard. Tell Skeet thanks, but I expect him to be just as impressive. I need him to have your back," Bailey swallowed. "Please be careful, here's Coop."

"What?" Coop asked impatiently.

"Don't bark at me," Rowdy scolded. "Skeet needs a word."

"I have arranged for Agent Jasper Mitani to respond to Mount Haven and retrieve our prisoners," Skeet advised. "Do not release them to anyone but Mitani. He's DEA. With any luck, we can tie them in with DeRossi and let Jasper deal with the duo from there."

"Why do you think there is any possible tie to DeRossi?" Coop asked. "I just got their names and they're not even from Detroit."

"Where are they from?" Skeet asked.

"New York."

"New York?" Skeet considered. "Well, there's your tie."

"Depiro," Rowdy considered. "Tell Coop to use that. Use the New York, Depiro angle to connect them to DeRossi. It doesn't matter if it sticks, he's just trying to figure out something to question them about. This will work. Plus, who cares if they put it all together and figure out he's the Andy Cooper that helped bring the man down?"

"I don't know," Skeet considered. "I mean I was all for making the connection when there wasn't a connection to be made. This complicates things."

"How?" Coop asked, catching Rowdy in the background.

Skeet switched the phone to speaker. "Because all three of us have a price on our heads."

"Really?" Coop asked, thrilled at the prospect. "How much?"

"I'm surrounded by infantile boys," Theresa grumbled.

Tony laughed.

"Enough," Skeet advised. "DeRossi put out an order the second his butt hit the mattress in that federal facility he now calls home. He wants us punished, severely. I'm just not sure that line of questioning is the answer."

"Sure it is," Rowdy disagreed. "If there's a connection, that DEA guy of yours might be able to make it. Let him push the DeRossi angle if you don't want Coop to. I think it's perfect. I mean, what more can the two of them do now? We're onto them and I know you'll keep Bay safe until I can get back there and do it myself."

"What happened to Bailey?" Tony jumped to his feet and moved to stand beside Rowdy.

"I'll play it by ear," Coop decided. "Trust me, Perkins. You know I can handle this."

"I have no doubt," Skeet agreed. "Just be careful and if things get too crazy, we can send Bryan and Maggie to stay with Angela."

"With Maggie pregnant, I just might take you up on that," Coop hadn't considered sending his family into hiding. It might be a good solution to the problem.

"Okay, give the phone back to Bailey. Rowdy wasn't finished apparently and I'm getting in deeper the longer I force him to wait."

Skeet handed the phone back to Rowdy and moved to explain the situation to Tony, Theresa and Blake who had just stepped into the room.

"I have to do something," Theresa stood to pace in frustration. "I am putting so many people in danger. We have to end this."

"We will," Rowdy assured her. He had finished up with Bailey and joined the group to strategize. "I think the key is in the evidence. Once we have enough, we can arrest Zarconi and get back to business as usual."

"That reminds me," Skeet looked at Theresa. "It's time."

"Okay," Theresa agreed. "While you watch that video, I'll work on going through the others. I can pick up where we left off." She grabbed a pad of paper and a pen then retreated to the back bedroom. Tony followed.

"What is this about?" Tony asked as he pulled her into his arms.

Theresa settled in closer. Somehow Tony always seemed to give her strength. She stood there, wrapped in the arms of a man she had come to love, knowing in a few minutes he was going to witness the death of the only other man she'd ever loved. She closed her eyes, took a deep breath and stepped back. "I didn't realize Shawn was saving the video to the cloud."

"The folders we couldn't access?"

"Yes," Theresa moved to the bed and settled onto the edge. "Carson and Marc figured out Shawn's password. Inside were videos, from the casino. Skeet and I started going through them earlier today. I've identified a couple of Dom's employees and I'm going to work on that while you watch with the others. You need to go back out there and watch the last video that was saved."

"And what is on that video?"

"Shawn's death," a single tear escaped her left eye and Theresa reached up and impatiently brushed it away.

Tony knelt in front of her and placed his hands on each side of her head, he used his thumbs to wipe away the tears that were now flowing freely. "I'm here for you, always. I will end this for you, for Bailey, for your techies. I am going to finish this." He leaned forward and pressed his lips to her forehead.

Theresa leaned back and locked eyes with Tony. She swallowed hard then shifted so she could stand. Tony straightened with her and once again pulled her into his arms.

Moondance Ridge

"I wish I could take away your pain," Tony whispered. "I would. I would do anything to make this better, I hope you know that."

"I do," Theresa nodded. "I know you have to watch that video. You have to do it so you know the kind of men you're dealing with. You have to do it because Tony Nazario thinks he should know everything. They have to do it because they're cops and its evidence. I know you have to watch it, but I don't. I can't. I've already seen it and I can never watch that video again."

"Rowdy is not watching that video because he's a cop and its evidence," Tony disagreed. "He's watching it for the same reason I will. Because he cares about you. Because you are important to all of us and we need to know. What we're dealing with, yes. But, it's more than that. We need to know our enemy so we can destroy him. I'm not sure you understand that and I'm glad for it. Just remember, we need to know. We won't be watching because we want to. We are watching because we have to."

"Thank you," Theresa once again settled onto the bed. "Now go, I have work to do." She placed the computer on her lap and clicked on the first video.

Tony stepped back into the makeshift conference room and settled into a chair. Blake had connected the necessary cords so the laptop screen was projected on the large screen television. The group watched in horror as Dominic Zarconi and his men tortured and eventually killed Shawn Regan. They continued to watch as Socks and Drago loaded up the body and left the area. Moments later, Theresa climbed from the tiny cupboard, stumbled then darted from the room. Silence filled the hotel office as each man tried to reconcile what they had just witnessed. Several minutes later, Tony stood and silently made his way down the hall.

Theresa looked up, understanding registered when she saw his face. "I knew this would happen once you saw it. I knew you'd change your mind. Tell me, which is it? You can't look at me the same? Your feelings have changed? Or is it the mission? You've changed your mind and you can no longer help? Maybe it's both?"

"Be quiet," Tony crossed the room and settled onto the bed next to Theresa. He snatched up the computer and set it on the floor before pulling her onto his lap. Then he just held her close, for her and for him. They sat that way for several seconds before Theresa straightened.

"It's okay if you want out," she swallowed hard. "I understand. I want out, I want nothing to do with that man and it's my problem. I do understand if you can never look at me the same again."

Tony studied Theresa, never taking his eyes off hers. He waited until she stopped talking then he pressed his mouth to hers. The kiss started out gentle, loving, full of so much promise. Then, he deepened the kiss, wrapped his arms tighter around her and soaked in the closeness. He needed her and he knew she needed him. Tonight, he was going to show her just how much he didn't want out. The timing was all wrong, it was always wrong. Sharing that kind of intimacy after all the ugliness he just witnessed was probably a bad idea, but he didn't care. He needed Theresa right now, and it seemed she felt the same way.

Chapter Ten

Several minutes passed before Blake finally stood and shut off the television. Rowdy looked at Skeet, then turned to Blake. "I'm sorry man, but Skeet and I need a few minutes alone. We're going for a walk." He stood and waited for his friend to follow. The two men exited the room and silently made their way to the sidewalk outside.

"You don't need to say anything," Skeet finally whispered. It was all he could do to say that much.

"I know," Rowdy gazed into the darkness. "But I'm going to."

Skeet looked at Rowdy and once again cherished the connection they had. He nodded and began to slowly walk away from the expensive hotel. They made their way to the park, the one just up the road where Zach had been killed. The reporter had been innocent and idealistic. A man on a mission without the means to succeed. He mistakenly believed he was walking into safety, instead he'd willingly ventured into danger -to the scene of his own demise.

"We really never talked about that time, after, I mean," Rowdy began.

"Rowdy," Skeet shook his head. "It's not necessary."

"I think It is," Rowdy disagreed. "Because watching that video reminded me of something."

"Please don't state the obvious," Skeet objected.

"I won't," Rowdy agreed. "Because it is obvious. That's not what I need to say. I know as well as you do the unspeakable horror your wife endured. We knew that going in. She was kidnapped by a madman, a serial killer who thrived on inflicting pain. You should not have watched that video tonight, but I know why you did."

"Then what is it you want to say?" Skeet snapped. He knew he was being unfair, but that video had brought back so many feelings he'd tried to bury, so much pain and heartache. But, the worst emotion of all was the intense feeling of guilt he still struggled with every day... knowing it was his fault Angela had been abducted in the first place.

"I met you during the worst time of your life," Rowdy began. "That's not unusual for a cop. I mean, it's our job to respond to calls for help. Calls by people who are experiencing pain, tragedy or their own personal horror."

"True," Skeet agreed. "I have to admit, I'm not sure where you're going with this."

"Just hear me out," Rowdy persisted. "Even when your world was falling apart, you couldn't help but be you. Skeeter Perkins, brilliant FBI Agent, world renowned investigator, and all around good guy. You were intensely loyal, focused and determined. You also never lost sight of who you were, what you believed in, and you never once compromised your integrity."

"I appreciate the moral boost but again, where are you going with this?"

"I respect you, Skeet. I always have," Rowdy said soberly. "I never told you that. I should have. When I was shot, when I lost my way, lost the job, my identity, my reason to live..."

"Rowdy," Skeet settled onto a nearby bench. "You always had a reason to live and the respect, it goes both ways."

"When I lost my way," Rowdy continued. "I thought a lot about you... and Angela. About what that woman went through and came out the other side beautiful and kind. About how you were able to bounce back... eventually. You are still you. She's an example for all of us. I'm so glad I was able to be there when we got her back."

"As I recall," Skeet focused on his friend. "You did a lot more than just be there. Maybe we should have talked afterwards because I owe you so much. You saved me in a way not many cops would have. You put everything on the line for a friend. You were right by the way, at the time I wasn't thinking straight. But, you were right."

"I thought we agreed never to discuss that," Rowdy stopped him. "I don't think we should go back on that now."

"If you insist," Skeet nodded. "But, I will be eternally grateful to you and Coop for all you did, then and now. We are going to get through this somehow. And in the end, we will both walk away with our character intact. We'll do that because of our mutual respect and admiration. But also, because we are better than Dominic Zarconi... morally and tactically."

"I agree, but that's not what this talk was about either," Rowdy sat down next to Skeet. "I do want to say one thing though."

"What's that?"

"There are few men I trust in this world. I mean, really trust," Rowdy settled against the back of the bench. "In fact, I'd say there are two - you and Coop... because of your character. I might eventually get there with Tony. He's a good man and like us, he has a few skeletons that make him... evasive, I guess. Certainly skeptical."

"I agree," Skeet settled in and stretched his legs. "I don't know him as well as you. I also think there's something he's hiding, something in the past he doesn't want to admit. I'm not worried about it if that's what you're asking."

"No," Rowdy glanced around. "I was just stating a fact. I did have a point. We all have skeletons. The way I mishandled my disability is one of mine. How I treated my family is another. Some might even lump in the men I've killed as unforgiveable. We can't let our skeletons define our life. I know you know that, deep down in your heart, you know it. But, I also think you still carry the guilt around your neck like an albatross. What happened to Angela was not your fault. You think it is because you were chasing him. Because he went after the woman you love to punish you. If you can't let it go, he wins. He is still punishing you from the grave."

"Let it go, Rowdy."

"No," Rowdy shook his head. "Because I saw it in your eyes when you watched that video tonight. Just like I saw it in Shawn's eyes as he endured blow after blow. He felt guilty for getting Theresa into that situation. He was wrong and so are you. He died not understanding the truth. Don't let the same happen to you. You can't carry that kind of burden around until your ninety or you're not going to make it to ninety. Do you blame yourself for the others? The ones that came before Angela? Were those your fault, too?"

"That's different and you know it," Skeet objected.

"Not really," Rowdy countered. "If you take a step back and look at this logically, he was going to abduct someone. He was finished with Darla Thompson. He needed another target, someone to experiment on. If it hadn't been Angela, it would have been some other vulnerable, kind, naïve young girl with her whole life ahead of her."

"I know you're right," Skeet agreed. "I've told myself the same thing a hundred times."

"But, you can't get past the guilt," Rowdy provided. "Guilt comes in a variety of sizes and colors. We all have to deal with it at one time or another. Tony told me today that I'm casual about death. I'm not, every time I'm forced to take a life, it drains a part of my soul. I'm not sure I can explain it."

"You don't have to," Skeet bumped his shoulder against Rowdy's. "I've been forced to kill, in the line of duty. Some you know about. Some were before we met. I get what you're saying but what I feel is different. I look at my beautiful wife, I see the amazing talent she has when she opens her heart and paints another glorious landscape; and I wonder how a man like me can be loved by a woman as pure and good as her. Sometimes, I struggle to live with myself knowing she had to endure so much evil because a madman was playing a sick, perverted game against me."

"Which is why you can't get past it," Rowdy bumped back. "You're thinking of this all wrong. As I said before, you know in your heart, even if it hasn't reached your head that you are not responsible. The killer and only the killer is responsible for the initial abduction and everything that happened afterwards. I bet every victim has someone out there playing the 'what if' game. It's a game you can never win. What if I had done a better job of protecting her? What if I hadn't gone to Texas? What if I had returned a day earlier?"

"All questions I've asked myself," Skeet admitted.

"What if I hadn't shot that kid? What if I had waited for backup? What if I had died?"

Skeet pivoted around and stared at his friend. "Did you really think that?"

"Tons of times," Rowdy admitted. "I was a burden. I wondered, would my family be better off if I had died that night. Those first few months, I convinced myself they would have been. I was wrong and so are you."

Skeet didn't know what to say, so he remained silent.

"You still think about what happened to Angela and blame yourself for every cut, every injection, every ounce of pain she was forced to power through and endure. Skeet," Rowdy studied his friend and waited. Finally, Skeet looked up. "If it was someone else, they would have died. Angela held on because she knew you would find her. She knew you would come for her. She knew you would never give up. She had something to live for. She had hope and faith in an amazing man that would never stop looking. That knowledge gave her the strength to hold on. If it had been another girl, it would have been another dead girl. He made a mistake when he took Angela. She doesn't blame you, stop blaming yourself."

Skeet hadn't considered that angle. It was certainly something to think about. It was also something he wasn't going to resolve tonight. "So," he stood. "While we're here, you want to take a look around. I mean, we might as well try to solve a murder while we're at it."

Rowdy stood and studied his surroundings. "The cops might have covered up the murder, but someone saw what happened. Look around, the place is scattered with people. Mostly young people, college students if I had to guess. We could get the geeks to do some digging. See if they can scrounge up a roster from Wayne State, students that may have been in the area the night Zach died. Theresa said she was still in college back then, it could be a good starting point. Let's track down a list of her graduating class."

"It's worth a shot," Skeet turned and started back toward the hotel.

Rowdy fell in beside his friend. He hoped Skeet would get past the guilt, Rowdy knew all too well how destructive it could be if you let it consume you.

"Thanks," Skeet said just before they reached the hotel.

"For?" Rowdy asked.

"I guess," Skeet glanced over. "For being you."

Rowdy grinned. "There's not much I can do about that one."

The two men stepped into the elevator and watched the door close. "I guess we should stop back by the office before we crash for the evening," Rowdy decided.

"Probably," Skeet pressed the button and waited patiently for the elevator to ascend. Within minutes, they were stepping into their new office space. Skeet frowned when he saw Tony and Theresa sitting on the couch. Blake had apparently turned in for the evening.

"I needed to talk to you," Theresa stood. "I think I might have found something." She moved to the table and clicked open the file with all the videos. "I asked Blake to leave it connected to the screen up there." She pointed to the flat screen on the wall.

"Okay," Skeet settled into a chair. Rowdy sat down next to him.

Theresa sat next to Tony and started the video. Within seconds, she paused the feed. "That first man, standing next to the stage is the guy I believe to be FBI."

"He is," Skeet confirmed. "His name is Troy Darrow."

"I think he's the man Zach met that night, the night he died," Theresa clarified. "The man standing next to him, I think he may also be a fed." She minimized the video and clicked on a second one. Within seconds, the same man appeared, standing next to Dominic in the casino.

"I don't know him," Skeet admitted. "He dresses like one of us. I need to get those to Stan. He'll be able to run him through face recognition using the Bureau's employee records and verify he's an agent. When Bryant called, he said there were two agents and maybe his boss. If you're right, we may have just discovered the second agent. Good work, Theresa. I'm still not sure bringing you here, to Detroit, was a wise move, but you have certainly proven to be resourceful and observant."

"Tony would probably agree with you, seeing as he expressed the same objection before we left Mount Haven," Theresa said, standing. "I'll tell you the same thing I told him, this is my problem and I know many of Dom's people. It's better to have me here, rather than back home. I think the events at the bar tonight went a long way in proving me right."

"Touché," Rowdy frowned at the reminder of what had happened with Bailey. "I'm beat, what do you say we all call it a night?"

"I'll be up in a minute," Skeet decided. "I need to call Stan, get him the videos and have him start working on uncovering that man's identity."

"I can wait," Rowdy offered.

"Naw," Skeet smiled. "It will only take a minute and then I'm turning in, too."

Tony, Theresa and Rowdy stepped from the room and headed for the stairs. Once the stairwell door shut behind him, Tony turned to study Rowdy. "Is our fed okay?"

"Skeet will power through this in spite of the personal cost," Rowdy answered.

"I'm not sure what that means," Tony pressed. "That video seemed to impact him more than it should have."

Rowdy stopped and considered. "Skeet's past is his story to tell, or not to tell as he deems fit. However, since we are working together, I will fill in the blank, in general terms anyway." He focused on Tony. "Do you remember me telling you, when we talked about bringing Skeet into all this, that we could trust him? I said we worked together in the past and that Coop and I helped rescue his wife after she was abducted. Then, he helped me rescue Bailey."

"Vaguely," Tony hadn't actually remembered that until now. "And she was tortured? Similar to Shawn in that video?"

"Yes," Rowdy agreed. "Similar and in some ways, worse. Watching that video was not an easy thing for Skeet to do. He had to do it but it was a sacrifice, one that will exact a personal toll."

"I'm so sorry," Theresa said, horrified. "I didn't know."

"It's not your fault," Rowdy turned to her. "Listen to me, Theresa. It is not your fault. None of this is your fault. I watched Shawn Regam dying tonight, I saw the guilt and regret in his eyes when he took his last breath. And to be honest, I've had more than enough of that from everyone on this team today. None of this is your doing. It wasn't Shawn's doing. If you take anything away from this experience, take that." He turned, ascended the stairs and disappeared into their suite.

"He's right," Tony said taking Theresa's hand. "I know you keep thinking it's all your fault, but it's not. As far as Skeet is concerned, you didn't ask him to come here. You didn't even know him. He was already here, working the job from a different angle. His assignment was completely out of your control. You can't absorb that responsibility. Not for Rowdy or me, either. We were already coming, you didn't ask for our help. In fact, I seem to recall you rejecting it vehemently. No matter the outcome, Rowdy is right. This is not on you. It's on him, Dominic Zarconi. He's the one to blame for all of it."

"I know," Theresa stepped through the door and waited while Tony secured the deadbolt and the chain. Then they walked hand in hand to their room. Once inside Theresa turned to study the man she once thought of as a nuisance but now loved with all her heart. *Tell him.* But she couldn't, not yet. The couple climbed into bed, each reflecting on the events of the day. Tony pulled Theresa closer, wrapping his strong arms around her in comfort. Within minutes they had both drifted off to sleep.

Skeet hung up the phone, moved to the computer and proceeded to upload the files. Stan had just authorized a secure folder on the Bureau's network to hide the information. They were the only two people in the entire department that had access to that particular drive. It was still a risk. Once it was in the FBI's hands, it became public record, but Skeet trusted Burns to add the necessary classification to keep it private. The video would never be released to anyone without the Director's signature. He wasn't only saving the two video's Theresa had identified from the casino, he also sent the one of Shawn's murder. He wasn't sure Theresa understood the gravity of the evidence she and her husband had collected. It was rare to obtain an actual recording of a murder. Even more so when it was a mob boss that didn't like to get his hands dirty. With that video, they'd hit gold and it was up to Skeet to preserve it. He powered down the computer, secured the room and made his way to the penthouse. Thoughts of Angela flooded his mind and sorrow engulfed him. He missed his wife and knew it would be a long time before he agreed to another out-of-town job. Not even Stanley Burns could change his mind on that front.

* * * *

Skeet hadn't slept well. His mind was flooded with the past, the present and a new perspective compliments of Rowdy Cooper. He climbed into the shower, hoping the water would refresh him and get his mind back on track. Dressed and ready for a day of baseball, Skeet exited his room and made a beeline for the kitchen and a fresh pot of coffee. When he rounded the corner, he realized Blake had beat him to it.

"You okay now?" Blake asked.

"Sorry about that," Skeet wasn't sure what he wanted to say.

"When Stan assigned me to this mission, he gave me a little background on you," Blake admitted. "Not much, but enough to know why that video struck a chord. I don't need an explanation. I'm just asking if you're okay."

"Thanks," Skeet poured himself a cup of coffee and settled in next to Blake. "And yes, I'm okay. That was a long time ago, but sometimes it hits when you least expect it. Don't worry, it won't impact the job."

"I wasn't worried," Blake said flatly. "And that wasn't the reason I asked."

"I appreciate that as well," Skeet took his first sip and closed his eyes. "There is nothing better than that first amazing sip of coffee in the morning. I seem to remember Tony mentioning a ballgame this afternoon, I think we could all use a little break."

"Right," Blake had forgotten about the game. "Is that okay? I mean are we supposed to accept gifts like this? He already provided the room and the office, now we're watching a game when we're supposed to be working."

Skeet grinned. "Absolutely, and I think it will be good for the soul."

"Then I guess I need to shower," Blake stood and left the room.

Skeet glanced at the clock, nearly seven. He wondered what time a successful businessman woke in the morning. *No time like the present to find out.*

Tony slid from the bed, careful not to wake the amazing woman still sleeping next to him. He loved her, there was no denying it and he was determined to have her by his side for the rest of his life. Hopefully now that they'd taken that last intimate step, she'd stop trying to push him away. He wasn't sure making love to Theresa on this trip was wise, but it happened and he didn't regret it. He just hoped she didn't, Detroit held a lot of memories for her. Maybe the timing wasn't perfect, but would it ever be? Probably not. After pulling on his favorite sweats, he silently made his way across the room and into the kitchen. He had just poured his first cup of steaming liquid when his phone rang. "Yeah?"

"You said we were going to a ballgame today," Skeet began. "Something about a suite."

"Right," Tony answered a little confused.

"I need a place to meet Theresa's tech advisors," Skeet continued. "Any chance there's room for two more?"

"Actually," Tony smiled. "I think that's an excellent idea."

"Do they need a pass or something?"

"No," Tony considered. "They just need to notify the ticket office they are part of the Tony Nazario group. I'll notify the officials I have two additions."

"Thanks," Skeet smiled. "I appreciate it."

"We'll meet you downstairs in a couple hours. We can stop for breakfast and maybe do a little shopping on the way," Tony disconnected the call and smiled. He couldn't wait to see Theresa's face when she finally hooked up with her two old friends. The stadium was a safe setting for the reunion and she needed a fun surprise after last night. Maybe it would help counter the stress and fear she'd been experiencing the past two days.

* * * *

Theresa stepped into the elaborate suite and smiled. She knew she should feel guilty, Tony must have spent a fortune renting it, but she didn't. The excitement of the crowd, the smell of freshly buttered popcorn, and hotdogs brought back some of her favorite memories. Growing up, they didn't have a lot of money; but the trips to see the Tiger's play had been special. Her mother never joined them, she was busy trying to prove herself as a prosecutor then the District Attorney. Plus, she had no interest in baseball. That meant quality time with her father. Steve Tanner was the biggest fan the Detroit Tiger's ever had. Theresa moved forward and stood before the plate glass window. Her father would have been in heaven up here. They were positioned just to the left of home plate where they could clearly see the entire field. She assumed the center suite was reserved for the owners, but this vantage point was just as good.

She relaxed against Tony's chest when he wrapped his arms around her waist and pulled her against him.

"I think I did good," he whispered near her ear.

"Better than good," she sighed. "Thank you. This is amazing."

"You look happy," Tony observed.

"I am," she admitted. "I can't stop thinking about dad. He would have loved this. He was such an avid Tiger fan. We came as often as we could, but our experience was somewhere in the nose bleed section. He would have loved you, I wish you could have met him."

"Me too," Tony said, surprised he meant it. He would have liked to meet the father of this amazing woman. He had to be strong and kind, just like Theresa. He wondered if she got her resilience from her mother or her father. Probably her mother, Jenny Tanner had to be resilient and strong to go after someone like Dominic Zarconi.

Tony saw two men enter the room out of the corner of his eye. He was about to point them out and reveal his surprise when Skeet stepped forward and pulled them into the corner. Clearly, this was more than a casual day at the ballpark for him.

* * * *

"You must be our tech experts," Skeet held out a hand in greeting.

"James Bond, I presume." Carson said flatly as he took the man's hand.

"Before we put work aside and enjoy the game, could I have a word?"

"Sure," Marc answered as the two of them followed the fed to the corner and settled onto a couch.

Skeet took a chair across from them, not sure how to make the request. "I talked to you about a contract."

"Yes," Carson acknowledged. "I told you we're in."

"I have a different offer," Skeet sat forward and rested his forearms on his thighs. "What I believe to be a better offer."

"We're listening," Marc prompted.

Skeet pulled out a sheet of paper and passed it to Carson.

"What's this?" Carson asked, confused. There were twenty-three names with what looked like account numbers listed.

"Those are Jeremy Haswell's victims," Skeet said pointedly.

Marc glanced at Carson, panic evident in his eyes. Jeremy Haswell was their latest hacking job.

"And?" Carson asked pointedly.

Moondance Ridge

"And nothing," Skeet replied. "I just thought you might be interested in knowing a little something about them. The first name, Nancy Cartwright, she's in her seventies. Has a bad heart. She's a widow, her husband left her a fairly significant nest egg, which Haswell conned her out of. She's now struggling and contemplating a return to the work force. Something she'll never survive at her age."

Marcos and Carson remained eerily quiet, not sure what the agent was getting at.

"The second couple, Devin and Marcy Tidwell, they have a son that is suffering with a genetic disorder. Little Tyson is only ten, but he's already gone through four major surgeries and is looking at one or two more if the Tidwell's can somehow come up with the finances to cover them. Unfortunately, Jeremy Haswell cleaned them out as well."

"Sounds like you know them, each person on this list, personally," Carson observed.

"Not personally," Skeet corrected. "I have met a couple of them, but I know their files backwards and forwards. I've read them many times and still, I haven't figured out a way to assist them. All twenty-three have similar stories-each facing a crisis-each teetering on the brink of destruction and pain. Unfortunately, it appears Haswell spent his fortune so there weren't any proceeds to return to the victims. It's a shame, really. A true tragedy for everyone involved."

"What does that have to do with us?" Carson asked.

Skeet shrugged. "Nothing, I suppose. Let's get down to business then." He passed a set of documents to each man. "Stanley Burns, the Director of the FBI has coordinated this offer with the

Department of Justice. It's an immunity agreement. Basically, it says if you are willing to be anonymous consultants to the FBI, you will be granted blanket immunity for any crimes you may have committed from the time you turned eighteen until the date of signature on the documents."

"For how long?" Marc asked.

"On our part, it's basically open-ended," Skeet said soberly. "On yours, it's a two-year commitment."

"So," Carson studied the top page. It was an official looking document. If he had to guess it was a memorandum of understanding of some kind. "What exactly do you mean by anonymous consultant?"

"The FBI already has computer techs working for the Bureau full-time. You would report directly to Burns. There are times, similar to this case, when we need an outside source. Someone we trust with confidentiality, experts in their field who can work on projects that are top secret and classified. Burns is willing to offer you one of these positions. Once you sign the documents, you'll have to be screened for clearance, but it shouldn't be a problem."

"Why?" Carson pressed. "This Burns guy doesn't know us, you don't really know us for that matter. Why would you trust us with classified information?"

"We know your work," Skeet replied. "We're willing to take the risk. Be sure to read through the agreement carefully before you accept. The most important restriction you will have to adhere to is the paragraph that deals with engaging in illegal activity while acting as a government consultant."

"Got it," Marc said dryly. "No hacking while employed by the fuzz."

Carson was studying the agent. He'd expected them to figure it out, eventually. He was a little surprised they discovered the secret so quickly. More surprising was the fact they knew and didn't just want to work with the duo on this case, but they wanted to work with them on others. And, what message was he trying to convey with that list?

"I don't want an answer today," Skeet continued. "In fact, I suggest you take a few days to think about it. The agreement is iron clad. No hacking of any kind once you agree to take on the job. Until then..." Skeet glanced at the list he had provided. "I hope you will still continue to work on our current case. With a little luck, maybe you can discover where Dominic Zarconi has his fortune stashed. Unfortunately, the Bureau hasn't been able to track down the details. We have no idea just how wealthy the mob boss really is. We suspect it's substantial, maybe a few mil considering the gun running on top of the casino, which is doing well by all accounts. The exact amount, however, that's a complete mystery. I hope it doesn't end up going to a colleague or even a relative that will continue the family business. There are too many others that could benefit from his fortune."

Marc looked to Carson in surprise. Was the agent seriously asking them to hack into Dom's finances and help out the victims on the list? The look on Carson's face mirrored the shock he was feeling. Clearly, Carson had received the same message. They had a lot to think about. Was this a trap? A way to trick them into hacking so they could be caught and arrested? Then why the immunity agreement? Was it possible Skeet's motives were simply benevolent?

"Now, I suggest you go say hello to Theresa," Skeet stood. "I think she'd enjoy spending time with the two of you while she's in town."

Carson stood and was immediately engulfed in a huge bear hug.

"Is it safe for you to be here?" Theresa asked.

"Relatively, I think." Carson smiled as he hugged her back. He had always liked Theresa Regan. To be honest, he had envied Shawn and the happiness he'd found so early in life. Now, he was glad his friend had found it. Shawn's life had been cut way too short. It was a comfort to know he'd been happy and in love for most of it.

Theresa turned and embraced Marcos. "I've missed you."

"We missed you, too." Marcos said as he returned the hug. He had always had a bit of a crush on Theresa and losing her completely when they were already reeling from the loss of Shawn had been difficult.

"I'm sorry I brought you into this," she began.

"We're glad you did," Carson objected.

"Yeah," Marc echoed. "You should have come to us immediately. We could have helped."

"I know," Theresa studied her hands. "I just wanted to keep you safe. I didn't want to drag you into all of this. Shawn worked so hard to keep you away from the danger. I felt like I needed to do the same, to honor his wishes I guess." She glanced up when Tony approached the group.

Moondance Ridge

Carson studied Tony intently, but didn't respond to the polished businessman.

"This is Tony Nazario," Theresa provided.

"I guess we have you to thank for the accommodations," Marc surmised.

Tony glanced at Marc, then back to Carson. It was pretty obvious Shawn's friends were skeptical of his relationship with Theresa. "No thanks necessary," Tony responded. "It seemed like a great way for Theresa to see some old friends while she's in town."

Theresa sensed Carson's reluctance and couldn't blame him. It had been hard for her to reconcile her feelings for Tony, it would be equally difficult for Shawn's closest friends. She leaned into Tony and relaxed when he wrapped an arm around her shoulder.

Carson and Marcos frowned. "Um, Tony?" Theresa said immediately.

Tony realized he was making the situation difficult. It was time to leave, to let Theresa enjoy the day with a couple old friends. He turned her around, so she was facing him and placed a hand on each of her shoulders. "I need to talk to Rowdy and you have a lot of catching up to do." He focused on the two men. "Make yourself at home, there's plenty of food and snacks to go around. I think the game will be starting soon." He leaned in and pressed a soft kiss to Theresa's lips then turned and walked away.

"So," Carson finally said.

"I understand," Theresa answered. "I know it's strange, but Tony has been amazing. When Shawn died, I thought my life was over, too. I honestly believed I would never care for another man again. We had so much history. I grew up with Shawn, I loved him with all my heart. I didn't think I'd find a man that could make me feel again."

"It's okay," Carson decided. "I mean, we didn't expect you to become a nun. Although, when we didn't hear from you... the thought crossed my mind."

"Funny," Theresa relaxed. "Tony is a wonderful man. I hope you will give him a chance. I hope you will take the time to get to know him."

Marcus watched as Tony walked away from the group and approached a third man they hadn't met. "He said he needed to talk to Rowdy. Is that the cop?"

"Ex-cop," Theresa corrected. "He was shot by a suspect before he moved to Mount Haven. Now he's my boss. I think you'd like him. He's a good man, too. Tony and Rowdy saved my life. I still can't believe how much they've done for me. Now, they're determined to deal with Dom. There aren't a lot of people like those two, not that I've met anyway."

"I'm glad," Carson decided. "What do you say we have a seat? Tony is right, the games about to start and we have a lot to catch up on."

The three of them moved to the front of the room and sat in the comfortable cushioned chairs that looked out over the ball field. For the next few hours, their world was filled with baseball instead of death, corruption and hacking. Tony and Rowdy joined them, Tony taking a seat to Theresa's left. The instant he sat down, she casually reached out and took his hand in hers. A signal to him and the rest of the guests that they were connected now. For the next several hours, the group forgot about work and simply enjoyed the game and the company of new friends and old. Unfortunately, the instant the game ended, so did their reprieve.

* * * *

The game had concluded and tentative bonds were formed over popcorn, hotdogs and soda. The group watched hundreds of patrons swarm the field while others made their escape onto the congested highways. Rowdy was entertaining them with an exaggerated story from his time in Chicago.

Skeet frowned when he heard the familiar sound of his phone. "Hello."

"I just received a briefing on a small arms deal going down near Detroit," Stan greeted. "It's taking place by boat; apparently, the merchandise is being delivered to a man in Canada. We've been cooperating with the ATF and the RCMP. Their informant just confirmed the deal is going down tonight. Are you in a position to intervene?"

"Intervene how?" Skeet asked. "We're not officially in Detroit, what are you asking us to do?"

"If we use local FBI, Darrow is going to know," Stan explained. "He may alert Zarconi and change the deal."

"I agree, but that still doesn't explain our role in all of this."

"ATF agents from Detroit are taking lead," Stan advised. "I just need you to make sure they intercept the boat. If you can use Rowdy and the billionaire, do it. It would be much cleaner if you and Blake kept your distance."

"Let me talk to them and see if we can figure something out," Skeet hesitated. "Are you sure you can trust the ATF? If they're operating out of Detroit, Zarconi could have infiltrated their ranks as well."

"I have it on good authority he's tried and failed. I tend to believe their clean," Stan sighed. "Watch your back; but I know Alecia Weise, she would not allow Zarconi to infiltrate her house."

Skeet had heard of Special Agent Weise and he was inclined to agree. "I'll get back to you."

"What's up?" Rowdy asked when Skeet disconnected with his boss.

"Arms deal on the river apparently," Skeet provided the necessary information and Stan's request to keep Skeet and Blake clear of the action. He included the part where Burns wanted Rowdy involved.

"You can't send Rowdy into danger without help," Theresa argued. "He needs you guys to keep anything he does legitimate."

"Will there ever come a time when you find it in your heart to trust me?" Rowdy asked.

"I trust you," Theresa disagreed. "I just don't want you out there alone."

"Which is why I'll be joining him," Tony told the group. "We can figure out a delay, some kind of stall tactic, until the cavalry arrives," he glanced at Rowdy. "We managed it at the warehouse. This should be no different."

Moondance Ridge

"With his money and my brains, I'm sure we can come up with something," Rowdy grinned. "Tell Stanley Burns we're in."

"Rowdy," Theresa argued. "I think we need to talk about this."

"No time," Rowdy disagreed. "Tony and I need to find a way out of this traffic. Any suggestions?"

Tony pulled out his cellphone and dialed a number.

"Now what?" John asked sarcastically.

"I need a lift," Tony requested.

"From?"

"Comerica Park Stadium," Tony laughed when John groaned.

"Glad to hear you decided to take some free time and catch a game while I'm stuck lounging on a rooftop watching a woman cut fabric," John said as he scrolled through his contacts.

"Thanks," Tony joked. "Glad you approve. Now, the lift?" He proceeded to explain the situation to John.

"Give me five," he disconnected and dialed an old friend. Tony knew John had contacts in every major city across the US. He just never thought he'd be the one to need them.

"Any luck?" Blake asked.

Before Tony could respond his phone rang.

"Make your way to the Grand Valley University building, Sticky will meet you on the roof with a chopper."

"I'm not even going to ask how you got permission for that," Tony shook his head.

"Who says we asked permission," John replied. "Make sure you're there waiting, otherwise things might get a little complicated."

"Yeah," Tony grinned. "I think I'll keep that info to myself. Thanks again. By the way, if things are stale with the designer why don't you bolt? Doesn't look like there's a threat, and I know you have your own work piling up."

"Actually," John shifted and settled against some kind of heating unit. "I do have a deal that's developing. I'll let you know, but I might need to clear out tomorrow, maybe take a day or two before I'm clear again. The fashionista doesn't seem to be in danger, so it shouldn't be a problem. We may have overestimated the danger here."

"That would be nice," Tony relaxed. "No need to call, I'll just assume you're heading out. Give me a shout when you get back, and I'll bring you up to speed."

"Later," John disconnected.

"Rowdy and I need to make our way to the University building across the street. The rest of you can hang out here or take off, whatever works for you."

"What happens at the University?" Skeet asked.

"We catch a ride to the nearest dock and charter a boat," Tony grinned as he left the room.

Rowdy followed, so did Skeet.

"Tony," Skeet called. "What kind of ride?"

"Sticky, an old military friend of John's will pick us up in a bird and transport us to the river. It would be nice if you and Blake shuttled the Beemer out somewhere along the way. Shoot Rowdy a text with the drop-off point. We'll need a ride back to the hotel when we're finished," Tony provided. "Now, we have to go. Apparently, our pilot is going solo; and we don't exactly have the proper approval for the landing."

"I'll take care of that," Skeet turned and headed back to the suite. He had already connected with Stan when he stepped into the room.

* * * *

The helicopter was flying along the US side of the Detroit River, looking for a drop-off point when Rowdy's phone rang.

"Have the pilot drop you at Riverside Park," Skeet said before Rowdy even got out a greeting. "Stan's arranged for a boat. It will be waiting at the dock just to the west of there."

"Riverside Park," Rowdy relayed. "Drop us off, then disappear. We'll take it from there." He paused and returned to Skeet. "We're on our way."

"Stan said the deal is supposed to go down sometime in the next hour. ATF is on the other side of town," Skeet advised. "They're close but might need a diversion. Do what you can, but stay safe. If we miss this one, we miss it."

"We're approaching the park now. Once you break through traffic, drop the car at the foot of Ambassador Bridge. We'll find a way to get back there when we're finished. Don't stick around, head back to the hotel so we know where to find you," Rowdy requested.

"Now what?" Tony asked as they stepped from the chopper and watched their only escape, at-the-moment, disappear into the smog filled sky.

"Now we make our way to the dock, snag the boat Stan provided and do a little recon while we wait," Rowdy decided.

"I'm still not sure how we're supposed to stall long enough to get the ATF agents in position without getting shot," Tony grumbled.

"You're the one that said we'll think of something," Rowdy reminded him. "So, start thinking."

The two of them made their way to the dock, boarded the boat and began their search. They hadn't gone far when Rowdy got a text from Skeet. "Let's head to Black Oak Prairie Heritage Park on the Canadian side," he told Tony. "Skeet says that's where the deal is supposed to go down."

"I don't suppose you're okay with a large forest fire," Tony suggested.

"No," Rowdy frowned, "I'm not."

"Well, we better think of something soon," Tony countered. "We're running out of time."

Rowdy disappeared into the cabin of the boat and returned with a light. "We might be able to use this somehow."

Tony glanced up then brightened. "That's a dive light."

"Okay," Rowdy frowned.

"Does there happen to be scuba equipment down there?"

"Actually, yes. That's about all there is, why?" Rowdy ascended the stairs and stood next to Tony.

"Take the wheel," Tony commanded. "I happen to be a diver and if we have the right equipment, I just might have an idea." He turned the boat over to Rowdy and disappeared into the cabin. Moments later, Tony surfaced wearing a wetsuit that was at least two sizes too big and carrying a large oxygen tank.

"Looks promising," Rowdy commented. "Mind telling me the plan?"

"I'm going diving," Tony provided. "It won't look suspicious as long as we keep our distance. Drop the light so I can find my way back. I'll maneuver to the boats, disconnect the gas line and drain their tanks. They'll be stuck. Neither party will be able to escape."

"Won't work," Rowdy disagreed. "Those tanks hold too much fuel. They might not get far; but with very little gas, they'll make it back to shore. Unless you plan to blow them up, then it might work."

"What if I disable the engines?" Tony ignored the taunt.

"Do you know how?" Rowdy asked skeptically. He was a suit... who drove a fancy new sports car.

"You have a serious blind spot when it comes to my money. Do we need to discuss my early years as a wily street rat again?"

"No," Rowdy shrugged. "I was just asking, I guess that's your way of saying yes."

"Yes," Rowdy shook his head. "I can disable an engine with my eyes shut. Now, let's figure out where to set up. And make sure you drop that light out of sight. They might get suspicious if they know I'm not sticking close to the boat."

"Aye, Aye Captain," Rowdy gave a quick solute. He sobered when his phone rang and he saw the display. "Please tell me you didn't have more trouble."

"Skeet called," Coop answered. "I thought I'd check in and see if you came up with a plan. Maybe help if you need it."

Rowdy relayed the plan and the two of them hammered out details. He jotted down the frequency the feds would be using to communicate and dialed it into the system attached to the boat. "Did Skeet tell you where he got the vessel on such short notice?"

"Retired cop," Coop provided. "And, the man's going to be livid if it comes back damaged."

"That shouldn't be a problem as long as Skeet's backup arrives in time."

"Be careful," Coop sobered. "There are so many things that could go wrong with this plan."

"I'll call when I get back to the hotel," Rowdy promised. "Watch my girls." He hung up and went over the details one more time with Tony. They both casually looked over when a boat marked with Casino deZarcon approached the area.

"A little bold, don't you think?"

"I think he's cocky," Rowdy grumbled. "Let's take him down a notch."

"With pleasure," Tony finished attaching his equipment and within seconds had disappeared over the side of the boat.

Rowdy waited, more than a little nervous about the plan. He just hoped Tony knew what he was doing, and the men on the boat didn't catch him in the act of sabotage.

* * * *

Theresa stepped into the large loft and was instantly hit with memories of the past. She'd spent so much time here, before Shawn got involved with Zarconi. The three computer whiz kids had frequently lost track of time and worked well into the night on their current project. Theresa learned the hard way that if she didn't interrupt, they could work all night without taking a break. Night after night, she'd stop for Italian or Chinese takeout... or their favorite pizza and arrived at the tech cave with dinner for four.

"Hasn't changed much," Carson admitted.

"Do you think they're going to be okay?" Theresa asked.

"I do," Marcos stated as he settled into his work chair. "I have an idea and wanted to run it by you before we get started."

"Okay," Theresa settled into a spare chair and waited.

"Well," Marc said hesitantly. "We haven't actually signed an agreement with the feds yet, but Skeet said to keep working the case. So far, they're sure we are looking at two agents and a supervisor."

"Right," Theresa agreed. "I guess Blake watched Agent Percy Seeger for days but he rarely leaves the office."

"I was thinking we should hack into his system and take a look around," Marc told his two friends. "I read that agreement we're supposed to sign; and even if it could get us into trouble, the immunity clause will cover us if we get caught."

"We wouldn't get caught," Carson settled into his chair. "And I like it. Let's see what we can do."

Theresa studied Shawn's two closest friends. "Are you sure there is no risk of getting caught? I mean, I'm not surprised Carson is on board; but the fact that you thought of it does surprise me."

"That's because Carson has always wanted to hack the government," Marc grinned. "He's always had me and Shawn to stop him. Breaking into a Special Agent's computer would be a dream come true for our friend over there."

"And your point?" Carson grinned.

"My point is you can't leave a trace," Theresa told him. "I have no doubt you can do this, but can you do it without Seeger knowing? If he's dirty, you can't tip him off."

"We can do it," Marc assured her. "I guess I just need your blessing before I do. I mean, Shawn was adamant about the rules."

"I know," Theresa sighed. "But, things change and just think, if you hook up with the FBI, months from now who knows how many government systems you might be hacking. And this way, it's legal."

"I hadn't thought of it that way," Carson considered. "I'm liking the plan more and more all the time."

"Then we do it?" Marc said for clarification. "We hack the Special Agent's computer and take a look around?"

"We do it," Theresa nodded.

The two men got to work, it was going to take time to track down the IP address. They had to open a back door into the government server and pinpoint the computer they needed to access. The process would be even slower because they could not leave a trace of their intrusion. Especially not their usual signature.

* * * *

Tony and Rowdy stepped into their makeshift office and glanced around. Skeet and Blake were impatiently waiting for an update.

"Tony will fill you in," Rowdy provided. "I need to call Coop."

"Not much to tell," Tony settled into one of the chairs and looked around. "Where's Theresa?"

"Still with the nerds," Blake provided.

Tony frowned. "Has anyone checked on them? Did you make sure everything was okay?"

"Yeah," Skeet nodded. "They're fine. She's safe there and the dynamic duo is working on some secret project they seem to be excited about."

"You're okay with that?" Rowdy asked, stepping back into the room. "I thought you didn't exactly trust them yet."

"I'm fine with it," Skeet told them. "We brought the two of them in to help with the investigation. I have to let them take ownership if this arrangement is going to work. I'm sure they'll eventually fill us in. Anyway, Theresa's with them... how much trouble can they get into with her there? Now, what happened with the arms deal? Stan said everyone is in custody and the whole thing went down cleaner than anyone could have imagined."

"I agree," Rowdy settled into one of the chairs. "In fact, I have to say I was a little disappointed. It should have been a lot more fun. It's not every day I get to stop an illegal arms deal on an international border."

"What can I say? I'm just that good." Tony smiled and pulled out his phone. He dialed Theresa.

"Are you back?" she asked anxiously.

"We're back, but you're not," Tony answered. "Do you need a ride?"

"Can I have Tony pick me up?" she asked the guys.

"Sure," Carson answered, engrossed in the system he was trying to set up.

Theresa rattled off the address and some basic directions.

"I'll be there in ten," Tony stood.

"That's all the explanation we get?" Blake asked. "What kind of debrief is that?"

"I'll debrief you after I pick up Theresa," Tony promised. "Shouldn't take long and that way I only have to tell it once."

"Go on," Rowdy smiled. "I'll relay the short version while you retrieve your woman."

"Stan said the engines were disabled," Skeet provided.

"Yeah," Rowdy settled in for the discussion. "It was actually pretty easy. Tony dove far enough down they didn't see him coming. Within minutes, he had the engines rigged and the boats immobilized. I'm sure he'll regale you with stories of sea urchins and Seymour like algae but it was actually pretty uneventful. Tony returned and we left the area just as the ATF arrived to arrest everyone involved. Looked like they recovered a fair amount of property in the raid. Zarconi has got to be livid."

"One of the biggest hits in recent history according to Agent Weise," Skeet relayed. "I have to wonder why they haven't caught him sooner. Is it possible Zarconi hasn't been in the arms business for long?"

"Maybe," Rowdy shrugged. They all glanced up when Tony and Theresa entered the room. As predicted, Tony spent the next hour spouting off about the dangerous world under the river and the harrowing adventure he'd barely survived all in the name of truth and justice and the American way.

* * * *

Dom was furious. He couldn't afford to lose those guns. And, The Phantom was not going to be happy when he learned his shipment had been snatched out from under him by the local ATF and RCMP. Darrow was looking into it, hopefully he'd have answers before the night was over. Dom had to have an explanation for The Phantom if he wanted to live to make another deal.

Luca Papworth was a mystery to the world, a man with a sketchy past and a moniker that described him perfectly. Most knew him as The Phantom, because he surfaced, conducted business then vanished without a trace. It had taken a lot of money and a great amount of effort for Dom to discover his true identity. Instead of providing insight, the knowledge had intensified Dom's fear and produced very little by way of details. He did know the man did not take disappointment well. And, if Dom didn't handle this situation correctly, he'd be dead before the end of the week. DeRossi had warned him not to get involved with the mysterious man, but Dom had mistakenly believed he could handle it. He thought having an insider within the ranks of the FBI would be enough. Obviously, he also needed a mole inside the ATF if he was going to make a go of the arms business. Something to think about later. Right now, he needed answers.

His mind shifted to the trouble at the paper, the explosion at the warehouse and the fact he still hadn't been able to reach Dreven or Talon. His organization was under attack, but was there one threat? A coordinated effort? Or, was it all a coincidence that he was connecting because of his paranoia? Being cautious had kept him in business, but was he letting it get out of control? There was only one way to answer that question, better information. Starting with Theresa Regan. He wanted that woman under his control, and he wanted it now. If he were lucky, she could shed some light on the mystery that surrounded her late brother-in-law, Zach Regan.

Moondance Ridge

* * * *

Carson stepped into the loft and froze. He'd thought the place would be empty. Instead, he spotted Marcos hard at work at his terminal.

"I couldn't sleep," Marc provided without so much as a backwards glance. "We need to talk."

"Okay," Carson agreed as he pulled up a chair.

"This is going to sound a little crazy," Marc warned.

"Crazier than hacking into a federal database and attaching a program to record all activity from a certain agent that might be associated with the mob?"

"Maybe," Marc straightened and turned to face his friend. "I woke up this morning around three after a strange dream. It was about Shawn, well Shawn and Danny J."

"That's understandable, not crazy. We've done a lot of nutty since we got involved in this case, but it all revolves around Shawn and the encryption stuff of Danny's. I don't think it's crazy at all," Carson disagreed.

"That's because I haven't told you the crazy part," Marc continued. "It was almost like a memory, not a dream. Remember years ago, when we competed against Danny J, and Shawn was trying to explain his complex reasoning. How he deciphered the pattern so quickly and could break the programming so easily?"

"Yeah," Carson nodded. "Neither one of us understood a word of it."

"Well," Marc glanced up. "I guess I understood more than I thought."

"Meaning?

"Meaning," Marc opened the companion program they'd developed to read the data collected through the keylogger program. "I guess you could say I channeled my inner Shawn Regan and fixed it. I woke up with an idea on how we could change the code in a couple key areas, and it worked."

Carson moved forward, shocked. "Show me."

Marc clicked the import button then moved to the cloud and clicked on a folder. Each one was labelled with a date. He chose the third day of the current month. "Since Dom hasn't upgraded his system, the keylogger program Shawn installed is still embedded in the background. It's still saving data." The screen filled with folders and web addresses. Marc clicked on a folder. "Since we don't have that data, nothing happens. We can go back to the others, the folders Shawn downloaded, and manually redirect the program to open the folder located in the cloud. With this program, it should crack the encryption for us. Unfortunately, if the folder has been moved or deleted, it's gone and we'll have to decrypt the data before we can view it."

"Okay," Carson studied the screen. "So, what happens when you hit on a web link?"

"That's where Shawn's brilliance comes in," Marc said, getting excited. "Remember Shawn said he wanted the program to identify the site, and then scan the system to automatically identify the username using their IP address?"

"Right," Carson glanced to the upper right corner of the screen and realized Marc had extracted Dominic's IP address and already entered it in the box. "So, click on one of the websites."

Marc smiled. "That's where it gets interesting." He clicked on one of the links and within seconds an offshore bank account opened.

"We don't need the user name or password because the program finds the username from the system with the IP and then extracts the keylogger info that contains the password automatically. Brilliant!" Carson exclaimed.

"Look," Marc pointed to the screen. "He has a substantial balance in this account."

Carson was still registering the amount when Marc added another column and imported a second folder from the sixth of the month. A new account located at a different bank opened. Within seconds he had repeated the action and had a third account open.

"There's over three hundred and fifty million," Carson marveled. "Should we take it?"

Marc pushed Skeet's list across the desk in front of Carson. "I was thinking we might make twenty-three people's dreams come true."

Carson glanced at the list then back to Marc. "Do you think it's a trap?"

"I don't see how it could be," Marc decided. "I've tried to look at every angle. I read the contract we're supposed to sign three times. If we take this, give it to those people and then sign the contract, we can't be prosecuted for the crime. No matter how many times I read it, I can't see a loophole that will cause us grief."

"Then Skeet actually wants us to take care of these people?" Carson surmised.

"I think he does," Marc agreed. "So, if you're in... you're up. Transferring the money, bouncing it around until there's no trace is your specialty. I was thinking ten million each."

"And the rest?"

"If you agree, we dump it into the slush fund. Just leave one million in each account to keep it open. Once we sign that document, once we agree to work for the FBI, we won't be able to skim for at least two years. Not even for a good cause. I'd like to have a buffer, a little rainy-day fund that we can draw on if we find a deserving recipient. A hundred mil would go a long way in covering emergencies."

"I agree," Carson shifted and pulled the keyboard toward him. "This is going to take a minute."

They both froze when a folder labeled with the current date suddenly appeared.

"He's online," Marc whispered. "Wait, let's see what he does."

"Give me a minute," Carson began frantically tapping the keyboard. Marc watched as his friend entered Zarconi's system through a backdoor created by the keylogger program.

"Be careful," Marc warned.

Moondance Ridge

Carson grunted as Dom's computer coding displayed on one of Marc's screens. Finally, he typed in a final command and Dom's monitor was mirrored to a second monitor... Marc's third screen. The two men watched, horrified as a photo of a young girl popped up.

"Give me that," Marc ordered. He used the mouse to open a new program, then typed in several commands. Within seconds, the images flashing across his screen were being recorded as a video. "What is he doing?" Marc asked.

Carson studied the transaction. Dominic pulled up a photo and attached it to an email address. Within seconds, he received a response. He logged into an underground internet site, posted a diagonal red box that said "unavailable" then replied to the email with a number. "Do you think that's another account?"

"If it is, he'll check it," Marc said confidently. "I found a pattern, each time he makes a deposit, he logs into the account to check the balance. Then, a couple days later, he makes sure the transaction is posted to the account. If he has another account, we'll take that too."

Carson pulled out his phone and dialed Skeet.

"Hello?" came a groggy voice.

"We need you here, at our office," Carson answered.

"What?" Skeet sat up and swung his legs off the bed. "What time is it?"

"Six," Carson said impatiently. "I'll text you the address, we need you... now! And, leave Theresa at the hotel, she can't see this."

Intrigued, Skeet climbed from the bed and pulled on fresh clothes. Something was up and the tech geeks were spooked. He hesitated, then called Rowdy.

"I'll meet you in the garage, at the car," Rowdy replied. "Give me five minutes."

"Make it three," Skeet corrected. "I'll have the car running."

By the time the two lawmen reached the loft, Dominic had sold five women. Well, one of them looked like a kid... a girl, fifteen -sixteen tops. Carson called out for the men to enter when he heard the brisk knock. Rowdy and Skeet approached the duo and studied the computer screens. Marc quickly minimized the bank info and pointed to the other screen. He and Carson quietly waited for the two men to realize what was happening and give them direction.

"Who are they?" Skeet asked, immediately spotting the photos of the five attractive girls. The oldest couldn't be more than twenty-five.

"We don't know," Carson answered. "We were working on something and realized Dom was logged in. We thought we'd take a look, careful like. He has no idea we're seeing this. I mirrored his screen. Once it started, Marc recorded it all."

"Is he done?" Rowdy asked.

"We think so," Marc said softly. "Did he really just sell those women?"

"Girls," Skeet objected. "He most likely just sold five girls. Can you show me the recording? Maybe stop the first one and start a new file just in case he does something we need to see?"

"Um, yeah," Marc hit stop, named the file then started a new video. He went to his first screen and opened his files, found the recording and double clicked. A video began playing.

Skeet and Rowdy settled into folding chairs and watched.

"Do you have someone you can send this to?" Rowdy finally asked. "The transaction just took place. If they can determine the exchange site, they still might be able to save those girls."

Skeet mentally filtered through each and every person on the task force, ultimately deciding it was safe. "I'm going to send this to Agent Sheila Jacobs. She heads up the Federal Human Trafficking Task Force. She'll have the resources to deal with it."

"Are you sure she can be trusted?" Carson asked.

"I am," Skeet assured him. "I handpicked the entire team myself."

"By the way, speaking of trust, we're monitoring your supervisor, um... Percy Seeger. He pulled the complete report on the raid yesterday and sent it to Darrow," Marc advised.

Skeet stared at the computer hacker. "I'm not sure I want to know how you did that. In the future, let me know before you monitor one of our agents."

"Is it going to be a problem?" Marc asked.

"No," Skeet sighed. "I'll advise Stan and he can do the necessary paperwork. We can monitor anyone at work, but it has to be approved. You're new and as far as I know you haven't officially agreed to contract with us, so I'll cut you a little slack on this one. Just let me know before you do something like that again."

"Got it," Carson grinned.

Rowdy laughed. "Hope you enjoyed that little stunt. You work with Skeeter Perkins now. Fun times are over, welcome to Skeeterville. Long hours for little pay and no recognition. Just think of it as a patriotic duty."

"Shut up," Skeet flipped Rowdy the bird as he dialed his boss. Within minutes Skeet was relaying the information for a secure database where the videos could be transferred. "Yes, I've advised them of the proper channels before violating a federal employee's privacy. I'm confident it will not happen again." Skeet winked at the guys. "Not yet. I think they are still considering it." Once he completed the call, he turned to Carson. "He's anxiously awaiting your answer on the consulting gig."

"I need another day to consider it," Marc said abruptly. "We'll let you know tomorrow."

"Are we covered on the girls?" Carson asked. "Do you want us to keep this up? There hasn't been any activity for a while. I think he left the room or something."

"You can shut it down," Skeet told him. "Sheila will pull the pertinent info from the video and track down the details. She'll be able to locate users with the email addresses and she has her own hackers that can monitor that site now that they know about it. You may have just saved a lot of lives. You certainly saved them from a tragic and horrific future. You should be proud of what you did today... of what you are now a part of."

"Thanks," Carson stood. "We'll let you know on the consulting job as soon as we make a decision."

Moondance Ridge

"Stan took care of the paperwork on that other thing so you won't catch anymore grief," Skeet added. "Do me a favor and keep monitoring Seeger. I need to know how deep his involvement goes. The report he sent over was a ruse. We wanted to know who accessed it. We knew they would eventually. It had information that pointed to contacts overseas. They are still in the dark as far as our investigation goes."

"Thanks for coming over on short notice," Marc stood. "We didn't really know what to do, or how to handle what was happening. It's a terrible feeling to witness something like that and know you can't stop it."

"You did stop it," Skeet corrected. "I'll talk to you tomorrow."

"Good job, guys." Rowdy added before heading out the door.

Once the two men were in the car, headed back to the hotel Rowdy voiced his concerns. "When Dom insisted Theresa work for him to pay off her debt, do you think he planned to sell her? She's older than any of those girls we saw today."

"I don't know," Skeet sighed. "I'm just glad the guys were active so early. They're certainly going to be a handful. The way they just casually mentioned they hacked into a secure government system and took a look around. He said it so nonchalantly, like the task was as simple as ordering a burger."

"For them it probably was," Rowdy paused. "There was a lot of money in that account. And, Marc didn't want us to know they'd accessed it. I hate to consider how many girls must have been sold to generate that kind of cash. Should we be worried about our hacker's motives?"

"I need a favor," Skeet was silent for several seconds before he turned to look at his friend. "I'm going to tell you something that could get me fired if anyone finds out I told you. What I asked those guys to do could get me fired as well, but I don't care."

"What?" Rowdy asked, worried.

"Almost the instant I logged onto their system and took a look around the programming, I knew they were good. The FBI has dubbed them Robin Hood. Their signature is all over that cloud system. They've only pulled a half-dozen jobs that we know of, but the jobs are always clean and untraceable. They go in, clean out the criminals, take nearly everything they have stashed away and then redistribute it to the poor."

"Okay," Rowdy nodded. "Doesn't sound that bad. In fact, I think I like them better already."

"The last guy they hit, Jeremy Haswell, defrauded twenty-three families. All of them are on the brink of disaster. We arrested Haswell; but between Robin Hood and his elaborate lifestyle, there was very little left. I gave those guys the names of his victim's along with personal bank account numbers. Then, I described some of the problems they are facing because Jeremy Haswell stole their money. I prompted them, in a roundabout way, to help if they had a chance. I specifically mentioned Zarconi and explained the uncertainty surrounding his fortune. The Bureau has no idea exactly how much money he has at any given time because his business is fluid."

"So, you want me to forget the bottom line?" Rowdy surmised. "Just in case it changes a bit over the next few hours."

"If you can live with it," Skeet studied Rowdy. He was crossing a line, and he knew it.

Moondance Ridge

"Skeet," Rowdy shrugged. "You and me... we've always had a different line. This is going to weigh on you far more than it will on me. I have no problem with those guys reaching into Zarconi's pocket and helping the victims of someone else's crimes. Sure, technically it's illegal; but do you think Dominic is going to report the theft? I'm pretty sure the answer is a resounding no. Which means, no victim... no crime."

"You truly believe that don't you?"

"I truly do," Rowdy affirmed. "And, you should too. You didn't tell those guys to hack, you certainly didn't do the stealing. And, it was Burns that decided to offer them an unrestricted immunity agreement. If they commit the crime before they sign on the dotted line, they're covered. Not your problem, and if anyone else has a problem with it, well... they can go talk to your boss or the DOJ. What may be about to go down, and let's be clear, you have no idea if they're going to act on your subtle suggestion or not..."

"True," Skeet agreed.

"What they may or may not do is not on you, and it certainly is not on me. So, no. I don't care one bit about a sadistic thug instantly losing a fortune. Plus, if they succeed, it adds one more cog to our wheel. Losing a fortune like that is only going to infuriate our favorite mob boss, and it might just push him to make a mistake."

"So, a win/win all around?" Skeet laughed. "I am always fascinated with the way your mind works Rowdy Cooper."

"Glad to be of service, Skeeter Perkins," Rowdy laughed. "You know, I'm beginning to see a pattern developing between you and me. So many of our conversations are exchanges that never really happened. I'll add this one to that list."

"I'd appreciate that," Skeet also smiled. Rowdy once again proved what Skeet had already known; he would never match the friendship he shared with the Coopers'. It was unique, intriguing and something he would value for the rest of his life.

* * * *

The entire group sat around the conference table in the office downstairs discussing their next move. They had certainly hit Zarconi where it counted, but they still had a lot to do.

"Theresa," Skeet decided. "We need a witness. Can you see if Carson or Marc can get you a roster of students attending Wayne State at the time of Zach's death? Rowdy and I saw a ton of kids hanging out and relaxing in the park. Some of them looked like they were studying. The timeframe was a close match to the time Zach would have been killed based on that police report. Someone had to see something and if you can get a roster, I'd like you to call each student. Tell them you're a fellow Warrior and you're looking for information on the death of your friend."

"Are you sure I'm the best one to do it?" Theresa asked. "What if I say something I shouldn't?"

"I know you'll be fine," Skeet said confidently. "You knew Zach personally. It gives you an edge the rest of us don't have. You can relate because you were a student and Zach was someone you had a personal relationship with. That kind of discussion can't be faked."

"Okay," Theresa agreed. "What are you guys going to do?"

"I have an idea," Tony spoke up.

"I'm sure this is something I'm not going to like," Theresa mumbled.

"No, but Rowdy might," Tony pressed a soft kiss to Theresa's cheek.

"I'm listening," Rowdy spoke up.

"I've been thinking," Tony stood. "We need to get into that warehouse. Upstairs if possible, the one we were headed to when we ran into happy feet over there."

Blake grunted.

"What did you have in mind?" Skeet asked skeptically.

"I was thinking Rowdy and I could pay another visit to the casino. If we launch a coordinated attack, we can take down several of the slot machines. Theresa said Dom has replacements in the warehouse; but if we sabotage enough of them, he'll have to order new ones."

"And, we deliver them," Rowdy provided. "Carson and Marc already gained access to Dom's hard drive. They should be able to determine who his supplier is. Then, we just hack the delivery schedule and make our move."

"And by move you mean?" Skeet wasn't sure it would hold up in court.

"By move I mean we intercept the truck and either ride along or make him an offer he can't resist," Tony answered.

"Be specific," Blake pushed. "Everything we do has to hold up in court. We can't lose this case because you stole the truck."

Tony rolled his eyes. "I'm not planning on stealing the thing, I'm planning on giving the guy a morning off with pay."

"Then I snap a few photos and if we get lucky, you have probable cause for a warrant," Rowdy provided. "It's solid, and you know it. We accept anonymous tips all the time. Just call me Mr. Anonymous."

"I have to run it by Stan," Skeet held up a hand when Tony started to object. "I have to. It's risky, and this is his call." Skeet stood and left the room. Fifteen minutes later, he returned. "We have a couple concerns."

"Which are?" Tony asked.

"The first one is Rowdy," Skeet told him. "He doesn't have jurisdiction here, but he's still a cop. He can't be the one snooping around and snapping photos."

"And two?" Tony asked.

"If you walk around the casino doing whatever it is you do to disable the slots, you are going to be caught on camera. If Zarconi gets suspicious, which he will when several machines go down, he's going to figure out they were tampered with. You have to find a way to accomplish the task without leaving a trace, and I can't know anything about it."

"I'm guessing that means I can't either," Blake stood. "I'll start going through video while Theresa works on the witnesses."

"Good idea," Skeet paused to study Rowdy and Tony. "I'm going to join them. Rowdy, I'm counting on you to protect our case. Don't do anything that Dominic can use to suppress evidence."

"I got this," Rowdy assured him. "Trust me, I'll figure something out."

"Why doesn't he trust me?" Tony asked when Skeet walked away.

"Let me think... oh, yeah. First, there's the explosion at the warehouse. Then, there's the hot cars you keep supplying."

"Those cars are not hot," Tony objected.

"I'm not sure I want to know the details," Rowdy stopped him.

"I don't know the details," Tony admitted. "But Wolf's solid. He was one of Conrad's projects and Con would never house a criminal. Wolf took off just after high school, decided to travel the world; and somehow, he ended up in California. He was in his twenties by then and had a run-in with Con. That's usually how Conrad found the next soul that needed saving. Anyway, I have no idea how they met. Con never revealed things like that to any of us. Wolf only stayed a few months, seven maybe. Then he learned his grandmother was sick. He immediately returned to Detroit and did his best to provide in-home care. Eventually, she deteriorated further and Wolf couldn't handle it on his own. She's in a nursing home now, just turned ninety-one. He works his butt off to pay her expenses and his, plus cover overhead at the garage."

"He provided you with a vehicle that was registered to a retired couple. They reside on the outskirts of town on a family farm," Rowdy pointed out.

"If you know that much," Tony countered. "You also know it's not hot. It shows legit. Like I said, I don't know the details; but whatever he's doing, it's not illegal. He might straddle the line, but he doesn't cross it."

Rowdy was satisfied with that explanation. The vehicle had come back legally registered. If Wolf had some kind of arrangement with the locals, he didn't really care. "How are we going to disable several machines at once without being noticed? Could we attach something to a breaker and force a surge through everything fed by that switch?"

"How would we find the electrical box?" Tony considered, that actually might work.

"There has to be blueprints somewhere," Rowdy decided.

"Most casinos have a central plug with the electrical running through a post. Then they run the lines behind the machine into an outlet," Tony considered. "If I could get to the outlet without being caught on camera, I might be able to force a surge through the main system and fry the entire row of machines."

"But how do we do that without being caught on film?" Rowdy pressed.

"I've got nothing," Tony admitted. The two of them sat in silence for several minutes trying to come up with a plan. Suddenly, Tony turned and focused on Rowdy. "What if we didn't do it all at once?" Tony's mind was racing, he had an idea but it was risky.

"What are you thinking?"

"Sulfuric acid," Tony explained. "You can buy it at any auto parts store in the battery aisle. We just need to figure out a distribution method, that's actually the hard part. The stuff is toxic. A few drops of liquid destruction and those machines will be toast. We could flush it through the coin slot, and the upside of using acid is time. It will take a while for the mechanisms to deteriorate. They'll never be able to track the damage to us because the slots will be operational until something fails."

Rowdy began to think through the plan. He couldn't run it past Skeet, the feds had to be kept in the dark. Could he ask Coop? No, better not to involve him either. They were on their own, or were they? "We need to get back to the loft and talk to the geeks."

"Why?"

"Because we need to study camera angles and make sure whatever we do is not captured as evidence," Rowdy stood. "I'll tell Skeet where we're going."

Rowdy stepped into the other room and approached Skeet. "I need Carson's number."

"Why?" Skeet asked. "Never mind." He pulled out his phone and scrolled through his contacts, holding the phone out for Rowdy to see.

"Thanks," Rowdy patted his pocket to make sure he had the room key and made his way to the door. Tony at his heels.

"What was that about?" Theresa asked when they left the room.

"We're not asking," Skeet sighed. "Whatever they're doing, none of us can know about it. We just need to trust them and hope it all works out."

"I'm really not liking that approach," Theresa said softly.

"None of us are," Skeet admitted. "But it's the way it has to be."

* * * *

"That has to be them," Carson said at the knock on the door.

"I'll get it," Marc said as he moved to the large metal door that slid, well actually clunked, to the side.

"You have our attention," Carson began. "We'd both like answers. For starters, tell us why you wanted to know if we've signed that document before you'll speak to us."

"We need to do something," Rowdy settled into a chair. "Something the FBI can't have any part in. We need it to be legal on their end. The last thing we need is for some slick lawyer to find a loophole and toss the evidence in court."

"Okay," Marc returned to his chair as Tony settled into the seat next to him.

"If you haven't signed the contract, you don't work for the feds," Tony provided.

"And, you need our help?" Carson asked.

"We do," Rowdy nodded. "But, this plan has to stay between us. Nobody but the four of us can know anything about it."

"I'm in," Carson agreed immediately.

Marc shook his head. "I'm shocked, my colleague wants to participate in a covert, slightly illegal mission."

"In or out," Tony asked Marc.

"In," Marc sighed. "I like to believe I'm more cautious and above board than Carson; but in all honesty, I too enjoy a good, slightly illegal, caper now and again."

Tony explained the plan, noting they hadn't figured out a way to introduce the acid into the machines yet. "Once the slots go down, Dom will have to order replacements."

"That's where you come in," Rowdy provided. "We need you to hack the system, determine who his supplier is and then hack their system for a deliver schedule."

"That's easy, but I think we can do one better," Marc informed them.

"Meaning?" Tony pressed.

"As Rowdy knows, we have already been in Dominic's computer," Carson glanced at Marc. "We can easily go through his system and determine how the security cameras work."

"Once we're in," Marc added. "We just dub the recording for a few seconds. If we find a machine that isn't occupied, we dub it. You step in, inject the acid then step away and the feed starts rolling again."

"We'd have to coordinate closely, it has to be perfectly synchronized but now days nobody is going to pay attention to an earpiece," Carson concluded.

"Okay," Tony nodded. "I can handle communications. We just use a cellphone and a high- quality Bluetooth. That takes care of the cameras, but we still need a way to introduce the stuff so nobody on the floor knows what we are doing."

"What about a syringe?" Carson asked. "You could buy several plastic syringes with a long enough tip that it will slide into the coin slot. Then, you put the syringe in the palm of your hand and act like you're slipping a coin into the slot. Anyone around you will just think you're gambling. It's pretty common to drop in a couple quarters then move to another machine. Once the acid has been introduced, move out-of-the-way."

"It might work," Rowdy considered. "If we don't have to worry about the cameras, we can focus on the people around us, make sure we're not getting unwanted attention. We'll need some kind of bag to put the used containers in. Tony, did you bring a suit?"

"No," he grinned. "But I brought cash, we can buy something off the rack." He frowned. "Something I haven't said in years, but desperate times..."

Rowdy laughed. "Are you sure you can handle the sacrifice?"

"It's going to be difficult," Tony grinned, "but I'll manage."

"When did you want to do this?" Marc asked.

"Today," Rowdy answered. "Tony and I will go round up the supplies. I need you to hack into the system and figure out the cameras. Is that doable?"

"We'll be ready when you return," Carson assured him. "It's going to take you awhile to purchase suits, get the acid, and the syringes. I'd also suggest you buy suit coats with large pockets. You can put the unused containers in the jacket pocket then have a plastic lined bag of some kind for the containers after you use them."

"Right," Tony stood. "We're just looking at five or six machines. If each of us take three syringes, this should be a piece of cake."

"As long as we lose the cameras," Rowdy glanced at Carson. He took a step forward then paused. "Tony, I'll meet you at the car."

Tony shot him a quizzical look then disappeared through the door.

"Have you taken care of that list yet?" Rowdy asked softly. "The twenty-three victims?"

Marc's head shot up in shock.

"We were working on it," Carson answered. "That's what you interrupted. Why?"

"Good," Rowdy nodded and turned. "We're trying to hit Zarconi from every angle. Taking his money is just another strike he won't see coming and if a few innocent victims benefit... that's even better." He continued out the door and slid into the car.

"Do I get to know?" Tony asked.

"What I can tell," Rowdy decided. "But not all. Skeet could get into a bit of trouble for some of it, so I'm not at liberty to share."

"Fair enough," Tony pulled onto the highway.

Rowdy explained what they had discovered that morning. "We don't want Theresa to know. Best case, she'll be upset because Dom is selling women."

"Worse case," Tony said soberly. "She'll realize that's what he has in mind for her."

"Exactly," Rowdy gazed out the window. "The geeks were working on the system this morning and located bank records. They were able to access the accounts."

"And you encouraged them to take it?"

"Something like that," Rowdy said absently.

"Another strike where it counts, I like it."

Rowdy turned to look at his new friend. "This conversation never happened."

"What conversation?" Tony smiled as he pulled into a designer suit store. "Let's shop."

* * * *

Several hours later, Tony and Rowdy returned to the loft outfitted in new, fancy suits. They had purchased dark blue Nalgene, wide-mouthed water bottles to hide the empty syringes after the acid was deployed into the machines. Each one came with a black outer cover attached to a long strap. They figured it would be less conspicuous for two men to walk around with a water bottle slung over their shoulder than some kind of purse under their coats. Tony had surfed the net and discovered acid wouldn't eat through Nalgene for some reason; so, it seemed like a good solution to their problem. To be safe, they'd purchased glass syringes rather than plastic and found a tactical pouch made from Nalgene as well. The plan was to cut the pouch into large rectangle strips and line the pocket of their suit coat to protect the lining if one of the full flasks leaked. Now they just needed to assemble their chemistry project and deliver the package.

"We're in," Marc said when they entered the loft. "Carson tested the system, and we've been able to dub the footage several times without detection. You're good to go on our end."

"What about the supplier?" Tony asked. "Any luck figuring out who they use to replace bad machines?"

"Yeah," Carson answered. "They'll have to have it overnighted, which gives us a little more time to track the delivery. We're monitoring the system for any large purchases. The second the order comes in, we'll be on it."

"Okay," Rowdy pulled out the various items and began filling tubes.

"You got any scissors?" Tony asked.

"There are industrial shears over there," Marc pointed to a shelf in the corner. "They'll work better on that pouch."

* * * *

Tony parked the vehicle in the middle of the lot and looked around. "We should be out of sight here."

"We don't go in together, and we don't leave together," Rowdy ordered. He pressed a button on his phone then slid it into his pocket. "Can you hear me, Marc?"

"Loud and clear," came the response in Rowdy's left ear.

Tony tested his equipment next. Carson came through crisp and clear in his earpiece as well. "Okay, we're on the move." He turned to Rowdy. "I'll go in first and head right. You go left."

"We get in and out," Rowdy said forcefully. "No matter what you see in there, in and out."

"Oh, really? I was so looking forward to a friendly game of roulette," Tony growled.

"There are so many other things that could go wrong in there, I wasn't talking about gambling," Rowdy stepped from the car and pressed the lock. He casually strolled through the parking lot and entered the casino through a large double door. Tony waited several seconds before heading for the opposite entrance.

"Okay," Marc said softly. "I have you in sight. There's a bank of machines to your right. I'm cutting the feed now. Three machines are available at the far end. Don't sit at the last one, sit down at least one machine in and drop a few quarters before you deliver the acid."

Rowdy rolled his eyes and continued to the area Marc described. He sat one seat in from the end and dropped a couple coins in the slot.

"Nobody is paying attention," Marc advised.

Rowdy ran a hand through his hair as a distraction. "How do you know that?"

"Oh," Marc smiled. "Because I'm still watching the real feed. I just dubbed the recording so they won't see what you're doing. You're clear for delivery any time."

Rowdy glanced around the room, realized Marc was correct and carefully slipped the syringe into the palm of his hand. He reached for the slot and made a swift motion, hoping if anyone did glance his way, they'd just think he dropped in another coin. Once the glass tube was empty, he lifted the lid on the bottle and dropped in the glass container. He was surprised that the noise of slot machines and lucky winners masked the sound as the tube landed at the bottom of the bottle with a thud. He dropped a couple more quarters into the machine and stood, ready to deliver his next blow.

* * * *

Tony had delivered two doses of acid and was headed for his third machine when a female voice stopped him. He closed his eyes and turned to face a woman he hoped he would never set eyes on again.

"Problem?" Carson asked. "Never mind, I can see the answer is yes. You need to get rid of her."

Way to state the obvious, Einstein. Tony thought to himself as he forced a smile and held out his hand in greeting.

Sabrina Goodwin stopped, studied Tony's hand and frowned. "What kind of greeting is that?"

432

"The kind you deserve," Tony said coolly.

Sabrina laughed. "Oh, Tony. You always were a tease."

Tony lowered his hand and studied the woman he once dated more closely. She had dressed to give off the appearance of wealth, but had fallen short of the mark. So, she was on the prowl again. He wasn't surprised her rendezvous with millionaire playboy Luc Thorne had ended. It was destined to fail from the start. "I'm guessing you're not here with Luc then?"

Sabrina flung her hair over her shoulder and huffed. "No, I got tired of Luc ages ago."

"Lucky him," Tony said flatly. "Well, good luck on your search and have a nice life."

"Tony?" Sabrina whined. "I've missed you. Can't you buy me a drink? I'd love to catch up."

"Let me think about that. No," Tony turned to leave but stopped when Sabrina placed a hand on his forearm.

"Don't be that way," she cooed. "I have a room upstairs. We could, I don't know, reconnect for old times' sake."

"Sabrina," Tony gritted his teeth and sucked air through his nose. "Whatever we had back then is not worth repeating. Not for me. You made your choice, now you get to live with it. Please, excuse me. I'm not really in the mood for gambling any longer." He walked away, knowing she would follow if he didn't leave the building.

"We got five of them," Carson said with too much understanding. "That should be enough."

Moondance Ridge

Tony silently made his way to the car and spotted Rowdy leaning against the passenger door. He knew he'd have to explain why he hadn't completed the task, but he really didn't want to discuss Sabrina Goodwin and the mistake he had made two years ago. He climbed behind the wheel and pulled the last syringe from his pocket. "I had to leave without delivering this one."

"That's okay," Rowdy took the syringe and dropped it into his plastic bottle. "We delivered five of them, it should be enough. Marc, we're signing off and heading back to the hotel. Thanks for all your help today. Give me a call when you figure out the delivery schedule."

"Will do," Marc said as he disconnected the call.

"Yeah," Tony agreed. "Thanks Carson. We could never have done this without you." Once he was sure Carson had disconnected, he glanced at Rowdy. "He told you?"

"Of course," Rowdy shrugged. "We went in as a team. The guys thought I needed to know why you got delayed."

Tony shook his head. "Of all the places to run into Sabrina, this was the worst one possible."

"Oh, I don't know," Rowdy grinned. "I'd say it was better to have that encounter while you're with me rather than Theresa."

"Good point," Tony conceded. "I dated her two years ago when I was at a low point in my life. Bailey had vanished and I wanted to move on, to leave the company I was with and start over. I do that a lot. Anyway, I had convinced myself I couldn't leave. I had to work for a guy that drove me nuts because if Bailey surfaced, I needed her to know where to find me."

"So, you dated Barbie in there and you got burned," Rowdy surmised.

Tony frowned. "How do you know what she looks like?"

Rowdy pulled out his phone and displayed his text. "Tech geeks."

Tony shook his head. "I should have known. Anyway, she's a gold-digger. It took me awhile to figure it out; but she's shallow, self-absorbed and always looking for the next guy with more than the last."

"Carson said something about Luc Thorne," Rowdy frowned. "He's not richer than you."

"Sabrina didn't know that," Tony laughed. "I was lonely and miserable, not stupid."

"And now?"

"Who knows," Tony shrugged. "She may have figured it out, she could be desperate, spotted me and thought I'd fall back into that old trap. I have no idea, I don't really care. My only concern was for the mission. I feel like I failed."

"Like I said before we stepped foot out of the car, in and out. We built in a contingency. Four probably would have been enough, but we aimed for six. We got five. I call that a successful mission. Now, we fall back and let the geeks do their job. Dominic has to place an order; the question is when. If he has enough replacement machines in storage, he might wait a few days."

"We better hope not," Tony replied. "We don't have anything that connects him to that building. It's our only hope of shutting the place down. We need this plan to work if we're going to hit him where it counts."

Rowdy smiled. "The geeks already did."

"The money?"

"Yeah," Rowdy nodded. "Marc told me it's done."

Chapter Eleven

"How did five machines go down in the same day?" Dom demanded.

"We don't know," Ike Krauss, the casino floor manager, admitted. "Maintenance opened up the back and didn't see anything obvious. We just had to roll them out. Hogan said he can do a complete diagnostic, but it's going to take time and there are five of them."

Dom threw the paperwork he'd been studying across his desk. "Fine," he decided. "Order new ones. I want them here tomorrow, expedite shipping. We can't have five of our most steady money makers down for more than one day."

"Yes, sir." Ike waited to be dismissed.

Dom ran a frustrated hand through his hair then pulled his phone from his pocket when it began to chime. "You're dismissed."

Ike turned and rushed out the door.

"Hello," Dom barked.

"How in the hell did my men end up in a cell in Podunk Montana?" Nico Depiro demanded. "When you asked for a couple guys to help out, I didn't hesitate to step in. I sent you two of my best; and now they are held up, IN MONTANA," Nico yelled. "Without bail."

"What?" Dom asked, confused. "I sent them out to pick up Theresa Regan. I have no idea how they ended up in a cage. What did they say?"

"Not a lot," Nico grumbled. "They called Blaze McCormick because they needed an attorney. Apparently, they've been locked away in some federal office building for two days."

"What office?" Zarconi demanded. Darrow should have known about that.

"DEA," Nico provided. "Once the locals traced them to New York and me, they decided to tug a thread and see if they could connect Dreven and Talon to Leon. This is a mess, Zarconi. One you created. The guys held up; but if I have any trouble over this, you'll be the one to pay the price."

"I'll handle it," Dominic promised. "And once they're out, free and clear, I'll have them return to New York. My guys will take care of the rest."

"I'm counting on it," Nico said before he violently ended the call.

Dominic stood and paced the room. That feeling he'd been ignoring for days, the one that told him he was under attack... returned. But, who was attacking him? Not Nico. He wouldn't sacrifice friends in an effort to destroy Dom's enterprise. The Phantom? Dom was pretty sure he'd smoothed that one over for now. David Sherman? The man was pissed about the death of his grandson but angry enough to start a war? That just didn't feel right. He needed information. Dom returned to his chair and considered, finally deciding on Joe. He picked up his phone and punched in Crazy Joe's number. It would leave him short, but it was the only way to get answers. Joe had to go back to Mount Haven.

* * * *

Tony and Rowdy were sitting in the penthouse when Rowdy's phone began to ring. "Yeah?"

"Two things," Carson began. "First, the purchase for the replacement machines has been placed. Just as I thought, Zarconi expedited the shipment and it arrives tomorrow morning. The delivery is scheduled for one in the afternoon."

"And?" Rowdy asked.

"Since we were mucking around inside Dom's computer and the security footage anyway, we decided to do a little checking."

"Are you sure nobody will know? I think that was reckless and unnecessary," Rowdy objected.

"You're talking to Carson Griggs and Marcos Cain; do you even have to ask?"

"My bad," Rowdy said sarcastically. "What did you find?"

"The security company only saves the feed for one month, then it's overwritten with new video. We searched Dominic's hard drive, that's clean too. Unless he watched Shawn's death within the first month after the murder, he has no idea Theresa was in the room."

Rowdy thought about that for a minute. "Then he doesn't know."

"How can you be so sure?" Carson asked.

"Because it took him just over a month to track her down and demand payment for a debt she didn't owe. If he knew she was a witness, he would have abducted her then... Or eliminated her. If I've learned nothing else from this case, I know that. Dominic Zarconi does not leave loose ends. He doesn't know she was there, trust me on this. I'm not wrong."

"We do trust you, and that's good news," Carson murmured. "About the delivery, it's a company called Full Throttle. The manager already filled out the schedule and a guy by the name of Brink Wright is driving the truck. He has a morning run, a break for lunch and is scheduled to make delivery to the warehouse at one tomorrow afternoon."

"Perfect," Rowdy said absently as he tried to come up with a plan of attack. "For the second time today, we couldn't have done this without you. Too bad you're going to work for the feds. This is more fun, fewer rules."

"I've decided to look at it from a different point of view," Carson disagreed.

"What's that?"

"I'm calling it a challenge," Carson declared. "Marc and I will figure out a way to accomplish our tasks within the confines of the law from now on."

"You're right," Rowdy agreed. "That will be a challenge. Thanks again for all your help. I'll let you know if we need anything else." The instant he disconnected, he filled Tony in on the schedule. "Now we just have to come up with a plan."

"Give me a minute," Tony pulled out his phone.

"Don't tell me you know the owner?"

"No," Tony hit send. "Hey, Vaughn. It's Tony Nazario. I need a favor." Several minutes later, Tony ended the call. "He'll call me back."

"I'm not sure I'm following your plan," Rowdy admitted.

"It's simple," Tony settled in, placing one ankle on his thigh. "If Vaughn can get me a ride-a-long with Full Throttle on the right truck, then it's all legal. I have a reason to be inside that warehouse. I take the photos we need, maybe run to the restroom while they unload the machines and we turn it all over to Skeet to work his magic. As long as we find something incriminating, Skeet will have probable cause and the feds get their warrant to shut the warehouse down."

"It could work," Rowdy didn't like it, though. Tony was hanging himself out there and if he got caught, Dom might shoot first and ask questions later.

"I'll be fine," Tony assured him. "You asked Skeet to trust you, now I'm asking you to trust me."

"And you trust this Vaughn guy not to give too much away?" Rowdy wondered.

"I do," Tony stretched out his legs. "I helped Vaughn a long time ago. He nearly lost his entire business. I was able to save it, and he's prospered because of it. Vaughn knows enough to get us what we need, and he'll do it without anyone at Full Throttle knowing why I'm there in the first place. He's using the favor angle on the owner. A guy by the name of Samuel Roseberg. Apparently, they have some kind of history and Vaughn thinks this Samuel guy will come through for him, which means he'll come through for us."

* * * *

"Hey Coop," Rowdy answered the phone and pushed the file he was reading to the side. "What's up?" Once everything had been arranged for Tony to accompany the driver on his run, the two of them had joined the others. Rowdy was sifting through documents hoping to find a clue in Zach's murder.

"I thought you should know, the two thugs have been returned."

"The ones that attacked Bailey?"

"Yeah," Coop confirmed. "DEA kept them hidden for as long as they dared. Then Jasper had to cut them loose. He decided to return them to me. Judge Harwick has refused bail. The DA convinced him they're a flight risk. For now, they're hanging out in Mount Haven's criminal hotel. Unfortunately, they got a phone call. Both of them spoke to an attorney, Blaze McCormick."

"Why do I know that name?" Rowdy asked.

"Because it's the same attorney Nico Depiro used to escape prosecution," Coop advised.

"What are the chances he'll win this one?" Rowdy asked. "You have him on the assault, right?"

"They'll do time, how much is another matter. I have no idea what kind of deal McCormick will work, but they're out of commission for now. I think it's safe to assume Zarconi is aware of their arrest."

"Good to know," Rowdy glanced up and realized the group was hanging on his every word. "That means you need to be even more vigilant. Dom still doesn't know we're in town. He's likely to bring his wrath down on you."

"I've got things covered," Coop scowled. "If he shows, I'll know it."

"If Maggie is in danger, I can make arrangements for her to stay with Angela," Skeet offered again.

"You ready to ship Maggie and Bryan out of town?" Rowdy asked. "Skeet says they can go stay with Angela and her friend."

"Let me talk to her and see," Coop said. "She went to the doctor and he switched her vitamins. Seems the pre-natal pill he originally prescribed was messing with her system. She's back on track and things are good, but I'm still worried. She insists on spending time at the bar; and so far, that seems to be the battleground of choice for your Detroit buddies."

"That's because they don't have anywhere else to go," Rowdy suggested. "For what it's worth, I think you should convince Mags to leave. If she wasn't carrying your kid it might be different, but she's vulnerable right now... and we're messing with the mob. You know how that ends, man. Get Mags out of town."

"And Bailey?"

"If I thought you could pull that one off, I'd say yes," Rowdy answered. "But we both know she's not going anywhere. Arguing with her would be futile. Just make sure Knight never leaves her side. I want her sleeping with that mutt until I get home."

"I'll watch out for her," Coop promised. "Is Skeet sure Angela's friend would be up for two more guests?"

"You sure there's room for Mags and Bry?" Rowdy asked his friend.

"Positive," Skeet answered immediately. "Say the word, and I'll make the arrangements. That means all of them. You get Maggie on the plane, and I'll have someone at the airport to pick her and the kid up and deliver them to safety."

"I caught that," Coop advised. "Let me talk to Maggie, and I'll let him know."

"Sounds good," Rowdy agreed. "Use Jase as you need to. He could be a big help out there."

"Don't worry about us," Coop advised. "I've got it covered. By the way, once McCormick learned about the arrest, he contacted Mayor Herlin. Jon played dumb but this could get dicey. Just know we've got things handled out here. There was no mention of you, Tony, Theresa or even Skeet and his side-kick."

"Good to know," Rowdy said, relieved. "That means I'm right and he still doesn't know we're here."

"I have no idea how that's possible," Coop grinned. "It's not like you're being discreet."

"We're wreaking havoc for sure," Rowdy agreed. "But either he hasn't put it all together, or he just hasn't figured out who it is yet."

"Be careful," Coop said before disconnecting.

"The good sheriff will call you directly if he can swing our plan to get Mags and Bryan out of town," Rowdy told Skeet.

"And Bailey?" Tony asked.

Rowdy frowned. "We both know she wouldn't go for it. I'm sure Coop will ask, but I know Bailey and she'll refuse."

"I agree," Tony said, disappointed. "But it's worth a shot."

The group worked well into the night, trying to tug any thread they could pull.

Moondance Ridge

* * * *

"Hey boss," Joe began. "I have bad news. Theresa Regan has left town."

"You're sure about that?"

"Positive," Joe affirmed. "I talked to a disgruntled patron last night at closing. He's not happy about it. Claims Theresa owes him a tumble, says she promised him a good time, but some guy got in the way."

"The same man that Socks and Drago encountered?" Dom asked.

"Couldn't say for sure," Joe replied. "But he doesn't work for the bar. I also got some details about Dreven and Talon's arrest. Seems they pushed a little too hard, assaulted a female bartender in their attempt to locate Theresa. She works with a large dog, one that bit the duo before the sheriff caught them in the act. I'm afraid Blaze will have a hard time working his magic on this one. Those two may have to serve some time after all. It's a small town, and they have a bar full of witnesses."

"Idiots," Dom grumbled. "I need you to stay out of sight. I'm sending Horatio and Geovanni out. They're dealing with something at the moment, but they'll be there in a day or two. Once they arrive, the three of you need to track that girl down. I want Theresa Regan back in Detroit before the end of the month."

"I'll start snooping around while I wait," Joe offered.

"Do it from a distance," Dom ordered. "There's too many things going on right now. I can't risk you landing in jail because some overzealous halfwit wants to make a name for himself. Steer clear of that sheriff."

"That's going to make things difficult," Joe advised.

"Start on the computer, you're good at that," Dom ordered. "We connected Theresa to Shawn and Zach Regan but we never really looked into her or her family. Find out if she has relatives out there. Find out where she would go to hide. Everyone has someone, and it just might be the reason she fled to Montana in the first place."

"I'll see what I can find," Joe clicked off. He hated causing problems for Theresa. He was rooting for her, hoping somehow she'd escape, but he knew better. Dom always got his way. So, Joe had to look into her connections. He didn't have a choice. It was either her or him... or his sister. It had to be Theresa.

* * * *

"I know you're worried, but I promise everything is going to be fine," Tony pulled a t-shirt over his head then settled onto the bed next to Theresa.

"There is no way you know that for sure," she objected.

Tony took her hand then leaned forward and gave her a soft, loving kiss. "Trust me."

"I do trust you," Theresa argued. "I do not trust Dominic Zarconi or his men."

Moondance Ridge

"I've got this under control," he insisted. "Rowdy and I are going to drive the route and he'll be close by. If anything happens, he'll be there."

Theresa sighed, knowing she couldn't change his mind. She hated this. They were all risking their lives for her and she hadn't even left the hotel.

Tony gripped her hips and pulled her closer, Theresa instinctively wrapped her arms around his neck. "I love you, baby. I got this. Stop worrying about me. I promised to protect you. I'm going to stop this man, and then we can talk about our future." He leaned forward, this time the kiss was hot, passionate and full of emotion.

Theresa pulled back, still shocked at Tony's words. She swallowed hard and looked into his eyes, needing to know if he was being serious. He was. "I love you, too," she whispered. "Please come back to me."

Tony sat back, a little surprised at her response. "Are you serious? Don't say it if you don't mean it."

"I mean it," Theresa said forcefully. "I am head over heels in love with you, Tony Nazario. Whether I like it or not and I need you to be safe. I don't think I could handle it if Dominic took you away, too."

"Which is why he won't," Tony promised. He smiled and pulled her in for one more kiss. "I gotta go. Trust me. I do love you, babe. I will come back. You have to believe that. This is nothing. I'm just riding in with the driver, snapping a few photos and then we'll leave. You're making more of this than you need to. Rowdy will be there; I'm not helpless and at the first sign of trouble, I'm sure the driver will bolt."

"Just be in the truck when he does," Theresa demanded. "I'll see you in a few hours."

Tony stood and walked to the door, then pivoted and blew Theresa a kiss.

* * * *

"Hey, Brink," Burt Johnson, the daytime manager for Full Throttle called out.

"What's up?" Brink asked, popping just his head in the door.

"Boss needs you to take Tony here with you on the run."

Brink stepped into the doorway and frowned. "Why?"

"No idea," Burt said as he looked at Tony.

"I'm helping a friend; and he can't have me riding with one of his guys, it will raise suspicion. I need to get a feel for the runs, the interaction and stuff like that. I will also need to snap a few photos."

Brink shrugged, "I'm pulling out in five. Be ready."

"The truck is parked around back," Burt explained as he pointed to the hallway. "Take a left, then a right and follow the long corridor to the back. Once you push through the door, you can't miss it."

Tony watched as the man turned and opened the top drawer of a file cabinet; clearly, he had just been dismissed. He turned, followed Burt's directions and ended up outside. He was now standing on a concrete loading dock. Two men were wheeling the last slot machine into the back of a truck. Tony descended the stairs and glanced inside the cab. Brink was already situated in the driver's seat ready to pull out at a moment's notice. Tony crossed in front of the vehicle and climbed in beside his driver, knowing he was an unwanted guest. He pulled out a small camera and began to snap photos. It might annoy the kid, but he had a plan. If he started now and got the guy used to Tony being snap happy, it wouldn't raise suspicion when he started taking shots at the warehouse.

"I don't like being part of this covert spy thing you have going," Brink said as he pulled away from the building. "If I find out you're using any of this to go after a driver, I won't look the other way."

Tony didn't answer. Seriously, this punk was trying to threaten him? Was that supposed to scare him off? He watched as a cocky grin spread across Brink's face. Apparently, it was.

Rowdy spotted the large truck as it drove past on its way to Dom's warehouse. *So far, so good.* He caught a glimpse of Nazario, silently watching the world go by. Rowdy started to turn away when he saw Tony's middle finger resting casually against the glass of the truck's passenger window. Did that man ever take anything seriously? He pulled in behind the vehicle and followed cautiously until he reached the last turnoff just before the warehouse. Within seconds, his vehicle was hidden behind some foliage; and he was in position just in case everything suddenly went south. He just hoped that didn't happen; because if he was forced to rescue Tony, things could get ugly.

Tony waited as the driver pulled through the large overhead doors. Then, he began to snap photo after photo. They wouldn't be perfect through the glass, but they should do. Brink shoved open his door and approached one of the workers. Tony snapped a picture of the man, careful to leave Brink's face out of the frame. He lowered the camera when the guy glanced up and scowled. Moments later, a second guy came forward, had a heated discussion with his co-worker then focused on Tony as he approached the truck.

Tony decided not to wait. He pushed open the door and lowered himself to the ground. Within seconds, he was standing next to Brink.

"Who is he?" one of the men demanded.

"I'm in training," Tony answered. "Just getting familiar with the truck, that's all. Is there a problem?"

"Listen punk," the guy took a step forward.

"Hey," Brink interjected. "I have five machines that need to be dropped. Am I leaving them here or returning to the warehouse?"

"You're leaving them," the man grumbled and backed away. He turned, took two steps then pivoted back around. "You stay here."

"Fine with me," Tony shrugged. He watched as the three men moved behind the truck. The instant they were out of sight, he began to once again snap photo after photo. He heard a sound behind him and spotted another man moving his way. That's when he noticed the crate. *Coffee, really?* They seriously needed to learn the phrase 'too much of a good thing'. Nobody would believe everything they smuggled was coffee, not in Detroit.

"Hey," a large, bald man barked. "What are you doing in here?"

Moondance Ridge

Brink poked his head around the back of the truck. "He's with me."

Tony approached the man, stopping directly in front of the crate. "Sorry, am I in the way? I can move," Tony said innocently.

"If you're not helping, get back in the truck," Baldie ordered.

Tony needed to see inside that crate. He glanced down, realized the lid wasn't secure and pretended to trip. He went down hard, landing against the crate. He flailed his arms, determined to knock the lid at least partially away. It worked. The wooden lid slid sideways far enough Tony could see the container was full of white powder.

The bald guy looked at Tony in disgust. "Get up and get back in the truck. I don't want to see you wandering around again. You will not like the consequences." He turned and marched away, taking the stairs two at a time before he disappeared down what looked like a hallway.

Tony didn't hesitate, he quickly snapped shot after shot, making sure to get a clear image of the markings on the package. When he was confident he had what he needed, he pushed himself off the ground and climbed back inside the cab of the truck. His ribs were killing him, hopefully he didn't break one of them in that fall.

Brink bounced into the driver seat and pulled away. Once they cleared the yard and entered the highway, he turned to study Tony. "Either you're one gutsy hombre or you're stupid, I can't decide which one."

"I like to think I'm just good at my job," Tony objected.

"Well, I hope you got whatever you needed because these guys don't mess around," Brink advised. "I have no doubt Rico already contacted Burt to inform him, in no uncertain terms, there will be no trainees accompanying driver's when they make deliveries for Casino deZarcon."

"They did seem a bit jumpy," Tony observed. "But, I guess it was a good test case. Do you have many clients that act that way or did I just get lucky? I mean, I had a limited window to get the data I needed, but that was a little intense."

"They're more particular than most," Brink said evasively.

"Well, maybe I should have switched some stuff around and joined you later this afternoon. I hope what happened back there doesn't cause you any trouble next time you make a delivery," Tony said, acting concerned.

"It should be fine," Brink shrugged it off. "You never answered, is a driver in hot water for something?"

"Not really," Tony answered. "And, the delay back there might help explain a few things. I think you just helped a fellow driver. I'm sure he'll be grateful when he sees my report."

Brink beamed with pride. "Good, that's real good." He pulled into the lot and backed up to the loading dock. "You want to grab a Coke or something?"

"I wish I could," Tony did his best to sound disappointed. "But, I have to hit the road or I'm going to miss an important meeting. Thanks again for letting me tag along. It was certainly enlightening."

"You're welcome any time, just call ahead next time. I'll make sure we hook up on a friendly run." Brink gave a casual wave then disappeared into the building.

Tony strolled to the side of the building and climbed into the waiting vehicle.

"Any luck?" Rowdy asked.

"I think we may have hit the jackpot," Tony explained what happened as they drove back to the hotel. The instant they stepped through the door, Theresa was out of her chair and in Tony's arms.

"Hey, I told you everything would be fine."

"Then why did you just cringe when I hugged you?" She reached down and began yanking Tony's t-shirt from the waist of his jeans.

Tony smiled and leaned in close. "We can take this to the bedroom if you want to keep going."

Theresa looked up and pinned him with a look that telegraphed impatience, annoyance and eagerness all at the same time.

Tony laughed and pressed a gentle kiss to the side of her neck. "You considered it, for the briefest moment, you seriously considered it," he whispered. He took a step back and pulled his shirt free. "Don't overreact. I had to fall onto a crate to get what we needed. The ribs are sore, could be bruised, but they're fine."

Theresa pulled up his shirt to investigate. She reached out and ran her finger over the deep red line that was starting to change to a dark bruise. "I knew this was a bad idea."

"I think it was a good idea," Tony disagreed. "Here Skeet, send those to someone that deals with drugs. I'm sure they can tell you what they're peddling from the markings. If I had to guess, I'd say cocaine."

"And you would know that how?" Blake asked.

Tony smiled. "I can't reveal all my secrets, now can I?"

Skeet pulled out his phone and dialed Burns. Once again, he provided the details and had Tony send the photos to an agent.

"What now?" Rowdy asked.

"Now we wait," Skeet advised. "However, Theresa had a breakthrough. We think we've located a witness that saw Zach's murder. He's hesitant to talk and needs a little push. You up for a friendly interrogation?"

"Lead the way," Rowdy held out his hand and pointed to the door.

"Why are you taking him?" Blake asked, offended.

"Because I need you here," Skeet advised. "I told Stan to call you if he needed anything else on what Tony just provided. I also need you to keep scanning the video. We have over a dozen shots of Agent Konner Ellison in the casino but none of them prove he's dirty. He's just talking to Dom's people. We need to figure out how involved he really is."

The moment the door closed, Tony took Theresa's hand. "We'll be back in a while."

"Where are you going?" Blake asked.

Moondance Ridge

"We're not leaving, we just have something important that we need to discuss. Knock on the door if you need us," Tony said absently over his shoulder as he pulled Theresa down the hall and into the adjourning bedroom, locking the door behind him.

The instant the door closed, Theresa turned on him. "What are you doing?"

"We need to talk," Tony kicked off his boots and settled onto the bed. When Theresa didn't follow, he patted the mattress, hoping she'd take the hint.

Theresa sighed, removed her own shoes then climbed up next to him.

"After I left, I realized my timing was off this morning," Tony began. "I shouldn't have sprung that on you just before I headed into danger. I'm sorry, it wasn't fair to you."

"I'm glad you told me," Theresa relaxed. "I'm glad I told you. I've been trying to figure out the right moment, but with everything going on... it just never seemed like the right time."

"Me too," Tony pulled her into his arms. "Which is why I blurted it out this morning. It was clumsy and rushed. I want a do-over." He reached up, resting his large hand against the back of her neck and gently pulled her forward. His mouth connected with hers and he nearly lost control. "I love you." He deepened the contact, desperate to show her how he felt in addition to telling her. Theresa moaned, then settled against him happy to comply.

* * * *

"Looks like you just identified your killer," Rowdy finally said as he and Skeet entered the highway on their way back to the hotel.

"Looks like," Skeet mumbled.

"You okay?" Rowdy turned to study his favorite agent.

"I was hoping we were wrong," Skeet admitted, taking the turn onto the on-ramp. "I know, it was a rookie move. But, I didn't want to believe they killed him. I wanted to think maybe they stood guard, protected someone else, anything but actually taking an innocent man's life."

"It's understandable," Rowdy settled back against the seat and stretched his leg. It was bothering him today. Probably all the time he'd spent in a car.

Skeet noted Rowdy's movement and realized he'd been pushing his friend too hard lately. It was easy to forget Rowdy still had a few medical issues to deal with. "Leg okay?"

"Yeah," Rowdy shifted again then settled and glanced at Skeet. "I know it sucks. I don't like it any more than you do. But the bottom line is clear, they did this. When we started out, Tony asked me if I'd have a problem taking down one of my own. We knew there were dirty cops in the mix. I don't because just like I explained to him, they aren't ours anymore. I know it sounds ironic, I mean you know most of my secrets. You were there when I straddled a line. But..."

"It's not the same," Skeet assured him. "We do things because we have to. We might cut a corner, tell a little fib, maybe take advantage of a situation to help someone else now and again; but neither one of us would ever get involved with something like this. I know that. I know they chose to go bad. I just hate it, that's all. I hate knowing two of the good guys have gone completely and irreparably bad."

"I know," Rowdy said softly. "And, that's why we're going to stop them. Because they did go bad. The reason doesn't matter. Money, prestige, power... doesn't matter. They are bad and we are going to take them down. All of them."

"It is different, right?"

"And there we have it," Rowdy shook his head. "Of course, it's different. You're feeling guilty and maybe a little vulnerable because you know you haven't always followed the rules. That's not the same as breaking the law and you know it. Sure, we've skirted policy now and again. Maybe we've manipulated a few facts for the greater good, but we aren't dirty. We're the good guys. Skeet, you know you have to think like they do if you want to catch them. Sometimes, you have to get a little mud on your hands that's all."

"It's amazing to me how you can look at a situation and be so sure you're doing the right thing," Skeet told him. "Even when you know an outsider looking at it from a distance may totally disagree with you. In your heart, you know you're right. And I know, in your heart you are good. For some reason, I have a hard time reconciling that with my own actions."

"Because you work for an agency that is worse than most when it comes to bureaucracy and red tape. Policy is golden somehow if you work for the FBI. I prefer to look at policy as a guide. A roadmap if you will. A suggestion of how to do things properly so the lawyers and the administration feel good about themselves and the way the department operates. None of them have spent two seconds in the real world; and they don't understand that when you spend time in the gutter, you might get your shoes wet."

"You know what scares me?"

"What?" Rowdy asked sincerely.

"That when I listen to you, it all sounds so reasonable," Skeet told him.

"That's because I am reasonable," Rowdy grinned. "And no matter what corners we cut, no matter what action we take, we always... always consider the safety and security of the innocent. We have never bent the rules to benefit ourselves. If we've straddled a line here and there, it was for the benefit of others."

"What about that thing we don't talk about?" Skeet asked. "That was to benefit me."

"I am going to make an exception, this one time because I think you need to hear this." Rowdy paused to consider exactly how to explain this one. "I guess you could say you benefited from what I did. I guess you could spin my actions and come out with a negative finding. That's not how I see it, though. And, it's not the way Coop sees it. Since we were both there, I'd say we have a say."

"Rowdy, you took the blame for something I did," Skeet pressed.

Moondance Ridge

"Yes," Rowdy agreed. "And, I've had a long time to think about it. At the time, it was a split-second decision. But, years later, I can say without hesitation... I'd do it all again. Because it was the right thing to do for everyone involved. My actions made the entire incident cleaner. There was no reason to muddy the waters. If you hadn't reacted, Coop would have taken care of the threat and all of this would be irrelevant. As far as I'm concerned, it is. There were four people in that drainage system. Three of us got out alive. That is all that matters. The rest... just let it go."

"What if I can't," Skeet sighed.

"Try harder," Rowdy suggested. "Because just like the guilt you feel over Angela's abduction, it's misplaced. It wasn't your choice, it was mine. I did the right thing, you did the right thing and Coop did the right thing. We can't change the past and I wouldn't even if I could. I took the blame for something you did. So what, I would have done it if I could have. Case closed."

"Sometimes it just feels like we're up against that line more than we should be," Skeet sighed.

"Like I said, to catch them, you have to think like them and sometimes you have to act like them. I know you're having some crisis of conscience because those guys are dirty, but there's no comparison. We are not bad, Skeet. We're just good at our job." As far as Rowdy was concerned the discussion was over.

Skeet pulled into the parking spot still pondering the conversation. It was the second time in as many days that they'd found themselves discussing something extremely personal. This time, he realized Rowdy was right. It wasn't like the guilt he felt because a madman had captured his wife. The events that unfolded in that damp musky drainage system didn't define him. He was a good cop, he tried to follow the rules, do the right thing and put the most evil, sadistic creatures that walked among us behind bars. He could live with the corners they cut because they would never break the law. And, that's what made them different from Darrow and Ellison. The two men a scared young man just picked out of a lineup as the guys who shot an innocent reporter. Only they knew how they'd arrived there; but a man had died because they were ordered to kill him by the mob; and they'd complied. He might get a little dirt on him now and again, but he would never be dirty.

Rowdy and Skeet were in the elevator, on their way back to the office when Skeet's phone rang.

"Perkins," he said out of habit.

Blake laughed, "Cochran."

"Why are you calling?" Skeet asked annoyed. "We're in the elevator. I'll see you in less than five minutes."

"It can wait," Blake ended the call and glanced up to see Tony and Theresa exiting the back bedroom. Good, he'd share the news all at once.

The group settled in to hear what Blake had to say. "Stan called. He was able to utilize DEA Agents out of Chicago to initiate the bust and subsequent investigation. He said the records are sealed for now because the drug guys out here are questionable. The DOJ is assisting where they can, but it's possible they're compromised too. The Attorney General approved the team herself. As we speak, the warehouse has been secured and agents are transporting the evidence to the Chicago office. From there, a team will sort through it and catalog everything. At least that's something we don't have to handle ourselves."

"Things are going to get dicey fast," Rowdy concluded. "We've hit every illegal enterprise Zarconi's running. And, we've hit him hard. The one thing we have going for us is anonymity. He has no idea who hit him. But, you better believe, he's going to put it together. I just hope our geeks came through and there's no evidence we were ever at those machines. Otherwise, shits about to get real."

"If they said they fixed it, you don't have anything to worry about," Theresa told them.

"I agree," Skeet nodded. He frowned when his phone chimed. "Hello."

"It's Marc. I just wanted to let you know Carson and I signed the agreement. We're official now."

"I'll let Stan know," Skeet said flatly. He wondered if they had taken care of that other item but didn't know how to ask and wasn't sure he wanted to know.

"We scanned them into the cloud, feel free to send him a copy if he needs one," Marc added.

"Just so you know, DEA hit the warehouse and confiscated everything. Or, they are in the process as we speak. I need to know, if Dom goes looking will he discover Tony or Rowdy anywhere near those damaged machines?"

"No," Marc said immediately. "We got that covered. They're in the clear. They might be spotted on the floor, we couldn't block that out unless we took down the system completely; but there's no record of them anywhere near those machines."

"Good, thanks."

"Do you need anything else from us?" Marc asked.

"No," Skeet sighed. "I think we've monopolized you enough today. I'll give you a call in the morning, once we determine our next move."

"We'll be waiting," Marc said and disconnected.

"Back to paperwork?" Blake asked.

"Why don't we take a break, head out to dinner? I think we've earned it," Skeet stood.

"I'm game," Blake agreed.

The rest of the crew stood and followed the feds out the door. "Any idea where we're going? We have to take two cars," Tony asked.

"Theresa, why don't you choose? This is your town after all," Skeet suggested. "In fact, if you want to invite those two friends of yours have them meet us there."

Theresa considered then suggested her parent's favorite restaurant. It was a fancy Italian place her family always went to when the Regan's came to town. She called Carson, who agreed to bring Marc and meet them in twenty minutes. The rest of the evening was casual and light. To anyone watching, it would seem like a group of friends had just stopped in for a cheerful get-together. Little did they know, somebody was watching.

Moondance Ridge

* * * *

"Come in," Dom told Troy Darrow. "We have a lot to talk about."

Darrow stepped into the room, wondering what this meeting was all about. He glanced around the room and realized Horatio and Geovanni were also in attendance.

"I called you here, because I'm confused," Dom began. "I know you've been paid for the services I require; but lately, I don't seem to be getting those services."

"I told you," Darrow countered. "The FBI and the ATF do not work together, not as a matter of routine. I don't have access to their system. I have no idea when they are about to hit a target. Didn't I tell you, when you decided to get into the arms business, that you needed a man on the inside?"

"You did," Dom answered. "And I told you to find me someone. As I recall, you failed."

"I'm still working on it, but those guys aren't easy to turn."

"Maybe we should talk about Drevon and Talon. I called in a favor from a friend. Now I'm in trouble with that friend, do you understand how grave the situation is?" Dom asked. "How did you miss that arrest? How did you not know they were being questioned? Held at a federal facility, grilled for hours... no, days. And, my guy didn't know a thing about it."

"Again, I'm with the FBI," Darrow pushed. "Not DEA. How was I supposed to know they'd go out to the middle of nowhere and get picked up for assault? I can't be everywhere, know everything that happens in every Podunk town across America."

"And tonight?" Dom gritted his teeth and waited. Tonight had been the worst debacle of all. How had the DEA learned he was trafficking cocaine out of his storage warehouse? The only place that was still safe was the secure complex that held his girls.

"Again," Darrow pointed out. "DEA. You told me you didn't want to waste money to buy off an agent. You made that call. I had one in the wings, ready to step up but you told me no. You said you've been in the drug business long enough to know how to run it without the help of the cops."

"I did say that, didn't I?" Dom had to admit he'd made a calculated mistake on that one. But, he'd mistakenly believed he was paying Darrow and Ellison to fill the void, why bring in more mouths to feed when he already had two feds in his pocket? His phone chimed. He glanced down and frowned. This better not be more trouble.

"What?"

"Yeah, my girls didn't show," Federico Rossello barked. "I told you I had a small window to do the deal. You assured me there wouldn't be a problem. So, what's the problem?"

"What!" Dominic flew out of his chair. He turned to Geovanni. "Did you make that call I told you to make?"

"Of course," Geovanni said immediately. The boss was in no mood to mess around tonight. "Murph assured me he'd handle it. That was over an hour ago, the deal should be done."

"Well, it's not," Dom held the phone away from his ear and counted to ten. "Go home, I'll look into it."

"What do I tell the buyers? The guys are waiting, expecting delivery. What do ya want me to tell the guys?" Federico demanded.

"Tell them there's been a delay," Dom said shortly. He threw his phone across the room and settled into his chair. "I don't suppose you know anything about that, either?"

"I can check into it, make sure we didn't have nothing to do with it," Darrow offered.

Dom slid the Glock from his holster and slowly pulled the trigger. The bullet hit Darrow directly between the eyes. "Clean that up," he demanded as he stood and walked across the room. "Then I need you in Mount Haven. Joe is waiting. Theresa has disappeared. Find her. The plane leaves in an hour." He walked out the door and never looked back.

"Hor," Geovanni asked, never taking his eyes off the dead man. "How do we dispose of a cop?"

"I don't know, but we better figure it out," Horatio answered. "Because that could be us if we miss that plane."

After loading the body into the car, the two men decided the best way to get rid of a federal agent was to dump him in the lake and hope the tide would take him far enough out into Lake Erie that it was never found. They drove south to the far edge of the lake and tossed him in, near the opening where the Detroit River connected to the lake. With any luck, he'd float away and sink to the bottom, eventually becoming fish food. Horatio and Geovanni stood at the edge of the water and watched the body sink. As soon as it disappeared, they jumped in the car and raced back to town. They didn't have much time left to stop home, pack a few essentials and get to the airport. As it was, they'd be arriving in Mount Haven pretty late.

"Should we call Joe?" Horatio asked.

"Naw," Geovanni decided. "Let's get into town and get situated before we touch base. Dom said he's working on something. We don't want to disturb him."

"Right, let's go. Dom hasn't been himself for the past week. His mood swings are giving me the creeps." Geovanni climbed from the car and approached the waiting plane.

"I agree," Horatio followed. "The slightest mistake and we might be fish food."

* * * *

Bailey gathered up the last of the trash and headed for the dumpster.

Jase stepped forward, "I got that."

"Thanks," she glanced around and spotted Maggie in what was obviously a serious conversation with Marnie. "What's up?" she asked as she approached the table.

"I'm trying to convince Marnie it would be best if she stayed at college for a couple weeks. We can manage without her, and it would be safer and better for Jase," Maggie answered clearly frustrated.

"And, I told her you are shorthanded and you need me here," Marnie objected.

"Actually," Bailey pulled out a chair and settled in to rest her feet. She patted Knight gently when he laid his head in her lap. "Maggie's right. We've had too many things happen here at the bar. Jase can't hold up much longer if he has to worry about your safety and mine."

"I was actually thinking I should shut the entire business down for a few days," Maggie admitted.

"Why?" Bailey asked, confused.

"Andy wants me to leave town," Maggie said softly. "And, I think I'm going to go. If I wasn't pregnant I would stay, but I have to think about my family."

"Which is even more reason for me to stay," Marnie objected.

"You should both go," Bailey said forcefully. "Jase can manage the kitchen, and I've got the bar. Casey can't leave anyway, even if she wanted to. She has that talent thing coming up. We've got this. It's a perfect solution, Coop can focus on the job and not go crazy with worry. Marnie, you can spend some quality time with that new boyfriend of yours; and Jase won't be so worried."

"You could come with me," Maggie suggested.

"I can't," Bailey shook her head. "Not even if I wanted. Pete and I are closing on the old cabin the day after tomorrow. Plus, I have Knight to take care of... and he'll take care of me. We can handle the bar, it hasn't been that busy the last couple days."

"I'm giving you the time off, Marnie. If you come to work, you won't get paid." Maggie finally decided.

"That's not fair," she objected. "It should be my choice."

"What should?" Jase asked.

"Maggie just gave your sister the next two weeks off," Bailey informed him. "We told her to stay at college because she won't get paid even if she stops in. And since I'll be here, I'll make sure she doesn't work."

"Thank you," Jase said to Maggie, relieved his sister would be far away from town.

"Fine," Marnie agreed. She could see just how worried Jase was and realized she was doing more damage than good by being here. "I'll drive out first thing tomorrow morning."

"That's perfect," Maggie turned to Bailey. "Are you sure you won't change your mind? I fly out early as well."

"I'm sure," Bailey stood and Knight perked up. "I couldn't if I wanted to. Jase and I have it all covered, right Jase?"

"We'll take care of your place Maggie, I promise."

"That's not what I'm worried about," Maggie also stood. "I'll check in and if things get too crazy, you can seriously just shut down for a few days. Now, I'm sure my husband is waiting." She leaned over and gave Bailey a hug. "Promise me you'll be careful."

"I promise," Bailey hugged her back. "Have a safe trip and don't worry about a thing." She was relieved things were finally back on track between the two of them. Spending so much time together under duress had forced them to talk things out.

Maggie turned and headed for the door. She was going to worry. Not about the business, they'd survive even if Bailey decided to shut down for a week. She was worried about Bailey and Knight. That dog was part of the family. One that had come to love Bailey enough that he'd risk his life for her. Maggie just hoped he didn't have to.

"I'm outta here too," Bailey turned to Jase. "See you at the regular time."

"I'll be here with bells on."

Chapter Twelve

Tony, Rowdy and Theresa were just finishing up their coffee when they heard a knock at the door. Rowdy glanced through the peephole, then swung the door open in welcome.

"Blake's starving, and I could eat," Skeet provided, the instant Rowdy opened the door. "We thought we'd head downstairs to the restaurant and have breakfast. You guys want to join us?"

"I do," Theresa stood.

"Sounds like a yes to me," Tony also stood.

"Actually," Rowdy shook his head. "I think I'll pass. Coop had to drive Maggie and Bry into Missoula to fly out this morning, and I want to check on Bailey before we start the day. I'll hook up with you guys downstairs, in say an hour or so."

"Tell Bailey hi for us," Theresa gave Rowdy a hug. "And, I'll order you takeout. You can eat in the office while we plan out our day."

"Thanks," he watched as his friends made their way out the door. Once he was alone, he pulled out his phone and dialed Bailey.

"Hey," she answered still a little tired, but glad to hear his voice.

"You doing okay?"

"We're fine," Bailey ran a hand over Knight's face and laughed when he batted her away with his paw. "I think your dog decided to be lazy for once."

"I'm guessing he's a little worn out," Rowdy grinned, glad she had Knight to protect her. "Has he stopped pacing the house in search of his dad?"

"For the most part," she climbed from the bed and walked to the kitchen to start a pot of coffee.

The couple talked for about an hour before Rowdy decided it was time to disengage and get back to work. "Hopefully, we won't be much longer," he missed her terribly and couldn't wait to get home.

"Be careful," she said softly. "I know you have Skeet and Tony, but please be careful. I love you and can't wait to see you. Stop playing with your prey. Take that monster down already and hurry home."

Rowdy laughed as he disconnected the call. He had just pulled up his contacts, planning to call Skeet when the door burst open and Kevin Laforge stepped into the room. Rowdy hit send, then placed the phone in his pocket. If Kevin knew he was here, they'd been burned somehow. Kevin was a low-level employee that used to live in Chicago. He used to work for Leon DeRossi and had been arrested several times by Rowdy and his brother. As soon as DeRossi was out of the picture, Kevin disappeared. Apparently, he relocated to Detroit.

"Kevin," Rowdy said calmly as he glanced at the gun pointed at his head.

"You should have gone to breakfast with your buddies," Kevin exclaimed, excitement evident in his voice.

"Hello," Skeet answered.

"That's okay," Kevin grinned. "I'm sure your buddy Agent Perkins will be back soon."

Skeet jumped to his feet and hurried out of the restaurant. Blake followed. Tony interrupted their waitress, who was dealing with another table, and asked that the check be added to the room bill. He handed her a fifty to cover the tip and the inconvenience.

"What makes you think Perkins is in town?" Rowdy replied.

"I saw him," Kevin answered, spittle spewed from the side of his mouth and landed on his chin. He was so excited he was literally salivating. "I saw all of you, last night at the restaurant. You weren't very observant, were you? Once Perkins gets here, I'm going to call this in. All I have to do is turn you over to Zarconi, then I can collect my million and bolt."

Moondance Ridge

"Huh," Rowdy pretended to think. "So that's the bounty? A million?"

"Are you kidding me?" Kevin yelled. "You ain't worth a full mil on your own. That's for both you and the fed."

"So," Rowdy sighed. "Kevin Laforge came all the way to Detroit just to pay me a visit. I'm touched. Although, that gun pointed at my head isn't very friendly. That's a felony by the way. Well, a couple of them. One for pointing it, the other for possessing it. As I recall, you're a restricted felon."

"Shut up," Kevin demanded. "You can't arrest me, you're not a cop here."

"True," Rowdy grinned. "That means no rules."

Kevin frowned. "Shut up and go sit over there." He motioned to the couch with his weapon.

"Not really in the mood to sit, but thanks anyway."

"You in the mood to get shot?"

"Are you sure that reward is a dead or alive thing?" Rowdy asked. "I mean, are you confident if you shoot me, you won't be throwing away half a million dollars just because you can't control your temper?"

"What's going on?" Tony asked Skeet once he spotted the feds in the foyer.

"Kevin Laforge, a thug that used to work for Leon DeRossi is in your room with a gun to Rowdy's head.

"Shit," he glanced at Theresa. "Maybe we should head to the office while we talk."

"Good idea," Blake moved to the elevator and punched the button. The group stepped inside and Tony blocked the opening as Blake hit the close button, ensuring they had the ride to themselves.

"He's waiting for me, then he plans to call Zarconi and collect the bounty," Skeet advised. "That means Kevin doesn't know we're responsible for Dom's trouble. Unfortunately, the instant Zarconi gets wind of our presence, he'll put it together in a matter of minutes."

They stepped out of the elevator and quickly moved down the hall into the office.

"What do we do?" Theresa asked.

"We're burned," Skeet decided. "We need to clean up everything from this room and transport it to the car. I'm going upstairs to see what I can do about Kevin."

"Bad idea," Blake objected.

"Why?" Skeet asked.

"Because that's what he's waiting for," Tony provided. "You help Theresa clean up the evidence. I'll go. The second you step foot in that room, he's liable to shoot you both."

"I have a better idea," Blake said as he looked around the room. "How 'bout I head up, snag a few supplies, then climb into the rafters and make my way to your room. I can set up and shoot the guy if I need to. I know, we have strict orders to keep Zarconi alive. I won't forget those orders when the mob boss arrives. I can handle this, I might have a few tricks up my sleeve. Something that should give Rowdy enough time to escape… a little distraction is really all we need."

"What kind of tricks?" Skeet asked.

"Nothing much," Blake shrugged. "Something Stan arranged before I left."

Skeet continued to stare.

"He got me a flash bang, just in case I needed it when I was out here alone."

"And what are you going to do?" Skeet asked Tony, satisfied with Blake's answer.

"Are you sure you can handle this?" Tony asked Blake.

"Positive," Blake said confidently. "I think you should stay with Theresa. If this Kevin guy is calling Dom, next to Rowdy she's in the most danger."

"I think it's safe to say the only two people in this group not in danger, are you and me," Tony corrected. "And that's only because he doesn't know we exist. I'll stay for now, Skeet let's get this stuff gathered up. Once Blake rescues Rowdy we'll need to get out of here as quickly as possible."

"I feel like I've just been benched," Skeet objected. "Did you forget I'm the one monitoring the call?"

"Put it on speaker for now," Tony requested. "I'd like to hear what's going on."

"I think Kevin is calling Dom," Skeet advised. "We need to get this stuff packed up. There's no telling how many men he'll bring with him."

Blake rushed toward the door.

* * * *

Rowdy was standing near the kitchen, his back against the wall, his right foot raised with the sole pressed against the wall in an attempt to appear unmoved my Kevin's threat. In reality, he was cursing himself for not having his gun within reach.

Kevin pulled out his phone and dialed a number. After advising the person on the other end of the situation, he disconnected. "Dominic Zarconi will be here soon. He didn't sound too happy when he learned a Chicago cop was in his town. Especially not the one who brought down his friend, Leon."

"You mean your friend?" Rowdy corrected. "I doubt Zarconi has friends."

Kevin frowned. "What do you know about Dom?"

"Enough," Rowdy shrugged. He was stuck, but hopefully Skeet was still listening and knew not to walk into a trap. With any luck, the group was now in the office where it was safe.

Blake yanked open his leather travel bag and pulled out his duty belt. It was one of the few items he'd kept from his time in the Army. It had been improvised to fit domestic life, but he believed in being prepared for anything. When Director Burns had called, Blake knew he'd be on his own for a while. So, he was careful to pack the essentials. He had his 9mm Government Issue with him at all times; but his weapon of choice was the beautiful, sleek .40 caliber Beretta. He tucked that into his belt and opened the large pouch that contained the flash bang. The cylinder-shaped diversion devise fit perfectly into a small slot on the belt. He had to do some fancy talking to get the director to issue him the restricted explosive, but he'd learned his lesson in Iraq. The best defense was a good offense. And, the best offense was taking your opponent by surprise. He double checked to make sure the device was secure; the thing only had a two second fuse. There was no room for mistakes. Blake removed one of the ceiling tiles and hoisted himself up, dropping the tile back into place before moving quietly over one beam after another. Within minutes, he was across the hall and in position. He was pretty sure he could incapacitate this Kevin guy in a pinch, but the angle wasn't great. He hunkered down, willing to be patient… for now.

* * * *

"He's on the computer," Marc called over his shoulder.

"What's he doing?" Carson asked, joining his friend.

"Pulling up a newspaper article on Leon DeRossi's arrest out of Chicago," Marc frowned.

"He knows," Carson decided. "He knows about Rowdy and Skeet."

Within seconds, Zarconi had closed out the article and was typing Rowdy Cooper's name into his search engine.

"Is someone telling him to look, or did he figure it out on his own?" Marc asked.

"Let me try something." Once again Carson hacked into the operating system of Dominic's computer, this time he had a specific mission in mind. Within seconds, the camera embedded in the front of Zarconi's monitor, flashed on; and the two men were staring into the eyes of their biggest enemy.

"Let's record it," Marc suggested as he clicked open a program and started the video.

Zarconi continued to open article after article on Rowdy, but so far, he wasn't looking for Skeet.

"Any idea what's going on here?" Marc asked.

"Somehow, he knows Rowdy's in town," Carson decided. "He's doing research. I need to call Skeet." Carson frowned at his phone when it clicked over to voicemail. "Do we have a number for Rowdy?"

"Shhh," Marc said annoyed. "He's calling someone."

* * * *

"Geovanni," Dom barked. "What's the status out there?"

"We just called Joe. He's meeting us at that bar, and we'll go from there. He doesn't think anyone will talk, but I think it's worth a try. We'll develop a plan and advise from there," Geovanni told him.

"Theresa isn't going anywhere," Dom began. "Put that on the back-burner. Right now, I need you to track down the woman from the other night. The bartender with the dog that attacked Nico's men. Shoot the mutt and get rid of the girl."

"Okay," Geovanni said hesitantly. "And what about the sheriff? Joe said he spends a lot of time at the bar. I think his wife is part owner or something."

"You got a name?"

"Sheriff Cooper," Geovanni provided.

"Shoot him too if you get the chance," Dom decided. "But, don't underestimate him. If he's the guy I think he is, he came from Chicago."

"You're sure you want me to take out the sheriff?" Geovanni asked, wanting to make sure Dom didn't change his mind later when it caused them problems. Once he shot a cop, every officer in the nation would be on the warpath, not just the locals.

"I'm sure," Dom growled. "I'm arranging for a plane, you'll have a dozen men out there as soon as I can get them off the ground. You and Horatio will need to find a place they can crash. We're going to make that town regret their interference in my business. When one of them messes with Dominic Zarconi, they all pay the price."

"Do you think they're tied to Theresa? Maybe she's staying with the sheriff or the woman with the dog." Geovanni suggested.

"If she's there, don't kill her," Dom ordered. "I want her for myself. She's in for a different kind of hell once I get my hands on her."

480

"I understand," Geovanni said before disconnecting.

"We need to get in touch with Skeet," Marc said urgently.

"I tried," Carson frowned. "It just goes to voicemail."

"I have another idea," Marc said as he picked up the phone. He called information, then dialed the Sheriff's Office in Mount Haven.

"Mount Haven Sheriff's Office," came a female voice.

"I need to talk to Sheriff Cooper, it's an emergency."

"I'm sorry, the sheriff isn't in today."

"Look," Marc pressed. "I'm a friend of his brother, Rowdy. This is an emergency. Can you give me his cell phone?"

"I don't know," the woman hesitated. "I could transfer you. Would that work?"

"That would be great," Marc waited as the line went silent.

"Sheriff Cooper," Andy said, wondering who was calling. He didn't recognize the number.

Marc explained who he was, why he was calling Coop instead of Skeet and relayed the details from Dom's call. He emphasized the danger Bailey was in as well as Coop. Their orders were shoot to kill, including the sheriff if he got in the way.

"He figured it out. Somehow, he knows I was involved with DeRossi in Chicago," Coop decided. "Thanks for the heads up. When you get in touch with my brother, tell him to call me."

"I will," Marc ended the call.

* * * *

Dom stepped into the foyer and glanced around. He knew you couldn't get to the penthouse without a key and that was precisely where he needed to go. He snagged the first bellhop and demanded access. The employee was about to refuse when the manager stepped forward. "I'll take care of this, Mr. Zarconi."

Dirk Swanson watched as his supervisor retrieved several master keys, handing them to the demanding mob boss, then escorted him to the elevator. Once they were out of sight, Dirk grabbed his phone and sent a text to Tony Nazario. *Incoming, Zarconi.* He hit send and turned to help the next customer just as his boss rounded the corner, gave Dirk his most threatening scowl, then walked away. Hopefully, the friendly rich guy would get the message in time.

* * * *

Tony glanced at his phone and frowned. "Zarconi's in the house."

"How do you know that?" Skeet asked.

"I slipped the bellhop a few bucks and asked him to warn me if we got company. Apparently, he's not a fan of the neighborhood crime boss.

"Can't you just go arrest him?" Theresa asked.

"Stan isn't ready for that yet," Skeet told them. "Apparently, he's working on something and still needs him on the outside. Something to do with the trafficking unit."

"Then what do we do?" she was so worried about Rowdy, the reference to trafficking didn't even register. She knew what Dom was going to do. He was going to waltz into the room, try to interrogate Rowdy the way he had Shawn, then he was going to shoot him - probably in the head. She couldn't let that happen. Maybe if she turned herself over to Dom, he'd let the rest of them go. She started for the door, but was stopped by Tony.

"What do you think you're doing?" he asked

"I have to save Rowdy," she tried to step around him.

"That's what Blake is doing," Skeet scowled.

"Clearly, he's not doing a very good job of it because Rowdy is still up in that room with a man holding a gun to his head," she pointed out. "Worse, he's about to come face to face with Dominic Zarconi."

"Give him time," Skeet told her. "These things are not as quick and easy in real life as they are in the movies."

Theresa plopped into a chair and brushed away a tear. She looked up when she heard Dom's voice.

"Hello, Kevin,"

"I don't have the other one yet, but this one is worth five hundred thousand. I just want my money, you can have the cop."

Dominic studied Rowdy, who clearly was not intimidated... not by him, not by Kevin. Maybe it was time for a little object lesson. He pulled out his Glock and shot Kevin in the middle of his forehead. He frowned when he realized Rowdy Cooper hadn't even flinched.

Theresa screamed, then started to cry.

"You keep offing the help," Rowdy drawled. "You might find nobody is willing to work for you."

"That might be a problem in your line of work, but I will always find willing participants in mine," Dom turned the gun on Rowdy.

"I doubt you're going to shoot me," Rowdy straightened and moved to sit in one of the kitchen chairs.

"And why is that, Rowdy Cooper?" He expected surprise, he expected some kind of reaction, but again the cop didn't bat an eye.

"Because you want answers, and I have them," he said casually. "And, because I know you well enough to know you didn't drive all the way over here to shoot the idiot on the floor over there, off me, then drive back to your place. If that's what you wanted, Kevin would have been given orders to eliminate me himself. Once he stepped foot in your office demanding payment, you would have taken him out in private. This..." he pointed to the dead man bleeding all over the floor. "This is messy and you want something for your trouble. So, what is it?"

Dom grinned and moved further into the room.

Blake adjusted. He now had a clean shot of Dominic Zarconi. His finger twitched, what he wouldn't do to pull the trigger and end this once and for all.

"You're right," Dom shrugged. "I want to know if you're the one that's been messing with my organization."

"I think you need to be a little more specific," Rowdy answered.

"What is he doing?" Theresa jumped to her feet and began to pace. "He's taunting that monster. Does he realize Dom will just shoot him if he doesn't like the answer?"

"Tony," Skeet said softly. "Why don't you take Theresa down to the car? You guys can load up this box, and I'll join you in a minute."

Tony studied Theresa, then picked up the box in one hand and took Theresa's hand in the other. He gave her a little tug and pulled her out the door. He didn't like this. He needed to be in that room with Rowdy, but he also had to protect Theresa. This was an impossible situation, and there were so many ways it could end in disaster.

Theresa let Tony pull her out the door. Once in the hallway, she turned toward the elevator.

"No," he said. "We're taking the stairs. Dom could have men waiting in the lobby."

"Right," Theresa nodded. As they made their way down one floor after another, Theresa became more and more frightened for Rowdy. They had no idea what they had gotten themselves into - the kind of man they were taunting. She was still lost in thought when three men stepped from the shadows and attacked. She screamed, turned and tried to run.

Moondance Ridge

Tony was prepared for the first blow, but he hadn't realized there were three of them. He was bogged down with the heavy box and needed his hands free. *Well, it can't be helped*, he thought as he dropped the box to the floor. The fight was on. He realized Theresa wasn't sticking with him, she had turned and started to run up the stairs. One of the men broke off and chased after her. Tony tried to follow, but was blocked by a second man. He was now being attacked by only two, but Theresa was vulnerable. He pivoted and kicked out, connecting with the man on the stairs below him. The guy stumbled backwards and teetered on the edge of a stair, Tony took advantage of his loss of balance and kicked out again, connecting with the aggressor's midsection. The man flailed his arms as he unceremoniously tumbled down the stairs. Tony turned just in time to dodge a sucker punch, came back around and slammed the man's head into the wall. Bad guy number two was out cold. Tony turned and ran.

Theresa nearly made it to the first door, the one directly above them, but as she grabbed the handle an arm wrapped around her waist and pulled her against her pursuer's chest. She didn't know this man, had never seen him before and already didn't like him. He had an evil look in his eyes as he dragged her out of the stairwell and marched her to the elevator. Within what seemed like seconds, they were standing in front of the penthouse door. The man knocked and waited.

"Apparently, we have company," Dom said hesitantly. "Answer it."

Rowdy walked to the door and frowned when a man stepped inside, dragging Theresa behind him.

"Who is she?" Rowdy asked.

"Don't play with me, Cooper. You know very well who that is. I believe she works for you; at that bar in Mount Haven. The one you own with another woman, I assume she's your sister-in-law," Dom frowned when he still didn't get a response. "I'm guessing the feisty woman with the dog is your wife."

Rowdy didn't bite.

"That's okay, you don't have to say anything," Dom turned to look at the newcomers. "Hello, Theresa."

Theresa? Skeet thought. Where was Tony? Something must have happened on their way to the car. He stepped into the hallway and pulled the fire alarm. There was no way to know how many men Zarconi had in the building, but a thousand hotel guests running around trying to escape might be enough to slow them down.

"Check it out," Dom ordered. Theresa's captor left the room.

"It's me you want," Theresa moved to stand next to Rowdy. "Let him go."

"I don't think you are in a position to give orders, sweetheart." He raised his pistol and pointed it at Rowdy's head. "He can join that pregnant partner of his. I sent my men to deal with her over an hour ago. I'm sure they've taken care of it by now."

Rowdy laughed.

"If you don't believe me, call your brother."

"I don't have to," Rowdy shrugged. "She left town ages ago. She's out of your reach. I'm at least five steps ahead of you, Zarconi. I know you, know your games and your tactics. It was only a matter of time before you'd go after my family."

"Well," Dom shrugged. "She might be long gone, but the vicious dog and that feisty woman of yours aren't safe. In fact, they probably both have a bullet hole between their eyes right about now. I'd be happy to provide a reunion."

Rowdy hoped Coop was back and had saved Bailey from Dom's goons. Otherwise, Knight would handle it, he had to believe that. He just hoped he didn't lose his dog in the process.

"Still no reaction," Dom was furious, but he didn't want this man to see just how angry he was. The cop was supposed to beg, he was supposed to express his agony over hearing the people he loved were dead. He was supposed to spill his guts. "That's okay, I know I can get a response from Theresa," he shifted and pointed the gun at her head. "Decisions, decisions. Who should I shoot first?" Dom gave Theresa an evil grin as he once again pointed the revolver at Rowdy's head.

The loud but distinct boom of a gunshot echoed throughout the room then everything went eerily silent. Suddenly, the room was filled with blinding light as an even louder explosion erupted.

* * * *

Tony struggled to get through the crowd. He had to find Theresa. Chances were pretty good their attackers worked for Dom, which meant they would take Theresa to their boss. He rounded the corner and nearly collided with Skeet. "Was that your doing?" he pointed to the speakers that were still sounding an alarm?

"Yeah," Skeet shrugged. "I thought it might help."

"It might have," Tony relented. "I have no idea how many of them are here."

"Theresa is in the room with Rowdy," Skeet provided as they moved in next to the door. The two men froze when they heard the gunshot. Tony frantically slid his key through the lock and yanked open the door. Theresa tumbled onto the floor at his feet.

"Get her clear," Skeet yelled as he glanced inside and spotted Dom on the floor, a large wound to his thigh was bleeding profusely. He had just located Rowdy, uninjured, when the world erupted. Bright light filled the room as the unbearably, loud boom echoed throughout the small space. He ducked his head in an attempt to protect his ringing ears, reached inside, grabbed Rowdy's arm and yanked him into the hallway.

They were all still trying to get their bearings when Blake dropped from the ceiling grinning. He yanked bright blue earplugs from each ear then frowned. "Run!" he called as he took off down the long corridor.

Tony helped Theresa to her feet, grabbed her hand and started to run. Rowdy and Skeet followed. The instant they reached the elevator, Blake pushed the button and the doors flew open.

One of the guest making their way to the stairwell called back to them. "If there's a fire, you shouldn't take the elevator."

The group stepped inside and waited impatiently as the car descended to the lobby. Skeet stepped from the elevator, glanced around and locked eyes with Ellison. The agent blinked, then turned and headed for the stairs. Skeet followed his friends into the garage and paused for a quick look around as they all gathered at the Beemer. "I'll drive," Skeet told them before climbing behind the wheel. "I need the keys."

Moondance Ridge

Blake climbed into the passenger seat, Rowdy and Tony slid into the back. Tony pulled Theresa onto his lap as he handed the keys to Blake.

They had just pulled onto the highway, headed to the outskirts of town when Rowdy asked the question on all of their minds. "Where in the hell did you get a flash bang? My ears are still ringing, you moron. I hope you know how to disappear, because if I end up deaf on top of everything else…"

Blake grinned. "You'll live."

"I'm not sure that's what Stan had in mind when he gave you that device," Skeet shot his fellow agent a look of censure.

Tony laughed. Theresa punched him, then sobered. The reality of what just happened, the fact that they all could have died, the knowledge that Dom was still out there…free, was all too much. Her eyes misted and she frantically tried to wipe the tears away wishing she was stronger, but knowing she wasn't.

"Hey," Tony said softly.

"This entire trip was a failure. You guys thought you could fight him, but you can't," she insisted. "After everything we did, Dom almost killed Rowdy."

"Where are we going?" Rowdy finally asked as he ended the call that had just gone to voicemail. Where was Coop and was Bailey and Knight okay? Dom knew far too much about his family.

"I need to find a place I can contact Stan," Skeet provided. "Since we've been working with the local AFT, I thought their building would do."

Rowdy dialed Coop's phone again at the same time Skeet's began to ring.

* * * *

Coop stepped on the gas, pushing his office vehicle to nearly a hundred. He had to get to Bailey before Zarconi's men did. He pumped the brakes, took the off-ramp as fast as he dared and careened around the corner. Once he was on the highway that lead to their ranch, he punched it again. Finally, he reached the entrance. He pumped the brakes again and took the turn onto the driveway a little too fast, the back tires slid, then caught and the vehicle lunged forward. That's when he saw them, three men approaching the front of Rowdy's residence. He pulled the car to the side, jumped out and took off, heading toward the back door at a full run.

Bailey had just slipped on her shoes, planning to take Knight for a walk when Coop burst through the back door. "What's wrong?"

Coop spotted Knight's leash and snapped it on the dog who was alert and focused on the front door. He gripped Bailey's wrist and pulled her back outside, dragging Knight behind them. They had barely reached the tree line when Bailey heard a loud crash. Knight pulled at the leash, desperate to return to the house. He let out a bark, then a low growl as Coop drug him through the trees by force.

"They found me?" she swallowed and let Coop pull her to the car, which was still running. Once inside, Coop flipped the vehicle around, bouncing over the edge of the driveway taking out a swath of newly grown foliage and dirt clods. Once the vehicle returned to the gravel drive, he accelerated and headed for the highway. He needed to get as far away as possible, as fast as possible, just in case they tried to follow.

"Car one," a male voice came over the radio.

"Go ahead, Derek," Coop answered.

"I saw you fly by and decided to follow. Do you need a back?"

"Meet me at the station," Coop decided.

"Uh..." Derek said. "A car with three occupants just pulled out of your lane. I'm not sure the station is your best option. Probably don't want a standoff with Mariah in the house."

Coop considered, Derek was right. He was out of options, they couldn't go to the bar, his house was too close to Rowdy's and Derek was right, the station was out. Where could he hole up until he formulated a plan to apprehend Zarconi's thugs?

"You could take her to my place," Derek offered, assuming Coop now had Bailey in the car with him. "I have a guest room and nobody will figure it out. I haven't transferred the title yet," he added cryptically, hoping if anyone was listening they wouldn't figure it out.

"Thanks," Coop agreed. "I'll meet you there. Don't engage with the suspects. They're armed and dangerous."

"Copy."

* * * *

Coop picked up after the first ring. "It's about time you called."

"What's wrong?" Rowdy asked, worried now.

"Haven't you talked to the computer guys?" Coop asked.

Rowdy frowned. "Skeet might be talking to them now, why?"

Coop outlined what had happened, how they intercepted the information and relayed the bad news that a dozen men were headed to Mount Haven to destroy anything in their wake.

"Is Bailey okay?"

"Yeah," Coop said. "I barely got there in time; if I hadn't been warned, the situation would have been a lot worse. There's no telling what might have gone down out there."

"But it wasn't," Rowdy looked at Tony who was clearly curious. "You owe the geeks something spectacular."

"They heard that," Skeet provided. "Are you talking to Coop?"

"Yeah," Rowdy said. "Thank them for me, Coop got there in time. Bailey and Knight are safe. They decided to close the bar down so nobody gets caught in the crosshairs. Marnie went back to college and Mags and Bryan should be hanging with Angie by now."

"We need a plan," Skeet grumbled.

"My plan is to go home," Tony advised the group. "If Dom is taking the war to Mount Haven, I'm going to Mount Haven."

"I agree," Rowdy said soberly. "Coop needs our help."

"Okay," Skeet agreed. "I'll advise Burns when we get to the AFT office."

"Did you hear that," Rowdy asked Coop. "We're coming home."

"I would never ask," Coop admitted. "But, that is music to my ears."

"I'll call you with specifics when I know more," Rowdy said. "And, thanks for taking care of my girl."

"You know I would do anything to keep her safe," Coop hung up and began to pace. A war was coming to his city, and he needed to be prepared.

* * * *

"Wow," Marc cringed as Zarconi slid one metal crutch across his desk, knocking the contents to the floor before he began to curse. "I'm not sure I've even heard some of those expletives and I'm pretty well versed in gutter talk."

Carson grinned. "Funny, we took his guns and he was a little annoyed, took his girls and he didn't seem to notice, took his drugs and he was pissed but still mostly in control. But, take his money... complete meltdown."

"You did notice he hasn't gone into the human trafficking account yet, didn't you?"

"Yeah," Carson shrugged. "That didn't escape my notice." He frowned, what was the next level of maniac after what they were witnessing? He wasn't sure he wanted to know, the answer might be more frightening than he could deal with.

"Maybe someone should tell him to look on the bright side," Marc turned his head to the side and watched the tantrum continue. "I mean, I left a million in each account. I left over a hundred million in the trafficking account so the feds could find it. We could have taken everything and left him completely destitute."

"Somehow, I don't think he'd appreciate our generosity," Carson dropped into the chair next to Marc. "We did do the right thing, didn't we?"

"As long as you did your job in the masterful way you always do, yes." Marc pivoted to look at his friend. "What? You're obviously having second thoughts. Which part is bothering you?"

He lifted his head toward the monitor. "That for one," he admitted. "We've never seen the aftermath before. I've never seen that kind of anger before. If he ever found out it was us."

"He won't," Marc said confidently. "And, I think I found something. A way to tie Zarconi to Danny J."

Carson moved his chair closer and listened as Marc explained Danny's system, the signature he left and how he had extracted the revision dates. The digital data was enough to convince them Danny Jones built this system. It wasn't conclusive, but it might be enough to tie Dominic to Danny J. He wasn't sure how it would help, but they now had a theoretical tie.

Moondance Ridge

"Burns," Stan answered after several rings.

"It's Skeet," he said immediately. "We're at the ATF building but we are heading out."

"What do you mean by that?" Stan asked.

"I mean we are all heading to Mount Haven to protect the town," Skeet advised. "Dom has nearly a dozen men headed that way. Actually, they might be there by now if he had access to a flight."

"What about Detroit?" Stan frowned. "We're not finished. I still haven't found the warehouse with the girls."

"We have enough to nail him for good," Skeet said confidently. "If you want, I'll go arrest him before I leave. Maybe he'll tell us where they are himself."

"Not yet. We can't risk it," Stan objected. "We're close on the human trafficking Op. Jacobs got a warrant to monitor the calls of Zarconi and several of his men. We need him mobile. We're... and by that, I mean she's... developing a plan to save the girls before we lock him up for good."

"And the agents?" Skeet asked. "The dirty cops? When are you going to deal with them?"

Stan sighed. "Darrow's body surfaced about an hour ago."

"He's dead," Skeet realized. "And Ellison?"

"He's still working, doesn't seem to realize we're closing in," Stan admitted. "We need to keep it that way. Once we tie this up with Jacobs, I'll take care of Ellison myself."

"Then it sounds like you don't need us in Detroit, anyway," Skeet surmised. "Can you tie Darrow to Zarconi?"

"Not so far," Stan admitted.

"Cause of death?"

"Bullet between the eyes," Burns provided.

"Maybe you can then," Skeet considered. "That seems to be his signature move. Snag Kevin's body from the hotel and see if the bullets match. If so, you have him."

"Kevin who?" Burns asked. "I think I'm missing something important. I wasn't aware there was a body at the hotel. Word is the place is still in chaos."

Skeet filled him in on what had happened, including Blake using the explosive Burn's had authorized as a diversion. "Kevin Laforge was stupid and greedy. He also kidnapped Rowdy, so he's not a saint; but I'd still like to see Zarconi pay for his death. He gunned that kid down in cold blood, and there's a witness. A credible one."

"Rowdy?" Stan clarified.

"Right," Skeet confirmed. "And Blake. If the bullet in Kevin matches the bullet in Darrow…"

"We can nail him," Burns agreed. "Okay, go to Montana and save the town. It looks like it was a smart move to get Maggie Cooper away for a while. Reassure Andy when you see him, I know he's going to be on edge. Don't worry, I'm not attached to this in any way other than the obvious. FBI Directors do not work cases themselves, they have people for that... as far as anyone knows. Everyone at the house is perfectly safe, and I've advised my security team to be on alert as an added precaution. They'll call the cops immediately, even on something minor."

"Thanks," Skeet sighed. "That gives me one less thing to worry about. We both know with a dozen hardened criminals in a small town, this could get ugly."

"Do what you have to do," Burns told him. "I've got your back. What happened to the documents? The files and the borrowed computers?"

"Oh," he turned to glance at Tony, "I don't know." He placed his hand over the mouthpiece. "Tony, what happened to the evidence and the computers?"

"Bellhop retrieved them for us. I had him lock them back in the office. He said everything was still in the box when he snagged it from the stairwell. Still had the lid attached; so the stuff is secure," Tony advised.

"There's not any actual evidence," Skeet informed. "Just reports, articles from Zach Regan, printouts of what is stored on that cloud system, stuff like that. It's located in the office we set up at the hotel. Tony got an employee to secure it for us."

"I'll send someone over to retrieve it," Burns assured him. "Call me when you touch down, and I'll give you an update."

Skeet disconnected the call and turned to take in the small group. "We're all set. Now, I just have to figure out how to get us there."

498

"Are you forgetting I own a jet?" Tony asked. "One that happens to be at the airport waiting for us to finish this mission and head home?"

"I'm not sure I actually knew that," Blake told him. "How soon can we leave?"

"I'll call the pilot and tell him to prepare for takeoff in two hours. That should give us enough time to gather our stuff and get to the airport," Tony walked away to make arrangements.

Rowdy stepped to the window and stared out at the city. Skeet moved in and studied his friend. They were silent for several minutes before Rowdy explained what was on his mind. "Darrow is dead?"

"He is," Skeet nodded.

"Ellison?"

"At work, as far as I know," Skeet assured him.

"You do realize it's because of us," Rowdy never turned from the window. "I should have anticipated that. We harassed Zarconi, took his guns, the drugs and those girls. He hired Darrow to intervene, to stop the feds from getting too close and he couldn't do that. Not with us calling the shots. Darrow couldn't give Dom advanced warning about anything in the pike coming his way because the feds didn't know our next move. An agent is dead because I did everything I could to hit Dom where it would hurt."

"We hit him where it hurt. It was a joint effort," Skeet sighed. "Agent Darrow is dead because he chose to work for the mob. And, because he made promises he never could have kept. He's dead, because he swore to uphold the law, then he decided to break it. As difficult as it is, you have to shake that sick feeling in your gut that's sitting there like a lead balloon."

Rowdy turned and glanced at Skeet, realizing his friend was experiencing the same guilt he was over the senseless death of an agent.

"Do it now, because we have bigger problems. The same man that shot Darrow, that killed Kevin right before your eyes and planned to kill you, has a dozen men headed to your town. He's targeting your family and you need to be on your game if we're going to stop him."

Rowdy turned back to look over the city, he stood there silently staring into the distance for several minutes before he nodded, turned and went in search of Tony.

* * * *

Tony was strolling across the tarmac when his phone rang. "Hey, everything go according to plan in Destination Unknown?"

"I'm gone for less than two days," John said clearly annoyed. "Two damn days and the instant I hit the states, I hear of chaos and mayhem in Detroit. Have you ever heard the word discreet? How about covert? Fire alarms, dead bodies and flash bangs?"

Tony laughed. "Glad you made it back okay."

"Clearly, you have a cluster on your hands," John persisted.

"Okay," Tony shrugged. "I get it. We're not discussing your secret mission. Things here got a little out of hand, but we're dealing with it." He motioned for Theresa to ascend the stairs and board the plane.

"If this is what you call dealing, I'm glad you went into business, buddy."

Theresa carefully climbed the metal stairs, took two steps inside the airplane and came to an abrupt stop. Who was that man? He was sitting so casually in one of the lounge chairs as if he owned Tony's jet.

Tony laughed. "Pays better," he was completely taken by surprise when he collided with Theresa's back. He wrapped an arm around her waist and pulled her against him, hoping it would steady them both and prevent a fall. The look on her face registered trouble. Tony followed the direction of her stare and smiled. He quickly maneuvered around Theresa's frozen form and pulled his friend into a tight embrace. "What are you doing here?"

"Like I said," John smiled. "I heard you had trouble."

Realization hit and Tony frowned. "You didn't cut your trip short because of me, did you?"

"Naw," John took a step back. "I told you it was a quick run. I was at the airport looking forward to a hot shower and a relaxing evening with a good Scotch when a buddy called. Said he heard Detroit was hot. When my name surfaced, Bandit called to see if I wanted help. Apparently, Sticky mentioned the bird drop over beers to a few friends and the rest ballooned from there. You know how it is, the line is active but usually reliable. I decided to take a detour. The New York side of this op seemed like a bust, anyway. I saw the jet when I arrived and figured you must be on your way. It seemed like as good a place as any to meet up." He placed a hand on Tony's shoulder and shook his head. "I'm glad you're okay."

"We're on our way out," Tony explained. "Dom sent over a dozen thugs to Mount Haven to take out Bailey."

John frowned and his eyes hardened. "Not gonna happen, not in this lifetime. That man has no idea who he's messing with. Putting a hit on our girl crossed a line and sealed the fate of more than a dozen thugs."

Rowdy frowned and narrowed his eyes at the newcomer.

Tony saw Rowdy's face and smiled. "Meet Rowdy Cooper, Bailey's number one man. I think he might take exception to your reference to our girl. But then again, he'd probably take issue with any reference that doesn't identify Bailey Zander as his and only his." Tony grinned and leaned in closer. "He's a little on the protective side. Kind of possessive and intolerant, too."

John stepped forward and held out a hand. "Great to finally meet you in person."

Rowdy studied Tony's friend as he accepted the greeting. "Haven't heard much about you, I have to say, but I will thank you for your service."

"Ditto," John turned to Theresa. "And, you must be the woman of the hour. The unfortunate soul that captured Tony's heart and threw in a little excitement for good measure."

Theresa cocked her head and looked at the stranger. She didn't know how to take his arrogance or his assessment of the situation.

"That's Blake Cochran and Skeeter Perkins," Tony pointed. "As you know, they're both FBI. This is the infamous John Buckley."

502

Blake stepped forward. "It's an honor to meet you in person. Do your friends still call you Buck?"

"Everyone but this guy," he pointed to Tony with his thumb. "Apparently, he's not that good at adapting."

Tony rolled his eyes and directed Theresa to one of the comfortable chairs. "We should get settled. I'll tell the pilot we're ready for take-off. We have a long flight." He turned to John. "Coming or staying? I can have Aero drop you anywhere you want."

"Coming," John settled back into the comfortable chair. "I'm in the mood for a little fun. Man, I can't believe your pilot let that nickname stick."

"What can I say?" Tony shrugged. "He worships me."

"Yeah," John mocked. "You just keep telling yourself that."

Rowdy shifted around the group and moved to the other side of the plane. He glanced around, then dropped into the chair next to a window. Their new addition just might end up being a liability. One, Rowdy and his family couldn't afford. What they were about to deal with wasn't going to be fun. And, the fact that John Buckley labelled it that way, spoke volumes.

"I think he's okay," Skeet said, settling in next to Rowdy. "I can read you like a book, you can't fool me... not about this. You're nervous about his involvement, but I think he's okay."

"Guess that depends on your definition of okay," Rowdy grumbled. "This is my family we're talking about. Ensuring their safety is not fun. It's essential."

Moondance Ridge

"I agree," Skeet stretched out his legs. "But for a guy like that, it's also a way of life. If you lived the way he does, punishing a few bad guys might seem fun. We both know he's seen and done things we couldn't imagine in our worst nightmare. I respect him… and I think I'm grateful he volunteered to join our humble group. We could certainly use the extra help."

Rowdy just nodded and prepared for take-off. Skeet stood and moved to settle in next to Blake.

"He doesn't seem to like me much," John said softly, watching Rowdy out of the corner of his eye.

Tony smiled. "His family is under attack, and you just said this was all about fun. What did you expect?"

John frowned, "I didn't mean it that way."

"As I see it," Tony continued. "It's good for you. Your ego could use a little reality check now and again. Rowdy's too grounded for hero worship. We both know, a typical reaction to the magnificent John Buckley is more in line with that greeting from Blake."

"I never said he should worship me," John objected. "But if we're going to work together, it might be nice if he didn't hate me."

"Well," Tony smiled. "I guess you're in luck. Hate is a pretty strong emotion and from the look on Rowdy's face… you're just not that important."

John flipped him the bird as he stood and made his way across the plane. He paused momentarily before settling in next to Rowdy.

"I think we got off on the wrong track," John said immediately. "I haven't seen Tony for a long time; and somehow when I'm near him, I tend to speak before I think. I guess... I hope you know I am taking this seriously. It's the reason I decided to join you. I'm sorry if my comment came across as insensitive and callous. I've dealt with guys like Zarconi before. His men should not be underestimated. I'm just saying I'm here to help, that's all. On a personal note, I'm told you're important to Bailey," he shrugged. "That would be enough. I have your back, you can count on that. You should also know, I looked into you... All of you. I needed to know what kind of people Tony was working with. Needed to assure myself he was safe and protected. Your history is complicated but respectable. Thanks for having his back, I appreciate it."

"You two go back pretty far, I assume," Rowdy asked.

"I can't remember a time I didn't know Tony," John smiled.

"He said the man that took him in, Conrad Werner had a way of rescuing lost souls. Are you one of Conrad's lost boys?" Rowdy asked.

John got a faraway look and sighed. "Con was unique. He was one of the smartest men I've ever known but his most admirable quality was his compassion. I suppose if you asked Con, he would have claimed me as one of his. But, I was never a street rat like Tony. I had a home if you want to call it that. I had a mother, again... if you want to call her that. She worked just hard enough to pay her way into the next party. I was on my own most of the time; and when I wasn't, her flavor of the month was usually knocking me around. Con always knew when I needed a place to escape. A refuge from reality, I guess," John gave a short laugh. "And, he somehow made it sound like I'd be doing him a favor if I crashed in his back bedroom."

"Sounds like a great guy," Rowdy observed.

"He was," John agreed. "It was a blow to all of us when we lost him."

"I'm a little surprised Tony stayed on track," Rowdy considered that a great accomplishment for a kid his age, especially once he was on his own again.

"He almost didn't," John admitted. "He got lost for a while, but Con pushed him, even from the grave. Conrad Werner knew Tony better than anyone. Knew what that kid would need to push forward and make something of his life. I'm proud of him, Tony has come a long way. I wish Con could see him now."

Rowdy studied John and realized he'd jumped to conclusions. Yes, John was tough and maybe a little hard around the edges; but he was also loyal and honorable. He thought about his own life, the trials, the split-second decisions that had altered his destiny. Then, he thought about the job, the things he had seen, been forced to do, the lives he'd altered when he gave them bad news, and he understood John a little better. "I'm sure it helped to have you in his corner."

"Mostly," John admitted. "I think it's helped me to have Tony in my corner."

Rowdy understood that, too. The two of them were like brothers, and John would walk through fire to protect Tony. It was the reason he climbed onto this plane, the reason he was flying to Montana instead of New York. Why he was walking into battle, instead of settling in with that bottle of Scotch. Rowdy glanced at

Skeet and relaxed. His friend would do the same for him; was doing the same. And, just like Tony and John, he knew Skeet would walk through fire for him. He'd do the same for Skeet. That was the reason they would prevail against Dom's men. Paid thugs could never understand the bond this group had. That lack of understanding was going to give their enemy a significant disadvantage.

"Hey," Tony stood and moved to settle in next to John. "You two good now? Looks to me like all the kinks have been worked out."

"We're good," Rowdy assured him.

"Great, I haven't seen this guy in months," he glanced at John to make sure he was content with the truce he'd made with Rowdy. Yep, back on top like always. Tony was still surprised that a man like John could find a way to get along with anyone. "It might be nice if we could catch up and, I don't know... have an actual conversation. Or are you going to ditch me for the hotshot cowboy?"

John glanced at Rowdy then back at Tony and shrugged. "He's probably more interesting. You? You're an open book that calls me so much these days, I haven't had time to miss you," John countered.

Rowdy grinned at the two friends' byplay and settled in for a long flight. If nothing else, it should be entertaining. After the last few weeks, Tony needed some relaxing fun with an old friend. Rowdy needed Bailey and his family. He couldn't wait to get home, to see for himself that Bailey was okay. To check on Knight and Coop. A feeling of foreboding settled over him. He was worried. They were flying into a hornets' nest, one that involved more than

Moondance Ridge

a dozen dangerous men; and they didn't have a plan. In fact, they didn't even have a place to stay.

Chapter Thirteen

The group was gathered in Derek's small living room, trying to come up with a plan. Not only did they need to combat Zarconi's men, they needed a safe place to hole up while they did it.

"What about that fishing lodge?" John asked Theresa.

"Nobody is supposed to know about that," she said in surprise.

"It wasn't hard to track," Tony admitted. "I'd guess Dominic even knows about it by now."

"It certainly has enough space for all of us," John continued. "Plus, the wilderness area gives me an edge."

"If he does know, wouldn't that be the first place they'll look?" she asked.

"Probably," Rowdy agreed. "But, I think he'll go out there anyway. Or send someone. I'm afraid he might do something drastic."

"Like what?" Theresa asked.

"Like try to destroy it," John agreed soberly. "Just another reason we should relocate. If we're there, we can stop them."

"Or die trying," Theresa mumbled.

* * * *

Several hours later, the group started trickling in at Moondance Ridge. They had split up, realizing they had a lot to do to prepare for a stay at the rustic resort that hadn't been functional for years. Theresa warned them she didn't have access to the buildings, so they would have to break in. There was a generator, but it would certainly need gas and could be clogged due to lack of use. The water was probably shut off... the list seemed to go on forever. There were so many obstacles, she wondered if moving to the neglected vacation getaway was a good idea.

One by one, the cars arrived. Everyone seemed to be confident it was the right plan... everyone but Theresa. She stepped from the vehicle and moved to the majestic stairs of the old lodge and settled near the top. Bailey climbed in next to her.

"You look upset," Bailey observed. "Melancholy for sure, but I'm getting the distinct impression you don't want to be here."

"I tried so hard to protect this place," Theresa glanced around and realized just how much she had to lose if they failed. Not only the resort, but the people helping her. They were all in so much danger and it was her fault. In her heart, she wondered if she should have surrendered years ago.

"Accepting help after shutting yourself off for so long isn't easy," Bailey said softly. "I understand, I've been there." She glanced up and smiled when Tony and the rest of the guys pulled up next to her car and began piling out of the vehicle. "It was probably the hardest thing I ever did when I called Tony and asked for help. I needed him, the company needed him, but it made me feel inadequate. Like I had failed my father and couldn't make it on my own. I've come to understand things a little better now."

"What do you mean?" Theresa asked, focusing on her uncle's old cabin off in the distance.

"I mean," Bailey followed her gaze. "I fled, like you did. It was the right thing to do at the time, I've finally accepted that reality as well. But, the guilt I felt when I learned of additional victims, the sorrow I experienced when I realized how serious the problems were in my father's company... my company, and all the rest got in the way for a while. In the end, I realized I had to run, I didn't have any other option. The same is true for you. You couldn't fight this Dominic guy alone. But, you've convinced yourself shutting everyone out makes you stronger. For the past two years, needing help of any kind was a sign of weakness and it put others in danger. I get it, but that's all over now. We are all here to help you. To defeat the monster that's been chasing you far too long so you can move forward. I suspect it's been a long time since you've been able to do that. Move forward I mean," Bailey paused. "What is that building you keep looking at?"

Moondance Ridge

"It's where Uncle Dean lived. His personal residence."

"Do you think he has a set of master keys in there?"

Theresa considered for several seconds. "Maybe," she finally decided. "He always kept a spare set in the mud room out back."

"Hey," Bailey yelled. "Tony, I need your help."

Tony's head appeared over the open door of the trunk. He smiled as he casually strolled over and stopped at the base of the stairs. "What's up?"

"Theresa's uncle lived over there in that cabin," Bailey pointed. "We were thinking he might have a master set of keys inside. If you can get in, we might not need to replace the locks after all."

Tony glanced at the modest structure situated up a small driveway and nestled against the majestic pines and rolling hills. "Let's take the car, you drive. I'll see what I can do." The three of them traveled the short distance together in silence. Tony jumped from the vehicle the instant it came to a stop. He began circling the structure, looking for a way to get inside. Theresa and Bailey moved to the front porch and peered through the crack in the curtains to get a better look. Both women jumped when the front door flew open.

"How did you get inside already?" Bailey asked immediately.

"Key," Tony held up the brass object for them to see as he lingered in the doorway. "You just had to know where to look."

"How did you know where to look?" Theresa asked.

Tony shrugged one shoulder. "Homeless kid."

"I don't even want to know what that means," Theresa said, pushing past Tony to step into her Uncle's domain. Memories and emotions flooded her. It had been so long since she'd been here, but she remembered the tiniest detail like it was yesterday. Once again, she wished she hadn't abandoned him. Wished she'd been here when he needed her. Wished they had time together after her mother's death.

Tony took Theresa's hand and pulled her further into the cabin. "No time for regrets, any idea where the keys might be?"

"He used to keep a spare set in the mud room out back."

"To the mud room," Tony intoned.

Bailey laughed and Theresa smiled.

"We've got keys." Tony declared, holding up a large keyring as he climbed out of the car. "The lodge, the rooms, the cabins... you name it, we can open it."

"I thought you said the keys didn't exist," John pushed off the truck he was casually leaning against, grabbed his bag from the bed, and shrugged. "Makes my job easier. Don't wait up." He turned and disappeared around the back of the house.

"Where is he going?" Bailey asked.

"He's setting up a few surprises for our friends. John's destruction... it's everywhere you want to be," Tony laughed. "I need to remember that one, he could use it in advertising."

"Should he go out there alone?" Theresa asked.

"He wouldn't have it any other way," Tony shrugged. "Trust him, he's a professional, and he knows what he's doing. We'll all be safer for it. He's gone for the rest of the night. Don't wait up, we won't see him again until morning."

Theresa frowned. Bailey gazed into the tree-lined wilderness, already worried about her friend.

"Okay, Coop and I will check out the generator," Rowdy decided. "Tony, you see if we have water. I'm pretty sure with the fresh lake and the river, Clawson would have opted for a well. It's more efficient with all the cabins and outbuildings, but it may need significant cleaning and repair. Nothing a slick businessman can't handle I'm sure," he added with a grin. Tony rolled his eyes and shook his head.

"Blake and I will unload the vehicles," Skeet provided. "Why don't you ladies go check on our accommodations?"

The group worked well into the night. By the time they were finished, the generator was running, the water was flowing and the beds were ready for company. Bailey had set out snack trays, deciding something light and easy was the way to go on their first night. One by one, they gathered in the lounge. Eventually, everyone was present and accounted for... except John.

"Should we check on him?" Bailey asked.

"Not unless you have a death wish," Tony said casually.

"I'm serious, what if he's in trouble?" Bailey persisted.

"Bailey," Tony sighed. "You know John, you know what he does, you know he won't be back until long after we've all fallen asleep. Stop worrying. He's fine. I know it's been awhile, but have you completely forgotten how that man lives?"

"No," she dropped into a comfortable chair. "But, that doesn't mean I have to like it."

* * * *

Dom slammed the phone on his desk and fumed. Every time he turned around, he was being hit with another problem. Now, some idiot doctor thought he was going to stay in bed for weeks. The imbecile. He had an organization to run. One that was under attack. It was bad enough he had to deal with those annoying crutches. If he couldn't handle the pain, he could always self-medicate. He shifted forward intending to log into his bank account when his phone rang... again.

"Yeah," he barked.

"Hey boss," Murph Bennet hesitated. Dom didn't sound happy today and he was about to make things worse.

"What's up, Murph?" Dom asked.

"We have a problem," he said tentatively.

"I don't need another problem," Dom barked. "What now?"

"Well uh..." he swallowed hard. "Federico just called. He's beyond livid. Said the girls never arrived. I told him that's not possible. I shipped them out personally, but he insists they've gone missing. Says his buyers are in a tizzy and it needs to be fixed."

"What exactly do you mean by shipped them out personally?" Dom growled.

Moondance Ridge

"I mean I pulled them out and loaded them in the back of the truck and watched it pull away headed for the drop-off. Everything went real smooth, no problems at all. I can't see how those women didn't arrive, but he insists I'm wrong," Murph answered. "I can't explain it. Women don't just vanish, I know that much."

"No," Dom gritted his teeth. "They don't. If Federico calls back, tell him to call me directly. I'll look into this."

"Sorry boss," Murph added. "I don't know what could have happened, but it sounds like you didn't need more trouble today."

Dom ended the call and logged into his bank account. The first step was making sure his buyers had paid him. If everything looked good, he may need to give them a partial refund. Further investigation would be essential. Worse case, if something went wrong on his end, he could always offer them a different product. A replacement girl for their trouble should appease them. Trafficking the girls was normally easy money. Oh, it had been a challenge initially, but these days his operation ran like a well-oiled machine. He'd perfected it quickly, just like he had his drug operation. The arms market was another story, he had more than a few setbacks on that front. He was managing them though. The Phantom worried him, but he could handle it... somehow. His business plan was right on track, by the end of the year his network would be in complete control. Nothing would come or go out of Detroit without his knowledge. Now, if he could just resolve the Theresa Regan problem, he could relax.

His stared at the screen in wide-eyed shock. That wasn't possible. He blinked, exited the account and logged back in. The screen refreshed with the same result, nearly half of his money was gone. Vanished completely. His mind raced, somebody was trying to destroy him. He still hadn't tracked the person who stole the funds from his secret accounts. Nearly three hundred and fifty million dollars siphoned down to three... now this. Dom began violently throwing things off his desk. The phone, a marble pen holder, a decorative crystal business card caddy all traveled across the room and smashed against the wall. It wasn't enough. He wanted to lash out against someone, anyone. He longed for some annoying, low-level employee to enter the room with one of their routine interruptions... he needed a target, any target he could shoot to relieve his anger.

Was it possible the investigation into his enterprise was more extensive than he originally believed? Had the feds taken his girls along with his money? All of his money. No, the legal system provided a means to freeze his accounts, not steal his balance. When he got to the bottom of this, the culprit was going to pay. His gut told him it had something to do with Theresa Regan and that ex-cop.

Dom turned and glanced out the window. He'd get Ellison working on it immediately, but first... he was going to teach Theresa a valuable lesson. He pulled out his phone and dialed a number.

"Hello," Joe answered on the second ring.

"I want you to go out to that fishing resort, Moondance Ridge or some nonsense, the one you found while researching Theresa's family. I think you said it belonged to her dead uncle. Burn the place down. Destroy every building, I want it leveled."

"Okay," Joe paused. "Do you want it anonymous like or should they know who did it?"

Dom considered. "Anonymous. I don't want that sheriff interfering any more than necessary."

Moondance Ridge

"I'll take care of it," Joe hung up and considered. Geo and Horatio should be back any minute with dinner. Once they returned, he'd enlist their help to develop a plan. He didn't like it, but these days he didn't like anything he was forced to do for Zarconi.

Dom dialed a second number. "Geovanni."

"Boss," Geo answered as he casually placed the takeout in the backseat.

"I told Joe to level Moondance Ridge," he advised. "Joe fills a need, but he's never had the stomach to do what's necessary. I need you and Horatio to make sure he follows through."

"Consider it done," Geovanni said as he climbed behind the wheel. He glanced at the phone and shook his head when he realized Dom had already disconnected.

Dominic continued to stare into the darkened nightscape sprinkled with dancing lights as he made another call. "Ellison, Darrow is gone. I need you to take his place."

"Okay," Ellison agreed. He didn't have a choice, he'd sold his soul to the devil long ago and was so deep in hell he'd never get out. He'd known this call was coming. His colleague had been missing for several days now. That wasn't like him, Darrow had his flaws, but he was always prompt and dependable. Somehow his associate crossed a line.

"I've had several raids on my property," Dom continued. "From the feds. Darrow failed to inform me of the incidents in time to avoid them. I hope you'll do a better job."

"I will," Ellison said, not really sure he could.

"Some of my girls have gone missing. I need to know if they've been intercepted by the cops. Don't worry about the locals, I'd know if they were involved. Check the federal level. In the past few days, I've had interference by ATF, DEA and the FBI. Access them all and find my girls." He hung up and returned to his chair. He needed to develop a plan. He'd give his men one night to resolve the problem. First thing, he'd have Socks take him to the warehouse. He needed to check out the setup for himself. If they were being watched, he'd know. He'd sense it. He always did.

Now, there was one more thing to take care of. He pulled out his phone and dialed his most reliable hitman; The Bull. The ringing stopped in Dom's ear, which was the only indication The Bull had answered. It was the usual greeting when contacting the notorious killer.

"I have a problem that needs to be addressed immediately," Dom said.

"How many?"

"There should be three. Danny Jones, his wife and her brother. They all live in the same home." He rattled off an address. "It's in Lexington just outside Louisville."

"You understand the terms?"

"Same fee as usual?"

"Correct."

"The first installment should post to the account by the end of the day."

"I'll notify you when it's done." The call was disconnected.

Moondance Ridge

Dominic sat back and took a deep breath. Things were in motion. The Bull would come through. His men better come through and by this time tomorrow his world would be back on track. His mind shifted to Ellison, he wasn't entirely sure the man was up for the challenge. *Oh, well*, he thought as he stood and headed for the casino floor. Either Ellison would learn to swim or he'd sink... literally, to the bottom of one of America's Great Lakes.

He frowned as he made his way through the long corridor. The action was in Mount Haven now. Joe did what he was told, but he always tried to cut corners and avoid collateral damage. Something that usually caused delays. Twenty-four hours, he'd give his men twenty-four hours, forty-eight tops. Surely, they would have the resort leveled and Theresa Regan on her way back to Detroit by then. He smiled, the lawman and his cronies believed they were rushing home to rescue their poor pathetic town. Unfortunately, they were headed directly into a trap... one that would prove deadly for everyone involved. Did the man seriously think he could sneak out on a private jet undetected? This was Zarconi's city, nothing happened in Detroit without him knowing about it, especially when it came to the airport. Unfortunately, his men hadn't been able to identify the owner of the jet? The cop's financial backer would have to pay as well. Dom paused to consider...Theresa would tell him, once she was under his control she would tell him everything he needed to know. He stepped onto the floor of the casino and relaxed. He loved the sounds of slot machines, jubilant chatter, entertainment and... Success.

* * * *

Marc jumped and looked at Carson when the knock sounded on the loft door. It was too early in the morning for company.

"Ignore it," Carson whispered.

The phone began to ring. Both men focused on the small device until it finally silenced.

The knocking grew louder, then Carson's cellphone chimed.

Carson pulled the device from his pocket and glanced at the screen. "Director Burns," he said before softly answering the call.

"Open the door," Burns demanded.

"What door?" Carson clarified.

"I'm outside your office."

"Sorry," Carson stood and made his way to the sliding door. Marc followed. "Good morning," Carson greeted.

Burns waited as the men shoved the heavy metal door closed and secured an ancient lock. The corner of his mouth twitched slightly before he sobered. That flimsy system might give the boys comfort but it would do nothing to provide protection. "Now that you work for me, we need to upgrade your security."

"We uh..." Marc glanced at Carson.

"We've looked into better security; but unless we do something illegal, for now, we can't afford a state of the art system," Carson provided. "We agreed to stay on the right side of the law, so I guess it has to wait."

"Like I said," Burns glanced around for a vacant chair.

"Oh," Marc rushed around the corner to their makeshift storage area and rolled out a chair. "Here, this was Shawn's."

Burns settled in, resting his elbows on his knees. "I'll send someone over. You're going to be dealing with sensitive information, I need to know it's secure."

"Okay," Carson shifted and studied the top cop. "But, that's not why you're here."

"No," Burns sighed. "There's been a murder, actually a triple murder. Late last night. I don't know if it's connected, but I wanted to make sure you two are being careful."

"Who died?" Marc asked.

"A guy by the name of Danny Jones. He no longer lives in the area, but he used to. I'm told he was a fellow hacker," Stan studied each of the men.

"He was," Carson stood and began to pace. "It's connected."

"You're sure?" Stan asked.

"Positive," Marc said softly as he accessed the information he'd pulled from Dom's system. "Danny J was the architect of Zarconi's encryption system."

"How can you be so sure?"

Carson returned to his chair and pulled it up next to Marcus. "We knew him, knew his style, knew his signature."

"I see," Burns studied the information Marc displayed on the screen.

"We all went to school together," Marc provided. "We've competed against Danny J. We beat him, with Shawn's help. He must have learned from his mistakes, but he didn't change his style, his tricks, his digital fingerprint I guess you could say. He just made it more sophisticated. Danny created that system. This is our proof."

"The most obvious evidence comes from the dates. Marc has isolated information on the system. This is when the code was installed, when it was revised, the last time Danny entered the system. It coincides with him leaving town," Carson provided. "Then add in the signature, Danny's fingerprints, the backdoor he always installs and there is no doubt this is Danny J's work."

"And now he's dead," Burns said solemnly. "Even more reason the two of you need to be careful and why you need top of the line security," Burns decided. "Is there any way he knows you're responsible? For anything," he added. He knew the duo would never admit they'd stolen funds from Zarconi and gifted it to twenty-three desperate victims of another man's crimes, but Burns knew they had. If Dominic realized who had taken his fortune, the two of them would disappear for good.

"No," Carson answered. "We've been inside his system several times but not through normal hacking channels, not even through Danny's backdoor. We went through the keylogger Shawn installed. Clearly, Zarconi doesn't know it's there or he would have removed it. He could simply uninstall the program to shut us out."

"Don't take any chances," Stan said as he stood. "I'm going to send a security team out here to handle the upgrades as soon as possible. In the meantime, I'll send a man around now and again to check on you. It would help if you opened the door."

"We were being cautious," Marc objected.

"This might be normal for you, but we haven't tormented a sadistic, murdering mob boss before," Carson said defensively. "We're a little out of our element and doing the best we can."

Stan's mouth twitched again. "Point taken," he turned and moved toward the door then pivoted. Once he had both men's attention he smiled. "I heard from a couple victims the other day; of a previous crime, I mean. Seems someone deposited ten million in each of their savings accounts. They stopped by to see if it was legal to keep it. Once I heard from four of the twenty-three victims, I did some checking. Seems they all got the same gift."

"Oh?" Carson said casually.

"Yeah," Stan smiled. "Too bad I don't know who did it, I'd like to thank them in person. Anyway, have a good day and be careful. Someone will be by this afternoon to take a preliminary look around. The installation should begin tomorrow, I'll tell them to start with the locks."

"What's wrong with our locks?" Carson called out as the Director slammed the metal door and made his way to a waiting vehicle.

"He knows," Marc said when Carson returned to his computer.

"He knows," Carson agreed. "But, he doesn't seem to mind; so, I plan to accept his thank you and forget it."

"I can forget it as far as the FBI goes," Marc agreed. "But, are you sure Dominic will never be able to trace the theft to us?"

"Positive," Carson turned to reassure his friend. "The FBI has never traced the funds. They recognized a pattern, our signature, but they had no idea who we were until we agreed to help Theresa. That's when they realized they had Robin Hood. By the way, I kind of like that name, too bad we're no longer in the business."

"So," Marc surmised. "You think if the FBI couldn't figure it out, Zarconi won't."

"I know he won't because I added a few layers of protection," Carson said confidently. "I'm not worried about Dom himself, if he knew computers, he wouldn't have hired Danny J. He won't figure it out, ever. But, he has the money to hire someone else. I added a few layers to my usual method to ensure nothing can be traced back to us. We're safe, I promise."

Marc silently studied his computer monitor for several seconds. "I was thinking.... at some point, we're going to be done with this. The FBI will arrest Zarconi; and they'll seize his computer and stuff, right?"

"Right," Carson nodded.

"And when that happens, they will no longer need us to hack in," Marc surmised.

"Not on this case," Carson agreed. "What are you getting at?"

"I think we should uninstall the keylogger," Marc said abruptly. "Once we gather everything we need, we uninstall the program then sneak out the backdoor and disappear.

Carson considered, what if they needed to get back in? "Let's think about it. I'd also like to run the plan past Burns. We'll tell him we're concerned. Explain that if we leave it open, another techie like us could find the door and discover our footprint. It's the safest way to ensure our safety."

Moondance Ridge

Marc studied Carson for a long time. That was the last response he'd expected from his lifelong friend. "You've changed."

"Yeah," Carson shrugged. "I guess I have. I thought long and hard about that contract before we signed it. I realized something, which was a big reason I ultimately agreed."

"What?"

"I knew if I accepted the FBI's terms... their offer, I could be part of something important. We can be part of a team that brings down the bad guys. We'd be helping to put criminals behind bars, not just stealing their money. I want to go legit, maybe permanently. I think I might be in as long as they will have me. Things could change, obviously. But, for now, I'm all in."

Marc smiled. "I agree. Let's get started on the encrypted files, if we succeed we just might prove we're worth it."

* * * *

Bailey sat next to Rowdy at the kitchen table, sipping coffee. She still hadn't seen John and she was worried. She was staring aimlessly out the window when she felt Knight's front paw land in her lap.

"He needs to run," Rowdy said, taking her hand. "I'm sure John's fine. Apparently, the two of you are closer than I originally thought."

"I met John through Tony when I was in college," Bailey said absently. "They saved me, life was difficult and a little overwhelming back then. John was in the military so I didn't get to see him that often. He was kind of like the amazing older brother that lives far away. When he visited, life was better somehow. He acts tough, I guess he is in a lot of ways, but he's also kind, loyal and extremely protective of those he loves. He would do anything to protect Tony, he'd sacrifice his own life if necessary."

"I'd do the same for you, Sweetpea," John said as he entered the room. "Any coffee left?"

Rowdy smiled. "Plenty."

John filled a travel mug, grabbed a small bag and disappeared out the back door. Bailey frowned. Knight humped his head against her thigh.

"I'll take him out," Rowdy stood.

"No," Bailey objected. "I need some air." She moved across the room, grabbed Knight's leash and headed for the door.

"Hey," Rowdy stood and moved to block her path. "Be careful. Keep Knight close and don't venture too far out back. Take the dog towards the lake, there's plenty of room for him to run out there. I'll join you in a minute."

Bailey headed for the door, Rowdy headed for his room, his shoes and his gun.

* * * *

Joe stepped from the truck and retrieved the small container of gasoline. This should be easy; hike to the lodge, splash as much gas as he could get onto the structure, and light a match. The lodge would be leveled, and he'd be spared Dom's wrath. He hated

Moondance Ridge

burning down such a beautiful building, but he wasn't willing to cross Dom to save it. The sadistic mobster would most likely kill him and then enslave his sister as punishment. No, like always, he had to follow through. He was nearly to the edge of the clearing when he heard the distinct sound of footsteps stomping through the foliage. Seconds later, a twig snapped. Another second and there was the flick of a branch snapping back in place. They were all subtle noises but distinct if you were familiar with the woods... Joe was familiar with the woods.

He slowed his pace and maneuvered to the left so he would be forced to climb over a large fallen tree. As he sat on the trunk and made a show of swinging his legs over, he spotted Horatio. Joe frowned, why was Horatio following him? Dom must have sent him. Did Zarconi doubt his loyalty? He was still thinking about his colleague as he approached the side of the building. If Horatio was here, Geo was too. Those two went everywhere together, but they were supposed to be in Missoula coordinating a plan of attack with the rest of the men. A sinking feeling settled in his gut, and he wondered if he would make it out of here alive. He was unscrewing the cap on the gas can when he heard a low menacing growl.

* * * *

Bailey was focused on securing Knight's leash around her waist as she approached the far side of their temporary home. Out here, she wouldn't need it and her favorite four-legged companion could get some much needed exercise. As she rounded the corner, she heard the distinct sound of Knight's warning growl. Her heart thudded in her chest as she came face to face with a large, imposing stranger.

"Why are you here?" he demanded. "Nobody is supposed to be here."

Bailey swallowed, frozen in fear. Knight started to bark, then returned to that low menacing growl he always used just before an attack.

* * * *

Rowdy had just stepped onto the back porch, trying to decide which direction Bailey and Knight had gone when he heard the familiar sound of his dog's warning bark followed by his signature growl. He pulled his pistol from the holster as he rounded the corner and nearly collided with Bailey. Instinctively, he maneuvered her behind him as he studied the stranger. No weapon, just a gas can, had he planned to smoke them out while his crew picked them off one-by-one from a distance? The plan might have worked if Bailey hadn't just foiled it. "Get inside," he ordered Bailey.

Moments later, he heard the back door slam shut and he relaxed... a little, knowing Bailey was safe. His relief was extremely short lived. Several things happened at once; the man lunged forward, Knight attacked and a shot rang out from somewhere in the distance.

* * * *

Joe spotted the man's gun and suddenly everything clicked, it all made sense. This was the cop. The one that owned the police dog, the dog currently focused on him. The woman must be the manager that fought back against the New York guys. Dom wanted this man, the dog and the woman dead. Horatio and Geo were only a few feet away, watching the situation as it developed. Horatio was a fairly good shot and he was always looking for ways to impress the boss. Killing a man that had caused Zarconi so much trouble would definitely impress the boss. Joe didn't think, he just lunged hoping he could save the man's life. The cop's only crime was crossing Zarconi. Joe had to protect him. If, in the end, Joe died? Well, at least he'd no longer owe Dominic Zarconi a debt. He heard the shot ring out at the same time pain radiated in his lower back. At almost the same moment, his thigh felt like it was on fire. He lost his balance and landed on the wooden patio with a thud. His head struck a large beam and everything went black.

* * * *

Rowdy glanced at the man who had just saved his life and realized the guy was either dead or unconscious. Adrenaline surged through him, he was under attack and the danger was coming from the tree-lined wilderness. He only had one option. Rowdy raised his weapon and took off toward the threat. He only made it halfway across the clearing when he spotted John in the shadows. Then, Knight brushed past him determined to catch the bad guy. Rowdy stopped, realizing John was in the way. He was about to encounter eighty pounds of canine furry and he wouldn't be prepared. "Knight, out," Rowdy called. The dog stopped, turned to look at his master for several seconds and took another tentative step in the direction of the fleeing suspect. "Out," Rowdy repeated. Knight focused on Rowdy, turned toward the trees and let out a high-pitched whine before slowly making his way back to Rowdy's side. "Heal," Rowdy said forcefully as he escorted the disappointed dog inside the rustic lodge. Once there, he slipped a doggy treat from his pocket and praised his companion for a job well done. He needed to get back outside, to check on the injured stranger, but this was more important. Knight had to know he'd done the right thing. His hesitation was a clear sign the dog was getting rusty. He was becoming a pet, not a working dog. Something to think about later. Rowdy slipped Knight one more treat before he stepped outside and shut the door securely behind him. He needed to check on the fallen man.

"What happened?" Tony demanded as he came to a sliding stop next to the unconscious body on the patio.

"I think he saved my life," Rowdy answered. He crouched down, determined the man still had a pulse and glanced back at Tony. "Help me get him inside."

"Looks like that beast of yours took a chunk out of his thigh," Tony observed. "Remind me never to save your life. Apparently, it's hazardous to your health."

"Just grab his arms," Rowdy frowned. "John went after the shooter. I assume he's okay out there alone?"

Tony glanced toward the wilderness, hoping his friend wasn't up against too many combatants. "How many?"

"Don't know for sure, but he'll have support," Rowdy assured him. "Coop's on the roof, John will have sniper cover as long as he's not hidden in those trees."

The two men managed to get Joe inside and settled onto a bed. One look at the gunshot and they knew they needed a doctor.

"Now what?" Tony asked.

"I'll call Skeet," Rowdy decided. "If he's headed back from Missoula, he can stop in town and escort Doc Brown in and out. Moondance isn't that far out of the way, but it's too dangerous for any of us to leave right now."

"Doesn't that make it too dangerous to bring in a doctor?" Tony asked.

"Good point," Rowdy ran his hand through his hair, trying to come up with a solution. His musing was cut short when he heard the distinct sound of Coop's rifle. Both men ran from the room in search of answers.

Tony entered the kitchen and spotted Theresa. She was biting her lower lip, obviously worried. Rowdy detoured to the lounge area. It had the largest window and he wanted to see if they had company.

"Is he going to be okay?" Theresa asked when Tony approached and wrapped his arms around her waist, pulling her against his chest.

"I don't know," Tony admitted. "We were discussing it when we heard the gunshot."

"Theresa," Bailey stepped in. "We need to at least clean the wound and see if we can get it bandaged.

"Wounds," Tony corrected.

"What?" Theresa asked. "He was shot more than once?"

"No," Rowdy stepped into the room. "Knight bit him in the thigh when he lunged at me." He pressed a soft kiss to Bailey's forehead. "If you can take care of the patient, I'll check in with Coop and find out what he's shooting at."

The women began gathering up supplies as Rowdy left the room, Tony followed.

Rowdy had just stepped onto the front porch when he spotted Coop descending the ladder with his rifle slung over his shoulder. His brother jumped to the ground and approached the duo soberly.

"I got one," he advised. "I don't think there are any others, none that I can see anyway. John's on his way back with the body."

"Why not leave it out there for now?" Tony asked.

"Because there will be others," Coop provided. "We know Zarconi sent out at least a dozen men and that's in addition to the three that were already here. If we start leaving dead men lying around, it's going to up the stakes, get their mindset on killing rather than negotiating. I'd like to keep the man's death undiscovered for a little longer."

"Wait," Tony said confused. "You just said three, what happened to the other one?"

"John," Coop said soberly.

"I saw an old stokes in one of the outbuildings," Rowdy said softly. "Let's get it and use the furthest cabin for the bodies. We can hide them from his friends and any wildlife scouting for an easy meal."

"I'll go get the keys," Tony told them as the two brothers made their way to the sturdy outbuilding west of the lodge. Once inside, Tony dialed Skeet.

"We're on our way back," he said in answer. "Just heading into Mount Haven as we speak."

"Any word on the dirty dozen?" Tony asked.

"I don't think they've left Missoula," Skeet provided. "Or at least they hadn't. One of the waitresses thought they were going out for a night on the town. They may not be heading to Mount Haven until tomorrow."

"Can you stop and convince the doctor... I think Rowdy said his name is Brown, to follow you out? We have a guy that needs immediate care," Tony provided.

"What kind of care?" Skeet asked. "What guy?"

"Tell him it's Joe," Theresa provided moving in next to Tony. Her hands were bloody and her face showed signs of tears. "The one Blake saw at the hotel."

"Theresa said it's Joe," Tony provided. "The guy that bugged your room in Detroit."

"And what are his injuries?" Skeet asked.

"Gunshot and a dog bite," Tony said flatly.

"Who shot him?"

"Don't know," Tony supplied. "Not us."

"One of his own?"

"It's a long story," Tony said impatiently. "What about the doc? You think it's safe?"

"Let me see what I can do," Skeet agreed. "It should be fine."

It was nearly an hour later when Skeet and Blake showed up followed by Doc Brown. The small group waited outside the room while the medical professional patched up their prisoner then left. Blake followed him to the main road then returned to the group.

"There was no sign of them," Blake announced. "I'd say there's a pretty good chance they won't be here until tomorrow."

"Tell me what happened," Skeet demanded.

Rowdy walked him through the events on the porch. John picked it up from there. He admitted to killing the first guy, the shooter. Horatio had called out to his companion for help just before John caught up to him. John glanced briefly at the second man's shadow as he disappeared into the forest. "When I glanced back, the idiot had leveled his gun at my torso. Fatal mistake," John said soberly. "I ducked and pivoted, ending up directly behind him. Within seconds, the threat was neutralized." John had reacted, if he hadn't, he'd be dead. He pushed away the image of his attacker crumpled on the ground, his body lying face down, draped over a rotting tree trunk, his broken neck resting to the side in an unnatural position. It was a lethal but silent maneuver John had perfected over the years. He never liked killing, but sometimes it was necessary. "I moved further into the forest silently searching for the second assailant," John continued. "I was approaching a small clearing when I heard the gunshot from Coop's rifle. The guy went down hard, collapsed over a large rock, and sandwiched his sporting rifle between his body and the large boulder."

Coop then walked them through his part in the entire ordeal. He'd seen the man with the gas can but realized the guy didn't have a gun so he decided to wait and see where things went. He heard the gunshot, the one that struck Joe, but wasn't able to spot the gunman through the trees. He was still scanning the area with his scope when he spotted Geo getting into position to ambush John. Coop neutralized the threat and descended his perch to assess the status of his group. He was relieved to learn the first shot had missed its intended target... his brother.

"We then got working on cleanup," Rowdy provided.

"And by cleanup you mean?" Skeet asked.

"We put both bodies in a single cabin at the far west end of the lake," John provided. "They'll be safe until we can get a Medical Examiner out to retrieve them."

"So now what?" Theresa asked, worried.

"They didn't know we were here," Bailey provided. "He said it was supposed to be empty. I think we have a little time. If these guys didn't know, the larger group couldn't either."

"Good," John stood. "We were caught by surprise today. Those two marched sporadically through the forest and didn't trip one of my obstacles. I have more work to do. I want to know the next time we have company."

"Can we help?" Tony asked.

"I'll take care of this," John shook his head. "You work on tactics. Trigger over there did a pretty good job on the roof. You might want to consider posting him up there again." He snatched a couple cookies off a tray and headed for the door. Suddenly, he stopped and turned to face the group. "I've marked the trees, green paint that blends into the forest. Spot one of the trees and you know there are traps beyond that point. I'd caution you to avoid going any further. I rigged them for damage, but hit the wrong spot and they could be deadly. If your target makes it beyond the markings, let him go. I'll take it from there." He didn't wait for a response, just turned and strolled out the door.

"Sheriff Trigger," Rowdy grinned. "I kind of like that."

"Don't even think about it," Coop grumbled. "He's right though, we need to finalize our tactical plan before we're invaded again. I'm hoping we can stop these men without killing all of them; but, ultimately that's going to be up to them. And, I honestly can't decide how I feel about that new revelation, or the man who set the traps."

"Let's focus on what we can control," Skeet decided. "We'll deal with the danger in the forest when it becomes necessary. What do we know about the men coming after us?"

"Not much," Blake grumbled. "We know they're killers and they're plotting our demise. Go team." He shrugged when Skeet scowled at his sarcasm.

"Joe might be able to help," Theresa provided.

"I'm not sure we can trust anything he says," Rowdy frowned.

"Can I try?" Theresa pressed. "I think he might talk to me."

"We'll try," Tony stood, took Theresa's hand and disappeared into the large bedroom currently housing Crazy Joe.

Moondance Ridge

* * * *

"I'm sorry about all this," Joe said when the couple stepped into the room. "You should have let me die. It's better for everyone."

"I don't see how," Tony disagreed. "This way you can cooperate and give us some answers."

Joe sighed. "Then it would have been better for me."

"You're trapped, aren't you?" Theresa asked. "Just like he's trying to trap me."

Joe hesitated for several seconds but decided he didn't have anything to lose by being honest. "I have to do what he says or he'll involve my kid sister. If I follow orders, she's safe. If I had died, the debt would be paid. You should have let me die."

"Maybe you still can," Tony provided.

Theresa gave him a shocked look.

"We'll figure that out later," Tony added cryptically. "For now, what can you tell us about the others? The men coming in from Missoula. Do you know how and when they plan to attack?"

"No," Joe sighed. "Horatio and Geo were supposed to be in Missoula developing a plan while I handled the lodge assignment. The fact they are here, tells me Dom has lost faith in me. You may have just saved my life only to give Zarconi the pleasure of killing me himself."

"Why?" Tony asked.

"I don't know," Joe admitted. "I've tried to walk the line. You know, follow orders but not cross a line I can't live with. Apparently, Dom isn't happy with my standards."

"Can we help somehow?" Theresa asked Tony.

"Why would you want to?" Joe asked, perplexed. "I harassed you, forced you out of your home, and took your money to give to that madman. Why would you even want to help me?"

"Because I understand," Theresa told him. "I know how it feels to protect someone. I know the lengths you have to go to when Dom is involved. You're protecting your sister. I admire that, and I think your sacrifice should be rewarded."

"I don't think anything I've done these past few years should be rewarded," Joe disagreed. "As far as the men - they won't have a plan, per se. They're... militants. Men without conscience. Dom sent them here to attack you... In other words, kill you. Nobody is supposed to leave here alive. The only way to stop them is to kill them before they kill you. If that makes you squeamish, you better rethink your strategy because if you hesitate, you'll lose. Dom never falters and neither will his men. Make no mistake, its kill or be killed."

"Good to know," Tony sighed. "We were hoping that could be avoided but considering the man we're dealing with, I'm not surprised. Do you know how many? We suspect around a dozen."

"Eleven," Joe told him. "Socks stayed in Detroit to help Dom deal with other problems," he paused to study Tony. "I believe you may have had something to do with that."

"Could have," Tony shrugged. "You're injured but not completely out of commission. What's your plan? While we're fighting the men, what will you be doing?"

Joe frowned. He hadn't considered that. "What are you asking?"

"Just what I said," Tony pressed. "Do we need to worry about you? Plan for an attack inside these walls as well as out? You just said you'd rather be dead. Do you plan to make sure that happens?"

"No," Joe glanced at Theresa. "Can I have some time to think about that?"

"What does that mean, Joe?" Theresa asked.

"It means if I had my way, if it was only me, I'd join up and help you," Joe said softly. "But I have Tiffany to consider. If any of them see me, if they report back to Dom, her life is over."

"We're not asking you to fight with us," Tony said, a little surprised. "But..."

"What?" Theresa asked. They couldn't ask him to risk so much.

"But, what if you knew Tiffany was safe?" Tony pressed.

"If I knew she couldn't be touched, I'd do what I could to help you. I hate Dominic Zarconi, and I feel the same about most of his men."

"What if we made a different deal?" Tony asked.

"What kind of deal?" Joe narrowed his eyes, realizing this man was a negotiator.

"What if I could ensure your sister's safety, and you agreed to stay out of the conflict completely? You don't join us, you don't join them. You just hang out here and stay clear of the fight. You're injured. In fact, with your two associates gone, nobody knows what happened to you. As far as they know, you are dead. I'm just asking you to keep it that way. If you do, I'll do everything I can to ensure you get a clean break. You and your sister," Tony added.

Joe focused on Tony. Was the man serious? Could he be trusted? He was right about one thing, if Horatio and Geo were dead, the rest of the men would assume he'd been killed as well. "What about the doctor? He knows I survived."

Tony shrugged. "He said it was touch and go. If infection sets in, you're more likely to die than live. We could simply tell him you didn't make it through the night."

"Impossible," Joe decided. "I won't fight. I can assure you of that, but it's impossible to hide from Dom. No matter where we go, he'll eventually find us."

"Not if you have a new identity," Tony said casually. "You steer clear, I'll send for Tiffany; and once this is over, we'll discuss the details."

"Why?" Joe asked reluctantly. "Let's say it is possible, why would you do that?"

"Because I happen to believe you've paid your debt to Zarconi," Tony turned to leave the room then paused. "And, I've always hated bullies."

"Tony," Theresa closed the bedroom door and put a hand on Tony's forearm. "Are you sure that's something you can promise? I mean we have a couple FBI agents, the sheriff, his brother and

Moondance Ridge

John... who happens to be former military. There are a lot of strong willed men to convince. I'm not sure they'll just let Joe walk out the door and disappear."

"Whatever happens," Tony pressed a kiss to her temple. "You had no part in it, you understand?"

"Tony," Theresa objected.

"No," Tony shook his head. "It has to be this way. If Joe holds up his part of the bargain and doesn't interfere, I'll do what I can to help him and his sister. But, you can't be a part of that... because of all the agents, cops, et cetera. I need space to do this my way. This is what you want, right?"

"Of course," Theresa nodded. "I just want it to be my fault, my doing not yours."

Tony smiled and shrugged. "Guess you can't always have what you want, baby. This one's on me." He continued into the lounge and dropped into a chair next to Rowdy. "Joe doesn't think the men will have a plan other than find us and attack. He's pretty sure the order will be shoot to kill, so that complicates things. I doubt we'll be able to negotiate with the enemy."

"Don't worry about that," Rowdy stretched and pulled a side lever on his chair to recline, crossing one ankle over the other. "Coop's being cautious, not necessarily realistic. He knows there will be carnage, he's just hoping to keep it to a minimum. Like he said, Dom's men will determine the extent of the damage they incur; not us. If they're hell-bent on destruction, we'll comply with their wishes."

"I can't..." Tony began.

Rowdy shook his head. "Don't start in on all that casual about death nonsense again. You're wrong. I'm not unconcerned, I'm reluctantly pragmatic."

"Sorry," Tony sensed Rowdy's objection to the assessment and decided he'd been wrong about Rowdy's approach to death. "Consider the topic closed."

Rowdy gave him a halfhearted smile before continuing with the conversation. "I assume John is adding a few more obstacles out there. Hopefully, that will slow down their approach and alert us to their presence. Coop will man the roof and I'm going to leave Bailey, Theresa and Knight to guard our injured friend in there." Rowdy studied Tony and Theresa. "Have you decided what to do with him when this is all over?"

"I have some ideas," Tony said evasively.

"Then I'll leave him to you," Rowdy released the lever and the recliner popped back into place. He stood and headed across the room. "I'm working on staging positions that will give us the best tactical advantage with Blake and Skeet if you want to join us."

Tony turned to Theresa and gave her a gentle hug. "We'll be fine. Go find Bailey and keep her company. It's going to be a long, stressful night; and she's going to be worried about Rowdy until this is all over."

"She's also going to be worried about you," Theresa headed for the door. "But we'll find something to keep us occupied for now."

Moondance Ridge

* * * *

"Hey, boss," Agent Stewart called out as he frantically made his way across the room. "I just intercepted a call between Socks and a guy named Murph."

Jacobs waited, knowing her man had something important.

"I think I have the location of the warehouse," he continued. "Unfortunately, Zarconi and Socks are headed that way. We don't have much time." He had reached the Special Agent in Charge and handed her his handwritten notes, including the address.

"Okay," Jacobs called out. "Listen up. We have a potential target, but there's not a lot of time. I need all available agents to respond to this address," she scribbled it onto the whiteboard. "We need to get in, rescue the girls and get into position around the building before Zarconi arrives. It's going to be tight boys, let's roll."

Every agent stood and immediately cleared the room.

* * * *

Dominic Zarconi climbed clumsily from his silver Lexus and scanned the area. It was just after sunrise and the place was eerily silent. Something wasn't right, but he couldn't put a finger on it. Socks jumped from the driver's seat and slammed the door before rushing around the back of the vehicle. He shoved open the passenger side door, yanked out the crutches and again slammed the door behind him. At least the fool stopped and waited for instructions before he rushed inside without a care.

"Do you want me to go check things out?" Socks asked helpfully.

"No," Dom slowly moved forward. "Follow me, but stay close and be ready for trouble. The place is too quiet." Dom glanced at the roadway and wondered where all the traffic was. Sure, it was early on a weekday and they were in the industrial section of town; but still, there should be a car here and there.

The two men eventually entered the warehouse and moved directly to the holding cells Dom had shipped in specifically for the girls. "Where is Murph?" he asked Socks.

"I don't know," Socks glanced around. "I called him when we left the casino, told him we were on the way. He said he'd be here waiting. I thought he'd greet us in the lot for sure."

Dom continued carefully down the line of cells until he reached one he knew should be occupied. He swung open the door and frowned. It was empty. He frantically began to open one cell after another. Every one of them was vacant. "Murph," Dom called out. No answer. "Let's go," he told Socks, knowing he wasn't going to like what was coming.

Socks headed for the outer door but was stopped a few feet from the first cell. Half a dozen men in suits, with guns blocked their path.

"Hands in the air," a female ordered. "And don't make any sudden moves or my men will shoot."

"Who are you?" Dom demanded. "You're trespassing," once again, his man inside the Bureau had failed him completely. Ellison was just as incompetent as Darrow had been.

"I'm Special Agent Jacobs," she held up a badge. "FBI, Human Trafficking to be specific. And you, Dominic Zarconi, are under arrest."

Dom's finger ran over the smooth surface of his Glock. His palm itched to pull out his favorite .40 caliber pistol and show the arrogant woman who was in charge, but he knew that would be lethal and he wasn't ready to die. He was outgunned and outnumbered six to one. He sighed and let the cocky agent take him into custody without incident, he'd be free within a matter of hours, anyway. Once he called his attorney, the firm would jump through fire to get him released. Then, he could enact a little vengeance. Ellison was going to pay dearly for this blunder. Once that was finished, he'd need to find a competent agent to replace him.

Dominic stared out the dirty side window as the familiar landscape flew by. He absently wondered if his men were having better success in that backwoods town in hillbilly Montana. He'd know soon enough. And if all went well, Theresa Regan would be standing in front of him enduring her own punishment before morning. He was looking forward to the reunion.

* * * *

"I can't get a hold of Dom and Geo's not answering either," Troy Mull told the group.

"Don't bother Dom," Tate Lockhart replied. "We have our orders. And, who cares about Geo? We finalize our plans and end this."

"I can't wait to get back to Detroit," Sammy Girman mumbled. "I hate the sticks."

"Don't we all," Greg Applebart agreed.

"Quiet," Tate ordered. "We leave in one hour. Listen up, we're going to storm Small-town USA, find the girl and hit the road. Cory, you and Troy ride with me. We'll head to that bar."

"I think that town had a café," Tristen offered. "You want me to check it out?"

"I want you to take Greg and Syco with you and hit any café, restaurant, or coffee shop in the area. I don't want you to stop and chow down while you're working."

"A man's gotta eat," Tristen complained.

"Sammy," Tate continued. "You take Ollie and see what you can find at the Hardware Store."

"And what do you want us to do?" Cale Brocato asked.

"You, Heath and Lynx stake out the police station," Tate decided. "Dom said he was having trouble with an ex-cop and the guy's brother is the sheriff. We need to know what they're up to. Make sure they don't get in our way."

"Why do I gotta take all the risks?" Cale asked. "You know how much trouble I'll have if I get arrested one more time."

"Then don't get arrested," Tate shrugged. "You have your assignments, be in the parking lot in one hour. Let's get this done."

The group convoyed into Mount Haven and dispersed, determined to locate Theresa and return to Detroit before the night was through.

* * * *

Tate pulled into the parking lot of the Spurs Bar & Grill. The place was obviously deserted, but it was a bar. Being closed didn't necessarily mean the drunks would stay home. He pulled to the side of the building and shut down the engine. "Cory, move into the driver's seat and don't move. We need a quick getaway just in case."

"What are you going to do?" Troy asked.

"We are going to take a look around," Tate pushed open the door and stepped onto the gravel lot. "You go that way, I'll head this way. We'll meet around back. Check the doors. We just need one body, and we'll have the answers we need."

The two men split up and disappeared around opposite corners. Tate came around the side of the building and spotted the large dumpster... and the man. He grinned as he moved forward, ready to have a little fun. Troy joined him seconds later and the two of them proceeded to beat the drunken patron nearly unconscious.

Tate took a step back, frustrated. Either the guy was too drunk or too stupid to give them what they needed. The only valuable information he got was the location of the owner's home. He was debating... finish this off, or head to the large ranch when he heard one beep of a car horn. That was the signal, Cory had summoned.

Troy turned and rushed toward the parked car. "Do you see anyone?" he asked Tate as they cautiously peeked around the corner.

"No," Tate growled. "He better have a good reason for using that horn." He threw open the passenger door and dropped inside. Troy climbed in the back and waited.

"Ollie called," Cory told them. "They got something from the Hardware Store. The group is out at the old fishing camp."

Tate frowned. "Then we're on our own."

"What?" Troy asked.

"Geo and the rest are dead," he said soberly. "What else did Ollie say?"

"He overheard a conversation with another shopper. Seems the guy wanted carb cleaner for his clogged lawnmower. The clerk said they were out on account of the men that came in the day before and bought every can they had. They said they had an old generator that needed an overhaul."

"And that told him they were at the old camp?" Troy asked, not convinced.

"No," Cory pushed. "A rough looking man told the clerk that's where they were headed. Said he was going to stay out there for a week or so and needed the generator while he was there. That's when the two locals began a long discussion about the camp, the previous owner and the state the place must be in. It's solid, Ollie was certain."

"We'll check it out," Tate decided. "I'm not convinced, it could be a red herring but we need to check anyway. I want the others to meet us out there. If that group is holed up in the wilderness, they're ready for us."

"I'll call Ollie and tell him to head that way," Troy decided.

"He already left," Cory provided. "We decided on the phone that we'd check it out. He'll be waiting up the road just before the turnoff."

"Call Cale," Tate ordered. "I need to know if there's been any activity at the police station."

* * * *

Cale slowed the car and moved past the large window, hoping his buddies would be able to see inside this time. They had already circled the old police station three times, but the windows were covered and they couldn't make out a thing.

"I think at least one guy is inside," Lynx decided.

"You think?" Cale said sarcastically. "I'm not going around again." He pulled to the side of the road and parked.

"What are you doing?" Heath asked in a panic.

"Holding surveillance," Cale said absently. "Watch the side door."

* * * *

"You know it's them," Matt told Derek.

"I agree," Derek said, moving a slat on the blind just enough to get a good look at the occupants. "There's three of them."

"I don't like it," Matt decided. "They're planning something. I think we should lure them away from the station. It's the only way to keep Mariah safe."

"Stay here, Matt," Mariah practically begged. "Don't leave me here alone. Last time you did that, I had to deal with two sadistic killers."

"Listen babe," Matt soothed. "This time will be different. I'm going to lock the doors before I leave. Don't open them for anyone. No matter what, you understand?"

Mariah nodded.

"I'm going to go out the back and take off toward Betty's motel," he glanced at Derek to make sure he was listening. "Derek will wait until they follow me, and then he'll take up the rear. I'll pull into the lot and see what they do. If they pull in behind me, Derek will be there to back me. If not, we'll both follow and see where they go. Either way, you'll be safe. Just keep the doors locked until we get back."

"What if they shoot you?" Mariah asked, worried more for Matt than she was herself.

"I'll shoot back," Matt grinned. "I doubt it will come to that. Derek?"

Derek shrugged. It was as good a plan as any. If Matt didn't mind being bait, he'd go along. "Once they pull out, I'm going to head to my car but that means I'll be a couple minutes behind you. Don't do anything crazy until I arrive. Just take a right onto the highway and pretend like you don't even know they're out there. Hug the speed limit and pull into Betty's place like you're responding to a call. Park your car at the far end just in case she has tenants. I'll be there as soon as I can."

Matt nodded, gave Mariah a quick kiss and headed for the back door.

* * * *

"What's he doing?" Heath asked.

The three men watched in silence as the officer stepped from the back door, climbed into his vehicle and headed in the opposite direction of town. He didn't even glance their way.

"Maybe he got a call," Lynx suggested.

"Maybe," Cale said shifting the vehicle into gear. "I guess we'll find out."

"Now what are you doing?" Heath protested. "Seems you're bound and determined to get us all arrested."

"Look at this town," Cale said as he pulled onto the highway behind the police car. "There can't be more than the sheriff and one other guy on duty, tops. If the sheriff's preoccupied... this guy's vulnerable and he's all ours."

"I don't like the sound of that," Heath mumbled.

Lynx grinned. "I do."

The trio followed the cop car until it pulled into the parking lot of a small motel. Cale drove past the entrance, careful to keep an eye on the lawman as he continued a few feet up the road. Once he was out of sight, he flipped a U-turn and pulled onto the shoulder of the highway. "Lynx, you get out and make your way through those trees. Heath, switch places with me. You stay in the car in case we need a quick get-away. I'm going to have a little chat with the fuzz."

Lynx jumped from the vehicle and darted into the shadows. Heath slid across the seat but he wasn't happy about it. Cale slid into the passenger seat and stared out the side window. Once the vehicle came to a stop next to the lawman, Cale jumped out and aggressively approached the officer who hadn't yet exited his vehicle.

Matt watched as the car came into view and pulled into Betty's drive. He immediately noticed they had lost a passenger. *Could be an ambush.* When the car stopped a few feet away and one of the occupants exited, he pushed open his door, stepped outside and casually leaned against the car.

Cale moved forward, determined to crowd the officer and get answers. "Where's your boss?"

Matt shifted, prepared to act if he needed to. "Busy." The suspect took a swing at him, but Matt was ready. He pivoted, forcing the blow to miss its mark. The man lost his balance and within seconds Matt had his arm behind his back. It didn't stop the guy from fighting. He yanked, ducked and twisted in an attempt to get free. Matt held on, barely. He was still wrestling with his assailant when he heard the sound of Derek's vehicle enter the gravel lot.

Heath watched as Cale took an aggressive stance against the young deputy. Things were going to spiral fast. He didn't need this. He wouldn't be spending the rest of his life in prison because Cale was a hothead. Dom told them to handle things, but he hadn't said kill a cop for no reason. That was just stupid and Heath wanted no part of it. He only hesitated another second before he shifted into gear, intent on leaving his two colleagues to fend for themselves. He'd gone less than ten feet when something struck him from behind. He lost control of the vehicle and slammed into a concrete barrier. His head hit the steering wheel and he blacked out.

Derek spotted the group, surprised it had already gone physical. He punched the gas just as the man inside the vehicle put the car in gear and started forward. Matt was busy trying to get his attacker under control, he'd never see the vehicle headed his way. Derek punched the gas and collided with the back bumper, pushing the car into a concrete barrier Betty had used to protect the wild grass that formed a play area for kids. The instant the car came to a stop, he took action. He was next to the car, pulling open the driver's side door before the guy inside knew what hit him. Derek ordered the driver out of the car but realized he was unconscious... or faking. He shoved the guys shoulder and his body fell to the right. The man was now sprawled across the front seat. Derek did a quick search and retrieved a .40 caliber handgun. He tucked it down the back of his pants, pulled out his cuffs and secured the suspect to the steering wheel. That should be good enough.

Derek straightened and spotted a man sneaking toward Matt. He must have cut through the forest. For a brief second, he wondered why the guy had fled from the car only to return minutes later. Didn't matter, Matt was in trouble. Derek took off at a dead run and tackled the second guy just before he cold-cocked Matt in the side of the head. The two of them went down, hard. The suspect started to fight, but doubled over instantly when his stomach collided with Derek's right knee. He reached for his cuffs and realized they were on the guy passed out in the car.

Matt frowned in understanding, Derek just saved him a world of hurt. If that sucker punch had connected with his temple, Derek would be dealing with two guys alone. Impatience surged through him and he decided he'd had more than enough. He pulled his asp from his duty belt and swung, the blow connected with the man's knee. The guy lost his balance and fell to the side, stopping the fall with his right hand. It was the chance Matt had needed to end the fight. He grabbed the guy's left arm and clicked on one cuff. Then, he yanked the second arm around and secured it as well. The perp was immobilized before he'd even had a chance to react. Seconds later, the man was shackled to the backseat, cursing up a storm. Matt glanced at Derek and frowned.

"Grab your spare cuffs," Derek ordered.

Matt snatched them off the handle of his spotlight and moved forward. Cuffing the last guy was easy with two of them. When it was all over, Matt let out a deep sigh. Derek held out a handkerchief. "Thanks," Matt took it and pressed it against his bloody lip. "Next time, I think we should spend a little more time on the con column of the plan."

"Why?" Derek grinned. "I think this turned out just fine."

"Yeah," Matt frowned. "But you're not the one with a fat lip."

"True," Derek's grin got even bigger. "But assault on a PO will stick a lot better now that one of us lost a little blood. Don't chuck the cloth, its evidence." He strolled back to the car containing the third suspect.

"What should we do with him?"

"I guess we better call out medical," Derek decided. "He's awake now, but still looks a little dazed. I think he hit his head on the steering wheel."

"I'll take those two and book them if you want to wait for Chuck," Matt offered.

"You wait for Chuck," Derek disagreed. "And while he's here, have him document your injuries."

"I have a fat lip," Matt objected. "I'm pretty sure a simple photo will be documentation enough."

Derek ignored his partner, grabbed his prisoner off the ground, and secured him in the back of his car. Then, he moved to Matt's unit and retrieved his prisoner as well. "While you wait, call Coop."

Matt was still frowning when Derek pulled out of the lot. He reached for his phone and dialed his boss.

Chapter Fourteen

"What now?" John asked as he pulled out another shotgun flare and attached it to the trip wire.

"I know you're busy," Tony began, stepping onto the back porch where he had privacy. "But, I need you to make arrangements for a woman to be picked up and brought to the airport. They can use my plane if you want."

"Who?"

Tony explained the situation with Joe and his sister, Tiffany, as briefly as he could.

"And you want what?" John straightened and sighed. Tony's need to save the world was becoming a problem.

"New identities," Tony admitted.

"Only if it ends here," John bargained. "I understand and for the record, I even agree, but this has to end. You can't save everyone."

"Deal," Tony said immediately. He knew John was right, he couldn't save everyone but his gut told him this was important.

"I hope you remember that the next time you stumble across another helpless cause," John headed for the next location.

"I'm not Conrad, I know that. I also know I can't save everyone," Tony conceded. "I just feel like this is important. I guess I'm invested. That's not typically the case, you know that."

"I'll call Bandit," John finally agreed. "But if the girl resists, he won't push it."

"I understand," Tony stared into the dark forest, wondering where his friend was at the moment. "If she says no, at least we tried."

"You can live with that?" John wasn't buying it.

"I can," Tony decided. "Does he need the jet?"

"Not now," John dismissed the idea. "I'll tell him to keep her hidden in the jet once they arrive in Montana. If that's it, I have work."

"That's it," Tony disconnected, thankful his friend had agreed. John would retrieve Joe's sister and prepare the new identities in a matter of hours. Once this mess was finished, he'd decide if Joe deserved them.

* * * *

"I'm not waiting any longer," Tate decided. "We're going in from the back, looks like that dirt road takes us to the edge of the property. Ollie, you two wait five minutes for us to get into position; then pull up the drive and head to the lodge. Keep the group distracted while we sneak up from behind. Tristen, I want the three of you to head up that road there. Approach through the forest and see if you can make it to the lodge. Time your hit on the same five-minute mark. Theresa has to be hiding inside. If you get bogged down, we'll be the second wave." He wondered where Cale and the others were but deep in his gut he knew. The idiot got himself arrested... again. They were down to eight men now, but that should be enough in this backwoods town. They'd go in, snatch up the girl and torch the place on the way out. He might even have time to hook up with that red head from the bar before they ditched this hell hole.

"What happens if Cale shows?" Ollie asked. "I don't need him messing up the plan, not while I'm hanging out that way."

"That idiot is in jail," Tate said confidently. "Otherwise, he'd answer the damn phone."

"I agree," Tristen said immediately. "That man does not have a lick of sense. PoPo got him, no doubt."

"Head out," Tate ordered. "I want this over and done."

The group split up, each taking their assigned routes, confident success was minutes away.

Moondance Ridge

* * * *

The group was gathered in the lounge area of the lodge, all except John who was still somewhere in the woods. They were going over the plan one more time before they got into position.

"I'm heading to the roof," Coop announced. "I want to be in place when they arrive. Matt said the men were casing the town, asking questions. They have to know our location by now."

"If they went to the Hardware store, they know," Tony said confidently.

"What makes you so sure?" Skeet asked.

"Because John made sure we left a trail," Tony grinned then frowned at what sounded like a shotgun blast. He rushed to the window just in time to see the red flare shoot into the air at the back of the property.

Blake stood behind Tony and immediately recognized the shotgun flare. "John's a genius and we have company."

Coop reached out and grabbed his rifle on his way to the back door. Blake and Skeet headed through the front, darting across the driveway just in time to get into position before the small compact car reached the end of the drive.

Tony pulled Theresa in close and gave her a quick peck before pulling away. "Stay in the back bedroom, no matter what."

"That means you, too." Rowdy handed Bailey Knight's leash and gave her a quick kiss, then a gentle push toward the bedroom.

"Be careful," Bailey ordered as she pulled Knight down the hallway. Theresa followed. The two women didn't step into Joe's room. Instead, they settled into the bedroom across the hall worried about the pending attack.

"The waiting is going to kill me," Theresa admitted as she settled onto the bed.

Bailey just nodded and settled onto the floor, next to Knight.

* * * *

Ollie stepped from the vehicle and waited, knowing he'd be confronted by someone within a matter of seconds. Sammy did the same. They moved to the front of the vehicle and surveyed the area.

"Think it's a trap?" Blake whispered.

"Yeah," Skeet nodded. "But, it's one we have to step into. Coop has our back, but be prepared for anything."

"We know you're armed," Skeet called out. "Place your weapons on the ground, slow and careful. Don't make any sudden moves. I'd hate to have to shoot you already."

Ollie glanced at Sammy and gave the slightest shake of his head. "Not gonna happen," he called out. "We don't want trouble, we're just here to negotiate a deal."

"Right," Blake grumbled. "And I'm the Pope."

Skeet grinned. "This is Agent Perkins with the FBI. I'm going to give you one more chance, surrender now and nobody has to get hurt."

Moondance Ridge

Sammy jerked around and stared at Ollie. "Nobody said anything about the FBI. Tate said we were dealing with locals. I'm out, this is not worth a dime in federal prison."

"I agree," Ollie whispered. "They've taken cover over there, in the trees. Head the other way and split up. If we get lucky, we just might get out of this alive. Go on three. If they start to catch up, double back. We'll try an ambush and escape."

Sammy didn't wait. He darted into the forest and took a left, Ollie went right. The two men sprinted, hoping to lose the agents and double back. The plan didn't have a chance, and they quickly realized a confrontation was their only hope.

Ollie glanced back and saw the agents closing in on them, he jumped over a fallen tree trunk, pivoted and doubled back. His only chance of success was a head-on assault. If they caught the agents by surprise, the delay might give them the lead they would need to reach the car. He bent over slightly and charged, hoping to connect with the youngest fed and take him out. Noise to his right told him Sammy had done the same. The two agents had to see them coming, but they didn't hesitate as they closed in on their targets.

Skeet knew this was going to hurt. Both men had realized the futility of running and were now in full-on attack mode. He hoped Blake was up for this because things were going to get ugly, real fast. He studied the man headed directly toward him and calculated carefully. Just as Sammy lunged, Skeet planted his feet, pivoted and ducked. The man missed him completely. Skeet reacted instinctively. He pivoted again, took two steps and flew through the air, landing on his target's back. He snapped on one cuff, then struggled for several seconds to get the other hand secured. He was just clicking the metal binding in place when a shot rang out, followed by a loud thud.

Skeet straightened and turned, careful to keep a tight grip on his man. Where was Blake? He shoved his prisoner forward as he slowly approached the large man lying on the ground, face down in the soggy leaves. Suddenly, the body was pushed to the side and Blake slid out from under the lifeless form of their second target.

Blake inhaled a deep breath and pushed up onto his knees. The air burned as it slid down his raw throat. If it wasn't for Andy Cooper, he'd be dead- choked to death by two hundred pounds of muscle. What was he thinking, taking a blow that way? It was a rookie mistake, one that nearly got him killed.

"You okay?" Skeet asked as he held out a hand to his partner.

"I'll live," Blake let Skeet pull him to his feet and forced another deep breath into his lungs. "Thanks to the sheriff."

"Doesn't matter why, only matters that you're still among the living," Skeet gave his prisoner another shove. "Keep going. I've had about all the attitude I'm going to take from you today."

Sammy grumbled but obeyed. Ollie was dead that was obvious. Sammy might go to jail, but he wasn't ready to end up dead, not even for Dominic Zarconi.

* * * *

Tristen moved slowly through the cover of trees as he approached the large structure. Greg and Syco were close behind him, but they didn't have a plan. If Ollie and Sammy did their job, the group should be distracted by their two associates. That would give them a clean opening to get inside, snatch the girl and get out of Dodge.

"Incoming," Rowdy whispered.

"There's three of them," Tony advised when he spotted the group. "We're going to have our hands full.

Rowdy took two steps to the side and crouched, ready to pounce the instant the group reached the clearing. Tony did the same, both men waiting for the right moment to attack. They would need the element of surprise if they were going to win this fight.

It only took a few seconds for the trio to emerge. Rowdy was on the first man immediately. Tony was two seconds behind him. The fight was on.

The three men started out looking cocky, but soon realized they were not dealing with amateurs. Tristen was fighting for his life and immediately realized he was dealing with a cop. That's when it clicked, this must be the ex-cop from Chicago Dom wanted eliminated. He reached for his gun, prepared to take the guy out for good. Suddenly, a foot collided with the side of his knee, something popped and he went down in complete agony. He hadn't expected the blow, he hadn't considered the possibility that a cop would fight dirty. Before he could recover, the guy had him in cuffs.

Rowdy glanced around and spotted the perfect tree limb. He pulled his prisoner forward and secured the cuffed hands to the tree with a zip tie. Once he was sure the guy wasn't going anywhere, he glanced around and spotted his two friends. They had doubled up, both of them attacking Tony in rapid succession. Tony was holding his own, but that couldn't last. Rowdy moved forward, hoping to catch one of them by surprise. Unfortunately, before he reached his prey, one of the men spotted him and took off deeper into the forest.

"I got this," Tony assured him. "Don't let him get away."

Rowdy hesitated, then bolted. All the men had to be captured... or killed. He couldn't risk an escape, not from this lot. The two men made their way deeper into the forest, each of them doing their best to out run the other.

Rowdy jumped over a large boulder, ducked under a low hanging branch and almost tripped over a fallen log. That's when he saw the green paint. He had a decision to make, follow his target into the woods and hope he survived or listen to John and let the man go. He slowed his pace, took two additional steps and stopped. It wasn't worth it. He had no idea what John had rigged out here, so it would be impossible to spot the danger. He was just about to turn around, head back to Tony and assist his friend when the world around him erupted. Rowdy was thrown backward with so much force, his feet actually left the ground. He landed on his back, hitting his head on the edge of a tree trunk. His ears were still ringing as he came to his senses. He forced his body to stand, took a tentative step and let out a relived breath when his leg held up under pressure. At least that blast hadn't re-injured his old wound. He surveyed the area and spotted his target lying face down about ten yards away.

Rowdy cautiously moved forward, careful to watch every step he took. The likelihood of a second trigger so close was remote, but he wasn't taking any chances. The instant he reached the lifeless body, he knelt beside it and felt for a pulse. He was a little surprised when he found one. The man was in bad shape; but at the moment, he was still alive. Rowdy pulled another zip tie from his back pocket and secured the injured man to a tree. If he survived, he'd get medical. If not, that couldn't be helped. Rowdy doubled back and had just reached the clearing when he spotted Tony. His friend was bent over and gripping his side as he leaned against a large tree.

Moondance Ridge

Tony was surprised, this guy was good but he was better. He ducked, shifted and planted an elbow in the man's ribs. The guy went down, hard. Tony moved forward, prepared to secure his prisoner when the guy shifted and knocked Tony's legs out from under him. Tony went down, but he wasn't out. He braced his weight on his hands and kicked backward, connecting with the guy's chest. The blow was enough to knock the wind out of his assailant.

Syco was in trouble. This guy had experience in fighting, more than Syco would have guessed. He struggled to suck air into his lungs and made a decision. He was going to end this once and for all. He dropped to the ground, careful to land on his right arm. The guy moved forward to issue a final blow, just like Syco knew he would. He waited, reaching carefully into his pocket until the man was only a foot away. That's when he lunged, pulling the switchblade from its hiding place as he released the blade and connected with the man's side. It wasn't a death blow, but it would give him enough time to escape. He jumped to his feet and took off at a dead run.

Tony grabbed his side in surprise. Where had that knife come from? He was in pain, more than he should be because the man had inadvertently connected with the worst spot possible. He had re-opened the wound Tony received weeks ago from Socks. A wound that was nearly healed until a few seconds ago. He leaned over and braced himself against a tree as he tried to put enough pressure on the cut to stop the bleeding. That's how Rowdy found him.

"You okay?" Rowdy asked as he stepped in next to Tony.

"I'll live," Tony grumbled. "But, I lost my guy. I take it yours found one of John's little gifts."

"You guessed right," Rowdy pushed Tony's hand away and studied his new cut. "Looks about the same, as the last time I mean. I'm thinking a little deeper, but I don't think he hit any major organs. You'll live."

Tony opened his mouth to respond then stopped when a large explosion echoed throughout the area. "That one was bigger than the last."

"Yeah," Rowdy frowned. "I don't think anyone could survive that one. Should I be worried about your friend?"

"No," Tony said confidently. "John's fine, he probably chased my guy into a trap."

"Let's hope you're right."

"I am," Tony was confident John was fine. He'd set the traps, he wouldn't accidentally trip over one. The guy was a pro. Plus, Tony knew for a fact John had survived much worse than the battle they were fighting at this small fishing resort. He had to believe that, the alternative was unacceptable.

* * * *

John spotted the three thugs from a distance and knew Rowdy and Tony would have their hands full. He was too far away to join the initial fight, but decided to head that way just in case he was needed. He watched from a distance as Rowdy secured one prisoner, turned and gave chase to a second man who had been

Moondance Ridge

engaged with Tony. That left his friend in a one-on-one battle John was sure he could win. He continued toward his friend but paused when he heard the beautiful sound of a claymore erupting. The ground shook and John grinned. It was nice when a plan came together, when his traps worked the way they were designed to work, when the bad guy didn't get away.

John turned, planning to head deeper into the woods, to check on Rowdy and assess the damage his trap inflicted on his target, when he saw Tony's opponent pull a knife and lash out at his friend. Tony went down instantly, the target fled. John took a step forward, intent on catching the man who had brought his friend down, but paused. Tony was still on the ground. Was he seriously injured? John's stomach clenched as emotion ran through him. Tony had to be okay. He pivoted and took several steps, afraid of what he would find when he reached his friend's motionless form. Suddenly, Tony shifted and put pressure on his wound as he pushed his body into a sitting position, then stood. John let out a relieved breath as he darted into the forest. He had a man to catch. Anger flowed through his entire body as he easily followed the man's trail. He took a deep, calming breath and forced his body to relax. In this state of mind, he wasn't sure what he'd do to the guy once he caught him. And, that would be hard to explain to the good sheriff. He wanted vengeance more than anything... well, except freedom. And, he wasn't going to fool himself; Sheriff Cooper would not hesitate. He'd cheerfully throw him in a cell and probably lose the key.

John continued, deeper into the forest and smiled when he realized where they were headed. His prey was making his way toward John's most lethal trap. One he would never survive, John would make sure of it. And he'd do it in such a way, not even the sheriff could cry foul. It took less than five minutes for John to catch up to the fleeing man. He quickened his pace and moved into position, making as much noise as he possibly could on purpose. It worked, the guy shifted, corrected course and made a beeline for the hidden line attached to the biggest claymore explosive John had in his arsenal.

Syco knew he was being followed, but he was way ahead of his pursuer. He slowed and altered his course, determined to make his way to the back end of the large property. Once he reached the river, he'd follow it to the highway and hitch a ride out of Montana. He didn't care what Dom said, he was never coming back to the country. He was so deep in thought, he almost didn't register the noise to his left. He glanced to the side and spotted the man instantly. Within seconds, he had altered his course and was headed straight for the water. The man must think he was stupid or something. It was obvious the guy was trying to get ahead of him, to cut him off and prevent his escape. Well, Syco was smarter than that. Just because he lived in the city, didn't make him an idiot. He quickened his pace and jumped gleefully over a large stump. Just before he landed, his foot caught on some kind of string; and he was catapulted forward. He landed with a thud, hitting his knee on a large, decomposing tree that had obviously fallen ages ago. That was his last thought, just before his world erupted.

John stood back, hidden behind a large tree and waited. The city slicker didn't disappoint. Within seconds, his explosive device erupted. Tony's attacker was dead. He didn't need to check, that blast was large enough to kill an elephant. Tony had rigged it to go off if anyone tried to escape from the path that led to the river. The long trip wire had taken nearly an hour to conceal. He never imagined one of Dom's men would venture this far into the thick shrub and fallen rocks to set the thing off so close to the charge. His intended victim should be another hundred yards away. At that distance, the blast would have injured a guy but it never would have killed him. This close, well... there was no need to check the body. It wasn't survivable and John wasn't interested enough to go looking. Bailey had been right about one thing, he'd give his life for Tony. And the man currently sprawled over the rocks and debris, he learned a hard lesson. Nobody messed with John's family and lived to talk about it... Nobody.

* * * *

Tate, Cory and Troy stepped from their vehicle and made their way into the thick cover of trees. They had only gone a few steps when Cory tripped over something. All three men froze in shock then dropped to the ground when the shot rang out. Troy was the first to realize it was a trap. A shotgun flare rigged to alert the current residents of an approaching threat.

"Good job, idiot," Troy grumbled as he stood and continued forward.

"What?" Cory asked, still unsure what had just happened.

"You set off the flare. Now they know we're coming and our exact location. If I get dead because of you, mark my words...I'm going to haunt you 'til the day you die."

"If you get dead, chances are pretty good I'll get dead, too."

"Shut up, you two," Tate barked. "We need to shift course. Head that way and see if we can throw them off our tail."

The three men silently made their way through the thick shrub and fallen trees. Eventually, they came to a tiny trail that led straight to the lodge.

"Should we take it?" Troy asked.

"Yeah," Tate decided. "But be alert and watch your step."

They were nearing the large building when they heard another explosion. All three of them froze and waited. After a minute of silence, Tate motioned for them to continue. They cautiously moved forward, pausing at the edge of the trees to take in their surroundings. Cory spotted the man on the roof. He pointed him out to the others and the three of them moved several yards to the right. Once they were situated at an angle where they couldn't see the sniper, they decided to make a run for it. If they couldn't see him; hopefully, he couldn't see them. When they reached the side door, Tate held out a hand to stop their advance. "I'll wait out here, deal with any trouble that comes our way. You two get inside, grab the girl and come back out this door. Once we have Theresa, we'll make our way into the forest over there. Tristen's car should be just on the other side of those trees."

Cory nodded in agreement, Troy frowned but obeyed. He pushed open the door and silently slipped inside. The two men made their way down the long hallway, searching for the woman they'd come for. They had nearly reached the end of the hall when Troy heard a noise. He pointed to a closed door and motioned for Cory to lead the way.

Cory reached out and cautiously turned the knob, worried what they were going to find on the other side of that door.

Theresa held her breath as the knob on the door slowly began to turn. She took a step backward, pushing her entire body into the tiny closet. Bailey unhooked Knight's leash and used the heels of her feet to push her body further into the corner. Her favorite K9 was now on full alert. He focused on the door and that low growl of his began to vibrate in the back of his throat. The instant the door

Moondance Ridge

slid open, Knight flew across the room and sunk his teeth into his target.

Cory wasn't sure what hit him. He opened the door and spotted a blurry ball of fur headed toward him. He tried to duck and pivot, but failed. Pain radiated in his thigh and he began to scream.

Bailey watched as Knight attacked the intruder. She started to move forward, to get out of the way; but Knight had sunk his teeth into the man's thigh and he was now dragging him away from the door. She didn't understand the movement until she spotted the gun. Was it possible Knight had been trained to separate his prey from a weapon? Knowing Rowdy, it was possible but still amazing. Knight released his hold, shifted into position and focused on the man still screaming on the floor. Once again, she thought she should move out-of-the-way. She glanced around the room, wondering where she should go and spotted the second man in the doorway. Panic set in and she wondered where Theresa was hiding.

Troy moved forward, focused on the violent animal guarding his companion. If he shot the dog, he could control the woman hiding in the corner. She'd tell him where Theresa was hiding. He took another step forward and was surprised when the closet door swung forcefully outward and collided with his head. He was a little dazed but saw the woman clearly.... Theresa Regan. She jumped from her hiding spot and moved toward him. *What was she planning to do now?* He didn't have to wait long for an answer. She raised a two-by-four over her head and swung. The weapon collided with his shoulder and knocked him backwards. Anger flowed through him and he lunged forward, tackling the woman who had now raised her make-shift weapon again; preparing for a second attack. The two of them fell to the ground with a thud. Theresa tried to shift, to squirm away from his grip, but he was determined to hang on. He wrapped his hands around her neck and began to tighten his grip as he straddled her back, pinning her to the floor.

Joe heard the commotion next door and knew he had to help. Two women and a dog were no match for Dom's men. He pushed himself out of bed and slowly made his way across the room. The moment he opened the door, he knew he'd made the right decision. Troy was on top of Theresa. He had her pinned to the ground and he was violently choking her. Was the idiot trying to kill her? Dom would not be pleased. Joe took another silent step forward and spotted the dog... and Cory. He glanced around the room, looking for a weapon when he spotted the gun. In one fluid motion, he crouched, snagged the weapon and continued forward. Within seconds, he had his arm wrapped around Troy's throat as he yanked backward.

The two men fell to the ground and began to wrestle for control. It looked like Joe had the upper hand until suddenly, the other man shifted and jumped to his feet. The fight moved into the hallway. Each man taking turns besting the other.

Bailey glanced at Theresa, her friend was still lying on the floor gasping for air. "You okay?"

"I think so," she pushed her body into a sitting position and leaned against the bed. "We need to get out of here."

"I don't think that's possible," Bailey glanced at Knight just as he lunged forward again. The injured man had obviously made the wrong move. "I'm stuck."

Theresa nearly jumped out of her skin when she heard the gunshot. She leapt to her feet and started to turn when strong arms wrapped around her midsection, pinning her arms at her side. She screamed then froze when she heard the menacing words Tate whispered in her ear.

"Shut up," Tate ordered. "Or I'll shut you up." He shoved the barrel of his gun further into Theresa's side as he forcefully pulled her down the hall. "We're leaving now. One peep out of you and Dom will get his prized possession in a body bag."

Theresa complied. Tate was nearly as bad as Drago. She hated him, feared him and knew Bailey's only chance at survival was if she let him drag her out of the building. She briefly wondered if Tate had shot Joe but decided it was more important to focus on her own problem at the moment. Somehow, she had to escape.

Both Tony and Rowdy panicked at the sound of gunfire inside the lodge. Neither man hesitated as they darted through the forest headed for the danger. They had just reached the clearing where the trees stopped and the yard began when they saw her. A man was dragging Theresa from the building. Coop was trying to get into position, shifting to get a shot; but Tony could see it was futile. The man knew the sniper was up there, and he was using Theresa as a shield as he made his way toward the trees.

"Stay back," Tate ordered. "I'll shoot her if you don't keep your distance."

Tony stopped momentarily but when the man disappeared into the shadows, he cautiously followed. Within seconds, he too had vanished into the forest.

Rowdy had a decision to make. Tony and Theresa needed his help, but where was Bailey and Knight? He was torn... check on the woman he loved or save his friend? He was spared the decision when Coop dropped to the ground and called out to him.

"Take care of those two," Coop ordered. "I'll see what's happening inside. I can't get a shot, anyway. Those trees are too thick. You'll have better luck than I will. Go, I got this."

Rowdy darted into the woods and followed the sound of voices. It didn't take long to spot the trio. The man had a gun to Theresa's head. Tony was standing behind a tree, attempting to negotiate with the gunman. Theresa was standing slightly to the man's left. Her eyes were wide, and she was obviously terrified.... for herself but also for Tony. Rowdy realized things were about to go south any second, and he had to intervene. He reached for his weapon, crouched behind a tree and fired. The bullet hit its mark... directly between the man's eyes and he fell to the ground, his gun slid from his hand as he collided with a tree, bounced off a rock and finally landed in a pile of moist leaves.

Tony rushed toward Theresa, pulling her into his arms as he comforted her. Theresa wrapped her arms around Tony and held on tight. They sat there, on the ground, feet away from the dead man as they tried to regain their composure.

Once he was sure the two of them would be okay, Rowdy turned and made his way to the lodge. He passed John in the clearing and knew Tony's friend would be there for the couple. He needed to find Bailey. He pushed through the door and rushed down the hallway pausing just inside the bedroom. The scene before him would have been funny if it wasn't so serious. Coop had ahold of Bailey's arm and he was helping her climb over the king-sized bed. Knight was focused on a man who had obviously been bitten... several times and was now screaming like a banshee. Rowdy moved forward, satisfied Bailey wasn't injured.

"Good boy, Knight." He praised as he reached into his pocket and pulled out another zip tie. "That's my boy." He crouched, pulled the man's arm behind him and secured the plastic tie around the guy's wrists. He may have secured it just a little too tight, but it couldn't be helped. Once he was confident the man was unarmed and couldn't move, he stood, took a step back and gave Knight the command. "Out."

Knight stood, glanced around, jumped onto the bed and made his way toward Rowdy. Once he reached his dad, he sat next to his leg and waited. Rowdy crouched and pulled Knight into an affectionate hug. "That's my boy." He rubbed behind his ears and straightened. Knight jumped forward, placing his front paws on Rowdy's chest as he tried to lick his master's face.

Rowdy laughed and moved toward Bailey. The instant Knight saw her, he dropped to the ground, rushed to her side and began licking her forearm as he pressed up against her leg. Rowdy took Bailey's hand and pulled her from the room. Knight obediently followed. Once in the hallway, Rowdy paused to glance at Coop. "You might want to tell that guy he has a right to remain silent. And, maybe suggest he exercise that right."

Bailey was laughing then sobered when Rowdy turned the corner and pulled her against him. He just stood there, holding her close as he tried to push the fear and anxiety out of his mind.

"I'm okay," Bailey finally said. "We're okay." She ran her hand through his hair in an attempt to comfort him. She'd never seen Rowdy like this before. "But are you?"

Rowdy pulled back, took her hand and led her to the couch. "The hardest thing I ever did was turn away from this house and go after that man. I knew Coop had things covered, that he would be there for you, but it wasn't enough. All I could think of was you. Not knowing if you were alive or dead, not knowing if I'd ever hold you in my arms again. It nearly killed me. I had to protect Tony and Theresa, but I was dying inside. Terrified of what I would find when I stepped in that room."

"I'm okay," Bailey settled onto Rowdy's lap and wrapped her arms around his neck before resting her head on his shoulder. "I was scared, but I also knew it was okay because Knight would never let anything happen to me. Did you catch him? Is Theresa okay?"

"He's dead," Rowdy confessed. "I had to shoot him. Theresa and Tony are safe. They were experiencing a little of the same, I think,... gratitude they both survived. They needed privacy and I needed you. Tony's injured. One of the men got him with a knife... same place Socks hit him at the bar, but he'll be okay. I saw John, too. He was headed for the woods as I rushed to the lodge. I think we all made it out alive. Which is a miracle, all things considered. He pulled her a little closer, not ready to let go just yet."

Tony finally stood and pulled Theresa to her feet. "Let's get inside, baby." He turned and spotted John walking towards them. Relief flooded his mind as he made his way forward, stopping directly in front of his friend. The two men locked eyes, hesitated, then embraced in the quick man-hug that only lasted seconds but telegraphed deep emotion and relief. Tony nodded once and gripped Theresa's hand again, grateful they had all made it out of this nightmare alive.

"You two get inside," John ordered. "I'll hook up with the sheriff and work on cleanup."

"How many?" Theresa asked. "Did we get them all?"

"Yes," John nodded. "Some are dead, others in custody but we have them all. And, just so you know, Tiffany is at the airport waiting for her brother. Once the coast is clear, we'll sneak him out of the house and turn him over to Sticky."

"Did he make it?" Theresa asked, not sure she wanted the answer.

John frowned. "I assumed he was still in bed."

Theresa explained the situation to the two men as they made their way to the lodge.

"I'll check on the prisoner," John decided. "You two join Rowdy and Bailey in the lounge. Once I've finished, I'll check in with the sheriff and see how he wants to proceed." He passed Skeet and Blake on his way through the large foyer.

* * * *

Coop was just disconnecting from a call when he stepped into the large room and glanced around. Everyone was present and accounted for... everyone but John. He turned to Tony, about to ask about his friend's whereabouts, when the man in question stepped into the room. "Okay, looks like we're all here." He glanced at the prisoners and frowned. "Derek and Matt are on their way to transport these men. I also requested medical, but it's going to take time coming from Missoula. In the meantime, Doc Brown is on his way out to look at the wounded and take possession of the bodies."

"Double duty," Rowdy observed.

"Yeah," Coop shrugged. "But, he knew what he was signing up for when he agreed to be Mount Haven's medical examiner."

"How's Joe?" Theresa asked.

"Gone," John advised as he settled into a chair. He exchanged a look with Tony then focused on Coop. "There's a man in the hallway, shot in the torso. He's still alive, but might not be for long. You may want to have that doc of yours check him out first."

"I also left a man secured to a tree," Rowdy provided. "He's injured, set off one of John's claymore traps; but he was alive when I left him. You also have the guy in the back bedroom. He's going to need a few stitches, but he'll live. It's unfortunate, really. But, Knight didn't hit an artery or a major vein."

Coop gave his brother a look of censure and moved on. "Skeet and Blake kept these guys contained while we dealt with the rest. Doesn't look like any of them have serious damage.

"Another thing I find unfortunate," Blake mumbled. Skeet gave the look of censure this time.

"Other than Tony, does anyone have any injuries?" Coop questioned. Once he was confident the group was okay, he focused on John. "Your explosives worked, saved the day more than once; but I have to call in the County to deal with the investigation."

"Why?" Blake asked. "I mean you already have the feds on scene."

"Skeet?" Coop looked at his friend. "This is your call."

"I'm comfortable handling this for now," he decided. "I didn't fire my weapon and neither did Blake. I don't see why we need to bring in another department."

"Well," Coop handed over his rifle. "I did, so did Rowdy." He focused once again on John. "Thanks to our token military guy over there I only had to kill one man today. His fancy footwork

579

Moondance Ridge

pushed my target into a blast zone and saved me from shooting the guy in the back."

John looked up, surprised by the comment. He studied Sheriff Cooper and realized he'd seen John's every move. He knew John had funneled that guy into danger on purpose... and he didn't seem to care. Would he really have shot the man in the back? John couldn't tell but from the cold look on the lawman's face... he decided it was a possibility. "Glad I could help. I mean, it's hard to defend a rifle shot to the back of a guy's head just because he's fleeing."

"He wouldn't have been shot for fleeing," Coop corrected. "He was nearly shot for that agg assault. I was concerned he might do the same to you. I was simply prepared to neutralize the threat."

Once again, John found himself shocked. This was the same sheriff who insisted they had to limit the casualties. Apparently, there was more to Andy Cooper than John originally believed.

* * * *

Several hours later, the prisoners had been transported, the wounded had been cared for and shuttled to the local clinic, and the dead had been removed. Skeet checked in with Burns and received his blessing to handle the case himself. They were classifying the entire situation as a continuation of a dynamic operation that started in Detroit. As long as Coop didn't object, nobody would complain. Coop was not objecting. Burns had already skimmed the reports and declared both shootings justifiable. The explosion? That was considered an unfortunate accident. The attorney's would have to sign off on the findings, but Stan didn't expect any issues.

Stan went on to inform them an arrest had been made; and Dominic Zarconi was going away for life. The evidence the feds had collected throughout the operation, combined with the stuff Theresa and Shawn gathered years ago, would make prosecuting the monster a slam dunk. Zarconi's top men were being rounded up as they spoke and most of them would be facing decades behind bars as well. Ellison confessed to his involvement in Zarconi's enterprise but was denying any knowledge or participation in the death of Zach Regan. The US Attorney wasn't worried. They had a witness. They may not get justice for Theresa's parents but Zach and Shawn's killers would pay for their crimes. Burns had the tech guys working around the clock now that they had cracked the encryption. Anything they could throw at that man would probably stick at this point.

"We made food," Bailey declared the moment Skeet disconnected with his boss and filled the group in on the developments. "Help me carry in these trays. I think we have cause for a celebration."

Tony pulled Theresa onto his lap and gave her a gentle kiss. "There's no more need for secrets. Moondance Ridge is yours, what are you planning to do with it?"

"I was thinking," Theresa tilted her head so she could read his expression. "Being a rich guy and an established businessman and all."

"Yes?"

"How would you feel about a partnership?" Theresa asked. "I'm broke, you know. And, I've dreamt of fixing the place up and starting fresh since the moment I stepped foot in this town. I can't think of anyone I'd want to share it with but you. Any chance you're up for a new venture? Partners maybe? Joint owners? I don't know."

"How about an investor?" Tony suggested. "I want this place to be yours... all yours. But, I'm willing to invest because it's a sure thing. You can pay me back," Tony grinned. "I'm pretty sure I can think of something I want from you. Then, there's the interest..."

Theresa shook her head. "No, that doesn't work for me. I want this place to be ours. I know I might be getting ahead of myself and if I scare you... well, that's too bad. I'm all in, Tony. I want a life with you and I want that life to include this..." she waived her hands in a circle. "All of it. Its partners or nothing."

Tony leaned forward and smiled, stopping just before he reached her lips. "Then partners it is and for the record, I'm not scared." He kissed her. Gentle at first but soon it turned into a deep, emotional gesture of his love. After a few seconds, he pulled away and smiled. "I think I'll finish that up later, when I can take my time and be a little more... thorough."

Theresa laughed. "I'm starved, let's eat."

* * * *

The group mingled as they enjoyed a meal with old friends and new ones, knowing they were finally safe and the threat was behind them. Conversation was light and occasionally humorous when Rowdy or Tony jumped in with a story about their misguided youth or the good old days. Finally, the banter ended and Blake and Bailey began to clean up.

John glanced around the room and suddenly felt claustrophobic. He stood and silently made his way onto the back porch.

Rowdy followed John outside and settled into one of the comfortable patio chairs.

"Got something on your mind, cowboy?" John asked.

"Yeah," Rowdy said casually. "Nate Voyt."

John studied the former cop a little surprised at the revelation. "Guess the two of you became closer than I thought in my absence."

"Life and death situations tend to do that. You know... create an unbreakable bond after very little time," Rowdy shrugged. "I trust Tony, I think the feeling is mutual."

"Then why are you asking me?"

"Because it was painfully obvious, the instant Tony mentioned the man, he was protecting someone. I think that someone is you," Rowdy observed.

"You would be right," John turned to face a man he had come to respect. "And, you thought what? The fact that we survived that fiasco would make me spill my guts?"

"No," Rowdy stretched his legs and crossed one over the other. "I was hoping you'd help me understand the situation so I can help Tony, a man I have come to care about, get past it and move on."

"What makes you think he hasn't moved on?" John bluffed. He knew for a fact Tony hadn't and probably never would.

"Personal observation," Rowdy provided.

John moved to the chair situated next to Rowdy. He settled in and rested his elbows on his thighs. "You're asking an awful lot. How do I know I can trust you with the information?"

"Mutual respect," Rowdy answered seriously. "Tony's part of my team now. I would protect that man with my life. I assumed someone like you would understand that."

"I understand," he gazed across the horizon and focused on the thick forest. "You're right, Tony hasn't come to grips with the entire incident. He's in an impossible position, and I'm not sure he ever will."

"I guarantee he won't as long as secrets surround the situation," Rowdy surmised.

"He's struggling with a crisis of conscience," John said softly. "Not about Voyt's death. I assume he already told you that man is dead. He agrees with me on that one, the guy got what he deserved."

"But?"

"But Conrad had a profound impact on Tony," John explained. "And Conrad's code was... unbreakable. You break the code, you didn't deserve Con's respect."

"And Tony broke the code?" That explained a lot. Rowdy understood how much Conrad Warner had given Nazario. If he thought he broke some kind of golden rule, he never would get past the guilt.

"He thinks he did," John corrected. "I disagree."

"Can you tell me how?"

584

"With his silence," John sighed. As little as twenty-four hours ago, he wouldn't even consider confiding in the man sitting next to him. Now, things had changed. Sheriff Cooper had surprised him. His brother... Rowdy? He was still an enigma, one John hadn't quite figured out. Had they let this go too long? John was certain the answer to that question was yes. But, how to resolve it? That was a conundrum. One, he hadn't been able to work out on his own. "Voyt was bad news, we both knew it from the start."

"But Tony hooked up with him, anyway?" Rowdy surmised.

"Out of desperation, yeah." John wasn't sure how to explain. "His mother, my mother... they were a lot alike with one important difference. They both lived to party, but my mother had a father who drilled responsibility into her from the second she was born. Tony's mom, she couldn't care less if he ate once a week - or never. It simply wasn't on the list. Viv, the Satan's spawn that gave birth to me, she at least ensured I had a hot meal and clothes on my back. That was the extent of her motherly love, but it was more than Tony got from Sky." John shook his head in disgust. "Don't for one minute think that was her real name. It was all part of the illusion she created. A cheap disguise to sound exotic."

"So, he learned to pick pockets?" Rowdy pressed.

"I think that kid was four, maybe five when he mastered that skill. It was the only way he had to survive," John said defensively.

"I get it," Rowdy did, all too well. How many times had he removed children from similar environments only to learn they'd been returned days later?

"Voyt wanted him, the instant he saw him, but Tony knew better," John continued. "Like I said, we knew he was trouble. Voyt sent his goons out, to harass him, bully him, torment him in any way possible but Tony held firm."

"Until his mother died," Rowdy realized.

"You are perceptive," John decided. "Until then it was tough, but at least he had a roof over his head and a warm bed to crash in. Suddenly, Tony was left with nothing. He did his best to make it, slept behind dumpsters or in old buildings. Avoided Voyt's territory and tried to steer clear of his thugs."

"It didn't work," Rowdy guessed.

"For a while it did, but Voyt was determined," John said softly. "I swear that kid had a new black eye every other day. He was a tough kid, for the most part he could hold his own, but Voyt started sending out groups. Local gangs who thought it was a real trip to beat a fourteen-year-old kid half to death then leave him alone and helpless in the street. Tony finally caved. He decided working as a runner for the sadistic prick was better than the alternative. The instant he agreed, the beatings stopped."

"So why was he still picking pockets? When he met Con, I mean?" Rowdy asked.

"Voyt wasn't satisfied with Tony just running his merchandise. He wanted him all in. He tried to set him up, trick him into breaking the law so he'd have something to hold over him, but Tony wouldn't bite. It infuriated Voyt, so he tried a different approach. He ordered Tony to start selling, dealing dope on the streets. Tony refused, knew he had to get out, so he went back to picking pockets. He planned to save enough cash to split town and find a new stomping ground."

"Enter Conrad Warner," Rowdy surmised.

"Yeah," John smiled. "Con was just what Tony needed. He saved him, in more ways than one. But, that just enraged Voyt. Not only had he failed to trap the kid, but some hotshot lawyer had swooped in and plucked him right out from under his nose."

"I can guess the rest," Rowdy frowned. "Voyt pursued Tony, Conrad protected him. That must have gone on for years. If I recall, Tony was seventeen when Warner was murdered."

"It did," John confirmed. "The attacks started up again. Tony couldn't go anywhere without getting into some kind of fight. Finally, Con had enough. He stepped in, went after every guy that laid a hand on Tony. Suddenly, Voyt's men were spending months in a cage. I swear, Conrad Warner never lost a case, no matter how weak the evidence. He was that good. Voyt's enterprise started to suffer. It's hard to rake in the dough when your men are wasting away behind bars instead of pushing dope to idiot kids."

"So, he sent Beynart in to deal with the problem," Rowdy had a better understanding of the situation now.

"He planned it out," John told him. "Cornered Tony outside the library. The two of them, Voyt and Tony, got into a massive argument. A final showdown I guess you could say. Voyt threatened retaliation, Tony told him to get lost. It was all for show on Voyt's part. He had a more sinister objective; he needed to stall, to keep Tony away from the house while Beynart did the deed. The guy was an idiot but effective. He broke in, hid out behind the furniture and the instant Con stepped through the door, he popped him. One shot to the chest and out. Took less than a minute and he was in the wind."

"How'd they know it was him?" Rowdy wondered. That was the type of crime that usually turned into a cold case.

Moondance Ridge

"The idiot left all kinds of evidence," John shook his head. "Finger prints all over the house for one. He even sat there for over an hour and smoked his favorite cigarettes. Left the butts in a tiny dish Con had on the mantel. DNA and prints nailed him. Travis Beynart is rotting in a cell. Because it was premeditated, he got life. He'll die behind bars but that's not enough for Tony."

"Why?"

"He wanted him dead," John sobered. "Tony wanted to kill him, in a way I guess he needed to. He became obsessed. I'd never seen Tony like that before. I guess you could say it worked, he was the one that flushed the rat out, brought him out in the open so the authorities could swoop in and snatch Beynart up. Tony went ballistic after that. Felt like he'd failed somehow. Like he had one shot to avenge Conrad's death and he'd blown it. It scared me, the defeat I saw in his eyes. The way he gave up and stopped living. I think it made it worse when he found out Con left him everything; the house, the car, his trust fund. It wasn't all that much, Con spent most of his fortune on lost souls like us, but it was enough to send Tony to the college of his choosing. Initially, he chose solitude. He locked himself up in that house and didn't leave for weeks."

"What happened?"

"I stepped in," John said with regret. "I was just a stupid kid myself. I was so desperate to help, but didn't know how. My so-called solution has haunted Tony ever since."

"What did you do?"

"I convinced him we should go after Voyt," John ran a frustrated hand through his hair. "Like I said, we were stupid. I had no idea the cops were after him. We had no idea they knew all Voyt's dirty little secrets. Apparently, Beynart sang like a canary before he was sentenced hoping to get a better deal. Didn't work, but it forced Voyt to run. We knew his schedule, he was vicious and ruthless; but he planned out his day to the minute and never deviated. We arrived at his house an hour before he typically left for the warehouse. I snuck into the garage and drained the brake fluid on his expensive sports car. Then, we hid down the road and waited. Right on time the man backed out of the garage and headed for work... or so we thought. Turns out he had other plans that morning."

"I get the stupid kid part, but what was the objective?" Rowdy asked.

"Fear," John shrugged. "Voyt operated on fear. We thought if we used that same tactic against him, he'd leave town or at least back off. I knew Tony had a future if he could only get past the tragedy. I was determined to get him into college and we needed Voyt off his back to do it. We didn't really have a plan other than drain the brakes then follow him to the warehouse and threaten him like he had threatened so many others. We thought no brakes would shake him, throw him off his game enough that he'd listen."

"You do realize that never would have worked," Rowdy frowned.

"I do now, but at the time we were sure it was the right thing to do," John sighed. "We followed him down his normal route but instead of turning at the fork to head to the warehouse, he took the opposite road and sped up the highway. The one that led to the coastline, with sharp turns and jagged cliffs. We both knew Voyt was in trouble long before he did. I apparently hadn't drained the entire reservoir because his brakes had worked fine up to that point. Suddenly, he took a sharp turn and we knew the instant Voyt realized his brakes had failed. He glanced around, frantically looking for an escape just before he hit a difficult switchback. The car spun out of control. It only took seconds for him to smash through the barrier and topple over the edge.

Tony insisted we stop, just to make sure. I wanted to leave as quickly as possible. Just continue down the road and never look back. Tony won that argument. We stood there, on the side of the roadway for several minutes as the fierce waves slammed that car into large boulders, over and over again. I'm confident the initial fall killed the man, it was over three hundred feet to the bottom. If not, he didn't live long. If the constant impact of that car against those rocks didn't do him in, he drowned within minutes. We didn't stay long but before we pulled away, the car was completely emerged-pulled out to sea and lost for eternity. I'm sure it's still resting somewhere out there, a rusted-out sports car settled on the ocean floor. With any luck, Voyt's body was devoured by sea life within the first month. I enjoy knowing that man spent his last days at the bottom of the sea... as fish food."

"You don't sound all that remorseful," Rowdy observed.

"I'm not," John said flatly. "And, don't for one minute think Tony feels guilty about that man's death. He doesn't. He feels guilty about the silence. Con was a lawman, sure he was a lawyer, but that's why the law meant everything to him. He taught each kid that stepped through his door the same lesson. No matter what you did, no matter how egregious it might be, you had a responsibility to stand up and deal with the consequences. Tony's suffering because of his silence, not the act itself."

Rowdy considered John's words. Almost immediately, he knew John was right. Tony wouldn't lose any sleep over Nate Voyt's death. He was struggling because he didn't do the right thing afterwards.

"What do you plan to do with this new-found knowledge?" John wondered.

"I plan to fix it," Rowdy shrugged. "Guess Tony's not the only fixer in these parts."

"Fix it how?"

"Most likely an anonymous tip," Rowdy considered. Maybe he'd bring in Skeet.

"There's something else you probably need to know," John stood and walked to the railing. "Something Tony doesn't know."

Rowdy waited silently.

"I'm in the clear," John turned back to Rowdy and sighed. "Tony doesn't know that because it's the only thing that has kept him from confessing. He's protecting me."

"And, you're protecting him," Rowdy realized. "You came clean, for the job. When you went into the Special Forces, you came clean?"

"I did," John leaned against the railing again. "In fact, it was Blake's father that handled the problem for me. Ty confronted me one day. Said he knew I was hiding something. Promised if I came clean, he'd handle it. If I didn't, I was on my own when it surfaced. I came clean. No matter what happens with Nate Voyt, I'm clear. I have a document that says so, official pardon from some uppity-up in the DOJ."

"But, Tony is still vulnerable," Rowdy decided. "The military couldn't save him because he was an outsider."

"You are a quick study," John grinned. "I won't let Tony spend one night in a cell for something I did. Not over that man's death. That's not justice, it's not what Con would have wanted. But if Tony knows there's no risk to me, he'll run to the nearest cop and spill his guts."

Rowdy grinned. "I think the nearest cop is my brother, so that's not necessarily a bad thing."

"I'll admit, I misjudged your brother," John frowned. "I'm just not sure he's going to surprise me twice in one day. Not with something like this. And then there's the fed. I think Blake would be cool with it, but he's not in charge. Perkin's calls the shots, he outranks Ty's kid."

"I find it interesting that a man who has spent his entire life as part of a team, doesn't understand the concept. Tony's one of ours now," Rowdy said forcefully. "And like it or not, so are you." Rowdy grinned. "I know that's not a comfortable notion for a loner like you, but I guess you'll just have to learn to deal with it."

John studied Rowdy for several minutes before he finally spoke again. "I guess I'll learn to deal with it then. And since I believe you when you say you'd protect Tony with your life, I'm going to trust you to handle this the way it needs to be handled. Just know, if Tony spends a single night in a cell, I'm going to hold you personally responsible."

"Now that's the team spirit," Rowdy stood. "I've taken up enough of your time and I'm pretty sure you came out here to finalize that covert mission involving Joe. I'll leave you to it." He turned and stepped back inside the lodge.

John frowned. That man was way too perceptive. Nobody was supposed to know about Joe... or his disappearance. He scrolled through his contacts and wondered if Rowdy was going to be a complication.

"Everything set?" he asked in greeting.

"We're headed down the runway as we speak," Bandit confirmed. "I'll hit you back when we land, let you know if we have trouble."

"Copy," John said, relieved the man was headed out of the state and on his way to a new life somewhere. "I'm out." He disconnected and settled into one of the wooden chairs, not ready to deal with a crowd just yet. He had a lot to think about. Foremost was Rowdy Cooper. Why had he just spilled his darkest secret to a man he barely knew.

* * * *

Rowdy settled onto the chair next to Tony. *Might as well go for broke.* "Tell me about Joe."

Tony glanced up in surprise, then quickly masked his reaction. "What about Joe? I agree with Theresa. The man must have snuck out in all the commotion. Took a chance when we were busy dealing with his associates and disappeared."

Rowdy frowned, more than a little hurt his friend had just lied to his face. He stood abruptly and turned to leave.

"Where are you going?"

Rowdy sighed. "If that's the way it's gonna be, I need some air." He pivoted then paused. "You know, one of these days you're going to realize I'm on your side. I know Rambo out there has been your confidant since childhood, but he's not your only friend."

Rowdy made his way to the front door and onto the majestic front porch. He leaned against the railing, surprised how much Tony's rejection hurt. He just met the man. Why did he care if Bailey's friend pushed him away? Because Tony was now his friend, too. And that should matter as much to Tony as it did Rowdy.

Theresa stepped in behind Tony's chair and leaned forward. "I don't know what you just did, but fix it."

Tony turned to respond but Theresa was already gone. He glanced at the front door and wondered just how he was supposed to do that. The answers Rowdy needed, Tony couldn't share. "Guess I better think of something," he mumbled as he stood and made his way outside. He paused just outside the door and realized Rowdy was upset. Still not knowing how to fix the problem, he moved forward and rested his arms on the large railing.

"If you don't want to talk about something, just say so," Rowdy said without glancing his way. "Don't lie to my face. That is one thing I can't forgive."

"I didn't..." Tony stopped. "Okay, I lied. It's just complicated. I can't answer your questions. It's out of my control."

Rowdy turned and studied Tony for several seconds. "I meant what I said in there. John is not your only friend. I suppose it never occurred to you... the possibility you could come to me. That we could have enlisted Skeet to do this right?"

Tony frowned. "I'm not going to lie again; so, no. It didn't occur to me. I thought you'd stand in my way, try to talk me out of it, obstruct somehow if I tried to move forward anyway."

"So, you relied on your fallback guy?" Rowdy said flatly.

"Look," Tony ran his hand through his hair in frustration. "I can't explain this. I just can't; so, I don't know what you want me to say."

"How about I explain it for you then," Rowdy offered. "You and Theresa went in for your talk with Joe. He confided in you. Told you something that hit a nerve. Instead of seeing him as the enemy, you saw him as a victim. One the two of you decided to help. How am I doing?"

"So far, you've hit the mark," Tony confirmed.

"The two of you came up with a plan to sneak Joe away, send him into the wind without anyone knowing," Rowdy continued.

"Close enough," Tony shrugged.

"And instead of bringing the problem to the people that could handle things properly, you turned to your good friend John," Rowdy surmised. "Now, Joe is out there, on the run, looking over his shoulder every minute of every day for the rest of his life when he could be living a new life. One where he has a new name, a new identity, a new history. One where the mob could never find him. All because you don't know how to trust anyone but him."

"Actually," Tony said slowly. "You are only partially correct. Joe is not on the run. He was reunited with his sister and the two of them are living a new life. A secure life and the mob... those who matter, they think he's dead."

Rowdy considered that. "I should have known Buckley would have contacts. People he could tap to create a new identity. Doesn't change anything with us, but I'm glad." He hesitated. "I realize they got a new life and a ride on that fancy jet of yours, but did you help them get established? Provide anything other than the few things they threw in a suitcase before they disappeared?"

"I set up an account," Tony admitted. Was Rowdy right? Okay, he had turned to John like he always did, but was that wrong? How would he feel if Rowdy had done the same to him? He'd probably be standing out here scowling at the lake just like his friend was now. "They have fifty thousand to help them get settled, buy furniture, shoes, the essentials."

"I guess that's a good start," Rowdy shrugged. "I would have done better."

Tony grinned. "You're awfully generous with my fortune. So, tell me, exactly how much would you have donated to the cause?"

"At least a full million," Rowdy decided. "I mean, the sob story he fed you must have had something to do with slavery and servitude to protect his sister. I'd say he deserves a little more compensation than fifty grand."

"A million?" Tony shook his head. "Like I said, you're awfully generous with my money."

"I wouldn't use your money," Rowdy said casually.

Tony considered, it took several minutes before it hit him. "Restitution, from Zarconi. Should have thought of that myself."

"Guess that's what you get for freezing me out," Rowdy turned to leave.

"I'm sorry," Tony said softly. "It wasn't my intention, but I can see I was wrong. I should have brought you in on this. Should have trusted you. Should have known you'd see things... well, the same as I did."

"Yeah," Rowdy turned to study Tony. "You should have. I'm not the enemy, I thought you knew that. I know John has been close, has been your only confidant since childhood, but like I said before... he's not your only friend."

"Any chance you're willing to help now?" Tony asked. "With the money? I like the idea of Dom funding a better life for Joe and Tiffany. He's the one that created the mess, he should contribute to their well-being."

Rowdy sighed. It was a start. He pulled his phone from his pocket and dialed up Carson.

"Yeah?" Carson answered.

"It's Rowdy."

"I know," Carson grumbled. "There's this thing called caller ID, I'm sure they even have it in Montana. I'm busy, what do you need?"

"Wow," Rowdy smiled. "Guess you're not up for that challenge."

"General Patton... I mean Director Burns, well let's just say that man never sleeps."

Rowdy laughed. "Let me repeat myself... slaving away, little pay and very little appreciation. Just look in the mirror every morning and chant 'patriotic duty' about five times. It might help, eventually."

Carson laughed. "Okay, you win. I'm exaggerating... slightly. What can I do for you?"

"Do you remember that bank account, the one you didn't access, the one I don't know about?"

"I have no idea what you're talking about."

"Don't mess with me, Carson."

"Okay, vaguely," Carson smiled. "You need a loan, cowboy?"

"No," Rowdy proceeded to explain the situation and asked for a little cash flow to get the siblings started.

"I'm not sure why you think I can help."

"I told you not to mess with me," Rowdy repeated.

"And I know, you know exactly what happened to those funds."

"I also know what the balance was initially, and what the balance was when the feds seized the account. Do you really want to have that conversation with one Stanley Burns?"

"How much are you thinking?" Carson frowned, he didn't like Rowdy knowing about his slush fund. "I mean, that's the guy that bugged the feds room. He extorted money from Theresa. I'm not feeling all that generous at the moment."

"I think we both know he didn't have a choice," Rowdy argued. "And, I very distinctly recall Theresa telling us she preferred dealing with Joe. He was always kind to her, never let Socks or Drago get out of hand. He was protecting his sister, Carson. Thanks to you, we know what he was protecting her from."

"Alright," Carson relented. Theresa had said Joe was good to her. "I'm willing to part with one million. Don't think that means I have more. Give me the specifics and I'll take care if it now, before I change my mind."

"Tony has them," Rowdy switched to speaker and motioned for Tony to provide the information.

Within seconds, Carson was in, studying the details. "Looks like someone already dumped fifty into the account. Was that you?"

"It was," Tony admitted. "You need to know, that information is classified. As far as anyone knows, Joe died in the battle. That name, his sister's name... they're off limits. The instant you log out of that account, you need to forget anything you see in there."

"You know," Carson grinned. "My memory is starting to get a little foggy. Who am I talking to?"

"Just take care of the transfer and get out," Tony pressed.

"You want the original fifty back? They're not going to need it."

"No," Tony said immediately. "Joe saved Theresa from one of Dom's thugs. It's a personal thank you from me for stepping in when I couldn't."

Moondance Ridge

"I forgot about that," Carson finished the transfer and logged out. "I'm feeling better about that transaction already. The deed is done, I didn't see anything, didn't do anything and we never had this conversation."

"Thanks for your help," Rowdy told him.

"You can thank me by forgetting where that money came from," Carson told him. "Anything else?"

"Just a small get-together. In a couple weeks. Nothing fancy, but it would mean a lot to Theresa if the two of you would join us."

"I'll check with Burns, see if we can get a couple days free," Carson agreed.

"General Patton will be attending as well, so I think you can probably swing it," Tony informed him. He rattled off the date. "Give me a call, let me know when you want it and I'll send out the jet."

"Sounds perfect already," Carson informed him. "Now, I really do have work. With any luck, I'll see you soon." He disconnected the call, leaving the two men grinning.

Tony turned to Rowdy. "I do trust you. With my life, my best friend... and even my secrets."

"I wish that were true," Rowdy sighed. "Because I think I could help you. Maybe someday you'll understand that."

"What are we talking about now?"

"Voyt," Rowdy said, then settled into a chair on the porch. "When you talk about him, you change. There's something you're hiding, something that still bothers you. Something that is eating at you and probably always will. We all have our secrets, but when they tear you apart the way that one does... it's unhealthy. I believe I could help, maybe someday you'll let me."

Tony settled into a chair next to Rowdy. Voyt's death did eat at him, no matter how many times he told John it didn't. But, revealing the truth wouldn't only risk his life, it would jeopardize his friend as well. "What if I told you I'd like to discuss it, but part of the story is not mine to tell? I can't risk another life just to clear my conscience. It wouldn't be fair."

"What if I told you John's life isn't on the line?"

"Did he already tell you?" Tony wondered. "I saw the two of you out back, did he explain what happened?"

"John and I talked about a wide range of things," Rowdy evaded. "I'm asking you to trust me. I'm asking you to take a leap of faith, without knowing what I know. I'm asking you to accept my friendship without restrictions. The way I have accepted yours."

Tony settled further into the chair and considered. He understood Rowdy's position and he wanted to comply. But would John forgive him? "How can you be so sure John's life is not on the line? If I come clean, how can you really know? You told me in Detroit you would never overlook murder."

"I won't," Rowdy confirmed. "But, I don't believe a homicide was committed; so, that fact is irrelevant under the circumstances."

Had John seriously confided in Rowdy? That fact alone shocked Tony. John was the most introverted, secretive person Tony had ever met. He studied Rowdy Cooper, wondering if it was possible. He finally concluded it was. Somehow, Rowdy had a way of making a person comfortable enough to share their deepest, darkest secrets. Maybe it was finally time to share his.

Tony began his story basically the same way John had. The two stories matched, not perfectly like they were rehearsed but close enough to give them credibility. When he finished, Rowdy was silent for several seconds.

"And you believe if you come clean, tell the authorities what really happened to Voyt, John will be charged criminally for his actions?" Rowdy finally asked.

"Wouldn't he?" Tony honestly didn't know the answer to that question. He wanted Rowdy's opinion. "I'm pretty sure I'd also be charged as an accomplice."

"Before I answer that," Rowdy considered. "Tell me what bothers you the most?"

"Seriously?" Tony looked at Rowdy in surprise. "I mean, you're a cop. Don't you know?"

"No," Rowdy admitted. "I could understand if you felt guilty about that man's death, but I don't think you do. I mean, he wasn't some innocent guy. He ordered a hit on the only father figure you had in your life. The way you told it, I don't sense regret... not about the loss of life."

"You're right," Tony sighed. "I don't regret Voyt dying. He got what he deserved. I guess I just regret John's role in it. I regret our role. John did it for me, to try to help me move forward somehow. We were stupid kids and looking back, the plan never could have worked. Voyt wouldn't have been afraid. He wouldn't have worried about our threats. We were dumb kids and we made a fatal mistake. As a result, Voyt ended up over a cliff. It's hard to explain my regrets over the whole thing. I guess, just the fact that I didn't come clean. I've been living with a lie for so long. Plus, the constant worry. One day, they're going to discover that vehicle. When they do, I don't want it to come back on John. If anyone has to pay for this, it should be me."

"And you know John would never let that happen," Rowdy pressed.

Tony shook his head. "The man would spend a lifetime in prison if it meant keeping me free."

"And if I could fix it?" Rowdy asked.

"I don't think that's possible."

"Actually, it is," Rowdy disagreed. "I only have one question. When you say you struggle because you didn't come clean, does that mean the only way to free yourself from the burden is to confess all your sins?"

Tony looked at Rowdy in confusion. "I don't understand the question."

"Well," Rowdy answered. "I'm specifically talking about the brake fluid. Do you have to confess to draining it to...I don't know sleep at night?"

"What are you asking? Be more specific."

"Here is what I propose," Rowdy began. "We bring Skeet in on this. Give him an anonymous tip. Tell him you saw the accident. We can even admit John was there. You two were kids, you didn't know what to do. When you saw the car go over the edge, you stopped. Once you realized the guy had to be dead, you bolted.

Moondance Ridge

Skeet will call the locals, have divers search the area looking for the wreckage. Once they find it, they'll close out Voyt's case as an accident. The point is, the case will be closed. Everyone will think he was driving too fast trying to get out of town and lost control. The cloud will no longer hang over your head. You won't have to worry about an arrest... yours or John's. You can finally move on with your life and put that unfortunate time behind you. If you can live with it, that is. Before you answer, ask yourself... would Conrad Warner want you to face charges over that man's death?"

"Con would want me to do the right thing," Tony said softly.

"And, who's to say what's right and wrong in this situation?" Rowdy asked.

"Could you do it?" Tony asked. "Could you leave out that important detail and live with yourself?"

"Absolutely," Rowdy said without hesitation. "But, I tend to look at the big picture. My actions might seem a little out of line to some but I always try to consider the greater good. It might surprise you, but I have a few secrets of my own. And, I sleep just fine at night, knowing I did the right thing. I'm just wondering if you can do the same." Rowdy didn't see the point in reporting the brake situation after all this time. Some local cop looking to make a name for himself might jump at the chance to prosecute a wealthy businessman for the decades old crime. Rowdy could live with the secret, he just hoped Tony could.

"I only have one question," Tony decided. "Are you sure they won't know? I mean the car won't have any brake fluid."

"After all this time?" Rowdy shook his head. "I doubt that car will have any fluid at all. Tranny, oil, gasoline... I bet the thing is completely dry. It won't matter. You do this? You come clean to Skeet, just tell the story the same as you told me. You knew Voyt, even had a beef with him. So, you were following him that morning to confront him at the warehouse. He took an unexpected turn and headed up the coast. Tell the truth, completely. Just leave out the part where John drained the fluid. Then, because you were scared kids... you bolted. I'd believe you because the story is true. Anyway, like you said... the part about John, his involvement... Well, that's not your story to tell. And, from what you said, you didn't see him drain that fluid, anyway. You were still in the car. Who says he actually drained it?"

Tony smiled at that. "We both know he did."

"I don't know that," Rowdy disagreed. "You don't either. You believe he did; but unless you witnessed a crime, you're not a credible witness."

"Don't take this the wrong way," Tony gave Rowdy a serious look. "But, I'm always amazed at the way your mind works."

"You know," Rowdy smiled. "Skeet told me the same thing just the other day."

"Speaking of Skeet," Tony decided. "Why don't we get this over with?"

"You sure?" Rowdy asked. "I mean it's okay if you want to take a little time to think it over."

"It's been long enough. I think it's time we put a plan in motion and let the chips fall where they may, so to speak."

"There won't be any falling chips," Rowdy stood. "Give me a minute, I'll snag Skeet. Once we're finished, I'd recommend a confidential discussion with Rambo."

Moondance Ridge

Tony laughed and wondered if Rowdy's nickname would stick. John might actually get a kick out of it. He sobered, his friend wasn't going to like it when he learned Tony brought in the feds. He wouldn't care about the lie of omission. John believed the entire situation should be left in the past where it belonged. Maybe, once he talked to Skeet... he'd finally be able to comply with his friends wishes and move on. He suddenly realized he already felt better. It was like a huge weight had been lifted the instant he confided in Rowdy. No matter what happened, he'd always believe he had done the right thing. His thoughts turned to Con. What would his friend and mentor think of his decision? Ultimately, Tony decided Con would approve... for the most part. And, that would have to be enough. One thing Con would definitely approve of was his relationship with Theresa. Maybe dealing with the past would help him redirect his focus on the future... a future with the woman he loved.

Chapter Fifteen

Two Weeks Later...

Theresa stood on the front porch of the lodge, anxiously waiting for their friends to arrive. Tonight was going to be a celebration. She couldn't believe how much had changed in less than a month. She'd quit the bar and was solely focused on remodeling the resort. Tony had talked her into officially moving into his house... formally known as the Wright Farm...currently known as the Nazario place to the locals. They were both busy. Tony decided to stay on with Drakker permanently and help Theresa run the resort as needed. Bailey's step-father and business partner, Peter, had brought in half a dozen new clients in their absence; so, Bailey was also spending less and less time at the bar. Rowdy didn't seem to mind, even with Maggie's restrictions due to her pregnancy.

Moondance Ridge

Speaking of Maggie, the woman had driven out to the resort in person to apologize for her behavior. Since then, everything had changed. More often than not, Theresa found herself entertaining both Bailey and Maggie each morning as she experimented with various breakfast options. So far, their favorite was Theresa's sweet rolls; her great grandmother's recipe that had been passed down to Theresa by her mother. For someone that had once considered herself the town outcast, it was nice to suddenly feel like she belonged.

Tony stepped from the lodge and wrapped his strong arms around her waist. "Before they arrive, I wanted to ask you something."

Theresa turned. "Okay."

"Are you happy? I mean, really happy?"

"You have no idea how happy I am, what's this about?" Theresa asked, perplexed.

"I have a feeling Bailey and Rowdy will be sharing big news tonight," Tony said cryptically. "It has me thinking, that's all."

"Did they finally get engaged?" Theresa wondered, sure the answer was yes.

"Maybe," Tony moved closer, wrapping his arms around her again. "I was thinking, once their big day is over maybe you and I could start planning our own special event."

"If that's a proposal Tony Nazario, you just failed miserably."

"It's not," Tony smiled. "I just want you to think about it. Be prepared when I decide to ask that's all. Maybe slosh it around, settle into the idea a bit."

Theresa smiled. She had hoped they were headed in that direction but didn't dare ask. Sometimes, Tony still had an itch... that subtle need to go... anywhere but here. He seemed to have it under control and scratched it by taking a trip to see one of their clients. Theresa just hoped it would be enough.

"What?" he frowned.

"I just sometimes wonder if this is enough," she admitted. "I mean to satisfy that need you told me about... that gypsy spirit, as you call it."

"It's enough," Tony gave her a gentle kiss. "It's more than enough. I rarely feel that need these days and when I do, a business trip cures me of the desire in about five minutes. The second I step through the door of the hotel, I find myself wanting to head for home. Love changes everything, baby. I miss you when I'm gone, I hope you know that."

"I do," Theresa smiled as the first car arrived. "Looks like Carson and Marc are here. The chaos is about to begin."

Skeet was driving the second car that pulled in. Tony was introduced to Angela Perkins and Stanley Burns' wife, Laney. Both couples had flown in together. Tony was headed into the kitchen to check on the caterers when Skeet stopped him.

"I just thought you'd like to know," Skeet said softly. "They found the car. Voyt's remains... what was left of them, have also been recovered. The detective called me twenty minutes ago to inform me, the case is closed. They've ruled it an unfortunate accident. Everyone involved believes Nate Voyt was speeding toward a secret, rarely used landing strip a few miles up the road. He took a corner too fast and careened over the edge of the cliff. Since there won't be any charges, it's not necessary to reveal the identity of my anonymous source. That chapter is closed, Tony. Stop worrying and move on."

"Thank you," Tony glanced at Rowdy and realized his friend already knew. Skeet had shared the results with Rowdy prior to informing him. He didn't mind, John would have done the same. And, speaking of his lifelong friend, John had just arrived. Tony excused himself, changed direction and headed for the parking lot. This was a conversation they needed to have away from listening ears.

* * * *

Hours later, Theresa was settled on a chaise lounge in front of Tony; relaxing under the flickering glow of the candles and the moonlight. She was happy, truly happy for the first time in years. She watched as Rowdy pulled Bailey to her feet and escorted her into the yard. The music was soft and romantic and the couple was taking advantage of the opportunity. They danced, out in the open all alone. Bailey was laughing, Rowdy was doing his best to hide a grin. Tony had been right, the couple announced their engagement earlier that evening. Then, Bailey begged Theresa to let her have the ceremony out here next to the lake. Theresa didn't hesitate, she couldn't deny her new best friend her dream wedding, after all. The fishermen would just have to adjust.

Tony stood and pulled Theresa to her feet then led her to the open expanse and joined his friends in a dance. Theresa laughed,

Tony grinned and maneuvered her into an exaggerated dip. Suddenly Skeet and Angela, Stan and Laney, and Coop and Maggie had joined in. The crowning achievement was when Carson and Marc stepped onto the field and instantly started to two step. Their moves were exaggerated and humorous. The group laughed at the lighthearted fun between two friends that had known each other forever.

Blake and John stood in the corner shaking their heads. Every group had to have a party pooper, apparently their group had two of them.

THE END

www.ingramcontent.com/pod-product-compliance
Lightning Source LLC
Chambersburg PA
CBHW052341020726
47503CB00001B/61